TALL, DARK,
Billionaire
TEXAN

TALL, DARK,
Billionaire
TEXAN

MANDY BAXTER

St. Martin's Paperbacks

This is a work of fiction. All of the characters, organizations, and events portrayed in this novel are either products of the author's imagination or are used fictitiously.

TALL, DARK, BILLIONAIRE TEXAN

Copyright © 2016 by Mandy Baxter.
"The Billionaire Cowboy" copyright © 2014 by Mandy Baxter.
"The Billion Dollar Player" copyright © 2014 by Mandy Baxter.
"Rocked by the Billionaire" copyright © 2014 by Mandy Baxter.
"Billionaire Sheriff" copyright © 2016 by Mandy Baxter.

All rights reserved.

For information address St. Martin's Press, 175 Fifth Avenue, New York, NY 10010.

ISBN: 978-1-250-07808-7

Printed in the United States of America

St. Martin's Paperbacks edition / March 2016

St. Martin's Paperbacks are published by St. Martin's Press, 175 Fifth Avenue, New York, NY 10010.

10 9 8 7 6 5 4 3 2 1

ACKNOWLEDGMENTS

Many thanks to everyone at St. Martin's Press, including my editor, Monique Patterson, Alexandra Sehulster, and the awesome cover designers, copy editors, and proof readers who helped to make this story shine. Also, huge thanks to my agent, Natanya Wheeler and everyone over at NYLA who continue to support me. I have to give a shout-out as well to Chelsea Meuller for sharing her knowledge of Texas with me and answering questions like, "So, is it t-shirt weather in Texas in December?" And for the record, in Idaho, fifty degrees is *totally* t-shirt weather.

THE
Billionaire
COWBOY

ONE

"You're about to have one pissed-off female on your hands, brother."

Ryder Blackwell looked askance at his younger brother before turning his attention back to the plume of dust rising in a rooster tail behind the Chevy pickup barreling down the road toward his ranch.

"You're probably right," he agreed. And that was the point. To get her out here. "She looked pretty pissed at the auction, didn't she?"

Jason snorted. "She looked like she wanted to take your head off. And while I like a violent streak in a woman, I don't think you're prepared for the heat she's gonna bring. You'll be lucky if she doesn't run you over with her truck."

A smile curved Ryder's lips as he considered the possibilities. The Chevy rounded the last turn on the ranch road and the back tires drifted to the left before correcting. "You're a faithless son of a bitch, Jase, betting against your brother like that. I can handle anything she dishes out."

Jason gave his brother a not-so-gentle nudge, connecting his fist with Ryder's shoulder. "You keep telling yourself that, big brother. As much as I'd like to stick around and watch you get your ass handed to you, I've got to get back to Dallas. The postseason is kicking my ass and I'm not giving Coach McNealy any reason not to start me."

It was Jase's third season with the Cowboys and Ryder knew that his brother protected his spot on the team with a ferocity that made a hornet look cuddly. He worked twice as hard as anyone else on the team and never gave anyone—including those asshole ESPN commentators who accused him of buying his way onto the team—any reason to cut him down. "Later, brother. Try to keep your fool head on your shoulders, all right?"

"Please." Jase sounded almost offended as he climbed into his Maserati. "Ain't no one gonna catch me."

The engine of the sports car roared to life and gravel sprayed out from under the tires as Jase took off down the road. When he passed the Chevy, Jase honked his horn a couple of times in a playful rhythm. Ryder snorted. No doubt that'd do a lot to cool Lara's jets.

As the Chevy skidded to a stop not three feet from where Ryder stood, a burst of adrenaline shot through his veins. There was something about her anger that got his blood up. And didn't that make him a sick son of a bitch?

"You bastard!" Lara Montgomery propelled herself from the truck like the little rocket she was and rounded on Ryder with the force of a tornado. "You knew I wanted her. I saved up for *a year* for that horse and you bought her out from under me!"

Something caught in Ryder's chest as he took in every detail of the woman standing before him: her face flushed with rage, her crystalline blue eyes full of fire. Her dark chestnut hair was wild and wind-tossed, framing her face with loose curls that he longed to smooth away from her cheeks. Goddamn, she was beautiful. And since the day he met her, she was an itch he'd been dying to scratch.

"You were at the auction to buy October Sky?" he asked, jerking his chin toward the corral where the thoroughbred mare cantered and tossed her head. "I had no idea."

When her eyes widened in disbelief and she blew out an aggravated breath, Ryder had to dig the heels of his boots into the driveway to keep from grabbing her and kissing those full lips of hers until she was breathless and begging for more. For months, he'd thought of nothing but kissing her. Touching and tasting her. He wanted to undress her slowly, like he was unwrapping one of the presents under his Christmas tree, fondle and fuck her until she screamed his name. Pissing her off might have been an unconventional way to get what he wanted, but Ryder liked to be unconventional when the occasion called for it.

"That's bullshit and you know it."

The words were spoken with a low edge that made Ryder yearn to have her say his name in the same way right at the moment she came. He was used to getting any woman he fancied. The fact that he couldn't have Lara Montgomery made him want her that much more and he planned on making sure that by the end of the weekend, she wanted him too.

Lara brushed past him, giving Ryder a nice view of her ass as she marched toward the corral. The sway of her hips was hypnotic, her jeans hugging every curve. And when she bent over to squeeze between the slats in the fence, giving him an even better view of that pert, round ass and the juncture between her thighs, his heart damn near stopped in his chest.

"You're still pissed off over the last time I was out here, aren't you?" Lara's bright blue eyes settled on him and Ryder bit back a smile. Her voice changed as she turned away from him and cooed soft comforting words to the mare, hand outstretched. The mare stomped a foot onto the ground and let out a nervous chuff of breath, but Lara didn't shy away. She laid her left hand on the mare's neck, her touch mesmerizing as she worked her right palm up and down her muzzle. Her strokes were gentle, yet full of purpose and the mare stilled, then leaned into Lara's touch. Never in all his life had Ryder been so damned envious of a horse.

"Ryder Blackwell, billionaire big shot rancher got schooled by the local vet and so he's gonna make her pay by throwing his money around, is that it?" Lara asked without turning to look at him.

Of course she'd make that assumption. Ever since the day Lara Montgomery tore him a new one over a calf that'd gotten stuck in a barbed wire fence on the back forty, Ryder couldn't stop thinking about her. No one ever dared to get up in his face about anything, yet that sassy little veterinarian went nose to nose with him without even thinking twice about it. But his plans had nothing to do with showing her up or throwing his weight around. In fact, ever since that day, he'd done everything in his power to convince her to go out to dinner with him. So far, she'd turned him down every single time without even so much as an explanation why.

A month ago, he'd hosted a fund-raiser for the local chapter of the Daughters of the Pioneers. Lara had been there, of course. With a date. Ryder had never been jealous of another man or what he had until that night. It drove him damned near crazy to see Lara in a tight black dress with a neckline that was tauntingly low. His eyes had been glued to her the entire night, the sight of the jutting points of her nipples pressing against the light fabric a cruel tease to his imagination. Thinking about the way she looked that night made his cock swell and throb against the fly of his jeans. What in the hell did that other guy have that he didn't? Seducing Lara became Ryder's single-minded obsession after that night. He wanted her so badly it hurt.

"I don't need to throw my money around," Ryder replied. "When I want something, I get it. It's as plain as that."

"Bullshit. You don't raise thoroughbreds. What you did is plain ol' mean."

Mean was standing there in a pair of tight jeans and tight v-neck top that showed off the swell of her breasts. Mean was shooting him down yet again after he'd asked her out for the tenth time after the fund-raiser. Mean was the sight of her tongue darting out to lick her full pink lips. *Mean* was making him come up with excuse after excuse to see her. Damn, it took all of his willpower not to close the distance between them and trace her full bottom lip with his tongue. "What can I say, Lara? Maybe I'm looking to expand from the cattle business."

"Well, sorry, but that explanation isn't going to fly with me, buddy."

Her cheeks flushed with anger and her chest rose and fell with quickened breaths. This was the closest he'd been to her in weeks. She was like a tumbler of expensive whiskey: heady, smooth, and she went straight to his head. He'd planned everything to the last detail and he'd be damned if he didn't bury himself in her slick heat by the end of the weekend. When he wanted something, he got it. And he wanted Lara Montgomery.

Lara spoke up and he gave his head a little shake to clear it. "Ryder, I want this mare and you're going to sell her to me."

He tilted his Stetson off his forehead and folded his arms across his chest. "No."

Lara whipped around to face him and the one word was enough to set her eyes ablaze. The more worked up she got, the more he wanted to get her good and naked and if he didn't slow down, Ryder wouldn't be able to hide the evidence of his arousal in his tight jeans. If she was this much of a challenge outside of the bedroom, he could only imagine what she'd be like between the sheets.

"No?" Lara repeated, incredulous.

He'd wanted her for far too long, his thoughts distracted by her too often to count. He needed to get his head on straight and flush her out of his system once and for all. Now. This weekend. Finally he had something *she* wanted. And he wondered how far she'd go to get it back.

"I might be willing to give up the mare," he drawled, "if you spend the rest of the weekend with me."

Lara stared at Ryder Blackwell, her jaw slack. Of all the low-down, arrogant, manipulative . . . *Ryder Blackwell is so low, he'd have to look up to see hell!* If he thought she'd simply hop in his bed and spread her legs in order to get the mare, he had another think coming.

Ryder strolled up to the fence, his rolling gait graceful and full of purpose like a wolf on the hunt. His gaze settled on her mouth and Lara kicked at the ground, because the way he was looking at her was doing nothing to help maintain her indignation over his ridiculous offer. His brown eyes smoldered, the heat stealing the breath from her lungs as it tingled across her skin. The man was sex personified, every hard muscular plane that defined him begging to be touched. She'd tried to keep her distance from him for weeks and kept up the pretense that she couldn't be bothered to give him the time of day because of the incident with the calf. But truth be told, she didn't trust herself around him. The attraction was too intense, the way his eyes devoured her like she was a slow-smoked brisket set every nerve ending on fire. Even now, her fingers itched to reach out and touch him, to see if the definition of muscle visible beneath his shirt was as iron-hard as it looked. And holy hell, his jeans were so tight she couldn't keep her eyes from the bulge of his fly. She licked her lips as she contemplated the outcome of releasing the button of his jeans and easing his zipper down, tooth by tooth. But Lara wasn't interested in a one-night stand with Wham, Bam, Thank You Ma'am Blackwell. Even if his skills in the bedroom were legendary. She was trying to build a reputation in town and a one-night stand with the area's most infamous bachelor wasn't going to help her out a single bit.

"I don't know what you've heard about me, Mr. Blackwell, but I'm not the sort of girl who sleeps with a man to get what she wants."

He studied her for a quiet moment, his face shaded by his Stetson, and Lara averted her gaze. Looking at her dusty boots was better than meeting the intense stare that promised all sorts of inappropriate things. "And I don't know what you've heard, *Miss* Montgomery, but I'm not the sort of man who has to pay a woman to sleep with him."

Lara bit the inside of her cheek so her amusement wouldn't show. Rich, drop-dead gorgeous, and not to mention charming in that self-assured sort of way, there was no doubt that Ryder had women throwing themselves at him daily. But she'd be damned if she was one of them, no matter how tempting he might be.

"So, if you're not suggesting I sleep with you in exchange for October, then what do you want?"

He flashed her a confident smile and his leather-brown eyes gleamed with a mischievous light. "The way I see it, you talk a good game, schooling me on how I ought to run my ranch and all. But can you back those words up? You think you can do a better job than me?"

So, they were back to the business with that damned calf? Lara didn't know the first thing about running a cattle ranch. And she'd only told him off because his flirtations made her realize that if she didn't put some distance between them, she'd wind up in his bed. Still, she'd rather die than admit to him that she couldn't run his ranch better than he could. "I know I can," she said, infusing every word with bravado. "At least under my watch, there won't be any calves left unattended."

Ryder's answering laughter sent a pleasant shiver down her spine. "Wanna bet?"

A challenge? Bring it on! "What are the terms?"

Ryder hopped up on the top rung of the fence and swung one long leg and then the other over, landing with a hop. She couldn't tear her eyes away from him as he walked up to her, his powerful thighs, confident stride, and that same hungry, predatory gaze causing her toes to curl in her boots. Sin incarnate. He stepped up beside her, so close that she had to look up to meet his face. He reached up to pet the mare and as his fingers brushed hers, Lara's pulse raced in her veins while her breath hitched in her chest.

"You stay here for the weekend," he said, his voice low and inviting, "and work my ranch. You do what I say, when I say it. If you last 'til Sunday, I'll give you the mare. End of story."

Lara cocked a brow as she reminded herself to take a breath. His proximity made her entire body come alive. A pleasant warmth radiated between her thighs; sweet Jesus, he could make her wet with nothing more than a glance. She prayed he wouldn't notice how her nipples puckered beneath the flimsy cotton fabric of her top, practically aching for his touch. Lara's gaze locked on his mouth, and all she could think about was taking his lip between her teeth. "And if I don't last?" she asked, a little too breathy.

Ryder gave her a lopsided grin that turned her bones soft. "If you can't hack it, you agree to work for me. And *only* me. As the exclusive vet to my ranch. Do we have a deal?"

Lara turned away and stroked October's neck. She couldn't think straight with those piercing brown eyes focused on her. Part of her wanted to scream, "Hell, yes!" at the prospect of being cooped up with Ryder Blackwell for an entire weekend. But logic stepped in and put the brakes on any wild imaginings of being at Ryder's mercy for almost forty-eight hours. The way he devoured her with his eyes made her realize that stepping up to the plate with him might be more than she could handle. It would be so easy to submit to her own silly crush and throw herself at the gorgeous cowboy and put those rumors about his sexual prowess to the test, though. Maybe a wild weekend with Ryder Blackwell was what she needed to finally get over her crush so she could focus on business. But no matter how much she wanted him, she couldn't risk what any sort of relationship with him would do to her reputation.

She passed her palm over October's silky soft, dappled-gray coat. The first time she saw the mare at the breeding stables, Lara was determined to own her. A single broodmare wasn't enough to build a successful stable of her own, but it was a start and that mare was the key to redeeming her family name. Even the most successful stables had to start somewhere, and October was Lara's somewhere.

"You'll be loading her up in a trailer for me by Sunday," Lara said with a smirk. "Because you've got yourself a deal."

TWO

Lara pulled back on the reins, stopping her horse at the top of a tall hill that looked out over the entire thousand or so acres of the Blackwell ranch. She rolled up the too-long sleeves on the thick wool shirt Ryder had loaned her—it's not like she'd come prepared to work outside in December's fifty degree weather—and tried to ignore the very male scent clinging to the garment. Her horse shifted on his feet as she stared out at a veritable ocean of cattle and wondered, *What in the hell did I get myself into?* She knew that Ryder Blackwell was a self-made man, working hard for everything he had, but until this moment, she'd never really considered the actual size of his cattle empire.

"Sort of tough to notice one calf out there, isn't it?" Ryder rested his arms on the pommel of his saddle as he stared out across the field, the wide brim of his hat shading his face. His tone wasn't snide or even mocking, more . . . awestruck. "And that's only about a quarter of the entire herd."

Lara's jaw went slack. "There's got to be three thousand head of cattle out there."

"Closer to five," he remarked. He shifted in his saddle and Lara couldn't help but notice the muscles in this thighs flexing against the tight denim as he pushed off the stirrups. This weekend would be a study in willpower, that was for sure. "The rest are at ranches in Idaho and Oregon. I could've put these somewhere else," he said, jutting his chin toward the herd. "Let some other cowboys be responsible for them. But I keep them here to remind me that success isn't possible without hard work."

His work ethic was something Lara respected. He might have been a player, notorious for bedding any woman who caught his fancy, but when it came to his ranch and the running of it, he was dead serious. "So, what's first on the agenda?" He might've scored a point or two with his down-to-earth work ethic, but she needed to remind herself why she was here. No doubt Blackwell would tip the odds in his favor. He wouldn't give October up without a fight.

"There's a few hundred head in that far pasture." He pointed out to a smaller fenced-in field about two miles or so from the main ranch. "We need to move them from where they are to the corrals at the ranch."

Lara stared at him, waiting for the punch line. They'd need at least five more bodies to move that many cows, wouldn't they? But instead of following up his statement with a "Gotcha!" or a round of laughter, he clicked his tongue a couple of times and shook out the reins, urging his horse down the hill.

"You're kidding, right?" Lara called as she spurred her own horse after him.

"Nope." His voice bounced in time with each step of his mount. "And there are probably fifty or so calves in that bunch. Best not leave any of 'em behind."

He might have dazzled her with his, "Behold, my kingdom!" moment at the top of the hill, but she wouldn't be so easily fooled again. This entire weekend would be about nothing other than retribution. Her humiliation as payment for his. She'd never run cows before in her life. Where would they even start?

Lara's horse, a five-year-old gelding named Samson, negotiated the hill with ease, picking his way down the incline as sure-footed as any mountain horse. Granted, the rolling Texas hills weren't treacherous by any means, but all it would take was a single misstep on a rock or gopher hole to send both horse and rider toppling down the hill. One hand gripping the reins, the other on the pommel, Lara leaned back in the saddle, helping Samson with her weight displacement. When they neared the bottom of the hill, he picked up his pace and headed after Ryder as though he knew his job and couldn't wait to get to work.

As she gained ground on Ryder, he turned in his saddle and called, "Get the gate, will ya?" and motioned to a section of barbed wire fence that had been fashioned into a makeshift gate. Well, he'd said she was there to work. Apparently, Ryder was planning on taking advantage of the situation. She steered Samson toward the gate and eased him to a stop. Ryder veered down the fence line to her left, looking over the rest of herd while he waited on her to open the gate for him.

Lara hopped down from the saddle and Samson took the opportunity to graze on the tall field grass. She eyed the fence and took one of the sections of wire in her hand, wiggling to test its strength. Ryder sure didn't scrimp when it came to building fence. The damned thing was taut, held in place by a section of wire that looped over a fence pole. She wasn't sure if she was strong enough to pull the fence posts close enough together to create the slack she'd need to lift the loop of wire and release the fence.

No way would she ask for help, though.

All the money in the world at his disposal, and Ryder Blackwell chose to use an antiquated homemade gate for his pastures? Lara took a deep breath, dug the balls of her feet into the ground, and wrapped her hands around the gate's fence post. Leaning all of her weight into the motion, she shoved the gate's pole closer to the fence's anchor pole, until she'd created just enough slack in the wire to lift it off the fence post. She reached for the wire and jimmied it up the pole, but it took away some of her leverage and the tension in the fence increased, keeping her from working the wire the rest of the way up the post. *Damn it.*

Attempt two at opening the gate ended much the same, with her panting, her arms shaking from the effort, and the fence mocking her with its very presence. A soft chuckle from behind her steeled her conviction, though, as she refused to let Ryder Blackwell get the best of her. She might not be strong enough to open his damned gate on her own, but she was smarter than all of his muscles combined were strong.

Ignoring him, Lara walked over to Samson and swung up into the saddle. She grabbed a length of rope and wound it around the fence's post before wrapping the other end several times around the saddle's pommel. She nudged her heels into Samson's flanks and his head bucked up before he took a step back, and then another, pulling the two fence posts together. Once the tension in the rope was taut, she hopped down from the saddle, counting on the horse's training to do the rest. A good roping horse knew when to stay put, and Samson did just that.

With more than enough slack in the wire, Lara lifted the loop off the fence post and gave a tug on the rope. Samson took a couple of steps forward and she threw the rope to the ground as she guided the barbed wire fence-gate wide open and let it fall to the ground. "After you," she said to Blackwell with a wide sweep of her hand.

* * *

Ryder had dated—well, more to the point, slept with—all sorts of women: wannabe cowgirls, rodeo queens, debutantes, hard-core business types, a cocktail waitress or three, and an elementary school teacher up in Lubbock, but there was something about watching Lara Montgomery open that gate that heated his blood to volcanic proportions. In tasking her with opening the gate, he'd hoped to give her no choice but to ask for his help. Hell, on a good day he had a hard time pulling those posts together himself. But the fiery vet refused to back down, and it was damned smart of her to get Samson to do the heavy lifting. He'd have to remember that trick the next time he was out here alone.

"So, why are we moving this group and leaving the others down here?" Lara asked as she maneuvered Samson into the pasture.

Her cold tone did little to cool his jets. On the contrary, it made Ryder more determined than ever to melt her icy exterior. "We separated this group last week. Most of these cows will be calving in the next few weeks. I want them closer to the main house. They're easier to take care of that way."

Ryder pushed his hat up on his forehead and turned in his saddle. A few miles wasn't far to ride, and even without Lara's help, he could have moved the herd with little to no trouble. They'd been moved back and forth between these pastures for years, and the cows knew what to do when he opened the gate. But he didn't want Lara to know that.

"Okay, so where do you want me?"

He couldn't ignore how her voice dropped a couple of decibels with the question, almost breathy, and Ryder thought of several places he wanted her, one of which was straddling his cock, riding him like she did that horse. Jesus, the way her ass came off the saddle and settled back down was enough to knock the air right out of his chest.

"Come around and flank the left side." Ryder's voice was strained, but it was nothing compared to the erection straining in his jeans. He cleared his throat and shifted in his saddle. "It'll push them out of the pasture and get them headed toward the ranch."

She shielded her eyes with her hand as she steered Samson toward the sun. Ryder pulled his Stetson from his head. He walked his horse, Dakota, up beside her and tossed the hat. "Here. You're gonna need it."

Without even a pause to consider the offer, Lara put his weathered Stetson on her head. It was a little big, and slid down her forehead, but Ryder couldn't deny that she looked damned fine in it. Seeing his hat and shirt on her body drove him crazy, scrambling his thoughts to the point that the entire herd could get away from him right here and now and he wouldn't give a single shit about it.

As if he wasn't even there, Lara steered Samson around the pasture, pushing the cows and calves out through the pasture gate and into the next field. He didn't know what he found more aggravating, the fact that she ignored him, or well, the fact that she'd *ignored him*. If Jase was here right now, he'd have fallen off of his horse laughing. What did he have to do to get a second glance from her?

Ryder never went into any situation half-cocked, though. He'd orchestrated the purchase of October Sky, knowing it would get Lara out here. He never left anything to chance. And as soon as the herd filed out of the gate, he sat back in his saddle and waited for Lara to lose that cool she so easily maintained.

"Whoa, where do you think you're going, little fella?"

Ryder smiled as one of the calves took off ahead of the group, frolicking toward the far fence line where the rest of the cattle grazed. Samson took off at a canter, showing off his training as he moved to cut the calf off and steer it in the right direction. Lara turned back to face him, a triumphant smirk curving her full lips when two more calves broke ranks and headed in opposite directions. Ryder couldn't have planned it better if he'd trained those little buggers to take off like that.

"Better round 'em up, doc. You wouldn't want one getting stuck in a fence somewhere."

She shot him a glare that further stirred his lusts as she maneuvered Samson toward the closest calf first. Wrong move. She should have brought the farther calf in line first to encourage the other to fall into step. Again, perfect.

"Dang it," Lara muttered as another calf kicked his back legs up and skittered off toward a patch of green grass on the outskirts of the herd. The mama released a drawn-out bellow as she stopped the flow of the herd in order to follow after her baby. "Come back, little guy," Lara crooned. "You're worrying your mama." She spun Samson around and sent him headlong into the middle of the herd.

"Damn it," Ryder ground out between clenched teeth as the once-ordered group fell quickly into chaos. So much for a well-orchestrated plan. There wouldn't be much use in trying to seduce Lara if she was trampled by a stampede first.

He whistled sharply, the sound echoing off the distant hills. The sound seemed to break Lara from her single-minded task and she looked up and around to find herself adrift in a sea of agitated cattle. Dust swirled up around her and she waved her hand in front of her face as she coughed. Samson reared up, none too happy about being pushed around, and damned near threw Lara from her seat.

Ryder chanced a quick look toward the ranch, relieved to see a streak of black-and-white fur racing down the hill, toward them. Pepper, the best cow dog he'd ever owned, bounded down the hill with a yip, clearly excited to show the herd who was boss. As the cows grew more agitated, their cries became a cacophony of sound, drowning out Lara's voice as she called out over the din.

Well, it wasn't how he'd imagined getting her close, but Ryder decided that improvisation had its merits. He pressed his heels into Dakota's flanks and sent him into the melee of cattle. Dakota pulled against the reins, throwing his head from side to side. Lara should have known better than to steer a horse into an agitated group of cows like that. Dakota grew nervous, stomping his hooves and raising his legs high as though worried he was about to get stepped on.

"Whoa, boy. Take it easy," Ryder crooned in her ear as he placed a comforting hand on the stallion's neck and maneuvered him right into the thick of the chaos. Samson spun wildly as he searched for a way out of the stampede and Lara's eyes were as big as silver dollars, her expression one of barely veiled fear. Through the press of cattle, Dakota soldiered his way through like any battle stallion worth his salt. No pesky cow was going to push him around and he gingerly picked his way through the stamping feet around him, ears perked and head held high.

Samson bucked again and Lara lost her grip on the reins, instead grabbing onto the pommel to stay in the saddle. Before he could try to pitch her again, Ryder maneuvered beside them and grabbed Samson's discarded rig before he wrapped his other arm around Lara's waist, pulling her onto his saddle. "You're lucky he didn't throw you," Ryder growled close to her ear. "Damn it, Lara, you could've been trampled."

He didn't mean to be so harsh with her. After all, he was the one who'd set her on that fool's errand. Ryder's heart beat wildly in his chest and his muscles tensed with unspent adrenaline. And what really rattled him—scared the ever loving shit out of him—was the fear he felt watching her out there and being almost too far away to help.

Talk about uncharted territory.

THREE

Lara's heart felt like it might explode out of her chest at any second. Her hands trembled at her sides and she gripped onto Ryder's shirt as he guided them away from the fray and clear of danger. Behind them, Samson skittered to one side, still a little rattled and out of sorts. An excited yip sounded from somewhere beside them and Ryder called out, "Round 'em up, Pep!"

A dark flash of color darted into Lara's line of sight and she turned to see a black dog with a white speckled band of fur around its neck and shoulders circumvent the agitated cows, nipping at ankles as she rounded them up into an orderly group.

"Good girl, Pepper," Ryder called out as the dog wagged her tail, pleased with the compliment. "Get 'em moving."

It only took Pepper a few moments to bring order to the chaos Lara had managed to create. Her cheeks flushed with embarrassment as Ryder's arm wound around her torso to hold her body tightly to his. *Great. Ryder Blackwell's dog is a better ranch hand than I am.*

"That was stupid," Lara stated without looking back. If

she had to admit to his face that she had no idea what she was doing she doubted she'd ever live it down. "I should have known better."

His voice was a low, sensual purr next to her ear when he said, "Round-up skills aside, doc, you sure know how to open a gate."

It shouldn't have made her insides turn to Jell-O when he called her "doc." And likewise, she shouldn't have wanted to lean back and rest her head on his shoulder. Lara shifted—saddles weren't made for more than one butt after all—and only managed to wedge her body between the pommel and Ryder, pressing her up against his groin in a way that made her very aware there was a well-built male right behind her.

They sure did grow 'em bigger in Texas.

Despite the clothes that separated their skin, Lara could feel every well-sculpted muscle of his body and then some. Her backside brushed up against his fly with each one of Dakota's steps, creating a friction that made her wonder what it might feel like to have Ryder Blackwell naked and thrusting into her from behind. So much for keeping her distance. She'd only been at the ranch for a little over an hour and already she was plastered up against him and thinking of ways to get closer still.

Samson seemed to have calmed down, his gait lazy as he walked behind them, but Ryder still held onto her, one arm wrapped protectively around her waist. His proximity made Lara's spine about as stiff as a cooked noodle, and the longer she stayed put, the more she wanted to nestle up and let her body mold itself to his. "I'm okay to ride now." Too bad her voice didn't echo the conviction of her words. "I don't think you'll have to worry about me starting another stampede. It looks like Pepper has the situation under control."

She felt more than heard the deep rumble of laughter

in Ryder's chest. A tremor that traveled the length of her body and settled low in her core. Lara sat bolt upright in the saddle, scrambling to hop down before she threw caution to the wind and straddled that cowboy like she had his horse. What was wrong with her? Lara had to remind herself that she was here for one reason and one reason only: to get back October Sky so she could rebuild her family's stables and reputation.

Ryder Blackwell did *not* figure into that equation.

As though reluctant to let her go, his fingers slid across her belly as she maneuvered one leg over the pommel until she was sitting sidesaddle. The contact sent delicious shivers over her skin and her abdomen clenched tightly with lust.

"Give me your hand."

Ryder's voice was as smooth and rich as Kentucky bourbon, every bit as heady too, because all it took was a few words in her ear to make Lara feel positively drunk. She reached her right hand across her body and his fingers brushed her palm before he gripped her hand in his. Her breath stalled in her chest as their eyes locked, their lips almost close enough for a kiss.

The rumor around town was that Ryder Blackwell could give a woman an orgasm just by smiling at her. His eyes crinkled at the corners as his lips spread into a sensual grin and for the first time since she'd heard it, Lara thought that the rumors might actually be true. "Watch your step, doc. I can't have my new ranch hand laid up on the first day of work."

Her brain went blank. She couldn't think past that smile, or the heated look in his eyes. "True," she said after a spell. "And I really wouldn't want to give the local hens anything to cluck about."

Rather than let her go, Ryder's grip tightened around her with those words. Something hardened in his gaze and he cocked his head to one side as he regarded her. "Is that why you've been giving me the brush-off? Because you're worried about what people might say about you?"

His expression was almost hurt and though it puzzled Lara to see him react this way, what did he expect? "Oh, come on, Ryder. You have to know that once a woman spends the night with you, she's the talk of the town by the next day. I'm trying to build a business here. A good reputation. No one will bring their animals to me if they don't respect me. Being one of your conquests doesn't exactly look good on a resume."

He released his grip and she slid down from his horse so unexpectedly that she almost didn't land on her feet. "What the hell do you care what people say, anyway? And besides, unless you're the one planning to spread the gossip, why does anyone need to know what you do in your spare time?"

Lara dusted her palms against her pants as though she could banish the lingering sensation of Ryder's touch and stalked over to Samson, grabbing up the reins. "Are you implying that I'd run around town and brag about spending the night with you?" As though a one-nighter with Ryder Blackwell was like winning a blue ribbon at the state fair.

"You said it, doc. Because I can guarantee you that any stories about what goes on in the privacy of my own bedroom aren't being spread by me."

Yeah, sure. What man didn't brag about his conquests? Especially one with the bragging rights Ryder supposedly had. "Knowing the damage it would cause, what woman in her right mind would go around blabbing to the entire town that she'd hooked up with you for the night?" She might have sounded disbelieving, but Lara had to admit that the biggest complaint from most of Ryder's former flames was that he rarely came calling a second time. And though it was totally unfair to lay all of the blame at his feet—it took two to tango, after all—Lara needed whatever flimsy excuse she could muster in order to keep her distance.

She hauled herself up into the saddle and put her heels into Samson's flanks to spur him into action. He took off at a trot and behind her, she heard Ryder urge Dakota to catch up. Within seconds he was riding beside her, his expression a notch below steam coming out of the ears. "I don't kiss and tell, doc. What I do in my bedroom is *my* business and no one else's. Including yours. But I can't control what people say about me and I'm not about to try."

No, it wasn't any of her business. Still, she couldn't help the twinge of jealousy that tugged her emotions in a direction she wasn't exactly thrilled about. Was it really the gossip that bothered her so much or the string of women who came before her, all vying for even a scrap of Ryder's affection? He never stayed with a girl for long, and as far as she knew, he'd never had a serious relationship. Lara didn't want to be simply another woman who walked through the revolving door of his bedroom, though.

"You know," Ryder shot back as he rode up ahead, "I can't help it if women are attracted to me. Or if I'm attracted to them. Should I become some sort of hermit, forsake all women just to appease the clucking hens as you called them?"

Yes, damn it! Lara didn't know why she was so worked up, but was it too much to ask that he not cat around town quite so much? The fact that she wanted Ryder despite her own rocky past, and despite what she was trying to do for her future was reason enough to keep him at arm's length. It was an unreasonable thought, sure. She was afraid to take him up on his many invitations because she didn't *want* to want him. That didn't mean she wanted any other woman to have him, though. "I just wonder if it's worth it, is all. Is your reputation worth a few meaningless one-night stands?"

By god, it was if it meant getting a woman like her all to himself. Nothing about Lara Montgomery was meaningless, though, and he was going to make sure she realized that by the end of the weekend. She was trying to antagonize him, erect a wall between them. But he wasn't going to let her do it. Lara could push his buttons all she wanted because he was going to be sure and push back.

"Maybe you're afraid," Ryder remarked as he steered Dakota around the herd to push them into the corral.

"Afraid of what?" she challenged.

"To acknowledge that someone might want you enough to not give a shit about anything else but having you all to himself."

Lara brought Samson to a stop beside him and said, "I don't want a man to own me, Ryder. I've had my fill of men who can't tell the difference between wanting a woman and treating her like a possession."

Her somber words gave him pause and Ryder sat astride Dakota, watching as she walked Samson toward the stables. The fear behind Lara's blue eyes was real, as was the slight quaver in her voice when she spoke. It wasn't Ryder who'd spooked her, but something—or perhaps, *someone*—else dredged up memories that it was obvious Lara would rather forget.

How could he possibly convince her that his interest in her had nothing to do with some petty conquest and "owning" her? If anything, she owned him. Hell, he'd spent thousands of dollars on a horse he had absolutely no use for just to get her out here. She owned his every waking thought and even his body, which responded to her in ways that no other woman had managed to coax from him. With nothing but a look Lara could awaken every nerve in Ryder's body. Own her? It wasn't ownership when you gave yourself over freely. And he was going to do everything in his power to make her see that.

Ryder decided to give her a few moments before heading after Lara into the stable. Though she'd thought to unveil some great revelation by letting him in on the not-so-secret details of his love life, he was well aware of what folks around town said about him. As well as the women he'd been with. You'd think they'd bagged a trophy buck—a top score on the Boone and Crockett scale—the way they talked about him. And whereas he'd never let the rumors get to him, he wondered what would prompt these women to so salaciously share their sexual exploits with anyone who'd listen.

One of the drawbacks of having money: you never really knew who wanted you for you or for what was sitting in your bank account.

Maybe that's why he was doing everything short of jumping through flaming hoops to get Lara's attention. She wasn't some silly cowboy groupie, like the women who frequented the rodeos in the hopes of landing a bull or bronc rider. And unlike the socialites who slipped him room keys at whatever swanky event he might find himself at, she didn't see him as a diversion to whatever boredom she suffered. If she wanted his money, like any other gold digger, she would've jumped on his cock the first time he asked her out.

Lara was beautiful, feisty, and intelligent. Fiercely independent and not a little stubborn. Ryder wanted her not only for those things, but because she wanted absolutely *nothing* from him. It was borderline perverse that he'd gone out of his way to buy October, giving Lara a reason to want something from him when he resented every other woman for the same reason. The hell with it, though. He'd started down this road. He had no choice but to follow it to the end.

He hopped down off of Dakota and took him by the reins, leading the stallion toward the stable. Through the large barn doors, he caught sight of Lara standing near one of the box stalls with Samson. The gelding stamped his foot and Lara spoke low next to his ear as she stroked his muzzle. The horse let out a chuff of breath and Lara laughed, the sound vibrating down the length of Ryder's spine and infusing him with a warmth that urged him to close the space between them. Dakota snorted as though mocking Ryder for his sappiness. *Stupid horse.* Lara cocked her head toward the sound but otherwise didn't give any outward sign to acknowledge Ryder's presence.

Her dismissal made him want to snatch her up in his arms. Lara's lips practically begged to be kissed, drawn into a stubborn pout. Every curve of her body called to him, countless secrets for him to uncover and explore. Maybe what she needed was for a man who knew her body to show her how good she could feel. And goddamn it, he was going to be the man to do it.

FOUR

Lara pulled the saddle off Samson's back and hung it on a stand in the stable. Without turning around to face Ryder she said, "Look, I'm playing your game, for whatever reasons, but that doesn't mean I have to sit back and let you humiliate me."

"This has nothing to do with humiliation," Ryder all but drawled. "All I gave you was honesty, doc. You should have told me first if you didn't think you could handle a truthful response."

Maybe he was right. Damn him. She unbuckled Samson's bridle and hung it on a hook before giving his backside a pat and sending him into the stall. The truth of Ryder's words stung. But why? She knew his reputation, had heard all of the stories about his insatiable sexual appetites and the number of women who'd wound up in his bed. So why now, when she had no intention of falling victim to her own desires would she give a single shit who he slept with and when?

"This was a stupid idea and I never should have agreed to it." She unbuttoned his shirt and already regretted that she was about to give it back. The scent of leather, freshly cut hay, and something else . . . an almost evergreen tang that was 100 percent male clung to the garment. She wanted to take that damned shirt home and sleep in it. Live in it. Revel in Ryder's scent until she wore the damned thing down to the threads. Lord, she was pathetic.

"Lara, goddamn it, would you quit being so stubborn and climb down off of your high horse for maybe one minute?" Ryder tossed Dakota's rig down on the ground in a tangled heap of metal and leather as he stalked toward her, his dark eyes burning with a heat that stole Lara's breath.

"I'm not being stubborn. I'm being practical. Do you know what people are going to say about me on Monday when they find out I spent the weekend out here?"

"I told you, I don't give a shit what people say," Ryder spat. "Never have."

He closed the distance between them until only a hairsbreadth separated them. The heat rising from his body buffeted her skin and a tremor of want shook Lara to her foundation. A rush of wetness spread between her thighs. It was almost humiliating how ready she was for him. How much she ached to have Ryder Blackwell inside of her. She was no better than any of the other women who shamelessly chased after him. But she'd be damned if she ever begged for his attention.

"Of course you don't care." Lara tried to infuse her voice with conviction but all she wanted right now was to submit. Do whatever he asked of her. "You can afford not to care. Whatever happens this weekend, you'll still be the legendary Ryder Blackwell. And I'll be nothing more than another notch on your bedpost."

He reached up and with his index finger, tipped his hat off her head. It tumbled somewhere behind her, but Lara couldn't be troubled to look. His eyes held her captive, that stare, so intense that it sent a pleasant shiver across her skin. "I'm not gonna lie to you, doc. I've wanted to fuck you since the moment I laid eyes on you. But you're more than a notch on *any* man's bedpost."

Well. That was . . . *up front*. Lara tried to swallow, but found her mouth too dry. Ryder was known for his no-holds-barred attitude. She just never expected to see it up close and personal.

"Ryder . . ." The words died on her tongue as he reached up and swept his shirt from her shoulders. Goosebumps broke out on her flesh as his calloused fingertips blazed a path down her arms and wrapped around her wrists.

He took a step forward and Lara instinctively took a step back. And then another. Her breath raced in her chest as he continued to send her backward until her back made contact with the rough wooden wall behind her. The unoccupied stall was dark and the scent of freshly laid straw invaded her nostrils. His grip on her wrists firm, Ryder lifted her arms above her head and pinned them there with one large hand as he brushed his body up against hers. Every square inch of Lara's body spiked into hyperawareness. Her nipples tightened, straining against the soft cotton fabric of her bra. Her skin tingled as Ryder bent over her, his heated breath caressing her throat. Her own breath came in shallow pants and she froze, hands pinned above her, as she waited for him to make his next move.

What are you doing? You should stop him. Now. Before you don't have a shred of dignity left.

His lips settled at her pulse point, his teeth grazing her skin and suddenly, dignity didn't seem all that important. "You can tell me to stop, you know." Ryder's voice was a husky growl that vibrated through her body. The grip on her wrists remained firm, as though he had no intention of letting her go, as his free hand worked its way between them to cup her breast through her shirt. "But I don't think you want me to." His thumb brushed her already stiff nipple and Lara gasped as a rush of wet warmth spread between her thighs. The hard length of his erection pressed through his jeans against her stomach and all rational thought left her mind as though sucked through a vacuum.

She arched against him as his fingers moved to her other breast, teasing the nipple through the fabric to an aching point. Lara bit her bottom lip to keep from moaning, but only because she knew that's what Ryder wanted from her. To make her moan and whimper and beg for his attention. And she wasn't about to give him the satisfaction.

He continued his unhurried path, his mouth a brand on her skin as he nipped at the rounded flesh swelling above the neckline of her shirt. Lara's breath sped in her chest as his free hand abandoned her breast and trailed downward, over her ribs and stomach to the waistline of her jeans. Her gaze locked with his and one corner of his mouth lifted in a self-satisfied smirk as he popped the button and eased down her zipper, her arms still caged above her. Though she wasn't helpless to stop him and was by no means being restrained against her will, the sheer excitement she felt at being held this way was unlike anything she'd ever experienced before.

Ryder's tongue flicked out at his bottom lip, a slow, languid motion as though savoring something delicious, and watching him made Lara's knees weak. His right hand slipped past her jeans and dove into her underwear and when his finger slid against her slick folds, she almost came for him right then and there.

"Is all that sweet honey for me, doc?" he asked next to her ear. He pressed his body into hers while his fingers danced across her clitoris, each pass sending a jolt of sensation zinging through her body. "Mmm . . ." Lara shuddered as his lips brushed her earlobe, his breath hot with his own labored breathing. "You feel so damned good. So slick and soft. I could pet you like this all day."

That sounded like a damned good plan. She'd been wound as tight as a spring for months, looking over her shoulder, worrying about things that weren't in her power to fix. Losing October had been the last straw, and the moment she felt the walls of her life closing in like a prison cell, Ryder Blackwell swooped in to set her free.

Lara gasped as he circled her swollen bud, applying the perfect amount of pressure before backing off. Would the price of this freedom be something she was willing to pay?

Good god in heaven the woman was perfection. Ryder breathed in deeply, taking her scent into his lungs and holding it there. She took her bottom lip between her teeth and arched into his touch, but he could tell she was holding back and that's not what he wanted from her. Ryder wanted to hear her moan, call out his name as she came. And the fact that she kept such a tight grip on her control made him more determined than ever to unravel her. He had a reputation to live up to, after all.

She squirmed beneath him, her hands releasing and contracting into fists in his grip. He kept her pinned to the wall, refusing himself any kind of physical pleasure while he rubbed that swollen knot of nerves at her core. The game was one he enjoyed, working himself up as he denied himself what he wanted until he couldn't wait any longer. And what he wanted more than anything was Lara's hands all over him, those soft fingers of hers wrapped tightly around his cock as she guided him into her sweet slick heat that dripped onto his fingers right now.

Holy hell, he could almost go off just thinking about it.

He pulled away so he could take in her expression while he touched her. Lara's blue eyes were heavily lidded before they fluttered closed, her dark lashes fanning against her flushed cheeks. She worked her bottom lip between her teeth, obviously determined not to cry out, but Ryder wasn't going to let that happen. He'd coax those sweet mewling sounds from her if he had to keep her up against this wall all damned day.

"Open your eyes," he commanded, brooking no argument.

As though shocked he'd tell her what to do, her eyes flew open, blue fire blazing in their depths. But she didn't argue, didn't even make a squeak of protest. She wanted him this way. If she didn't, she would have told him to go to hell the second he backed her against the stable wall. A slow smile grew on his lips as he locked his gaze with hers and slowly eased off the pressure, teasing her clit with feather-light strokes that would bring her close to the edge without sending her past it. Her breath labored in her chest and he bent over her, nipping at one taut nipple through the fabric of her shirt. She sucked in a startled gasp and his cock throbbed almost painfully from the sound. It wouldn't be long before he had her sobbing with pleasure.

He pulled back a bit more, and she ground her hips against his hand in frustration. Ryder leaned in, his gaze locked on Lara's, so close that their lips almost touched. "I'm not going to let you come until I hear you, doc. I can keep you this way until you're dying for me to finish you off."

It wouldn't take much. She was already close, her body vibrating against his with each soft stroke of his finger. She urged her hips toward his hand, sliding her clit against him but he shimmied his knee between them, bracing her leg against his. He wanted to dip his finger inside of her, feel the tight constriction of her channel, but he refused himself even that small pleasure. He wanted to leave her sated but wanting more. Because as far as he was concerned, they were just getting started.

"Tell me you want more," Ryder growled next to her ear. Her breathing grew more ragged as he increased the pressure, sliding his finger through her folds and stopping short of entering her. Lara's body tensed and he pulled away, taunting her with a feather-light stroke.

"Tell me."

He repeated the motions again and Lara's full lips parted in a silent *O* that made him want to kiss her until neither of them could breathe. But he held back, his own well-practiced restraint keeping him in control of the situation and himself. He circled her entrance with the pad of his finger, working the over-sensitized flesh and her knees buckled as she let out a whimper not much louder than a whisper. She excited him past the point of reason. His previous partners had relented so easily, playing the game for his benefit, only to give in after a few moments. But Lara was different. Her will rivaled his own and Ryder couldn't wait to see where the weekend would lead. "Come on, doc. Tell me you want it and I'll let you come. It's that simple."

Her eyes met his, the bright blue depths smoldering with heat. "If you think I'll give you the satisfaction of hearing me beg, you've got another think coming, Blackwell." Her voice was a husky purr that shot straight to his balls, drawing them painfully tight.

The urge to open his fly and pound into her was almost too strong to resist. And while Ryder hadn't been shy about riding bareback in his more wild past, he wasn't about to ruin his chances with Lara by throwing caution to the wind. He respected her too much for that. But, god, how he wanted to bury himself deep inside of her, fuck her up against the wall until she was out of her mind with pleasure and screaming any damned thing he wanted her to scream.

"I don't want you to beg," he said, grazing his teeth against her throat. "I want you to *tell* me what you want. And then, I'll give it to you."

He kissed her jawline, her throat, the swell of her breasts, but restrained himself from claiming her mouth like he wanted to. Lara arched her neck, rested her head on the wall behind her and a soft, almost resigned groan worked its way up her throat. "What I want," she said without looking at him, "is for you to stop playing games and make me come."

The simple command damn near brought him to his knees. No one dared to order him around, not *the* Ryder Blackwell. He was treated with a certain level of respect and sometimes fear because he was a shrewd businessman and went after what he wanted. And the women he'd been with . . . well, they saw nothing more than a chance to get their hands in his wallet. They rolled over and begged. Gladly. But not Lara. She refused to beg for anything. She didn't give a damn about his money or his reputation. And that's why he wanted her more than any other woman he'd ever met.

He worked her stiff bud in earnest, sliding his fingers over her flesh in tight little circles. Lara let out a long, drawn-out moan, the sound so goddamned sweet that a pleasant shudder shook Ryder's body. Her muscles went rigid as stone against him, and then melted with her release as she pressed her hips into his hand, crying out over and over again as she came. Ryder brought her down slowly, easing into soft, feathery caresses. He released his grip on her wrists and she relaxed against him, holding onto his shoulders for support as her breath sped in her chest.

"Oh my god." The words were barely a whisper, but her warm breath against his neck heated Ryder's blood to boiling. He couldn't wait to do it all over again, a battle of wills that ended up with her soft and willing in his arms. She raised her head from his shoulder, alert. "Did you hear that?"

The sound of tires crunching on gravel was followed by a car door slamming. An agitated female voice called out, "Ryder Blackwell, where in the hell are you?" and he groaned into Lara's hair.

"Who is that?" she asked, her tone just north of horrified.

He pulled away to give her a grin and shrugged a shoulder. "My mother."

FIVE

Lord have mercy. Despite the fact that she'd been caught—literally—with her pants down, Lara couldn't help but find it amusing to see the oh-so-tough Ryder jump to attention like a wayward calf at the sound of his mama's holler. And that guilty, boyish grin he'd flashed her before hightailing it out of the stable . . . she almost came again from the sight of it.

So much for keeping him at arm's length.

Lara had vowed not to let Ryder Blackwell get to her, as he had so many others, but now that she was here alone with him, she found him too hard to resist. As evidenced by the mind-blowing orgasm he'd given her. She'd heard the rumors that he knew how to pleasure a woman. In fact, tales of the attention paid to his lovers was practically the stuff of legend. And when it came to his own pleasure, Ryder was known to be down to business. Lara had certainly come face-to-face with part of that legend today. As she tried to make herself look presentable, she wondered at his restraint. She could feel his erection through the tight denim of his jeans, saw the evidence of his arousal burning in his gaze, and heard the intensity of it in his voice.

Why did he hold back? Was it to add insult to injury? Take October from her and then tease her with his sexual prowess? No. If that had been the case, his only concern would have been making sure he got off, not the other way around. Maybe there was more to Ryder Blackwell than the rumors circulated around town. As she headed out of the stable, a smile curved Lara's lips. She had all weekend to find out, didn't she?

"Jason stopped by the house this morning on his way to Dallas. Told me a few things too. Ryder James Blackwell, did you buy a horse at auction this morning just to spite that poor little gal?"

As Lara approached, she swallowed down the laughter that threatened. A man was in serious trouble when his mama triple named him, and seeing the nearly thirty-year-old Ryder cower in his mother's presence was a sight she'd cherish for weeks to come.

"Jase has a big mouth," Ryder grumbled, casting a sheepish grin Lara's way. Her chest swelled with emotion at the openness of his expression and she couldn't help but smile back. "And I'm a grown man, Mom. If I want to buy a horse at auction—any horse—I will."

"Pfft." His mother swatted at him and Ryder jumped back barely missing his mother's hand. "You need a thoroughbred like you need a hole in the head, son. What are you up to?"

"Apparently," Lara said as she approached, "he's getting into the horse-breeding business."

"Well. I hope you're here to whoop his butt, Dr. Montgomery," Ryder's mom said with a smile. She reminded her of him: same light brown eyes and intelligent features. "I'm Rayanne Blackwell, by the way."

Lara reached out and shook her hand, trying not to let her gaze wander to Ryder as it seemed to want to do on its own. "Nice to meet you, Mrs. Blackwell."

"Please. You call me Rayanne or nothin' at all."

It was also quite apparent where Ryder got his charm. "All right, then. Rayanne."

"Well, since I'm here, you might as well show me what all the fuss is about." She headed in the direction of the stables and Ryder jogged to catch up with her.

"October's in the corral," he said, turning her shoulders to navigate her in the right direction. "Over there."

"Well," she said on an exhale. "How 'bout that. She's a beautiful mare, isn't she?"

Rayanne strode up to the fence, clucking her tongue and cooing at October Sky. A pang of regret shot through Lara's chest. What if she lost her bet to Ryder? And what if—even after what had happened between them—he still refused to sell the mare to her? Lara couldn't bear to think of losing October. Not when she'd worked so hard to buy her.

"So, tell me, Dr. Montgomery, why did you have your eye on this particular mare?" There was something about the way Rayanne asked the question, as though she already knew the answer but wanted Lara to tell her for someone else's benefit. Perhaps Ryder's?

"First off, if I'm calling you Rayanne, you'd better call me Lara." Rayanne gave her a wink and she continued, "October Sky is descended from Diamond Dancer." From behind her, she heard Ryder approach and he settled in beside his mom, leaning his arms on the fence post as he watched October trot around the corral.

"He won the Triple Crown, didn't he?" Rayanne asked.

"Yep," Lara said with pride. "My grandpa owned the stables that bred him. A few others who made names for themselves too. At one time, people came from all over the world to buy his horses."

"I'd say that's a pretty interesting fact, wouldn't you, son?"

Ryder didn't answer, simply nodded his head. His eyes met Lara's, his brow furrowed as he studied her. She wondered what he'd think of her when he heard the rest of her family's sob story.

"So, what happened to your granddaddy's stables, Lara?" Rayanne continued.

"Long story short," Lara said as she peeled her gaze away from Ryder's, "he trusted the wrong person and lost everything. His ranch, his livelihood, and every last horse in his stable. I saved up to buy October so I could rebuild his legacy. Maybe even redeem my family's name."

"Honey." Rayanne laid a comforting hand on Lara's shoulder. "It ain't your name that makes you what you are. And don't you forget that."

Lara's lips quirked in a half smile. If that wasn't a ranch mother's logic, she didn't know what was. Those same words could have come from her own mother or grandmother. She just wished she believed it. If Rayanne knew her family's story—and who knew, maybe she did—then she'd know how people had treated her family after everyone found out that the trainers at the stable had been injecting the horses with steroids, not to mention forging breeding records and fabricating lineages. In essence, they were selling poor stock for top dollar. By the time it all came out, her grandpa was too old to take an active role at the stables, and couldn't fix the damage. When all was said and done, he was forced to answer to several lawsuits and had to sell everything to pay off the many judgments.

"Sometimes," Lara replied, "your name and the reputation affixed to it is all you've got."

"What do you think about that, Ryder?" Rayanne asked, turning to face her son. "Do you think a person should be judged by their name and the reputation hitched to it?"

Lara had a feeling that Rayanne Blackwell was the kind of woman who liked to point out life lessons on the sly. And as she sensed that Rayanne had coaxed Lara's history out of her for her son's benefit, likewise, there was something in her words to Ryder that made her think she wanted Lara to know a little something about the Blackwells as well.

A sordid past, perhaps? What sort of dark cloud could possibly be hovering over the lives of the town's most prominent cattle family?

Ryder locked eyes with his mom, well aware of the message she was sending. It was one she'd been conveying to him all his life. That he was more than just his name and the by-product of the man who'd given it to him. A man was the sum of his actions and convictions. And the name Blackwell—while something he'd never been proud of as a boy—was one he'd built apart from his father's contribution to it.

His mom was never shy about voicing her disappointment over some of his antics over the years. Apparently, today was no exception.

"I think a name is only as good as the person wearing it," Ryder finally said. "And that worrying about the past or what you could or couldn't have changed for whatever reason brings a person nothing but a lot of pointless heartache."

His mom gave him a pointed look. "And don't forget it, kiddo. Now, I left a stockpot here the last time we had Sunday dinner and I need it for a batch of chili I offered to take over to the Senior Center for their Christmas Eve dinner. I'm going to go fetch it and head home." She turned toward the main house and added over her shoulder, "You best behave yourself, you hear me?"

Ryder gave his mom an affectionate smile as he watched her amble toward the main house. She had at least four stockpots at her own house; no doubt she was using the one she'd left here as an excuse to butt into his business and get a look at Lara. As if she needed an excuse to be nosy.

He scooted down the fence line to where Lara gazed out at the corral, watching with a wistful expression as October pranced around. "I feel like I'm fifteen again, caught doin' something I shouldn't with someone I shouldn't be doin' it with."

"Your family is close, aren't they?"

She didn't look at him, just kept staring at some unknown point, lost in her thoughts. Ryder used to think that no one could have as dark a shadow on their past as he did. But maybe he was wrong about that. "My mom and my brothers and I are." No need to dredge up too much of the past. If Lara knew all of the dark details, she'd jump in her truck and hightail it out of there, horse or not. "I've got some cousins on my mom's side of the family that I'm pretty close with too. Aunts, uncles . . ."

"I'm not very close with mine," she said on a sigh. "Maybe I ought to hit up the Senior Center for some Christmas Eve chili next week. It's not like I'll be spending the holiday with any of my own relatives." Ryder hated how the moment managed to turn so somber. He wanted back the fiery, passionate woman he'd explored in the stables. The sadness she exuded now sent a pang straight through his chest. "My grandpa and I used to be close . . . before. After he died, I sort of drifted away."

"Mom made it sound like she knew your family," Ryder remarked. "I didn't know you were local."

"I'm not," she scoffed. "Not really. My grandparents

were local, but my dad moved to Houston after Grandpa lost everything and they stopped bringing me here. I guess without his money and reputation for my dad to live off of, he didn't see much point in staying here."

Ryder had known people like that most of his adult life. Those who measured others' worth based on the numbers in their bank account and nothing more. No doubt none of them would give him the time of day if he lost everything. He could only imagine the kind of alienation Lara must have felt growing up with that hanging over her head. "You know, it's not the mare that's gonna redeem your family name, doc."

"And what would you know about that?" She still refused to look at him and Ryder resisted the urge to grab her by the shoulders and spin her toward him.

"You'd be surprised."

"Right," she scoffed. "What's next on the chore list, boss?" She looked at him now, her expression one of fierce determination. "Let's get back to work. I've got a brood-mare to win."

SIX

Lara was an idiot. With nothing more than a few heated looks and seductive words whispered in that smooth bourbon voice of his, she'd spread her legs and let Ryder entice her into one hell of a distraction. And at the corral a moment ago, he'd tried to distract her again, opening the conversation to suggest that Lara should give up on owning October Sky and get herself some other horse to build her stables with. Because it wasn't about reclaiming her family's legacy, apparently. No, the foundation of a good reputation was all about pulling yourself up by the bootstraps and making do with what you had. Or maybe, what you could *afford*.

Yeah, right.

She waited patiently by the stables as Ryder said goodbye to his mama. Lara didn't know much about the Blackwell family—aside from the fact that they had more money than God—and frankly she didn't care. She needed to stay focused, remember why she was here, and steel herself against Ryder's seductive ploys. If she wasn't careful, by Monday, she'd be nothing more than another name to add to his long list of conquests, and she'd walk away as empty-handed as when she'd arrived.

As soon as Rayanne's little pickup took off down the road, Ryder turned toward the stable, his rolling gait as relaxed and confident as a champion bull strolling through a feedlot. He strode past her into the stable, and Lara turned to watch him retrieve his Stetson from where he'd knocked it off her head right before he'd backed her into the stall. A pleasant shiver raced down her spine as she thought about what had happened in there and how alive with pleasure he'd made her feel.

It was no doubt merely a taste of what he was capable of, but whether or not she was interested in sampling the entire menu, a taste was all she was going to allow herself to have. Ever again. And if he came away from their encounter with nothing more than a serious case of blue balls, well, too damned bad. She was through with him.

"Back the truck in here," Ryder all but commanded. "We need to load up thirty alfalfa bales and take them over to the far pasture."

His cool tone didn't do much for Lara's attitude. Though, what did she expect? She'd treated him with the same detachment not a moment before. She deserved everything he dished out, and now that she'd practically rejected him, Lara expected him to put her through the wringer. No doubt he'd dish out a list of chores designed to make her want to give up.

Well, that wasn't going to happen.

She wasn't leaving this ranch without October Sky.

The ranch truck wasn't an impressive, tricked-out, luxury ranch pickup like she'd expected it might be. Rather, it was an old, beat-up flatbed with one white door, one blue door, and a green hood. A smile curved her lips as she headed for the old Ford that looked like it would be more at home on a tiny, run-down, three-acre ranch, rather than Ryder Blackwell's sprawling estate.

"Keys are in it!" His voice echoed from somewhere deep inside the stables.

Lara hopped into the truck, the door hinges resisting as they creaked in protest. "You know what Ford stands for, don't you?" she called back toward the stables. "Found on the road dead." Ryder's soft laughter made it to her ears and she settled herself on the worn bench seat, adjusted her position to avoid a spring poking through the upholstery, and turned the key in the ignition. The engine whined and whirred, as though reluctant to get to work, and Lara pumped the gas pedal in quick succession. "Come on, you can do it. Fire up." On her third try, the engine roared to life and knocked and spluttered for a few minutes before it began to idle at a steady pace.

Woot! Ryder probably thought she'd have trouble starting the old ranch rig, but she showed him. She may have failed at running cows, but she'd owned enough beater vehicles in her life to know how to coax one into starting. Lara threw the truck into gear and slowly backed it in through the wide barn doors. Careful not to back into anything, she negotiated the narrow middle section until the flatbed sat directly under the loft stacked with dark green bales of alfalfa.

"Stay out of the way," Ryder called from the loft, his tone not a little bossy. She supposed that was a good thing. Distance would be a hell of a lot easier if he was too pissed off with her to be charming. "I'm going to drop these bales down."

"You need someone to stack them, though," Lara remarked with a smirk. "I'm pretty sure I can manage to not be crushed by a bale of hay. Just toss them down. I'll stack them."

The derisive snort that answered her made her wish she had something to chuck at the cocky cowboy. She welcomed the chance to exercise her muscles and maybe work out a little of the frustration she was feeling. Granted, her legs were damned near useless after the shattering orgasm Ryder had given her, but she didn't want him to know that. No use bolstering an ego that already got its fair share of strokes.

Ryder stepped to the edge of the loft, a bale of alfalfa held firmly in his grasp. She couldn't deny it was quite an impressive sight, each muscle cut and defined, corded from the effort of holding up the eighty-pound bale of hay. He tossed it down as though it weighed nothing at all and it bounced once on the flatbed before rolling to a stop at Lara's feet. She gripped the twine that held the bale together in both of her hands and was sure to lift with her legs as she maneuvered the heavy rectangle of hay to the back of the flatbed, the first of her soon-to-be-organized stack. Granted, she couldn't haul them around the way Ryder could, but she was holding her own just the same.

"Here." Ryder threw down a pair of well-worn leather gloves. "Use those."

Of all the stubborn, pigheaded women.

Though he always welcomed a social call from his mother, today's not-so-impromptu visit had thrown a huge monkey wrench into his plans. He'd had Lara right where he wanted her: soft, dripping wet, and oh-so-willing. But his mom's sermon on family and reputations had managed to squash all of Ryder's hard work.

Speaking of hard . . .

His cock pulsed in his jeans, his own raging desire reminding him that as far as he was concerned, he and Lara had only just begun their erotic play. He welcomed the discomfort, used it as motivation to continue on his course.

He refused to stop this game until he had her every way imaginable. And maybe even a few he'd never thought of.

"Are you tired, Blackwell? Need to take a little breather after exerting yourself over that one bale?"

Lara's sarcastic comment broke through his musing, and he looked down to find her smirking up at him, an expression that made him want to strip her bare and do all sorts of dirty things to her until she was as pliant and agreeable as a newly broke filly. Damn it, with all of the women who'd gladly jump into his bed without so much as a wink, why was he so obsessed with the one who didn't seem to want anything to do with him?

Well, it didn't take a mind like Freud's to figure that one out.

He hoisted another bale into his grip and dropped it down onto the flatbed. Lara slipped his gloves on and moved the alfalfa next to the first bale. One thing was for certain: Lara Montgomery was damned tough.

It took half as long to load the truck as he'd expected. And though there'd been next to no conversation, it was a companionable silence. Something he rarely experienced with other women. He enjoyed working alongside Lara. And wasn't that damned domestic of him? "Ready?" he asked as Lara hefted the last bale into place. He hopped down onto the truck from the loft and pushed his hat back on his forehead.

"To the feedlot?" she asked.

Down to business. She could deflect all she wanted, but Ryder was more determined than Lara was stubborn. "Yup. We'll feed and then break for dinner."

It took all of about an hour to throw out thirty bales of alfalfa for the cows and calves they'd moved to the north pasture. The supplemental feeding was important, and for some stupid reason, Ryder wanted Lara to know that he was looking out for his stock and making sure they were well taken care of. When the last bale was spread and followed the long line of strewn alfalfa he'd constructed, he had her circle back around toward the house.

Ryder sat on the flatbed, legs dangling off the edge as the old truck rocked and teetered on the unsteady ground. It was a piece of shit and only ran about half the time, but he kept it to remind him of his roots. And a few other things. He pulled off his gloves and brought his hand to his temple, tracing the scar above his left eyebrow. It took eight stitches to close the split in his head, an injury sustained when his dad got pissed at his brother Luke and Ryder stepped in to take the brunt of his father's rage. His eyes wandered to the corner of the flatbed, to the very spot he'd smacked his head when his dad shoved him and he'd tripped into it.

He couldn't erase the past. But he could damn well make sure history didn't repeat itself. Ryder had been only sixteen when he finally took matters into his own hands. It had been the first and last time that he'd let his own rage spur him to violence. And he vowed he'd never lose control like that again.

"Where do you want me to park?"

Lara's words cut into his thoughts like a soft rain on a sultry afternoon. Only now did Ryder realize that his fists were clenched tight, and his heart raced in his chest. He banished the unpleasant memories that threatened to suck him into a dark place he rarely visited and focused his attention instead on the sound of Lara's voice. "You can pull up to the main house."

The truck rounded the stables and approached the house, and Pepper shimmied her little black body out from her doghouse and bounded next to the pickup, tail wagging as she yipped in welcome. "Somebody's glad to see you," Lara remarked as she killed the engine and hopped out of the truck. "Come here, girl."

Ryder watched as Lara snuggled Pepper, ruffling the fur at her ears. "She's a mixed breed, isn't she?"

"She's a mutt all right," Ryder said with affection as he bent down beside Lara to stroke Pepper's fur. "Blue heeler and border collie. She's smart as a whip and the best-tempered dog I've ever owned."

"I believe it," Lara said with a laugh. "You sure showed those ornery cows who's boss this morning, didn't you, girl?"

Pepper wagged her tail and pushed her snout under Lara's arm, getting close enough to give her cheek a couple of licks. Lara laughed and wrapped her arms around Pepper's neck, enjoying the affection, and something tightened in Ryder's chest. Maybe this weekend wasn't such a good idea. Because with every moment he spent with her, Ryder was afraid that Lara was anchoring herself deeper into his system rather than working herself out the way he'd hoped.

"Did you train her to run cattle?" Lara's eyes met his and for a moment, some of the iciness melted away, replaced with a glow that seemed to soak right into him, igniting every inch of Ryder's body with fiery warmth.

"Sort of," he said with a shrug. "She was born to chase and herd, so it comes naturally to her. Dogs like Pep need something to get after, you know?"

Lara smiled. "I do. I've treated more than a couple ambitious cow dogs who thought they could take on a truck tire or two. It's good that she has plenty of space to roam around and get all of that energy out of her system."

Ryder looked around—there wasn't another house for miles—at the acres and acres of land. "You got that right. Guess we both need a little space to roam."

Lara's expression darkened and she averted her gaze. "Guess so. No chance of any ex-girlfriends dropping by for a quick visit when you live all the way out here."

He was good and ready to put talk of his past relation-
ships away once and for all. Yes, he'd been with more than
a few women in his life. They both knew it, no point in
beating a dead horse. But he was curious at Lara's sharp
tone. "What's the matter, doc?" he teased. "Jealous?"

She didn't look at him when she said, "Hardly. Though
I have to wonder how many women have gotten the Ryder
Blackwell treatment in such a low-rent place." She ran her
fingers absently through Pepper's fur. "Maybe you figure
the local vet wouldn't mind if you took her right there in
the barn."

Low rent? That stable cost him a fortune, and the place
was almost as clean as his house. He wasn't sure what Lara
thought—maybe that he wined and dined the women he
slept with, bathed them in expensive gifts before they fell
into bed with him. But what she didn't know was that she
was the first woman he'd ever actually entertained at his
place. *Ever.* "You're making a mighty big assumption,
don't you think?"

"Am I?" Her eyes met his, serious and almost . . . sad.

"Jesus Christ, Lara." Ryder stood and snatched his Stetson off his head, smacking it against his thigh. She frustrated him past the point of reason and maybe it was her
up-front, down-to-business attitude that made him want
her even more. "For someone who's trying so hard to rebuild a reputation tarnished by cheap, cruel gossip, you're
sure jumping on that bandwagon pretty damned quick."

"See, that's the thing, Ryder," Lara said, giving Pepper
one last scratch behind the ear before she stood to face him.
"All the gossip about my family happened to be true.
People don't generally talk about someone unless they give
'em something to talk about."

"Well, if that's what you think, I suppose there's nothing I can say to change your mind." He let out a derisive
snort. "Let's eat." Ryder snapped his fingers and Pepper

fell into step beside him, wagging her tail and bouncing as he headed for the house.

Never before had Ryder bothered with worrying over the shit people said about him. It was just talk after all, and he'd be willing to bet his "many" conquests were way overexaggerated in the public opinion. But now, after being hit over the head with it repeatedly by the woman he was trying to impress, Ryder wished for the first time that people would've kept their big mouths shut.

SEVEN

Lara didn't know why her mood had turned so sour. Especially since she'd already decided that she wasn't going to let Ryder Blackwell touch her in any way more intimate than a handshake ever again. Still . . . her mind rebelled against logic, reminding her of their time in the stable and the way his fingers worked her sensitive flesh, bringing her fevered body to heights of pleasure she'd never experienced before.

With nothing more than the artful caress of his fingertips he'd given her the most intense orgasm of her life. And there was a part of her that yearned for more. That need to have a little more of him was enough to sour Lara's mood. *So much for being stone-cold.*

The Blackwell ranch was impressive in and of itself. Over nine hundred acres of lush pastures and rolling hills dotted with trees. Ryder's house stood like a sentinel at the head of it all, a sprawling ranch-style mansion that might have been considered modest by billionaire standards. Even when her family had been at its wealthiest, they'd never known luxury like this.

Ryder led the way across a wraparound porch to the side of the house. A cottage door led to a small mudroom, complete with coat hooks fashioned from discarded horseshoes and a bench made from cut lodge poles lined with cubbies for boots. Pepper scrambled across the hardwood floor into the depths of the house while Ryder kicked off his boots. Lara followed suit, stuffing them into one of the empty cubbies and tried not to look too nosy as she followed him into the kitchen.

Wow.

"I think your kitchen is as big as my entire apartment." The words escaped Lara's mouth before she could think better of it. "I mean . . ."

Ryder chuckled. "It's definitely bigger than the house I grew up in."

Lara strolled into the kitchen, her fingers skimming the shiny granite countertops as she walked. If she had a kitchen like this, she'd live in it. Top-of-the-line appliances, an island counter big enough to roll out ten pie crusts, windows that let in the perfect amount of sunlight, and a gorgeous porcelain basin sink that looked like the only antique in the place.

"My mom salvaged that sink from my grandma's place," Ryder said when he noticed her eyeing it. "We reclaimed a bunch of stuff from the old house when we built this one. There are little bits and pieces of my family in every room."

Ryder might have been a lowlife for buying her horse, but Lara admired his love for his family. And there was something about a nostalgic man that made her feel all warm and fuzzy inside. If he cared enough to save his grandma's sink, maybe there was more to him than the heartless womanizer she'd sized him up to be.

"Well, let's get to cooking." Excitement pooled in Lara's stomach at the prospect of putting Ryder's kitchen to good use. "Though I have to admit, I half-expected to see a team of professional chefs waiting to cook our meals to order."

Ryder rolled his eyes at her ribbing, a half smile curving his lips, and it only intensified the butterflies swirling in Lara's stomach. "I know how to cook, thank you very much. Sit down, and I'll whip us up something."

"Uh-uh," Lara said with an emphatic shake of her head. "No way am I not going to take the opportunity to play in a kitchen like this."

"All right." Ryder flashed her a wide smile that went straight to her head. How could a man make her feel giddy from nothing more than a grin? "We'll cook together, then. You grab the steaks and veggies from the fridge and I'll rustle up the pans."

"Deal."

Ryder's "fridge" was a double glass door, industrial Frigidaire that looked like it belonged in a five-star restaurant. Stocked full of pretty much anything she could possibly want, Lara dug through its confines, worried that she might get lost before she managed to gather all of the ingredients for dinner. After some hard-core foraging, Lara managed to retrieve a couple of T-bone steaks, onions, mushrooms, and a trio of peppers.

"There's rice in the pantry," Ryder said as he pulled a pan from a baker's rack above the island. "Unless you want beans or pasta, or something else."

"Rice is fine." She set her haul on the counter next to the stove and riffled through the walk-in pantry left of the refrigerator, marveling at the neat rows of sundry items. Really, Ryder's kitchen was better stocked than the local grocery store.

"Why did you turn me down when I asked you out last month?" Ryder asked out of nowhere as he tore into the package of steaks and seasoned them. He didn't make eye contact, just focused on the task at hand. Huh. A little out of character for the usually self-assured cowboy.

"You know why," Lara said. She filled a pot with water and set it to boil on the stove. "Why did you buy October when you knew I wanted her?"

Ryder paused as he set one of the steaks aside. "You know why."

She probably deserved that. A heavy sigh escaped her lips and she said, "I turned you down because I knew what people would say about me if I went out with you. I've worked hard to rebuild my family's reputation. Once I get my stable up and running, I don't want anyone to have a reason not to do business with me."

"And you think a date with a successful cattle rancher would've tarnished your reputation?"

"You know what I mean." Lara grabbed a knife from the butcher block and went to work slicing peppers. "It's different for a man. You can date as many women as you want with a revolving door into your bedroom and no one would bat a lash. Your reputation as a businessman is good and intact. But the second a woman acts like she might want to play the field, everyone treats her like she's a leper. Not exactly the best way to start a business. Plus, I didn't want people to think I was . . ."

"What?"

Lara cringed. "A gold digger. I'm not exactly rolling in money, you know."

Ryder set aside the steaks and turned toward Lara, his light brown eyes alight with a heat that she wished she could ignore. He stalked toward her, and she took a few steps back until he'd effectively pinned her against the island counter. The intensity of his gaze stole her breath and Lara tried to avert her eyes but he held her captive. "I don't give a good goddamn what anyone says about me and neither should you."

"That's easy for you to say," Lara remarked. "You've already made your fortune."

"And I could lose it tomorrow." The warm timbre of his voice shot straight through her, settling between Lara's legs in a slow thrum that stirred her desire. "Life is short and I refuse to waste it on a lot of needless worry. I'm not going to deny myself the things I want because of some nosy assholes who don't know how to mind their own business. I do what I want, when I want, and the rest of the world can go fuck itself."

"And what do you want, Ryder?" It was a dangerous question, one Lara wasn't sure she wanted him to answer because she was looking for an excuse to disregard her own coached detachment. Her breath hitched in her chest, her body hyperaware as he reached up and smoothed his thumb across her cheek.

"I want *you*."

Dinner took a backseat to a more primal hunger as Ryder stared into Lara's bright blue eyes. His hands found their way to her hips and he gripped her tight, hoisting her pert little ass onto the countertop. The thought of laying her out, savoring every inch of her like she was his last meal made his head spin and his cock swell in his jeans. And Ryder could think of no better way to put the wide marble countertop to good use.

He reached up and without a word stripped Lara's shirt up and over her head. Her chest rose and fell with her breath and he stared greedily at the soft round flesh swelling above her bra. With his eyes still locked on hers, he took a step closer and she spread her legs as though in invitation. Ryder cradled himself against her and placed a lazy kiss between her breasts as he reached behind her and released the clasp.

With the straps clutched in his grasp, Ryder leaned back

and paused. It took all of his restraint not to jerk the garment free of her skin, but that was the point, wasn't it? To test the limits of his control, see how long he could hold out. For a moment, he simply stood there. Drank her in. Let his eyes roam over the flesh his fingers itched to reach out and caress. And when his hands began to shake from the effort of restraint, Ryder slowly dragged the straps down Lara's arms and pulled her bra away to reveal her breasts.

Mary mother of god.

Her nipples puckered tight as they were exposed to the air and Ryder reached out, cupping the delicious weight of one breast in his hand while he took the other into his mouth. He sucked deeply, swirling his tongue over the pearled peak and Lara arched into him, her breath catching in a desperate gasp. His cock responded to the sound, growing almost painfully hard and throbbing against his fly. He wanted inside of her so bad, he didn't know how long he'd be able to wait. But he was going to do his damnedest to make sure she was screaming his name long before he dove into her sweet, wet heat.

Goddamn. If having her was half as good as the anticipation, Ryder doubted he'd be able to let her leave once the weekend was over.

As he suckled her, he rolled her other nipple between his thumb and forefinger, stopping to give her a light pinch before he resumed the rhythm. A slow whimper worked its way up Lara's throat and she braced her arms behind her on the counter as she rolled her head back on her shoulders. She spread her legs wider, inviting him even closer.

Well, don't mind if I do . . .

Ryder eased her back until she was lying on the countertop, legs dangling over the edge. With much less restraint than he'd previously exhibited, he unbuttoned her jeans and peeled them off of her—along with her underwear—in a single swipe. If her naked breasts were enough to drive him to a near-frenzy, the sight of her bare, glistening sex sent him completely over the edge. He traced the pad of his finger over her mound, the skin soft and nearly bereft of hair. He paused for a moment, remembering the man she'd been with at the benefit and wondered if she'd groomed her gorgeous pussy for him.

It didn't matter now. After this weekend, Ryder was going to make damned sure that no other man laid a hand on Lara Montgomery ever again.

She was ready for him, so wet the evidence of her arousal had spread over her thighs. He ran his finger down her soft skin and up, taking some of that sweet honey onto his finger as he worked it into her folds and the swollen knot of nerves at her center.

Lara's back arched off the countertop with the first tentative touch and her hands balled into fists at her sides. She came alive from that one touch, her body so responsive to him that she trembled. It was a heady thing, one that Ryder enjoyed almost more than the sex itself: the knowledge that he was responsible for her pleasure. That *he* awakened that response in her. As though her body lay dormant until he provided what she needed to spark to life. It was that power that Ryder craved. Needed. And with such a strong-willed woman as Lara, the rush he felt pleasuring her intensified by leaps and bounds.

While he stoked her soft pink flesh, Ryder's free hand traveled up Lara's torso, pausing to grip the curve of her hip before passing along her ribs. His palm closed over her left breast and a contented sigh escaped Lara's lips. He slowed his ministrations, eyes locked on her face. Her little pants of breath caused his own to speed in his chest. Lara spread her legs wider and urged her hips toward his hand and Ryder took the cue, circling her bud with the pad of his finger. He took her nipple between his fingers and teased the already stiff peak, plucking at it, all the while gauging Lara's reaction.

It was instant and intense. She cried out from the contact, her back bowing off the countertop. The sound of her voice, ragged little sobs of pleasure, shot straight through Ryder's body and tightened his balls to the point that he was aching for release. But he promised himself that first she'd be screaming his name and he was going to make sure that happened before he allowed himself to enjoy her.

When he abandoned her breast, Lara whimpered in protest. A smile curved Ryder's lips. He'd give her whatever she needed—and maybe even a few things she didn't know she needed—in good time. Right now, he wanted nothing more than to taste her, to work her into a frenzy so that when he finally took her, they'd both be mindless with need.

Ryder pressed his palm, fingers splayed, on the flat of Lara's stomach. Her muscles flexed beneath his hand as he traveled upward between her breasts to her throat. He cupped the back of her neck, his grip firm as he stroked his thumb along her jawline. She was so responsive, so fucking beautiful it damned near stole his breath. "Oh god, Ryder, I need to come."

Lara's heavy-lidded eyes locked on his and her tongue darted out to lick her lips. He imagined her soft pink tongue swirling over the head of his cock and he let out a groan. She was everything he wanted in a woman: sensual, strong-willed, intelligent. She knew what she wanted and how she wanted it. Unlike the other women he'd bedded, she didn't give a shit about his money and likewise, she didn't judge or measure him based on the numbers in his bank account. She told him she wouldn't sleep with him in exchange for the horse and he believed her. And knowing that she was here, naked, and willing because she wanted to be and not because she thought she'd get something out of the deal meant more to him than any conquest in his past.

Ryder leaned over her and put his mouth close to her ear. She nipped at his earlobe and the contact was electric. If he didn't fuck her soon, he was going to explode. "I want you, Lara. I want you so fucking bad I can't stand it," he said, low. "I'm going to touch you, taste you, lick every inch of you and then fuck you until you can't even imagine having another man's hands on you."

"You talk a good game." Lara's voice was a husky murmur that vibrated through Ryder's body. "Now, let's see you back it up."

EIGHT

So much for sticking to her guns. Lara should have been ashamed at how easily she managed to succumb to Ryder's charms, but when he touched her she couldn't seem to remember why. His heated, almost crass words in her ear only managed to prove that when Ryder Blackwell set out to do something, he gave it his all. He didn't want her thinking of other men? No. Problem. He was so unlike any man she'd ever been with. As though he'd made it his life's ambition to learn the intricacies of her body and how to give her pleasure. And if she did say so herself, the man was a freaking master at his craft. If he could evoke so much from her with a simple touch, she could only imagine what he'd be like buried deep inside of her.

She sure as hell hoped he was a man who kept his promises.

Her body vibrated with need, every inch of her skin sparked into awareness. He circled her clit with the pad of his finger and a shudder traveled the length of her spine and settled low in her core, a deep throbbing need that drove her past the point of reason. "Make me come, Ryder."

As though repeating herself would spur him into action. Lara knew better. No one pushed Ryder Blackwell or made him do anything before he was damn good and ready to do it. His breath was hot in her ear as a satisfied growl rumbled in his chest. Knowing which places on her body were the most sensitive, his mouth brushed the skin at her throat and then moved lower across her collarbone. Each contact was a brand, the heat traveling through her veins like liquid fire. His tongue dipped at her belly button and Lara gasped at her sensitivity there. Their eyes met for the briefest moment and a satisfied smirk spread across Ryder's lips. He gripped her thighs, the rasp of his calloused hands on her skin a delicious torture as he dipped his head between her legs and paused.

Oh god, yes.

"Tell me what you want."

Apparently the powerful Mr. Blackwell enjoyed having her boss him around. He'd been the same way with her in the stable, holding off, teasing her until she gave him a command. Not that Lara had any problem voicing what she wanted. On the contrary, her previous partners had practically needed a detailed map and voice-activated GPS to bring her to orgasm.

But not Ryder.

"I want you to make me come," Lara said, her voice breathy with anticipation.

"How?"

"You know how." He brushed his thumb against her clit and Lara's hips bucked at the intense sensation. Damn him. Once again, he refused to go further until she played his game.

"Maybe I don't," he teased. "How will I know what you like if you won't tell me?"

"You'll know," Lara said. He brushed his thumb against her sensitive flesh once again and she let out a low moan.

"Don't worry, if you're doing it wrong, I'll be sure to tell you."

The low chuckle that answered her caused a rush of warmth to radiate low in Lara's stomach. She enjoyed his playful side and wondered what it would be like to stick around long enough to learn more about him. "I have no doubt you would, doc."

"I'm not going to beg."

He stroked her once more. Slowly. "I don't want you to."

Ryder certainly wasn't a selfish lover, but she'd known that. When you managed to rock a woman's world the way he did, word got around. It was the other part of the rumors that Lara was really curious about, that when it came to his own pleasure, he got down to business and that was that. If Lara had any say in the matter, she was going to make sure Ryder enjoyed himself as much as she did.

"I want your mouth on me," she said after a moment, "when I come."

His lips curved into a wicked grin. "Oh, I can do that."

When he sealed his mouth over her sex, Lara let out a low, drawn-out moan. The marble countertop chilled her overheated skin as she relaxed back on its surface, the extreme sensations only heightening her enjoyment. Ryder circled her clit with his tongue before taking it into his mouth and sucking gently. He increased the pressure and when Lara felt the soft rasp of his teeth, it almost sent her over the edge.

"That feels so good, Ryder. Don't stop."

He grabbed her hips, his fingers curling around her ass as he angled her hips up toward his mouth. Lara reached behind her and gripped onto the edge of the counter as though it would anchor her and keep her from floating away on a cloud of bliss.

His assault was unhurried, calculated to gain the results he wanted. For a brief moment, a pang of jealousy stabbed at Lara's chest as she imagined the number of women he must have been with in order to hone his skills to so sharp an edge. *He's not with those other women now. He's with you.*

"Oh, god. Just like that."

Lara's brain spluttered. Short-circuited as Ryder did wicked things to her with his mouth. He lapped at her mercilessly, circling her clit only to reward her with a long, languid pass with the flat of his tongue. He lifted her ass up off the counter and repositioned her, scooting her higher until she was damned near laid out like a sacrificial offering on the cool marble surface. He bent over her, propping one of her legs up on his shoulder while his free hand wandered up her torso toward her breasts. They tingled with anticipation, her nipples puckering tight as though anxious for his touch. When his skillful fingers found a pearled peak, her breath caught in her chest.

"I'm so close, Ryder," she gasped. "Don't stop."

There'd be no "please" from her. No pleading words, only urgent commands. He groaned as his tongue flicked out at her and Lara felt the vibration of it travel through her sex and up her spine in a delicious shiver that left her panting as she threaded her fingers through his thick hair to urge him on. "Harder . . . yes, like that . . ."

Ryder reacted to her words as though he could barely restrain himself. She wondered at his control. Any other guy would have been on top of her and pounding away by now, totally unconcerned with whether or not she got off. But she already knew that Ryder was a rare breed. She didn't bother to stifle her moans, the intense pleasure of Ryder rolling her nipples between his thumbs and forefingers as he lapped at her, stealing all coherent thought. Her body tensed, the sensation of coiling in on herself almost unbearable. She rocked her hips against his mouth and his name burst from her lips as she came. "Oh, god, Ryder! I'm coming."

He didn't relent, but pressed his face tighter against her as the orgasm rolled through her body, wave after wave until her limbs were heavy and her breath sped in her chest. She doubted she could move even if she wanted to, though she might float away without the use of her limbs. "Ryder, you're going to kill me."

Lara couldn't help the laughter that bubbled up in her chest. Boy was in his own little world down there . . . He looked up and when their gazes locked the grin he gave her was enough to melt every bone in her body until she was nothing more than a helpless puddle of goo.

Damn. She was in deep trouble with this one.

Right about now would be the time that Ryder unzipped his pants and went to town. The faster he came, the faster he could leave his partner a happy girl. Most women failed to notice that he never stayed the night. Why would they when he paid so much attention to their needs prior to seeing to his own? He left them with smiles on their faces, and he didn't feel as guilty for the quick, *wham-bam* encounter.

But Lara wasn't like any of the others. Christ, he didn't want this moment to end. He wasn't interested in getting off and sending her home. He wanted to savor her, again and again. Take his time with her. Fuck her for hours until neither of them could stand and they'd have no choice but to fall into bed together. Ryder wanted to hold her. Take her clover-honey scent into his lungs and wake her with plying kisses before he buried himself deep inside of her and started all over again.

Holy shit. These thoughts were completely out of character. And it scared the shit out of him.

"Ryder, maybe we could go to your room?"

Lara's words woke him from his reverie and for a moment he drank her in. She was something to look at, naked and lounging on his kitchen counter, her skin flushed and her sex soft and glistening. Her full breasts were perfect, the dusky nipples still erect and Ryder reached out and cupped one, brushing his thumb across the peak. Lara's head rolled back on her shoulders and a sweet half-moan, half-sigh escaped her lips. "Ryder, let's go to your room. *Now.*"

The urgency in her tone stirred the glowing embers of his lust and he lifted her insubstantial weight off the counter and set her to her feet in between his legs. She didn't seem bothered by the fact that she was bare as the day she was born while he was still wearing all of his clothes. He admired her confidence and it only added to his need to have her.

His gaze wandered to her full lips and the urge to kiss her was so intense that it damned near took him to the floor. But Ryder held back, and instead ripped at his shirt, popping a couple of the buttons in his haste to get it off. He tossed it on the counter. Lara's eyes took in his naked torso, her expression hungry and it spurred him to new heights of need as he seized her hand and led her through the house, up the stairs, and past the second-story landing to his bedroom at the end of the hallway.

No time to see the sights. He'd give her the grand tour later.

Lara looked around his bedroom with wide eyes, pausing at the king-sized bed. "And I thought your kitchen was impressive," she said with a laugh.

Ryder never liked the fuss people made over his wealth. He worked hard and got lucky. That was about all there was to it. And it bothered him that a lot of people forgot about the fact that the Blackwells had been one of the poorest families in town at one point. But Ryder never forgot. Those memories of growing up would blight his soul until the day he died.

Lara sauntered up to him, her blue eyes shining and limpid, and a soft smile curved her full lips. She reached for the button on his jeans and unfastened them with a muted "pop" as the brass button slid through the denim. Her tongue darted out to lick her lips as she pulled down his zipper, tooth by agonizing tooth, and Ryder's lungs all but seized up as she slid his jeans and underwear down, her palms lingering on his ass, before she pushed them down past his thighs. It only took a moment for Ryder to kick the restrictive clothes the rest of the way off and when he stood before her, naked and hard as stone, she closed the distance between them and wrapped her hand around his cock.

Ho-ly shit.

Her touch was like a brand, stoking the flames of his need until Ryder's brain went damned near blank and all that remained was a haze of primal lust. Lara smoothed the pad of her thumb over his swollen head, already slick with a bead of pre cum and Ryder groaned, long and low. "Don't stop what you're doin', doc. Because that feels damned good."

A half-smile, half-smirk lit her features and the expression heated every molecule of his body to the point of combustion. While her tight fist worked up and down his shaft with slow precision, she backed him up to the bed and eased him down on the mattress.

"Sit."

Hell yeah he was going to sit, because honestly, he wasn't sure he legs could hold him upright for another second. She knelt between his legs and Ryder leaned back on his arms so he could see her face. Their eyes met for a long moment and then she took his length into her mouth.

Ryder sucked in a sharp breath. The heat of her mouth was amazing, the wet warmth like satin sliding over his cock. She swirled her tongue over the crown and he bucked his hips toward her, the sensation so intense that he felt a tingle run the length of his spine. None of his other partners ever went down on him. They sort of expected the Ryder Blackwell treatment and waited for his legendary "servicing." The fact that Lara would be interested not only in receiving pleasure, but in giving it was one more thing to set her apart from all of the others.

"Oh . . . yeah . . ." Jesus, she had him speechless. "You're driving me crazy, doc."

Her eyes met his. Watching her while she worked his length with her mouth caused his balls to draw up tight. She increased the suction and speed, gripping onto his thighs, the bite of her fingernails giving him the slightest bit of discomfort and the right amount of edge. He'd thought this weekend would give him an opportunity to work her out of his system once and for all. But as he sat up and wound his fists in the silky strands of her hair, Ryder realized that he was too far gone to be anything other than hopelessly addicted to Lara Montgomery.

A long moan vibrated in Ryder's chest as her teeth grazed his shaft and nipped at the swollen crown. He was going to come if she kept it up and he wanted to be buried to the root inside of her slick heat when that happened. He tossed his head back, a low growl rumbling in his chest as she sucked a little harder, slowing her pace until Ryder's thighs shook and his muscles tensed. "Faster. Don't stop."

Of course she did the opposite, pausing to run the flat of her tongue up the backside of his shaft. A deep growl resonated in Ryder's chest as she licked him once more. Slowly. Then she took him into her mouth and sucked. Stopped. Licked him again. And sucked. Ryder's jaw clenched tight. He didn't know how much more of her merciless teasing he could take. With his fists still wound in her hair, he eased her back and then moved his grip to her shoulders as he urged her to stand. She gave him a be-mused look but he didn't give her time to question him. Instead, he spun her around to the side of the bed and leaned her over the mattress, her tight little ass jutting up in the air. He jerked opened the drawer on the bedside table and grabbed a condom, tearing the package with his teeth in his haste. With shaking hands, Ryder rolled it over his cock and positioned himself at her opening.

And drove home in a single thrust.

She was so wound up, so utterly ready for him that her body accepted him with ease. He seated himself deep inside of her and paused, breathing through the intense sensation of her inner walls clenching him tight. She felt like heaven wrapped around him.

Lara reached back and gripped his thighs. He moved slowly at first, pulling out almost completely before plunging back in. The sound of her low moans as he fucked her spurred him on and Ryder increased his pace, her cries of pleasure mingling with the sounds of their flesh meeting and parting again and again. The need to come overwhelmed him and he gripped tightly to her hips as he thrust.

"Oh, god, Ryder, harder." Lara pushed into him, urging him on and he went as deep as he could go, pausing only long enough to feel the pulsing constriction of her pussy before he pulled out and thrust again.

"You feel so good," Ryder panted. Sweat trickled down his brow and neck. If he didn't come soon he was pretty sure he'd burst into flames. "Just a few more strokes and I'll be there."

His words triggered a response and she pulled away, de-nying him what he wanted most. Frustration coiled tight in Ryder's stomach and he grabbed her hips, pulling her back against him as he thrust deep inside of her. Lara moaned low, but pulled away once again. She crawled up on the bed, rolling onto her back. "You need to slow down, cowboy. No need to rush."

Jesus. If she thought talking to him like that was going to do anything to slow him down she was sorely mistaken. Ryder climbed up on the bed, settling himself between her hips. He thrust inside of her and she arched up to meet him then pulled away. "Fuck me hard and slow."

When she told him what do to without an ounce of shame or embarrassment, he had no choice but to obey. He thrust as deep as he could go, grinding his hips against hers as he rode her. Lara gripped his shoulders, her nails biting into his skin as she rolled up to meet him, grinding her pussy against his cock in a hot slick caress that caused his back to bow as his spine went stiff. Again and again he drove into her. Deep. Slow. And all the while, her low moans and whispered words urged him on as she both encouraged and denied him.

"I want you to come, Ryder. Oh, god, I want you to come."

Lara's body arched up off the bed as she cried out and her sex constricted tightly around him, pulsing as she came. His thin string of control snapped and Ryder increased his pace, fucking into her with zeal until he followed her over the edge. His own orgasm rocked through his body with the force of a hurricane, blasting through every pore, every nerve ending until his thighs vibrated from the strain of holding him upright. He collapsed on top of her, their labored breath keeping time with one another. Ryder wrapped his arms around her and remained still for a long moment, unwilling to withdraw from her body. When he finally pulled out, he regretted the separation. Already he missed her heat, her body, the intense sensation that he was right where he belonged.

A shrill alarm pierced the peaceful quiet and Lara started beneath him. "What is that?"

"Aw, shit. It's the fire alarm," Ryder said with a laugh. "I think we burned dinner."

NINE

Ryder strolled through the door of his bedroom looking almost more confident naked than he did with his clothes on. And why wouldn't he? The man was built like a god, all taut muscles, defined lines, and solid strength. Lara doubted he'd spent a day in the gym, which was all the more appealing to her. It meant that Ryder achieved the body he had through manual labor and hard work.

Total turn-on.

"We could have burned your house down," she remarked as he slid into bed beside her. It was probably a little too early to turn in but she was exhausted and needed at least a catnap. The problem was, she was wide awake. Her body still thrummed with pleasure and all she really wanted to do was lie here and listen to the sound of Ryder's voice.

"Lucky for us we didn't put the steaks on the grill." He laughed as he gathered her up in his arms. She enjoyed the feeling of security she felt with him, so unlike her previous relationship that had run her out of Houston and back home in the first place. "The rice is toast, though. And I'm pretty sure I'll have to toss the pot."

"I'm so sorry," Lara said with a groan. "I'll buy you a new one if you want."

"Please," Ryder scoffed. "We could've burned the place to the ground and I wouldn't have noticed."

"Me neither." The admission wasn't hard to make. Nothing, not even a burning house could have stopped them. "It was definitely worth a scalded pot. Your kitchen island is another story, though." She laughed. "No way can anyone ever prepare food on that surface ever again. You're going to have to tear it out and replace it."

Ryder flashed her a wicked grin that did wonderful things to Lara's body. "Oh, no. I'm fencing it off and preserving it for posterity. That counter isn't going anywhere."

His words ignited something deep inside of her. A resurgence of lust, but something else too. A depth of emotion she hadn't let herself feel in a very long time. "I hadn't planned on moving back here, you know." For some reason, the words tumbled from Lara's mouth as though she had no choice but to lay herself bare. "Do you remember when I told you that someone tarnished my granddaddy's name by forging records and selling bad stock?"

"Yeah."

"Well, it was my dad that did it. He was basically selling the good horses on the sly and pocketing the money while he duped others into buying useless stock for top dollar. Double-dipping, I guess you'd say. We left town because my grandfather ran him out of town."

"So why'd you come back?"

"You asked why I turned you down every time you asked me out? Well, it wasn't only because I was trying to keep my reputation untarnished. I left Houston because my previous boyfriend was a little . . ." There really wasn't a nice way to put it. "Insane. Possessive, abusive, you name it. I filed a restraining order against him but he pushed the boundaries too many times. He wasn't going to move, so I did. I had to get away from him."

Ryder's brows drew sharply down and his jaw clenched. "He hit you?"

Lara averted her gaze. Admitting that she'd stayed with someone for so long who'd physically and mentally put her through the wringer was tough. "Tom was okay in the beginning, but I guess most assholes are. By the time things got really bad I didn't know if I'd have the strength to leave. Thank god I did, though."

He stared at her for a quiet moment, the emotion present in his expression almost too intense for her to acknowledge. "Jesus Christ, Lara. I had no idea."

She gave a rueful laugh. "How could you? It's not something I'm proud of and I don't go around talking about it. If I went out with you and you found out I had all of this baggage, I figured you wouldn't be able to run fast enough and I'd be left to explain our one-night stand as I fought to rebuild my reputation in the community."

"You think you're the only one with baggage?" His understanding tone tore through her, causing a deep aching cavern to open up in her chest.

"What sorts of skeletons could the perfect Ryder Blackwell possibly have in his closet?"

He stroked his fingertips along her jaw, his gaze wistful. "You'd be surprised."

"I'm the daughter of a son who cheated his own father and destroyed him, the ex of an abusive stalker, and the crazy woman who thought she could work a cattle ranch single-handedly in order to win a horse. A horse that probably won't rebuild her reputation no matter what the pedigree. I doubt there's anything you can say that would surprise me."

"I never cheated my dad out of anything, but I did almost kill the bastard."

Okay, so maybe he could surprise her. Lara's brow furrowed as she searched for the truth in Ryder's words. His face bore the serious expression of a man making a confession and the leather-brown depths of his eyes echoed dark secrets of a past she couldn't comprehend. "Oh my god, Ryder. How?"

He shifted as though the discomfort of revealing so much to her was almost painful. "He used to beat us. Mom the most. He was a nasty, drunk, worthless piece of shit who never did a damn thing for any of us. One night when I was sixteen, he came home half-crocked and went off on my mom because dinner wasn't on the table. It was almost midnight. He dragged her out of bed and beat her within an inch of her life. So, I grabbed his rifle from the closet and leveled it on him. I gave him a choice: get the hell out and never come back or take the beating of his life. He lunged for the rifle and I smacked him right in the face with the stock. And then I hit him again. And again. And again. It took both Luke and Jase to pull me off of him and by the time I was done he had four broken ribs, a fractured jaw, and a concussion."

Lara's heart broke for him. She could only imagine what sort of daily torture they must have endured to push a boy to such lengths. But she'd seen firsthand the love he felt for his mother and she for him. And it wasn't hard to picture Ryder stepping up to take on the role of head of the family. "Did he press charges?"

Ryder snorted. "No. When he got out of the hospital, he took off and never came back. After that, I finished high school and busted my ass to build this family and this ranch up and make a life for us that we could all be proud of."

When it came right down to it, Lara supposed that she

and Ryder weren't all that different. They'd both lived through a family betrayal of a sort and they both were stronger—and maybe a little harder—for it. "Well, you certainly did that." She reached out and traced a lazy pattern on his stomach with her fingertip and smiled as the muscles tensed beneath her touch. "You became the man your father refused to be. And I know your family loves you for it."

Ryder tucked his finger under her chin and raised Lara's gaze to his. "Is that what you're trying to do? Be the man your father refused to be?"

His expression was dead serious but she couldn't help her amusement. "Something like that," Lara said with a laugh, "though I lack the equipment needed to be a proper man."

"And thank god for that," Ryder said solemnly.

They talked through the evening and into the night. Naked, limbs entwined, voices soft in the quiet darkness. Ryder held nothing back, answering every question and asking a few of his own until there wasn't much they didn't know about one another. He'd never shared himself with another person so completely before. But with Lara, he felt as though he could tell her anything and she would never pass judgment or think less of him because of it.

She was more than just a conquest to him. He'd thought of her as an itch he needed to scratch but with each passing hour he spent with her, Ryder realized that there was nothing, no amount of time spent, no number of trysts, not a thing in this world that would ever flush his want of this woman out of his system.

Wonders never cease.

When the conversation waned, a companionable silence settled. In the total darkness of his room, there were only their bodies and mingled breaths. He explored her body with slow precision, loving how her breath would hitch or tense when he passed a sensitive spot or did something she liked. Up one arm, across her collarbone, and down the other arm to the tips of her fingers. Across the ridges of her ribs and over the flat expanse of her stomach. He followed the curve of her hip, down the outside of her thigh to her knee. She tensed, ticklish there, and the sound of her throaty laughter warmed him from the inside out. Up the inside of her thigh, Ryder let his fingertips dance across her soft skin and Lara opened herself to him. So damned responsive, so unafraid to show him—and even tell him—what she wanted. He found her slick center and her breath hitched as he stroked her.

Lara reached up and cupped the back of Ryder's neck, drawing him closer. Their mouths met and her lips were like rose petals against his own. He kissed her deeply, and as he circled her swollen nub with his fingers, his tongue entwined with hers in a sensual meeting that left them both trembling and breathless with need.

He was going to take his time with her. Savor every minute of it. And tonight was only the beginning.

The sounds of gravel crunching under tires stirred Lara from a contented sleep, the likes of which she hadn't known in a long time. For a moment she lay still, listening to the sounds of Ryder's even breaths beside her. A smile curved her lips as she relived the hours they'd spent together. Resisting Ryder's charm had obviously been a wasted effort, but never had Lara been so thankful for a lack of willpower in her life.

Curiosity won out over sleepiness as she slipped out from under Ryder's arm. She padded across his bedroom—the space was bigger than her entire living room—to the window. In the gray light of dawn, the car was difficult to make out, especially from the tall second-story window. Lara's heart skipped a beat and then kicked into overdrive as she watched a man jump out of the car and head toward the house.

No.

It couldn't be him. Could it?

Tom was crazy, but was he that stupid? It wouldn't be a far stretch to assume he'd been following her. Maybe he'd been at the auction yesterday and trailed her out to the Blackwell ranch. It was the only house for miles, it's not like it would have been hard for him to discern where she was once he got out this way. Damn it. She'd gone months without hearing from him and had begun to hope that maybe the asshole had given up. But apparently, Tom was just getting his second wind.

Her cell was in her truck and the last thing she wanted to do was wake Ryder up to deal with her crazy ex. That'd send him running for the hills for sure. The house was equipped with a top-of-the-line security system, but it wouldn't deter Tom for long. Lara needed to get him the hell out of here before the shit hit the fan. She looked around and realized that all of her clothes were downstairs in a heap on Ryder's kitchen floor. Confronting an ex with a penchant for terrorizing and stalking would be a helluva lot easier if she had some damned clothes on.

Careful not to wake Ryder, Lara grabbed his boxer briefs and discarded shirt and slipped them on. The shirt smelled like him and it distracted her as she made her way down the stairs. She held the garment to her nose, breathing deeply of his intoxicating masculine scent. How she wished she was upstairs with him right now, curled up against his body and sound asleep.

Lara crossed through the kitchen, her gaze pausing on the kitchen island counter as a pleasant shiver passed the length of her body. Ryder Blackwell certainly was one of a kind. And now, what could have been a really good thing was about to be squashed because of Tom. Now that she knew more about Ryder's history, his childhood, the last thing she wanted was to darken his door with her drama. Especially after he'd worked so hard to overcome so much.

If she had to call 911, she would. Lara wasn't stupid and she'd experienced enough of Tom's abuse to know that he didn't mess around. But if she could get him to leave without involving the local cops, it would be better for everyone. Especially her. The gossips would eat her alive if they got wind that not only had she spent the weekend with Ryder, but the police had to come out to settle a domestic dispute with her ex. She might as well kiss her future here good-bye if that happened.

The sound of footsteps on the porch outside gave Lara a start and she clutched Ryder's shirt tightly to her throat as though that simple part of him on her body would keep her safe. Her hands trembled and she found it difficult to catch her breath. Memories assaulted her of Tom's fingers biting into her skin, his face looming over hers as he snarled his threats. The aftermath of his rages and physical violence that finally convinced her to file the restraining order. Screw her reputation, she was calling the cops.

Lara changed course in search of a phone when the sound of glass shattering sent her reeling backward. Her heart jumped up into her throat as an alarm began to wail, echoing throughout the house so loudly that she pressed the heels of her palms against her ears.

Adrenaline dumped into her bloodstream in a rush, muddling Lara's thoughts as the fight-or-flight instinct overwhelmed her. She needed to get out of the kitchen and the hell back to Ryder. Now. With a quick turn to her left, Lara sprinted for the stairs when her body met a solid form that sent her sprawling backward on the floor. In the low morning light, she made out the sneer curving Tom's cruel lips.

"No more games, Lara. It's time for you to come home."

TEN

Ryder sat bolt upright in bed, his heart hammering against his rib cage. In all of the years he'd lived in this house, he couldn't remember a single time the alarm had been tripped. His first thought, after the near–heart attack was that Lara was probably scared shitless.

He looked over to tell her that everything was okay when he noticed he was alone in his bed. "Lara?" he called over the din of the alarm. Then again, louder, "Lara!"

A tidal wave of panic crested over Ryder as he shot out of bed. He threw on his jeans and didn't bother to fasten them as he made a beeline for the gun safe in the far corner of his bedroom. His hand was steady as he entered the combination, though his heart was still racing. With no time to be picky, he grabbed the first thing his hand made contact with, a Ruger 270 rifle, a handful of shells, and rushed out the door and down the stairs.

"Lara?"

Jesus Christ, that damned alarm was drilling into his skull. The white lights of the Christmas tree twinkled softly in the living room but didn't provide enough light for him to see much more than the outline of shadows. Ryder steered toward the foyer, his bare feet slapping on the wood floor as he jogged for the security system panel at the front door. He flipped on a light and entered the code, the sweet silence that descended a godsend. A deep sigh escaped his chest and he headed back the way he came, flipping on lights as he went.

"Lara, you down here?"

A sharp stab of pain radiated through Ryder's heel and he stumbled as he lifted his foot to check it out. He plucked the shard of glass from his foot and noticed for the first time the broken window in the formal dining room. "Son of a bitch," Ryder ground out from between clenched teeth. He slid several long bullets into the magazine before pulling the bolt action on the 270, loading a shell into the chamber. "Lara!"

The sounds of a scuffle came from somewhere near the kitchen and Ryder brought the rifle up in his grip, ready for anything and scared to death of what he might find. As the sun rose higher in the sky, the muddled gray of dawn began to slowly melt away, casting enough daylight through the kitchen windows to see Lara struggling against an assailant who was dragging her bodily from the house. "Goddamn it, Tom, let me go!"

"Don't fucking move."

Lara looked about as surprised to see Ryder standing there as her attacker did. They both froze in place, her expression one of abject terror, while his was a barely restrained rage that Ryder knew all too well. He'd seen that same expression on his dad more times than he could count.

"I don't want any trouble, buddy." His confident tone made Ryder want to laugh in the bastard's face. Pretty ballsy talk for a guy with a 270 leveled on him.

"Then let my friend go and we won't have any," Ryder replied.

"Look, I don't know what she told you, but this is my lady. She gets out of line sometimes and I'm just here to get what's mine. I ain't stealin' nothing, Lara and I are going home is all."

Good lord almighty, how did someone as confident and intelligent as Lara wind up with a lowlife hick like that? Anger pooled in Ryder's gut, the urge to tear into the asshole almost too strong to resist. "Doc, is that true? You wanna leave with this guy?"

"No." The word was barely louder than a whisper, spoken with so much fear that Ryder had to bite the inside of his cheek to keep from letting loose a string of expletives that would no doubt do nothing but agitate an already half-crazed man. And to be honest, at the moment Ryder wasn't sure if the crazed son of a bitch was him or the guy holding Lara against her will.

"Doc?" Tom said in an angry, incredulous tone that caused Lara to shrink away from him. "Sounds like the two of you got pretty cozy, huh? Guess I shoulda figured she'd whore herself off to the first guy who could give her a leg up."

"My rifle here is a little over eighty years old," Ryder remarked as casually as if he was talking about the weather, "and it's got a hair trigger. So let Lara go before I blow a hole in your head the size of a crater. You hear me?"

Their eyes met and Ryder knew he was being sized up. His gaze didn't falter as he held the rifle steady. He wanted the fucker to *know* he wouldn't hesitate to blow his head off if he got a clean shot.

"Doesn't matter," Tom scoffed as he loosened his grip on Lara's waist. She squirmed and kicked, slapping at his arms. "She has to leave here sometime. And when she does, I'm takin' her home."

He let her go with a shove and Lara sprawled to the

floor. Ryder looked down, briefly taking stock of her reddened and puffy left cheek. A haze of unsuppressed rage clouded Ryder's thoughts, the likes of which he'd only known one other time in his life.

"Ryder, don't."

Lara's pleading words fell on deaf ears. He set the rifle down on the counter and charged without a second thought to his actions. The asshole had the nerve to look surprised. Ryder rushed past Lara and grabbed Tom by the collar of his shirt, ramming him into the wall with all the force of a charging bull. "You think you're *ever* going to lay your hands on her again?" Ryder's voice sounded foreign in his own ears. "There's over nine hundred acres of ranch out there, and I can bury your body where no one will ever find it."

Mocking laughter answered the threat, adding fuel to an already raging fire. "Did you seriously threaten to kill me? You might have money, but it's not enough to save you from assault charges. I bet the cops around here take death threats pretty seriously too."

Assault? Oh, he hadn't seen anything yet. Ryder slammed him against the wall, hard enough to rattle what little brain he had in his head. Tom coughed and gasped as the breath was knocked out of him and because Ryder didn't want him getting too comfortable, he rammed his fist into the other man's stomach for good measure.

Tom let out a *whoof!* of breath and doubled over, hands wrapped around his gut. Ryder took a step back and before he could defend himself, Tom came at him with an uppercut that sent him listing to one side. *Well, that one's gonna leave a mark.* His tongue flicked out at his split and swelling lip and he tasted the coppery tang of blood.

Logical thought evaporated from Ryder's mind, replaced by a violent urge to hurt this man who had given Lara a reason to feel so much fear. The passing moments were a blur, nothing but flying fists, flailing limbs, and more than a few solid connections. Pain didn't register as Ryder took a fist to the ribs and he gave as good as he got. Better. Taller with more body mass than the smaller man, it wasn't long before Ryder had the advantage and Tom dropped to his knees. It only confirmed what a coward he was that he could so easily hit a woman but tucked tail as soon as he was faced with an equal opponent.

"Ryder."

He laid his fist into Tom's face.

"Ryder."

He felt something tugging at his arm and he fought against the restraint.

"Ryder!"

And then his vision was filled with Lara's face, full of concern as she threw herself between him and Tom. Her brow was furrowed and tears streamed down her face. "Stop." Her voice was a firm command, nothing pleading or afraid as she spoke. Every inch of him seemed to shake as he looked down on her, the unspent adrenaline looking for a way out. She wrapped her arms around him and pulled him close. "You're too good for this, Ryder. Don't let him tempt you into lowering yourself to his level. It's not worth it."

Lara's voice vibrated through him like a soothing balm, a breeze that cleansed him of all irrational thought and brought him back into the present. He looked over her shoulder at Tom, slumped over on all fours and slowly scooting himself toward the far wall. As though she'd woken him from a nightmare, the clarity of the moment settled on Ryder like a heavy mantle and he released a shuddering breath as he wrapped his arms around her and pulled her close. "Are you all right?" he said next to her ear. "Did he hurt you?"

"I'm okay." She gripped his shoulders, holding on so tight that he could feel the tremor that shook her slight form. "I'm okay."

Lara watched from a distance as Tom was loaded into the patrol car by one sheriff's deputy while the other finished up talking to Ryder. She'd already answered all of their questions and sat in the swing on Ryder's front porch, wrapped up in a blanket to ward off the chill that still clung to her skin in the late December morning. She held an ice pack to her cheek and said a silent prayer of thanks that Tom hadn't roughed her up too much. In addition to violating the restraining order, he could add breaking and entering and assault to his list of charges and the deputy assured Lara that he'd see some definite jail time. Though she wasn't foolish enough to believe it would be much, it might deter him from seeking her out again. At least, she hoped.

"Hey."

Lara looked up to find Ryder standing in front of her and she glanced past him to see the patrol car backing out of the driveway. "Hey." She felt like the walking dead, way too exhausted both emotionally and physically for more than a mindless shuffle.

Ryder held out his hand and she accepted it gladly, pushing herself out of the swing as he led her back into the house. Her slow steps didn't help her to keep up with his pace though, and Ryder paused halfway through the kitchen. "What?" Lara asked as he gazed down at her. "Is everything okay?"

He didn't respond, simply scooped her up in his arms. "Ryder, put me down." It was ridiculous for him to carry her through the house like she was a child. "I can walk. I told you, I'm fine."

"Shush." His response didn't open the door for conversation. "I'm taking you to bed and you're going to get some rest. And then I'm going to make you breakfast and take care of you for the rest of the day."

Warm emotion bloomed in Lara's chest. She'd let the town gossips paint a picture of Ryder in her mind. One that portrayed him as nothing more than a cocky, selfish playboy. But there was so much more to him than anyone knew. He was gentle. Caring. Strong and compassionate. Her arms tightened around his neck as he negotiated the stairs, holding her body tightly to his. For years Lara had punished herself for mistakes that weren't hers, carrying the guilt of her father's actions around her neck like a heavy stone. Maybe that's why she'd ended up with someone like Tom in the first place. Because she'd convinced herself she didn't deserve any better. In the long run, though, being with Tom had led her home. Led her to gather the courage to shed her father's betrayals and rebuild her life. And that led her to Ryder.

Once in his bedroom, he set her down on the bed as though she was the most precious and fragile thing in the world. He tucked the blankets around her and his light brown eyes warmed when he said, "Would it be totally inappropriate to tell you that you look fantastic wearing my shirt and underwear?"

Lara laughed, loving the way the tension melted out of her body with nothing more than a look and a few words from him. "I think that's the best compliment I've ever received."

"The only way you could possibly look any better is if you were wearing my boots too." He leaned in and placed a gentle kiss on her cheek. "Maybe I can talk you into trying them on a little later?"

A smile curved her lips as she took his hand in hers and kissed each one of his bruised knuckles. "Absolutely."

* * *

Ryder set four strips of bacon onto a plate, next to the scrambled eggs and toast before placing it on a serving tray. He poured a glass of orange juice and set a small carafe of coffee along with cream and sugar next to the carefully assembled breakfast presentation and balanced it all with careful precision as he made his way back up the stairs. His eyes wandered to the piece of paper he'd placed under the napkin and silverware and smiled.

When he'd lured Lara Montgomery to his ranch with the promise of winning back her horse it had been with single-minded purpose. He'd thought to get the lively brunette into his bed and out of his head once and for all, but over the course of twenty-four hours, she'd managed to anchor herself firmly in his heart.

"Look at you, showing off your cooking skills," Lara remarked as he set the tray in front of her. A few hours' sleep had done her good and her face no longer bore the shadows of exhaustion. He settled in beside her on the bed, snatching up a piece of bacon and popping it into his mouth.

"I can do more than cook."

Lara smiled at the innuendo as she offered him another slice of bacon before taking one for herself. "Oh, don't I know it," she teased back. "You're a true Renaissance man, Mr. Blackwell."

He leaned back against his pillow, folding his arms behind his head. He hoped that today was the first of many more mornings spent in bed with Lara, and he was going to do everything in his power from here on out to make her his. "That I am."

Lara reached for her napkin and Ryder leaned up to gauge her reaction. As she smoothed the linen over her lap, her eyes darted to the paper. Lara gave him a sidelong glance as she took the paper in her hand, skimming the words written there. His stomach did a pleasant flip at her reaction as she turned to look at him, her blue eyes wide and shining with emotion.

"This is the certification of bloodline for October," she said with awe. "I'm named as her owner."

"Wow, you catch on quick, doc," Ryder said. "You might make a decent horse breeder yet."

She studied him for a long moment as though trying to read his mind. "You couldn't have transferred ownership this morning."

"Nope." Ryder leaned back on the pillow and let out a contented sigh. "She's been yours since the auction. I had you listed as the owner when I bought her."

"But the bet . . . ?"

"Doc, you're the worst cattle rancher I've ever seen, though you can stack hay better than both of my brothers combined. Do you really think I was such an asshole that I would have taken her from you? I knew how badly you wanted her, but since you kept turning me down for dinner, I had to get you out here somehow."

The smile she gave him warmed Ryder from the inside out. She was by far the finest woman he'd ever known and he'd do it all again if he had to. "I don't know what to say . . . I'll pay you for her, of course."

"No." She gave him a puzzled look and he said, "Think of October as an early Christmas present. You're going to take the money you saved up for her and put it into building your stables. I won't let you pay me for her and if you try, I'll buy you another horse, and another, and I won't stop until you accept my gifts. Understand?"

Lara pushed the tray away and leaned in to Ryder until their lips almost touched. "Well, I'm not opposed to having a partner." The low sensual tone in her voice stirred Ryder's body and a low growl vibrated in his throat. Damn, she was sexy without even trying. "Whaddya say, Black-well? You interested?"

Their lips met in a slow and sultry kiss. Ryder loved a challenge and Lara was presenting him with a new adventure, and with someone he yearned to share it with. "You know what, doc? That sounds damned perfect to me."

She kissed him again and her tongue slid against the seam of his lips. "Funny, I was thinking the same thing. This might be the start of something, don't you think?"

He pulled her onto his lap and Lara squealed with delight before he slipped his hands under her—well, his—shirt, greedy for her soft skin. "It sure is, doc. It sure as hell is."

THE
Billion Dollar
PLAYER

ONE

"How's the groin, Jason? You gonna be one hundred percent for Sunday, son?"

Steve McNealy, the offensive coordinator, always talked to Jase like he was still in Pee-Wee football instead of a twenty-seven-year-old man with a college career and four years of pro ball under his belt. Though, in relation to the years with the NFL that Steve could claim, Jase guessed he was sort of a pup.

"I'm good to go, Coach. I'll be tearin' it up next week."

Steve gave him a pat on the shoulder. "That's good, son. Glad to hear it."

It had been one bitch of a week: ice, physical therapy, and more ice. He was surprised his dick hadn't sustained frostbite by now. And with the playoffs just around the corner, Jase couldn't afford to show any signs of weakness. Especially when Malcolm Willis, second-round draft pick and hotshot prospect out of Stanford was waiting in the wings to take his place on the field.

He had a hard enough time maintaining his position on the team without the added pressure, thank you very much.

Tonight's party was a kickoff for the post-season. One of many get-togethers aimed at boosting morale and ensuring that they'd be an even more cohesive team in the playoffs. Truth be told, Jase didn't see these functions as anything more than an excuse to get shitfaced and blow off some steam away from the prying eyes of the press. And from the looks of some of the women parading around, someone had dug deep to provide more than alcohol for tonight's entertainment.

"Hey, man. 'Sup? You feelin' all right?"

If one more person asked him how the fuck he was feeling, he was going to go *off*. "Yup. Right as rain." Jase turned toward Carson Rader, the starting quarterback and gave him a nudge with his shoulder. "You're not getting rid of me yet, dude."

"Nah, man, you got it wrong. I'd throw a first-class bitch fit if McNealy put anyone else on my line. Especially that little shit, Willis. His ego's still too big to be on my field."

"That's because there's no room," Jase said with a laugh. "Your ego's already too big for the field."

"Truth." Carson flashed him the million-dollar grin that had earned him the title of Prince Charming and grabbed a glass of champagne from a tray as the waitress walked by. "I'm not about sharing the spotlight."

It was spoken in good humor, but as the highest-paid quarterback in the NFL, Carson Rader knew his worth and wasn't afraid to own his ego. Thanks to him, the Cowboys might be getting a bid to the Super Bowl this year. Jase wanted that ring so damned badly he could practically taste the gold on the tip of his tongue and he'd ride the wave of Carson's ego all the way to the playoffs. "You can have all the spotlight you want, buddy."

Carson wasn't the only guy in the league with a nickname. Being known as Billion Dollar Blackwell wasn't exactly an honor and it sure as shit didn't have anything to do with Jase's paycheck or his talent. Rather, he'd earned the nickname after an ESPN anchor commented that the Cowboys had drafted him not because of his talent, but because he had the money to buy a spot on the team. It hadn't helped that his brother Ryder owned one of the most expensive boxes in Cowboys Stadium.

Jase was firmly of the belief that money didn't solve everything. In his case, his family's money had done him more harm than good. His reputation, his value as a player had taken a hit and it meant that he had to work three times harder than the hardest-working player just to prove himself. Those were the breaks though, and if he'd let that sort of shit get under his skin, he would have quit his freshman year of college.

A companionable silence settled, each of them taking in the sights. Carson didn't make eye contact, just sipped from his glass. "But really, Jase. How are you feeling?"

He never could get anything over on Carson. Jase stretched his neck from side to side in an effort to banish some of the tension pulling his shoulders tight. "I'm feeling like if I don't get my shit together, I'm going to be riding the bench for the duration. I'm sore, my game is shit, and I'm stressed the hell out." He gave a rueful laugh. "That about cover it for you?"

Carson didn't seem in the least bit fazed. At least one of them was keeping a level head. Jase could feel his place on the field slipping through his fingers. He needed something—anything—to pull him out of the damned slump he'd been in for the past few months.

"You need something to take the edge off, that's all," Carson replied. "There's plenty of talent here tonight." He gave Jase a pointed look. "Fuck this shit out of your system, blow off some steam. A piece of ass will do wonders for your attitude."

A lot of guys used sex to take the edge off during the

playoffs. They called them "good-luck fucks" or "playoff poontang." Crude, sure. But athletes were superstitious creatures by nature and more players than not swore by the power of some good ol'-fashioned sex magic for luck.

"I don't want the typical 'talent.'" Jase was a red-blooded American man, but even he had standards. He could have dragged any number of the women here tonight into the bathroom and gone to town. But pounding into some honey up against a bathroom wall wasn't going to get his mojo back.

"Just get it done, Jase." Carson spoke as though he needed to get in to have his teeth cleaned or car serviced or some shit. "I need you on the field to keep my ass from getting sacked. You do that, and I'll keep putting the ball in your hands, brother. You're the best tight end on the field, Jase, and I don't give a flying fuck what anyone has to say about it."

Jase thought about making a joke about Carson's balls, but thought better of it. He never could out-snark Prince Charming. Another server passed with a tray of drinks and Jase snatched one up in his palm. He loved Carson like the pain-in-the-ass brother he never wanted, and it meant a lot that he wanted him on the field, but Jase would never give him the satisfaction of knowing it. Dude's ego was too big as it was.

The sound of shattering glass and metal clanging on the marble floor interrupted any further conversation and Jase turned with the collective body of players and guests toward the source of the commotion.

"Oh my god, I'm so sorry!"

Jase rose up on his tiptoes and scanned the crowd until his gaze landed on the woman frantically scooping up bits of broken glass with a dripping wet rag. One of the girls for hire looked like she'd taken a champagne bath—probably not the first time—and was spluttering and glaring daggers down on the flustered waitress. "You ruined my dress, you stupid little skank!"

Classy.

Jase had been an underdog for most of his life, so watching as someone was bullied dug under his skin like a chigger, irritating him past the point of reason. The waitress obviously felt bad; her face was as red as the Texas state flag and she was stuttering out apology after apology as she tried without success to clean the floor with the soaking wet rag.

"She's the one," Carson asserted as though he'd found a ruby in a sack of rocks. "If you hook up with her, I guarantee you'll be right as rain for the playoffs."

Jase hiked a casual shoulder. It was the only part of his body that hadn't gone rigid. Christ, even his gut was coiled up tight as a fist. "Could be." Short, coffee-brown hair brushed her chin as she tucked the locks behind her ear. Her cheeks were flushed with embarrassment, but it just as easily could have been passion. She licked her full lips, biting down on the bottom one as though using the pain to distract her from the moment. And her eyes . . . bright emerald gems that shone from behind dark lashes. Like a full-body tackle, the sight of her stole the air from his lungs. "There's a lot of tail walking around tonight, though." He didn't want to seem too anxious but there was something about her that damned near had him bouncing with excitement.

"Yeah." Carson snorted. "But you said yourself, you don't want typical. She's far from it if you ask me."

Jase could agree with Carson on that point. "She looks like she could use some help."

Carson chuckled. "And you're just the man to give her a hand."

He pushed his way through the crowd, shaking his head at the fools who didn't have the good sense to turn away from the scene as the girl continued to mop up her mess. Didn't they know they were just helping to turn a simple mistake into a spectacle? His wide strides and sweeping arms cleared the crowd and he crossed the fifty or so feet between them in a couple of seconds.

"You might want to wring that rag out before you go to mopping stuff up again," he said with a smile. "Here, let me help you."

Avery Lockhart looked up from the pool of champagne she was currently stranded in, jaw slack and eyes wide. As if she wasn't already mortified to the point of speechlessness, now she was face-to-face with the one and only Billion Dollar Blackwell. Holy cats, he was even better looking up close than he was from a distance.

"No!" You'd think that champagne was acid the way she screeched at him, but if he got down on all fours to help her sweep up broken glass, she'd die of embarrassment for sure. His slacks looked like they cost more than her entire wardrobe. "R-really, please, I can clean this up. I'm the one who made the mess, and you're going to ruin your pants."

Oh sweet Jesus, she wished that people would stop staring at her. The hussy sporting the dress that looked like it came from the Jenna Jameson private wardrobe collection was still fuming, her talon-like acrylic nails tapping a quick staccato on the sequined waistline of her dress. If she could, Avery would have melted right into the marble floor tiles and disappeared.

"I've got other pants at home. And you know, there's this thing called a washing machine. It's revolutionary. You just throw dirty clothes inside, turn it on, and in an hour? Clean clothes!"

Avery paused, her stomach somersaulting through her rib cage. She resisted the urge to smile at his attempt at levity while she swallowed down a groan. The sound of his voice, as dark and rich as grade-A Belgian chocolate, did something wonderful and terrifying to her insides all at the same time. This was torture. Pure, unmitigated, hellish abuse. "Um . . ." *Say something, Avery. Anything would be good.* Her mind drew a blank, her vision filled with Jason Blackwell in all of his glory. Christ Almighty he was good looking. "Seriously, I've got this. This is your party. Go enjoy yourself."

She wanted to look away. She really did. But he was like the sun, holding her in orbit with his magnificence. And likewise, everyone else within a twenty-foot radius. Avery's gaze shifted and her cheeks flushed with renewed heat. It was easy to forget there wasn't a crowd watching her every move when she stared into his gorgeous whiskey-brown eyes.

But the annoyed and somewhat breathy tone of Porn Star Barbie's words was enough to break the spell. "Oh, god, I'm absolutely *dripping* wet."

Avery hid a smirk. Probably not the first time she'd ever said that in front of an audience. Her gaze met Jason's and she could have sworn they were having a moment. His eyes crinkled at the corners and his lips twitched as though suppressing a smile. It shouldn't be funny. Really, Avery was mortified. So why did she suddenly feel like laughing?

"Can someone please get this lovely lady a towel or something?" Jason seemed oblivious to the expression of smug pleasure that blossomed on the Barbie's face. "And as for the rest of you yahoos, go find something worth staring at. I thought this was a party!"

Nervous laughter followed and the crowd quickly dispersed. Avery had a feeling that Jason Blackwell was used to people doing as he said. Especially when it came to women. As she continued to sweep the shards of glass into a manageable pile, Avery caught sight of someone coming from the kitchen with a large, fluffy towel. Thank god.

She was afraid she was going to have to mop up the champagne with her own shirt.

"Here you go, sweetie."

The towel that Avery thought had been brought for her was draped over the Barbie doll's shoulders by one of the waitstaff. Lovely. Could this night get any worse? Wait. She probably didn't want an answer to that.

"Jase, could you show me to the bathroom?" Barbie cooed. "I want to rinse some of the sticky off me."

Avery rolled her eyes. *Seriously?* One more crack like that and she was going to lose her cool. She refused to meet Blackwell's gaze this time. They weren't sharing a "moment" or anything else. She was the hired help and he was the football star. Fraternization wasn't only far-fetched, it was flat-out impossible.

Jase. It was obvious that Barbie was on a nickname basis with him. Avery tried not to think of how cute it was or how the name suited him so much better than Jason. And likewise, she kept her eyes drilled to the mess in front of her as he pushed up from the floor to escort little miss wet 'n' sticky to the bathroom. *Gag.* Avery was willing to bet that she looked just like a Barbie without her clothes, too. Hard plastic parts and not an inch of her the body that god and her mama gave her. Just the way guys like Jason Blackwell liked their women, no doubt.

"I hate to break it to you, but you're not making any progress."

Avery's heart stuttered in her chest as she looked up the length of Jason's considerable frame. Dang. They really did grow 'em bigger in Texas. "Shouldn't you be in the bathroom helping my unfortunate victim to disrobe?"

He squatted down beside her and was still a good foot and a half taller. He had to be pushing six and a half feet if he was an inch, and carrying at least two hundred and fifty pounds of muscle around on his large frame. *Close your mouth and stop staring, you idiot!* Jason Blackwell was a tower of masculine perfection.

"There were more than a few able bodies ready and willing to help your victim out of her dress," Jason remarked with a mischievous glint in his eyes. "I left them to it so I could bring you this."

He pulled a stack of white kitchen towels from behind his back and Avery almost squealed with delight. The rest of the waitstaff had treated her as though she were all but invisible, leaving her to flounder in a pool of champagne and a pile of broken glass as if her clumsiness was a communicable disease. She'd been just about to go on a quest for a mop and bucket before Jason showed up with the towels. "Would it be cheesy to say that you are officially my hero?"

"Hell no," Jason replied. "In fact, I demand official hero status from here on out. But I do think you owe me a reward for my gallantry."

"A reward, huh?" Avery wasn't sure what he was angling for, but she sure as hell wasn't going to pull up her skirt as a thank you. "Don't heroes usually perform good deeds out of the kindness of their hearts?"

He flashed her a wicked grin and Avery was pretty sure that if she wasn't already on her knees, that smile would have gotten the job done. "What's your name?"

"Avery," she remarked.

"Avery? Really?"

Aaaand enter the jokes, teasing, and comments that she had a boy's name. She'd heard them all. "I take it your parents hadn't planned on you being anything but an Avery, am I right?"

Stunned silence followed. Wow. Not even a single wisecrack. "Um, yeah. That's pretty much it. My dad was planning on naming me after my great-grandpa. When I wasn't a boy like they'd thought, he slapped my name on the birth certificate before my mom had a say."

"Avery. I like it. I'm Jase Blackwell, by the way. Also known as the hero of the night." He motioned to the stack of towels. "How about you let me take you to dinner tomorrow night? I'll even help you mop up the champagne."

"Yeah, that's probably not a good idea. I mean, you're—and I'm—" How could she possibly explain to him why a date was the worst idea ever? She took the towels out of his hands and averted her gaze. "It probably wouldn't work."

"You're gonna shoot me down, just like that? You wouldn't believe what I had to do for those towels."

His nonplussed expression only solidified why it wasn't a good idea for Avery to go out with him. Guys like Jase Blackwell got what they wanted when they wanted it. And the girls they dated were equally self-confident and just as gorgeous. Avery wasn't exactly arm candy material. She wouldn't last a second on a date with Jase before he realized what a monumental mistake it was. Ultimately, she was doing them both a favor by turning him down.

"You don't have to do me any favors, really. This isn't the first time and it sure as hell won't be the last time I make a fool of myself in public. You don't have to feel obligated to help me. I can wrap this up all by myself. Thanks for the towels, Jase. You'd better get back to the party."

TWO

"Obligated? What the fuck does that even mean?"

The burn of Avery's cool rebuff was still simmering just under Jase's skin even after having a week to cool down. He couldn't get her out of his head, his memory overwhelmed with images of her dark hair cut into an edgy bob, and the most gorgeous green eyes he'd ever seen. There was a pretty good chance he could have bench-pressed her petite frame with one arm she was so tiny, and she had the cutest button nose he'd ever laid eyes on. In a word, she was stunning. And the fact that he couldn't have her, made him want her that much more.

"How in the hell should I know what it means?" Carson sat on his couch, watching game footage. There wasn't a day of the week the guy wasn't eating, breathing, or sleeping football. "I know I said she was the one, but maybe you should have cut your losses and moved on. The room was full of supermodel-gorgeous women."

Supermodel-gorgeous? Hardly. More like rode hard and put away wet. The tension and bad-luck streak he'd hoped to end with a wild romp with Avery had crashed and burned. And rather than find some other woman to get the job done, convincing Avery to go out with him had become Jase's single-minded obsession. "Can you just give me the name of the catering company?"

"I can, but I gotta say, this isn't the best time to start anything. You were supposed to hit it and quit it, dude. Not chase after her like a lovesick puppy. The playoffs are around the corner and I want your brain getting the necessary blood flow. Know what I mean?"

"Dude. I don't even want you thinking about where my blood is flowing. Know what *I* mean? Just give me the damned number and get back to your home movies."

"You're going to appreciate these home movies come next week. Especially when I decide to throw an outside right pass."

Translation: give me any more shit and you won't even touch the ball next game. "Have I ever mentioned how much I love the fact that you watch so much game footage? I mean—"

"All Occasions Catering. Now get lost."

"Thanks," Jase said as he headed for the door. "See you at practice tomorrow."

"Don't be late!" Carson called after him. "Cuz we're going to the Super Bowl, baby!"

Another reason why Jase loved Carson: his unfailing optimism.

Throwing together yet *another* last-minute party wasn't as easy as it seemed. Especially since most of the people he'd invited had already been to one of the three he'd thrown last week or they had other plans. What had started out as a full-on bash was now more like a dinner party on steroids. Just a little bigger and bulkier than you might expect. Definitely not the sort of shindig that would warrant a handful of waitresses. Of course, just like for the past three parties, there was only one waitress that Jase wanted in attendance tonight.

He'd requested her again specifically and since the team—and now Jase—had thrown a lot of business their way, the caterer had assured Jase that Avery would be there without question. Jesus, he was nervous as a newborn calf, all wobbly legs and unsure steps. Twice already tonight he'd tripped on his own damned feet and he doubted that would do much to make an impression.

Unless he was planning to send her running the other way.

At half past six, the caterers arrived, carrying in boxes full of food that made Jase's stomach growl. He'd requested good old-fashioned Texas barbeque tonight, the kind like his mom used to make. Brisket, beans, potato salad, and cornbread. Tailgating food.

"I swear, I've been here so many times in the past week, I feel like this is my own kitchen. I don't even have to ask where the plates and silverware are anymore. I'll go ahead and get the table set."

Jase looked over at the caterer—Penny? No, Peyton. He'd been preoccupied, searching for one face in particular. "Sorry, what was that?"

Peyton repeated herself, but again Jase didn't hear a word. Avery walked into the kitchen beside another woman, each of them carrying a cardboard box. His gut clenched tight and his mouth went dry. Damn, just the sight of her sent him reeling, like the rush of taking a shot of top-shelf bourbon. He was drunk on nothing more than her nearness.

"Mr. Blackwell?" the caterer gave him a quizzical look.

"Sorry?" Jesus, he wasn't doing much to come across as a guy who had his shit together. He forced his gaze from Avery and let Peyton lead him toward the patio. Right, she'd asked something about where he'd wanted her to set up the buffet. "I've got tables ready to go over here."

"I think someone has a crush," Kristie whispered in a sing-song tone into Avery's ear. Her stomach was slowly clawing its way to her throat and no matter how many times she swallowed, she couldn't seem to get rid of the lump.

"I seriously doubt that," Avery replied with a grin. "Just because he asked me out once, doesn't mean he meant anything by it. He only took pity on me because I'd made a fool out of myself."

"Uh-huh. Right." Kristie's rueful tone rang out in the expansive kitchen that gleamed with polished granite and stainless steel appliances. It was the sort of gourmet layout that was every aspiring chef's dream. She'd kill for a kitchen like this. "This is the guy's fourth dinner party in just over a week, Avery. And Peyton told me that he's requested that you work every single one. I doubt it was your superior serving skills that put you at the top of his list."

"Ha. Ha. Thanks." Avery knew she wasn't the world's most graceful person. Her middle name was klutz. And as a server, she sucked. She'd taken this job with the hopes that Peyton would eventually put her in the kitchen doing what she loved most: creating culinary masterpieces. But so far, she'd done little more than arrange hors d'oeuvres on serving platters. Not exactly fulfilling her life's ambition. "I think you're wrong, but I'm not going to complain about the extra hours. It'll be a nice pad to my paycheck."

"Oh, I'm not wrong," Kristie replied. "And I think I owe you a *big* thank you. Four Dallas Cowboys parties in less than a week. Bring on the man candy!"

From the French doors that led out to the patio, Jase Blackwell stared over the heads of everyone in the kitchen, those light-brown eyes zeroed in on her. A pleasant shiver rippled from the top of Avery's head and slid down her spine. His back had been turned to her when she'd first walked into the kitchen, but even so, her heart fluttered when she'd recognized the defined muscles, the curve of his neck, and shock of tawny hair that was just the right amount of messy. When he turned and noticed her? Her knees had buckled. His effect on her was undeniable.

After a week of thinking of nothing but the sexy football star, how pathetic was it that she'd known him with his back turned to her? Their gazes locked and his lips spread into a slow smile. It was that wicked, confident, I-get-what-I-want-when-I-want-it expression that had nearly curled Avery's toes when they'd first met.

"Look at the size of his hands," Kristie said under her breath as she started to unload the boxes. "How would you like to have those palms cupped around your ass?"

Avery could think of worse ways to spend an evening. "Pro ballers are notorious for screwing around." It was better to remind herself of why Jase Blackwell was off-limits rather than entertain any fantasies about what it would be like to have his hands on her. "Would you really want to subject yourself to that sort of revolving-door hookup, Kristie?"

"He could revolve my door anytime."

Avery laughed. "Gross."

"What? Are you seriously trying to tell me that you wouldn't let *the* Billion Dollar Blackwell ring your bell into the wee hours of the morning if you had the chance?"

She'd had the chance. Sort of. And she'd sent him packing. "I don't know. Wouldn't you feel self-conscious? I mean, the guy must get propositioned by hotties all the time." Women a thousand times more put together than she was. "I'd be so worried about measuring up that I probably wouldn't enjoy myself."

"You're a total hottie, Avery." Kristie nudged her hip

into Avery's as she took the foil off a pan of sliced smoked brisket. "You already measure up."

Avery wiped an imaginary tear from her eye and sniffed. "And that is why you're my BFF."

"Damn straight," Kristie said. "A girl can dream, right? I say go for it, Avery. When are you ever going to get another opportunity like this again? Live a little! In fact, I *dare* you to go after him."

Avery had never been one to back down from a challenge and Kristie knew it. She had to admit, she was tempted. What could it hurt to spend a little quality time with the gorgeous pro football star? As long as she went into it knowing that it would never be anything more than a casual one-night stand. She continued to ready serving platters for the night's fifteen guests, and Avery was careful to keep her eyes on her work. The urge to look up, to search the kitchen for any sign of Jase was almost too hard to resist and she didn't need to complicate her life by chasing after something that was out of her reach. But, oh man, she couldn't help but think that a night with Jase Blackwell would be one she'd never forget.

"Okay, I think we're ready to roll." Avery's boss, Peyton, breezed into the kitchen, a fluttering mass of excited energy. She loved her job and it showed, but Avery could have done without the hyperactive flapping of arms as she ushered her and Kristie toward the patio.

Here goes. Try not to spill anything . . . Nothing conveyed professionalism like dumping a plateful of barbeque on one of the dinner guests. But the second she walked out onto the tiled patio, her hands began to shake. *Abort! Abort!* Was it too late to turn around and head back for the kitchen? Probably. Damn it.

She felt Jase's eyes on her without even having to look up to confirm the fact. His gaze burned through her, igniting all of her nerve endings until her skin tingled with a pleasant warmth that settled between her thighs. She tried again to remind herself why it wasn't a good idea to give in to Jase Blackwell's advances but her body was giving her a hell of a counterargument.

"Holy crap, Avery. He's eyeballing you like you're his next meal. *Rawr.*" Kristie nudged her with an elbow as they returned to the kitchen to grab the side dishes. "How many times has he asked you out?"

"Since last week?" Avery said. "Three." At every dinner party he'd thrown, he'd asked her out at the end of the night. And Avery had turned him down each and every time.

"And you haven't accepted why?"

That was a good question. Avery set a tray of brisket on the buffet table and followed Kristie back into the kitchen. She grabbed the king-sized bowl of potato salad and headed for the patio. "I'm really not sure if it's a good idea or not."

Kristie came up behind her carting a pot of baked beans. "Let me answer that for you, Ave. It's *definitely* a good idea."

Across the expanse of the well-manicured lawn, Avery caught sight of Jase from the corner of her eye. He was chatting up a group of guys and their dates, or wives, or whatever, but somehow, she felt his attention on her as a vibration that traveled the length of her body. Every inch of her was painfully aware of him, dialed in to his exact location like metal seeking out a magnet.

What would it hurt to give in to her attraction? Even if it was just for one night?

Again, she caught his eye from a distance and her breath caught at the intensity of his stare. Her heart clenched at the thought of what it would be like to be discarded by a man like Jason Blackwell once he was done with her. She didn't think her self-esteem would be able to take a hit like that. He could throw a million dinner parties for all she cared, Avery wasn't going to give in no matter how charming—or sexy—he might have been. Jase Blackwell was simply going to have to remain one item on her bucket list that went uncrossed.

Distance was the only option.

THREE

"Come *on* you piece of junk. Start!"

If ever Avery had wanted to firebomb her own car it was right now. Kristie and Peyton had already taken off for the night, leaving Avery officially stranded. And apparently dead was the theme of the night because when she fished her phone from the bottom of her purse, she found that it had rolled over and kicked the bucket sometime in the past few hours as well.

Great.

She stared through the windshield at the looming three-story mansion that was Jason Blackwell's house. The place was a castle in comparison to her own modest apartment. Avery's stomach clenched at the thought of knocking on the door and asking him for help. Wouldn't that be the icing on tonight's cake? She rested her head against the steering wheel and let out a groan. A do-over would be so welcome right about now.

Avery squealed at the sound of a knock on her window and her head snapped back from the steering wheel with the force of a rattlesnake strike. Her heart jumped up into her throat and her fear slowly transformed to annoyance when she came face-to-face with Jase's smiling countenance. *Glad I could entertain you. Ugh.*

"Car won't start?"

Avery rolled down the window, cringing at its squeaky protest. "Oh, no. I just like to round out a night of waitressing by hanging out in customers' driveways. It's sort of my thing. You don't mind, do you?"

Jase laughed and the sound rippled through Avery's body, settling low in her abdomen. She hadn't felt that sort of spark in a long time. And it scared the crap out of her. "Believe it or not, that wouldn't be the strangest thing a woman has done in my driveway."

Avery gave him a wry smile. "Somehow, I wouldn't doubt it."

Jase opened the car door and Avery stiffened. For some reason the barrier of the door between them put her at ease. As though protecting her from the image of perfection on the other side. She was willing to bet those feathery locks were silky soft. He was so tall that it looked uncomfortable for him to hunch down to eye level with her. His body just seemed to go on forever. And when he smiled . . . sweet Jesus. A rush of liquid heat spread from her belly outward, bathing her in delicious warmth. If a grin made her feel that good, she could only imagine how his hands would make her feel . . .

"Far be it from me to interrupt a woman's post-waitressing rituals, but if you want, I can give you a ride home."

As she saw it, Avery had two options. One, she could ask Jase to use his phone and call Kristie to come pick her up. In which case, she'd be alone with him in his house. Two, she could let him drive her home. In which case, she'd be alone with him in his car. Crap. Either way they'd be alone together and Avery seriously doubted she'd have the willpower to turn him down again if he asked her out. Holy crap, she was sure her cheeks were flushed from the heat in his gaze. The rest of her body sure as hell was.

"Avery? I'm sensing a moral dilemma. It's just a ride home. I'm not asking you to knock off a bank with me or anything."

She cocked a brow. "What? You mean that's not what this is about? I brought along a black catsuit, a ski mask, and everything. You know, just in case."

Jase's resounding laughter melted Avery's insides. "Oh, sugar. I would pay good money to see you in that getup."

It was a joke of course, but the way his voice got low and husky with the words caused Avery to shudder. His accent even got a little thicker, slow and sweet like honey fresh from the comb. She wondered what it would be like to hear that voice low in her ear, whispering passionate, dirty things and Avery shifted in her seat. Just thinking about sex with Jase made her body burn and her clit throb. If the simple thought of him made her wet, she could only imagine what the real thing would be like.

She gave a nervous laugh. She could talk a good game, but her snark was a shield she wore to hide the lack of confidence she felt on a daily basis. "I doubt it would be too impressive. I bet you'd pay more just to get me to take it off." *Oh god.* "Wait. That came out wrong. I don't mean that you'd want me to—Not that I think you'd want to see me—" Could the seat just fold her up and swallow her already? "That's totally not what I meant."

Jase's answering amusement rippled over her, open and good-natured. "I'd say something to that but somehow I doubt I could give you a response that wouldn't get me into trouble."

Avery grinned and her cheeks flushed with renewed heat. "Probably not."

"Okay, so how about that ride? Or would you rather

camp out in my driveway until someone sends a search party out for you?"

She let out a slow breath and tried to slow her racing heart. "Thanks. A ride would be great."

Jase extended his hand and his palm swallowed hers as he helped her out of the car. He held on just a little too long, the lingering contact causing sparks of sensation to tingle along Avery's nerve endings. She cleared her throat and he gave her a sheepish grin as he released her hand, which she rubbed against her thigh. As though the simple act could banish the sensation of his touch. She'd need to cut her hand off at the wrist for that to happen.

Jase led her into the garage that was at least twice the size of her apartment. The contents were a gearhead's wet dream: a Maserati parked at the far end, a Harley-Davidson toward the rear, and a vintage '67 Corvette in mint condition occupied the center space. Jase didn't pay them any mind as he made his way toward the older-model Chevy pickup in the far right bay. It seemed so out of place among the other cars and high-priced toys. Caked with mud and much too practical and lusterless, like a rock nestled in a bed of diamonds.

"This poor truck looks like it's run the gauntlet," Avery remarked as she opened the door. What was it with Texas boys that they all had to jack their pickups up a mile off the ground? She was going to need a damned stepladder to get inside. Even up on her tiptoes, she couldn't grab the oh-shit handle on the frame to hoist herself up. "For some reason," she grunted as she reached up again, "I doubt there are many mud bogs around this swanky subdivision."

A quick yip escaped Avery's throat as strong hands encircled her waist. Jase's hands were so big that the tips of his fingers almost met, and he lifted her up into the truck as though she were nothing more than a rag doll. "Sugar, you're just barely knee high to a grasshopper. You sure you don't need a booster seat to ride up front?"

Holy cats, he was *killing* her. Pouring on that Texas charm, it's not like he knew that sort of good-natured teasing turned Avery's insides to Jell-O. No, that was just Jase's personality, and it wasn't doing anything to cool her lust. Looks *and* personality? He was almost too good to be true.

"As if I haven't heard that one before." She forced herself to tease back. To hide the fact that she was nervous and sweating bullets from the attention. "Come on, Blackwell. You can do better than that."

"A challenge, huh?"

He stretched out the seat belt and leaned over her to buckle it, his arm brushing against her breasts. Avery inhaled a sharp breath as her nipples tightened beneath the cotton fabric of her bra. "If you want to call it that."

"You do realize that I have an insane drive to win at all costs, right? Challenge accepted."

Nothing got his blood up like a little healthy competition. And as Jase rounded the backside of the truck, his blood was damned near humming in his veins. For the fourth time this week, Avery had all but ignored him through dinner, intentionally avoiding his gaze. After dinner, she'd kept to the kitchen, cleaning up and packing it in quicker than a pony heading for the barn. By the time he'd ushered the last of his teammates out the door, she was gone. But the automotive gods had been smiling down on him tonight. He was going to kiss that little junker of hers on the bumper when he got home. This was just the opportunity he needed to get to know her better. And already he found her irresistible.

Even in the dim light of the cab, Jase noticed her body language change the closer they got to her apartment.

Their conversation dwindled, no longer playful as Avery devolved to answering his questions in one- or two-word sentences. She was uncomfortable. But why?

"You probably don't come down this way much." Her voice was quiet as she spoke toward the window. "My part of town is a far cry from million-dollar mansions with car dealership–sized garages, huh?"

That was the reason behind her change in attitude? She was embarrassed? "Avery, believe it or not, but I was so poor growing up that there were days my brother and I had to share the same lunch. We didn't have much, and Mom would pack one sandwich and a banana if we were lucky. My brother Luke and I would fight over who got the bigger half. I swear," he said with a laugh. "More than once I thought about gnawing my own arm off. I was always hungry."

Avery turned to look at him, her green eyes luminous in the dark interior of the truck. "Really?"

"Oh yeah. We were dirt poor. My dad was a worthless son of a bitch and I spent a lot of years gettin' teased for my older brother's hand-me-downs that barely fit. And for the record, cozying up to your twin while you share a sandwich isn't exactly something that's gonna keep a guy from getting smacked around. My brother Ryder saved our family. After Dad left, he picked us up by our bootstraps and turned our ranch into a cattle empire. Thank god, too, because by the time I hit high school, I was eating seven meals a day."

It wasn't a story he told often. In fact, if you asked the sports media, Jase was nothing more than a spoiled rich kid who'd not only bought his way onto his college team but into the NFL as well. And even though he didn't know Avery very well, he sensed that her social standing—poor neighborhood, junker car, waitressing job—bothered her. Jase never thought of his money in terms of it giving him a leg up over anyone. Rather, he valued it more because of what he'd had to go without when he was a kid. And likewise, he tried to share the wealth, donating to charities, schools, libraries, whenever he could.

"Were your hand-me-downs too big or too small?" Her tone had regained some of its pluck, putting a smile on Jase's face.

"Too small. Ryder is only four years older than me and by the time I was fourteen, I was already bigger than him. I don't know what my mom was thinking. Really, Ryder should've gotten our old clothes."

"I didn't know you had a twin."

Jase laughed. "Don't tell me you've never heard of the infamous Lucas 'Lucifer' Blackwell."

"Should I have?"

She had to be shitting him. When it came to bands of female worshipers, Luke took the cake. "He's the lead singer of Riot 59. Girls happily throw their high-priced panties at him on a damned near daily basis."

"Sorry, I'm not familiar. Do they sing country music?"

As if Luke would be caught dead singing a country ballad. "You'd think so, but my brother is all about the angsty rock. Sensitive like Coldplay, One Republic, but edgy and retro like Bastille with a little punk flavor. At least, that's how he describes it. Probably why the ladies love him."

"That's quite the musical combo," Avery said with a wry smirk. "But if he's your twin, I doubt it's just his musical chops that have the girls swooning."

Jase couldn't resist the opportunity to tease her. "Are you sayin' I'm pretty, sugar?"

Her eyes met his for a brief moment and Jase's breath hitched. "I'm saying that any woman with eyes in her head would be hard pressed not to look at you, Jason Blackwell."

Hot. Damn. The sound of his name on her lips was as

sweet and rich as whipped cream. Her intense emerald gaze was enough to stir his cock and the damned thing pressed against his fly like it was trying to escape the confinement of his jeans. This was a bad idea. The temptation to do something reckless was too great. Jase didn't want to scare Avery off. But damn it, all he could think of was getting her closer. On top of him would be good. Naked, even better.

"Take a left here," Avery said, pointing to a small apartment complex. "My unit is in the second building, one-B."

As he pulled into a parking space, Jase's gut bottomed out. The thought of just dropping her off and calling it a night was unbearable. He wanted her. Right now. Right in the fucking front seat of this truck if he thought he could get away with it.

"Thanks for the ride," Avery said as she unbuckled her seat belt. "I'm sorry my car is loitering in your driveway. I'll get it towed out of there first thing in the morning." Jase moved to unbuckle his own belt and she said, "Oh, you don't have to walk me, Jase. I'm a big girl."

If only she knew the action had less to do with any show of gallantry and more to do with his plan to get a hell of a lot closer. "Don't worry about your car. I'll have it taken to a shop tomorrow."

"Oh, no, thanks. Really, don't." She seemed appalled that he'd offer. Well, that was too bad, wasn't it? "I can't let you do that. It might be a while before I can afford to have it fixed. I don't want it sitting at a garage for who knows how long."

He scooted across the bench seat. A couple of inches. A couple more. Avery's lips parted, her bottom lip just a little too full and practically begging Jase to take it into his mouth and suck. Another inch. Two. Jase stretched his arm out on the headrest and her eyes darted to the motion for the barest second. "Jase . . ."

She averted her gaze, her body drawing in on itself. What did she have to be so self-conscious about? Did she not realize how fucking beautiful she was?

"Avery, look at me." Her eyes met his, curious. "Now don't move."

"Why?" she whispered.

"Because I'm going to fucking explode if I don't kiss you right now."

FOUR

Holy cats, Avery, this is happening right now.

Avery had never been the super-confident woman. Oh, she knew she wasn't bad looking, but guys weren't tripping over themselves to ask her out. And likewise, she was such a klutz that it tended to turn people off. When Jase looked at her with such intensity, such longing, it made her feel like maybe she could be that girl. The confident one. Someone who knew her worth and wasn't afraid to own it. Jase took his time, studied her face for the briefest moment before tracing his fingers from her temple to her chin. And then, he cupped her face, holding her still as though she were made of glass. When his lips met hers it was an unhurried, deliberate kiss that she felt in every nerve ending of her body.

A slow tease, his lips met hers in a rhythmic dance that flooded Avery with a heat that she felt right to her core. Desire ignited inside of her, raging like a fire through dry timber as Jase's thumbs stroked up her jaw, feathering over her earlobes and Avery shuddered as a pleasant chill chased down her spine, meeting the heat of her body in a way that made her feel as though she'd become a gossamer thing, steam swirling in the clashing temperatures.

Jase's breath mingled with her own as he continued to kiss her. His tongue played at the seam of her lips, as measured as his kiss, coaxing her to open for him. Avery's lips parted, but rather than deepen this kiss, he continued to take his time. The tip of his tongue flicked out at hers, the contact so innocent and yet so intimate that it caused Avery's breath to hitch in her chest. No one had ever kissed her like this. And the fact that she barely knew the man who shared this wonderful thing with her left her feeling rattled and unsure. She didn't want to be used and discarded by Jase. Treated as though she wasn't worth the time for an honest-to-god first date let alone a second one.

But that didn't mean she possessed the desire or the willpower to stop him, either.

Jase abandoned her mouth, kissing the corner of her lips and across her jaw. She tilted her head to one side and he continued on, his lips blazing a trail across her flesh as he settled his mouth at her pulse point and sucked.

Wow. Oh wow, oh wow, oh wow. Avery let out a quiet moan. She couldn't help herself, it just felt so good. The little sound seemed to urge Jase on. He groaned into her skin, a low rumble that she felt all the way to her pussy. If Jase Blackwell played football half as well as he kissed, the Cowboys were guaranteed a Super Bowl win this year.

"Jase," she breathed. "That feels amazing."

She felt him smile against her skin. "Sugar, that isn't even my best effort."

Cocky. Her lips curved into a reluctant smile as he took her earlobe into his mouth and sucked. Her sex clenched with need and her hips gave a shallow thrust as though acting of their own volition. "I don't warrant your A-game, Blackwell?" Her shield of snark shot up, protecting her from feeling anything that might eventually hurt her. "That makes me sad. It really does."

He nipped at her throat, soothing the sting with the wet heat of his tongue. Avery didn't need to be naked to know that her sex was slick, her lips swelling around her throbbing clit. Could she go through with this? Her body was 100 percent on board, cheering her on like it was the home stretch and she was mere feet from the finish line. Avery could think of worse decisions than inviting Jase inside her apartment. They were both consenting adults, after all. It's not like she was the first woman in the history of sex to contemplate the appeal of a one-night stand. And though she'd spent all week convincing herself of why being with him was a bad idea, right now, she couldn't think of a single reason to stop.

"I can't show you all my tricks at once, sugar," Jase murmured against her skin. "No self-respecting athlete goes into any situation without a carefully planned strategy."

Jase made his way back to Avery's lips and she released a contented sigh. He kissed her deeper this time, though no less methodically, his tongue plunging deep into her mouth, stroking along hers in a slippery caress before withdrawing and plunging back in again. Another wave of heat stole over Avery's body. The way he was kissing her now was downright lewd. Using his tongue to fuck her mouth with painstaking precision.

If he kept kissing her this way, she'd come before he even laid a hand on her.

"I could kiss you for days," Jase said against her mouth, the vibration of his words tickling her lips. "Weeks. Just kiss you and kiss you until we both passed out from exhaustion."

Avery's stomach fluttered. No one had ever said anything so sweet to her. If it was part of his plan to ply her into sleeping with him, it was working. She was getting closer to that point of mindless need that superseded common sense and caution. "Jason Blackwell," she whispered. "Are you trying to manage me?"

"That depends," he said in a husky tone. "Is it working?"

He was as charming as he was sexy. Avery was helpless against him. Why not give in? Live out a fantasy with a man built like a warrior. She could have the experience of her life as long as she didn't allow herself any sort of emotional attachment; she wouldn't have to worry about having her heart broken when Jase moved on to someone else. And she had no doubt that he would. Men had emotionless sex all the time. Why couldn't she?

Decision made, she reached down to flip the lever and moved the bench seat back. If she was going to keep this emotionless, inviting him inside wasn't an option. With their combined weight, as soon as Avery released the latch, the seat fell backward with a jolt. Jase's gaze met hers, his lips quirked in a half-smile and a brow raised in question. Rather than explain herself, Avery put her finger to his lips. He took the digit into his mouth, enveloping her finger with the warmth of his mouth as he sucked. His tongue traced the underside of her finger and Avery's lids drifted shut for a blissful moment.

It was now or never.

Thanks to the club cab—and the fact that she'd moved the seat back—Avery had plenty of space to move in the spacious truck. She swung one leg across Jase's waist and settled onto his lap. He bucked his hips, scooting over fully onto the passenger side, and Avery sucked in a sharp breath as the hard length of his erection rubbed against her core. Even through his jeans she could feel every long inch of him and it sent a thrill through her body at the thought of having him deep inside of her.

Jase's brow furrowed as he looked at her. Avery began

to unfasten the buttons on her white work shirt, her heart racing in her chest. "I think you're doing a pretty good job of managing me."

He sucked in a breath as she shrugged off the shirt, leaving her bare except for the lacy fabric of her white bra. His gaze heated, the whiskey brown of his eyes glinting with hints of molten honey. Avery leaned back, her lids drooping as the angle only helped to press his erection firmly against her. She shifted her hips just so, releasing a quick breath at the sharp stab of pleasure that shot through her from the friction.

"Jesus, Avery." Jase's nostrils flared as he gripped her waist in his hands. "What are you doing to me?"

Her stomach flipped as confidence surged through her. No man had ever made her feel so brazen. "That depends," she said. "Is it working?"

"Hell yeah," he said on a groan.

Jase's cock pulsed in his jeans, so fucking hard it was a wonder the damned thing hadn't ripped through the denim. With every meeting of their lips, he wanted more. With every touch, he craved another inch of bare skin. And when she climbed up on his lap, any common sense he might have had took off like a spooked mare. He couldn't have thought in a straight line if he'd wanted to.

The woman tied him into knots.

She leaned over him, the short curtain of her hair brushing over his face. When her mouth slanted against his, he sighed into her mouth, their breaths mingling until they were one. Slowly, he slid his palms up her rib cage, her skin like satin on his calloused palms. He cupped her breasts, flicking his thumbs over the pearls of her nipples through the fabric and Avery let out a low moan that shot straight through Jase's shaft and settled in his balls.

He'd never wanted a woman the way he wanted Avery.

Passion clouded his thoughts until Jase was consumed. He needed every inch of her exposed. Wanted to suck, and lick, and fuck her until she screamed his name. Was dying to feel her pussy clench around his cock as she came. In a frenzy, he tugged at the cups of her bra, freeing those full, beautiful breasts from the restraining fabric. Their weight in his palms was heaven, the heat of her skin branding him. Tonight Avery would surely scar him, leave her mark permanently upon his body. And Jase couldn't wait to feel the burn.

In the dark interior of the cab, only the streetlight outside illuminated Avery's body. Her skin was like cream, pale and smooth, the dusky nipples standing proud and erect as he pinched them.

"Oh god," Avery gasped.

Her response only spurred him on and he eased her back, cradling her body in his arms as he bent his head to suckle her. He took her nipple into his mouth, rolling it with his tongue and Avery let out a soft, mewling sound that sent the blood racing to Jase's cock. So much for having anything left over to support brain function. Her skin was sweet with just the slightest salt tang and smelled of ripe clover. With each pass of his tongue, each nibble of teeth, her cries grew louder and more desperate, filling his ears with the sweetest sounds he'd ever heard.

Avery braced her hands on his chest, her palms kneading his pecs before her fingers trailed down his ribs. His stomach clenched reflexively and his breath caught in his chest as her fingers grazed his fly and she fumbled for the button. God, how was he ever going to keep it together? He'd go off the second she took him into her hand.

As she popped the button and eased the zipper of his jeans down, Jase switched to her other breast, taking as much of her into his mouth as he could and drawing on the flesh with deep, hungry sucks. He pulled back slowly, clamping his lips down on her nipple and Avery cried out, "Jase, oh god, Jase." His name on her lips was heaven. He wanted her to say it again and again.

She eased him back, and Jase craned his neck forward, stroking the tip of her nipple with his tongue. He was rewarded for his effort with a tight whimper just before Avery put her weight behind her actions and settled him back against the seat. Their eyes met, and those green limpid pools consumed him, the expression so heated Jase thought for a moment he might be dreaming. She was so responsive, so passionate. Perfect.

Avery shifted her body so that her ass rested at the edge of Jase's knees. In the close quarters of the truck, she leaned back against the dash for support as she finished pulling his zipper down. Slowly, she slid her fingers past the waistband of his underwear and his abdomen twitched. When she took him into her hand, his head rolled back on the rest and Jase's eyes drifted shut. "Ah, sugar," he moaned. "Stroke me. Nice and slow."

He looked up to find her studying his expression. She appeared unsure, her brow furrowed as she worried her bottom lip between her teeth. He placed his hand over hers, urging her to take him in a firm grip and guided her hand to stroke down from the swollen head of his cock, right down to the base. Jase's thigh muscles went taut as pleasure shot through him. He released his grip and she stroked back up, slowly, and then rubbed her thumb over the crown, spreading a bead of moisture over the engorged head before stroking back down. Jase shivered at his sensitivity. "That's it, sugar. Just like that." If she kept up her pace, he'd come in her hand and there wouldn't be a damned thing he could do to stop it. On and on it went, the torture delicious and unrelenting. All the while, she kept her gaze locked with his, her lips parted and eyes wide in silent wonder.

Sweet Jesus, she was too good to be true.

Jase slid his palms up her thighs as he dove beneath the hem of her skirt. His thumbs brushed the juncture between her legs, the silk of her underwear already damp with arousal. "Avery." His voice was a harsh whisper in the quiet cab of the truck. He swallowed against the dryness in his throat. She moaned as his thumbs brushed against her clit, so swollen he could feel the little bud through the fabric. He wanted inside of her. Now. Buried as deep as he could go. He wanted her to ride his cock until they were both too exhausted to move. He needed to fuck her like he needed his next breath. "I want you. Tell me you want me, too. Tell me to fuck you, Avery."

"I do." Avery slanted her mouth over his in a desperate, feverish kiss. "I want you, Jase. Fuck me. Now."

Haste took on a new meaning as he fumbled, one-handed, with his jeans. Jase dragged his wallet out of his back pocket, while shimmying both the pants and his underwear down off his ass. Avery rose up on her knees, head bent in the crowded cab as she helped to pull the denim past his knees. He fumbled with his wallet and gave a sheepish laugh. "Jesus, sugar, I want you so bad I can't even get my hands to work right."

Avery smiled, her expression lighting up like the sunrise. With a last triumphant tug, Jase managed to free the foil packet from the wallet and he tore into it like his survival depended on it. He rolled the condom over his erection and cupped Avery's face in his hands before kissing her with renewed vigor. She threaded her fingers through his hair, the scrape of her nails causing pleasant chills to cascade over his shoulders and down his back. He took her tiny waist in his hands and she rose up on her knees, settling herself over the engorged head. Jase's fingers once again brushed the dampened silk of her underwear and he groaned into her mouth before jerking the fabric aside.

He wanted to pound into her, bury himself to the root. But Jase waited, giving Avery control of the situation. His body shook with both restraint and passion, his mouth greedy for hers in an insatiable way that he couldn't explain. When her slick heat brushed his cock, Jase sucked in a breath.

"Avery." Her name on his lips was like a fifty year old scotch, heady and intoxicating.

"I know, Jase," she murmured against his mouth. "I feel the same way."

FIVE

Was she really going to go through with this?

She'd never been so forward with a man, so completely wanton. It went against her nature, but Jase was just too commanding. His touch, addictive. He was a force of nature that Avery was helpless to fight.

Jase's thighs twitched against hers, the muscles unyielding stone. His fingers dug into the flesh at her hips, gripping and releasing, gripping and releasing as though it took all of the self-control he could muster not to impale her body on his cock. Avery's abdomen tightened at the thought, another rush of wet warmth spreading between her thighs. She didn't know how he did it, but being with Jase made her feel brave.

Slowly, she rocked over the head of his erection, the shock of heat from the contact causing every nerve in her body to ignite. Jase reached up and peeled his T-shirt from his body, offering up another distraction as Avery took in the sculpted form of his pecs, the narrow ridges of his abdomen and the tight taper of his waist. Hesitation warred with need, common sense and self-preservation scratching at the back of her brain. How could she keep this encounter emotionless when every look, every gentle touch made her *feel* so much? The desire to put her palms on those hardened hills and planes nearly distracted her from the moment. Would acquainting herself with his body—all of it—be a mistake?

Oh, who the hell cared!

Avery braced her palms on his shoulders, her attention focused on the way he felt beneath her hands, the contraction and release of each individual muscle, the smoothness of his skin. She rocked against him once again, this time lowering herself on top of him. A tortured moan vibrated in Jase's chest as his head leaned back on the headrest. "Just like that, sugar. Oh, shit that feels so good."

His words urged her on, the strained timbre of his voice vibrating every tendon in Avery's body. She took him deeper and stilled, giving herself a moment to adjust to his size. She was so wet, so ready for him, that her own impatience won over and she took him fully inside of her as she settled down onto his lap.

He cupped her breasts as she rode him, his palms so large that they engulfed her. With gentle precision he massaged her sensitive flesh, kneading and working his way to her nipples, which he rolled between his fingers, sending a pulse of sensation straight though Avery's core and into her throbbing clit.

"Harder, sugar. Don't stop."

When he called her sugar in that slow, honeyed voice, it nearly drove her over the edge. She'd give him anything he asked for, as long as he kept talking to her like that. Her fingertips dug into the flesh at his shoulders as she held onto him like a lifeline. He thrust up to meet her, the sounds of their bodies meeting and parting only adding to her pleasure. The windows fogged in the truck's cab as their labored breath heated the air. Sweat trickled down

Avery's throat and between her breasts. Down the back of her neck and along the ridge of her spine. She'd never experienced sex in such a visceral, all-consuming way. She was lost to Jase Blackwell. She no longer knew where her own body ended and his began.

Her head lolled back on her shoulders and Avery braced her arms behind her on Jase's knees. He leaned forward, capturing one aching nipple in his mouth and laved her in time with each thrust. A languid pass of his tongue, followed by the sensual sting of his teeth as he nibbled at the hardened peak.

Avery was mindless. Past the point of reason and spurred only by desire. Her throat was raw from her ragged cries, and she couldn't even be bothered to care about anyone seeing or hearing them. In this moment there was only Jase. She couldn't get enough of him. Couldn't take him deep enough inside of her. Avery rode him with abandon and he gripped her hips firmly in his palms, guiding her actions as he suckled unmercifully at her breasts.

"I'm going to come. Oh, god, Jase, I'm going to come."

The words were a mantra, building in intensity with each deep thrust.

Avery closed her eyes, shut out everything but the sensation of pleasure building to a fever pitch, the sound of Jase's body meeting hers and his labored breath. The wet heat of his mouth on her skin and the way his hands moved her hips in a sensual dance on his erection. Her world spiraled, careening into darkness, shrinking until her skin, her very veins were tight and constricted. The wave crested within her and rolled, breaking her apart into thousands of tiny pieces.

The orgasm took her like a riptide. "Jase!" His name burst from her lips in a strangled gasp and he held her tight, refusing to slow his pace.

"That's so good, sugar. Come for me. Ah, god, you're

squeezing me so tight." He let out a low moan and Avery looked up to find his expression strained, forehead pinched, and jaw clenched. His hips bucked in a wild thrust and then another before a primal shout ripped from his throat, his body going rigid as the orgasm took him.

"Oh, Christ!" His thighs were like oaks beneath her. He buried his face between her breasts and his thrusts became shallower. "That's good," he murmured. "So fucking good."

He wrapped his arms around her, and leaned back in the seat, pulling her against his body. Avery's arms were limp, nearly numb from being braced behind her for so long, and her legs were deliciously fatigued and warm. Chills chased across her flesh as Jase caressed up and down her spine in a slow and easy rhythm. His breath was labored and hot against her throat and his lips soft where he planted lazy kisses right beneath her ear. Avery couldn't have moved if she'd wanted to. And right now, she was completely content to stay here, with Jase still inside of her, held tight in his embrace.

"I'm moving into this truck," Jase said absently, his fingers still traveling the highway of Avery's spine. "I'm just going to throw a sleeping bag in here and set up camp. And *no one* else is ever allowed to sit on this seat again."

Avery answered with soft, sluggish laughter. "I hate to point this out, but there's no shower in here. After a few days, no one will *want* to ride in this truck."

Jase chuckled. "Good. Because I don't want anyone other than you in this seat ever again."

Avery's pulse picked up its frantic pace and it had nothing to do with their previous exertion. Ever again? Like, *ever*? Jase's words struck a chord. One that plucked at the thin strings of panic that connected Avery's brain to her emotions. She'd coached herself to remain detached. Treat this encounter like the one-night stand she was sure it would be. Hell, she'd half expected him to boot her out the door the second he'd come. Wasn't that the pro-athlete M.O.? Hit it and quit it?

Quiet descended, settling over Avery like a too-warm blanket. Jase continued to hold her, his embrace so gentle, his breath warm on her neck. For a moment, she could almost believe this intimate lie. Jase was still riding the high of his orgasm and that euphoric burst of endorphins that made him think he was experiencing emotions that he didn't really feel. In the morning his head would be clear. He'd realize that tonight was nothing more than a good time. And Avery was willing to bet that by this time tomorrow, he'd be promising some other woman that no one would ever set foot in his pickup truck again.

Texas chivalry, y'all.

"Are you cold?"

Of course Jase would assume the tremor that ran the length of Avery's body was due to the cold. He held her tighter, cupping her shoulders and ribs in his large palms. The contrast between them was laughable. She could only imagine what people would say if they saw them together. Her petite five foot, four inch frame was dwarfed by his six and a half feet of towering bulk.

You don't have to worry about it, Avery. There's a snowball's chance in hell you'll ever be seen out in public with him. She was a waitress, for Christ's sake! The withdrawn, accident-prone girl who worked at his team's private parties. All she would ever get from Jase Blackwell was a drive home and an amazing few minutes in the front seat of his truck. Her mother would be so proud.

God. What have I done?

Avery's demeanor cooled with the air. The chill soaked right into Jase's chest, permeating his bones. Now that she wasn't driven by lust, was she having second thoughts?

Regrets? The thought that she would soured his stomach, because he regretted nothing.

Jase wasn't some blushing virgin and he'd never make apologies for that fact. He'd experienced all that life had to offer and then some. But no woman had ever managed to get under his skin like Avery had. Hell, he'd spent close to ten thousand dollars over the past week on dinner parties he didn't even want to attend just to get a glimpse of her. To exchange even one word with her.

He'd never expected things to go this far with her tonight, but Christ Almighty he was sure glad that they had. She was perfection. Every straight line and voluptuous curve of her body was made for him. True, he didn't know much about her, and his mom would slap him right upside his head if she knew that he hadn't properly courted Avery before . . . um . . . giving her a ride in his truck. But Jase had never been much for convention. So they'd gone about this a little backward. So what? They had all the time in the world to get to know each other. Jase wasn't going anywhere.

"I'd better take you inside, sugar. You're shivering."

She hadn't answered his initial question but from the slight tremor that shook her, she had to be chilled. Her fingers idly teased the strands of his hair where they brushed the back of Jase's neck. His cock stirred inside of her, growing harder by the second. He wanted her again. And as much as he would've liked to resume where they'd left off, Jase had been taught better than to be a selfish dick. Avery was cold and their position in the truck couldn't be all that comfortable for her. True, his tall, bulky frame was cramped as well, but he would have fucked her in a clown car if she'd asked. Who cared about a leg cramp or two? The pleasure Avery had given him trumped any of his previous sexual encounters. By miles.

She deserved better than a wild toss in the front seat of his truck like they were a couple of horny teenagers, but Jase wouldn't take back what happened for even a Super Bowl ring. Avery shifted, rising up on her knees. He couldn't stand the thought of being separated from her just yet and hugged her tight, easing her back down on his cock. "Don't leave," he murmured into her hair. "Not yet."

Avery gave a nervous laugh, her tension rippling over Jase's skin. Her voice was shy, tentative when she said, "I don't want to give my neighbors any more of a show than they've already gotten. Besides, it's late. You probably have an early practice tomorrow and I don't want to keep you."

Was she brushing him off? Because he sure as hell felt the bite of bristles in her words. "Not that early." He planted a kiss below her ear and she stiffened. "At least let me walk you to your apartment." Where he'd do his damnedest to seduce her into a repeat performance.

"Oh, no. It's okay."

In a heartbeat she'd gone from fiery and passionate to cool and shy. Had he misinterpreted her earlier? No. She'd wanted him as much as he wanted her. There was no doubt in his mind. She pulled away and he let her this time, gauging by her nervous behavior that she needed a little space. "I want to walk you," he said. When her body left his, Jase ached with the need to pull her back to him. Jesus, what was wrong with him? Tonight was supposed to be about scratching an itch and nothing more. The good-luck fuck Carson sent him after in order to get his game tight. "I won't take no for an answer, sugar." He should have let her out of his truck—and his life—right now. Clean with no strings attached. Instead, he was trailing after her like a calf with a lead rope around his neck.

One wild romp and he was under her spell.

An awkward silence descended as they took a few

moments to put themselves back together. The air in his pickup was thick with Avery's scent and his body responded, his cock still thick and hard as he tried to zip up his jeans that frankly, weren't cooperating. Avery's gaze caught his and her expression brightened as the sweetest shy smile curled her lips.

"Having a little trouble with your pants?" she asked in a playful tone that did nothing to calm his raging hard-on. Damn. Her strange combination of unsure and unabashed turned him on. So unlike the mewling, overconfident groupies he was used to.

"More like a problem with my body," he replied sheepishly.

The comment earned him the pleasure of Avery's soft laughter and his gut clenched. She finished buttoning up her shirt, and Jase found himself drawn to the motion of her fingertips as they hovered between the breasts that he'd just licked and sucked in a greedy rush. If he didn't have her again soon, his body was likely to implode from the pressure. "Ready?" he asked, his voice still rough with passion.

She let out a barely audible sigh. "Ready."

Jase got out of the truck first so he could help her down. His hands lingered at her waist, his fingers digging in as though anchoring his body to hers. Avery cleared her throat and he let her go. *Classy, dude. Way to rock the intense vibe.* It was a wonder she wasn't sprinting full speed for her front door.

They stopped at the door to her apartment and she fiddled with the hair at the nape of her neck as though nervous. Christ, a kiss good-bye was nothing compared to the downright dirty things they'd done in his truck.

"Good night." So sweet.

"'Night, sugar."

Jase leaned in and placed a gentle kiss on Avery's mouth.

"Thanks for taking care of my car." She leaned up, kissed him again.

"I'll let you know when it's fixed." One more kiss. And another. This one deeper, intense.

Avery unlocked the door and eased it open before winding her fists in Jase's shirt. She took a step back and then another, dragging him through the door.

Well, whaddya know. His night wasn't quite over yet.

SIX

"Be sure to wait for your cream to reach one hundred and ninety degrees before adding the lemon juice," Chef Isaacs, the head pastry chef, said as he strolled through the maze of cooking stations. "If you add it too soon, your cream won't thicken properly and we want perfect, creamy mascarpone to result."

Avery checked the thermometer as she continued to stir the heating cream, her attention only half on today's lesson. Memories of the previous night assaulted her, heating her blood and sending a renewed sense of warmth through her limbs. Once Jase walked her to her apartment, her resolve had crumbled under the onslaught of his kisses along with her plans to keep him at arm's length. She didn't regret her decision for a second, either. Their second time had been better than the first and though he'd left shortly after, Avery had floated toward sleep on a cloud of bliss that carried her over into morning. Her limbs were still deliciously heavy, her body sated. It should be illegal to feel this good without an ounce of guilt.

Hands down, the best night of her life.

"Be sure to stir constantly," Chef Isaacs continued. "You will begin to notice that your cream is starting to foam as it reaches the near-boiling point."

And though washing Jase's masculine scent from her body was the last thing Avery wanted to do, she'd reluctantly showered, removing every trace of him from her this morning. She figured her fellow students would appreciate it if she showed up to class clean. Personal hygiene was pretty damned important in the food industry. Besides, no one wanted to advertise that they'd spent a wild night in bed, even though Avery had earned some serious bragging rights.

Jason freaking Blackwell. *Ho-ly cats.*

The sound of cream sizzling on the burner pulled Avery from her thoughts and she scrambled to turn down the heat as her pot boiled over. "Too hot, Ms. Lockhart," Chef chided as he passed her station. "You'll have to start over and heat it to the proper temperature before you add the lemon juice now."

"Yes, Chef." She felt the eyes of her classmates on her as she set the pot of scalded cream aside and mopped up the mess. This wasn't the first time she'd made a spectacle of herself after spilling or dropping something, but for some reason, she was more embarrassed than usual. As though everyone around her knew every dirty thought that had distracted her focus. God, she was such a *loser*.

How could she possibly concentrate while images of Jase's perfect body butted their way into her thoughts? It was hard enough to convey an aura of confidence without the distraction.

"Someone's got her head in the clouds today," Kristie remarked as she measured out a tablespoon of lemon juice and added it to her cream. "Don't tell me, Billion Dollar Blackwell gave you the private tour of his bedroom after everyone left last night."

Avery cringed and her friend's eyes widened to the size of serving platters. "Oh my god," she exclaimed, nearly tipping her own saucepan over in the process. "He did! You slept with him!"

"Shh!" Avery seethed, looking around to make sure no one overheard. "I'm not trying to share the details of my love life with the entire room, Kristie."

"Maybe not," she remarked, "but you sure as hell better share them with me. Spill."

Avery checked the temperature of her cream to make sure it had cooled to one-ninety and put the saucepan back on the burner as she measured out a portion of lemon juice. "It just sort of happened," she said. Usually, she wouldn't have thought twice about divulging to Kristie the dirty details of her romantic encounters, but this was different. Jase was a secret she wanted to keep to herself. "My car wouldn't start and—"

"Ah!" Kristie exclaimed. "So lucky. I wish my car was a piece of shit."

Avery cut her a look.

"What? I *so* would have loved to have been stranded in his driveway. I take it he gave you a jump?"

She laughed as Kristie waggled her eyebrows. "He's actually really . . ." Sexy? Amazing in bed? Built like a freaking Greek god? All of the above. "Sweet," she finally said. "Nothing like what I expected."

"And . . . ?" Kristie looked as though the suspense might cause her to spontaneously combust.

"And what?" Avery said with a laugh.

"Are you going to see him again?"

Definitely not. Last night couldn't be anything more than a one-night stand. Avery knew it was best to cut her losses now before she got too involved and gave Jase the opportunity to hurt her like she knew he'd inevitably do.

"I doubt it." She kept her attention on the saucepan in

front of her. "I think last night was a once in a lifetime thing."

"All right, everyone. Your cream should be properly thickened by now and can be transferred into your sieves. Be sure to line them with cheesecloth first, people."

At Chef's instructions, Avery switched gears, preparing for the step that would separate the whey from the cream and make the mascarpone cheese. Tomorrow they were making tiramisu, and she wanted her mascarpone to come out perfectly. She'd yet to impress Chef Isaacs and she was desperate for her instructor to see beyond her scattered appearance and clumsiness. On the flip side, she'd tried not to think too hard about last night, but Kristie had managed to send Avery's already frazzled thoughts into overtime. Jase didn't ask for her number. He didn't even say he'd see her later. Why should it matter if she never saw him again when she'd convinced herself that she didn't care either way?

"Oh god." Avery brought her hand up to her face, completely oblivious to the fact that she still held a spoon in her fist. The spoon smacked her forehead, bathing her face in too warm and too thick cream that clung to her face like plaster. "Ow! Ow, ow, ow." She grabbed a towel and wiped her face, rinsing it under cool water before wringing it out. Of all the bone-headed, clumsy . . .

"You've got it bad," Kristie said as she helped to wipe down Avery's hair. "That boy's got you tied in *knots*."

One night with Jase Blackwell, and Avery was as good as ruined. So much for emotional detachment. That plan had backfired in a grand fashion. "No, I don't." Just because Kristie could see it didn't mean Avery was about to admit it. "I couldn't care less about him."

"Uh-huh. *Sure*." Kristie returned to her station and began to ladle her soon-to-be cheese into the sieve. "You just keep telling yourself that, Ave."

She would. Because she didn't think her heart could take being broken by Jason Blackwell.

Hands down, it had been the best practice of Jase's entire football career. The offensive staff as a whole had been beyond impressed with his performance and convinced that he was ready to start tomorrow's game. And despite the fact that his place on the team finally felt secure, up until last night there had still been a nagging insecurity that Willis would be starting their first game of the play-offs and not him. So to say that he was relieved was the understatement of the year. Avery really was his good-luck charm.

Fuck. Yeah!

Jase pulled up to Avery's apartment complex, still flying high on the endorphins and anticipation for tomorrow's game. Thank god they were playing at home because right now, all he could think of was the fiery brunette who'd rocked his world not once, but twice last night. And despite the fact that he'd been instructed by his friend to "hit it and quit it," he was dying to see her again. As he locked his pickup, Jase gave himself a precursory sniff. Damn it, he should've showered. But in his haste to get to Avery, he was lucky he'd had the presence of mind to change out of his damned cleats. Hopefully she wouldn't mind.

Jase's fist hovered at the door as his stomach twisted into a knot. What if she wasn't happy to see him? What if she'd realized that last night was a mistake? Or she'd been after nothing more than a one-nighter like so many other football groupies. Just another conquest to add to her list. *Jesus, nut up, dude.* Luke would mock him unmercifully if he could see him getting all twisted up over a woman like this. The problem was . . . after only one night with her, Jase knew that Avery was more than just a random hookup.

He knocked three times and held his breath.

When she opened the door, Avery's brow furrowed. "Hey," she greeted, clearly bemused as though she was surprised to see him standing in her doorway or some shit. Seriously? How could his presence come as a shock?

Jase's mouth hung slack. He'd planned to say something but words failed him. Instead, he was possessed with a need that overrode any brain function. Avery was too damned beautiful. Too desirable. So instead of saying hi, or any other civilized thing, Jase rushed through the doorway and took Avery in his arms, kissing her like his next breath depended on it.

She answered his impassioned kisses with a matching fervor. Gripping the hem of his shirt, she broke their contact for only as long as it took to drag it up and off his body. Likewise, Jase wasted no time in freeing the buttons of Avery's shirt, popping a couple in his haste to get her good and naked. He kicked a leg behind him and the door closed with a resounding slam that neither of them seemed to notice as they continued to claw and tear at each other's clothes.

Jase lost his balance as he toed off his shoes, taking Avery with him as they tumbled down onto her couch. If he didn't get inside of her soon, he'd lose his damned mind. Her tongue slid against his in a wet tangle and Jase groaned into her mouth. Sweet lord, her scent, her taste drove him into a frenzy of mindlessness and he cupped her flesh as he slid her stretchy yoga pants over the curves of her ass and down her thighs.

"Oh, god, Jase, now," Avery breathed as she broke their kiss. "Fuck me right now."

Her urgency spurred him on and he spun her around and positioned her so she was draped over the arm of the couch. His fingers shook as he unhooked her bra, leaving her to pull the straps down over her shoulders as he fished in his pocket for a condom just before he shucked his jeans and underwear. With his teeth, he tore open the foil packet and rolled the condom onto his cock, entering Avery in a single desperate thrust.

"You're so wet," Jase panted as he pulled out and drove home again, eliciting a low moan from Avery that tightened his balls. "So damned tight. Sugar, you're gonna be the death of me."

She answered him with a whimper that only stoked his lust, a sound that echoed his own need to a tee. Words died on his tongue as he fucked into her, at first a slow and measured action that bordered on torture and ending in quick, fierce thrusts that left them both gasping for breath. Jase leaned over Avery, cupping her breasts in his palms, her back sculpted to his chest. He couldn't get close enough. Deep enough. He growled his frustration from between gnashed teeth, her slick tight heat gripping him with every pump of his hips.

"Oh, Jase, just like that," Avery panted. "Don't stop. Harder."

His body slammed into hers and the sound, mingled with their guttural cries, drove him closer to the edge. Avery's pussy clenched him tight as she came, her entire body shuddering with each renewed spasm and her voice raw and ragged as she called out his name over and again.

"That's it, sugar. Come for me," Jase said against her ear. His own pleasure crested, his shaft damned near aching as his balls grew tight. The orgasm ripped through him on the heels of Avery's pleasure. The tidal wave crashed over him and swamped Jase with intense sensation that ignited all of his nerve endings and left him weak and trembling on top of her.

Each time with Avery was better than the last.

He eased her up from the couch and leaned back onto

the cushions, taking her with him. "Hi," he said with a grin, smoothing her hair from her face.

"Hi." The smile Avery gave him in return was equal parts sinful and sweet, a combination that stoked Jase's lust anew. "How was your day?"

"I'd say it was good, but now? It's perfect."

The flush on her cheeks deepened with Jase's words and his chest swelled with emotion at the realization that he could affect her in that way. He was telling the truth, though. Today had been great. Better than. But one look at Avery and even the best day of his life paled in her presence.

"How was your day?" He leaned in and kissed her forehead, her temple, the hollow of her cheek.

"Mmm." Her eyes drifted shut as she leaned in to his kisses. "Good. But better now, too." Jase kissed the corner of her mouth and her lips curved into a soft smile. He moved downward across her jaw to her throat and she shivered against him. "Did you come straight from practice?"

"Uh-huh. Why? Do I smell?"

"Like a locker room," she said with a laugh.

"Sorry." For the record, he totally wasn't sorry. "I was anxious to see you and a shower would've taken too long."

Avery sighed, her warm breath fanning across his cheek. "I bet you say that sort of flattering stuff to all the girls."

Her voice was still husky with desire, lazy and low. The sound rippled through him, tightening his skin and prickling with a heat that settled low in his gut. "You're the only one, sugar."

She gave a little snort as though she didn't believe a word of it, but he couldn't have spoken truer words. Jase wasn't some inexperienced kid and he sure as hell didn't have to work hard to get a date. Hell, he didn't have to work at all. He'd never paid any of them a compliment that equated to more than "nice ass."

And whereas Avery had the finest ass he'd ever had the privilege to lay eyes—or his palms—on, she deserved more than some vapid comment about her body. She intrigued him, and he found that beyond his blinding lust, he simply wanted to be with her. Talk to her. Spend whatever free time he had with her. Could it be that this would be the beginning of a real relationship with Avery? Holy shit. He'd been after nothing more than a casual fling. A one-nighter to steer his luck in the right direction. What was quickly developing between them was so much more than Jase had bargained for. And it scared the fuck out of him.

"Not that I'm not happy you decided to come over, but don't you have a playoff game tomorrow? I might be wrong, but I heard it's sort of a big deal."

How could Jase think about football, or anything else when she touched him that way? Avery's fingertips danced across his skin, skimming over the surface of his pecs, down his ribs, and the ridges of his stomach. She ventured lower, past his torso and the trail of hair that led from his belly button and Jase held his breath. His cock twitched as though it had been trained to respond to her touch. *Jesus.* "I, uh." His voice cracked and she stifled a laugh. He cleared his throat and started over, trying to ignore the sensation of her fingers flirting along the border of where his hips met his thighs. "I do have a game tomorrow. And yes, it is a big deal."

She reached between them and cupped his sac. Jase let out a slow groan as she kneaded his flesh in her palm, her skin so damned soft. He wanted her again, but he couldn't press his luck this close to a game. His legs felt like Jell-O already. Another go with Avery and he'd be useless on the field tomorrow.

"Home game?"

"Uh-huh." She stroked down between his thighs and Jase's brain went blank. Her hand ventured back to his cock and he thrust into her hand, his body committing all-out treason against his mind. "You should come." No, he should come. Again. Right now. He needed to get his mind out of the gutter, but how, when Avery was performing magic on him with her hands? She worked the condom free of his renewed erection and her hand slid across his stiff flesh.

Jase swallowed audibly, stifling a groan. "I'll get you tickets. Front row. Fifty yard line." Hell, if she kept stroking him like that, he'd get her down on the goddamned field if she wanted him to.

"I can't." Her voice was nothing more than a whisper in his ear. "I have to work back-to-back events. But maybe we could go out to dinner tonight? Hang out until your bedtime?"

Her teasing tone didn't go unnoticed. But the thought of having to get dressed up and spend time fending off fans and autograph hounds just didn't appeal to him. He wanted to stay right here with her, naked on the couch, for as long as possible. "How about I take a shower, so I don't stink up your apartment, and we order in?"

"Oh, okay." Jase wondered at her disappointed tone. "Sure."

A nasty thought took root in Jase's mind. What if what was really important to Avery was that she be seen with him? He didn't want to believe that she was just like all of the other users out there, and it soured his stomach. He wanted her to be different.

No. He *needed* her to be.

SEVEN

"Shouldn't you be fueling up on something healthier? Carbo-loading on whole grain pasta and power foods for tomorrow?"

Jase folded the wide slice of pizza into his mouth and took half of it off in a single bite. "I'm totally carbo-loading. I plan to eat this entire pizza by myself. It's a good thing we ordered a second one for you."

He gave her a wink and Avery couldn't help but smile at his easy charm. In fact, it was too easy to be with Jase. Too comfortable. Her plan to keep him at arm's length was failing miserably. She tried not to let her disappointment ruin the evening. The fact that Jase had turned down her suggestion to go out stung despite the fact that she'd coached herself into believing what was happening between them was nothing more than a fling. You didn't go out on dinner dates with a guy you were sowing your oats with. Her heart didn't need to be in the equation. Keep it light. Fun. No strings attached so she wouldn't get hurt.

"Your car should be ready by the end of the week. I told

the guy at the garage to deliver it here when they're done. I hope that's okay."

Okay? Was he kidding? She wouldn't even have to find someone to take her to pick it up. It was better than okay. "Can I get his number? I'll need to talk to him about working out some kind of payment plan."

Jase waved her off. "Already taken care of."

The last thing she needed was for him to think she expected him to spend his money on her. She wasn't that sort of woman and she didn't want him to get that impression. "Jase—"

"It's already taken care of." When she opened her mouth to protest, he shushed her. "And if you argue with me, I'll just go out and buy you a new car."

"I'll pay you back."

"Do you like Mercedes or BMW better?"

Avery grinned but kept her mouth shut. She had a feeling he'd go out and buy her a damned car just to prove he could. His triumphant grin caused her stomach to rocket up into her throat and float back down to her toes. "Good. I'm glad that's settled," he remarked before snatching up another slice of pizza.

So far, their evening together had been anything but impersonal. Avery studied Jase from the corner of her eye, so at ease, lounging on her couch with his long legs propped up on her coffee table as though he hung out in rat hole apartments like hers all the time. You'd never think he had a fifteen-thousand-square-foot mansion on the other side of the city. "So, what did you do today?"

The question threw Avery for a loop. No strings attached meant he wasn't required to ask questions about her day. "Um, I had class today."

"What sort of class?"

This was dangerous territory. He was opening the door for their relationship to venture past meaningless sex. And whereas it might not have seemed like a big deal to Jase, for Avery, it was a different story. What would happen once he set her aside? "I'm attending Le Cordon Bleu."

"Cooking school?" he asked with a grin that melted Avery's spine.

"Culinary academy," she replied. "I'm not just learning how to flip an egg over there."

"You know, I love food. Eating is my second favorite pastime. Well . . ." He stroked one long finger along Avery's jaw and she suppressed a shudder. "After today, I think I need to amend the list and make eating my third favorite pastime."

She gave a nervous laugh. When he talked to her in that seductive, smoky tone, it was all she could do to keep from tackling him to the floor. "I love to cook. It's my second favorite pastime."

"What's your first?" His eyes sparked with heat and he licked his lips.

Avery's gaze locked on Jase's mouth. God, how she loved kissing those lips. She looked away. "My new favorite pastime *might* have something to do with a certain football star."

"Oh really? Anyone I know?"

She answered him with an enigmatic smile. "Could be."

"Are you sure you can't come to the game tomorrow?"

Avery didn't miss the disappointment in his tone, or the way his eyes conveyed emotion that was too deep for what she needed this to be between them. "Gotta pay the bills," she replied. "That tuition doesn't pay for itself, you know."

He looked away as though embarrassed. "Ryder paid my college tuition. I was offered a scholarship but I turned it down. I didn't think it was fair to accept a free ride when there were other guys on the team who could benefit from the financial aid."

"I think that's great, Jase. Especially that your brother would help you out."

He snorted. "You'd think so. But the shitty thing is that I might have gotten a hell of a lot more respect if I'd just taken the damned scholarship. For all four years of my college career I had to field questions from smart-assed sports reporters asking if my brother had bought my position on the team."

"That's awful!" Avery couldn't believe that the media would try to persecute Jase and his family for doing something good.

He hiked one massive shoulder and Avery resisted the urge to reach out and touch. "It is what it is. It's how I got my nickname."

"You don't like it, do you?" Even Avery had to admit that a tag like "Billion Dollar Blackwell" probably wasn't complimentary. She regretted using the nickname herself when she'd talked about him with Kristie.

Jase snorted. "Not so much. I'd like for the media to see past my family's bank account and acknowledge my skill on the field. I mean, it's not like any of the guys in the NFL are living paycheck to paycheck. I don't know why they continue to fixate on mine."

Avery had failed to consider that Jase's life might not be a cakewalk. After all, money didn't solve every problem. "I'm sure that the people who matter recognize your skills. Everyone else can piss off."

Jase leaned forward to snag another piece of pizza from the box. "What about you?" he asked. "Have you ever seen me play?"

Again, Avery wondered at his tone. Tentative, yet hopeful, as though both anxious and afraid of her response. "I have." She wasn't exactly an avid football fan, but she'd watched more than her fair share of games. Football was a Texas institution, after all.

His unsure expression tore at her heart. "And?"

"Well." She stroked her fingers along his arm, mapping the topography of muscles that flexed beneath her touch. "I'm no expert, but I'd say you're pretty amazing."

His answering smile was as brilliant as the sun and Avery was powerless to fight his magnetic pull. She leaned in to his chest and though she knew allowing him to fold her into his arms would surely lead her further toward ruin, she didn't care.

"What about you, sugar?" His deep voice rumbled in his chest and she shivered. "How do you rate your chef skills?"

"I'm not a chef yet," she replied. "But someday. I don't know . . . most days I feel like I'm barely cracking a three. I'm so clumsy and scatterbrained sometimes. I spill and burn stuff, but when I'm focused, I can definitely hold my own in the kitchen."

"I have a feeling you're selling yourself short," Jase remarked. "I think you're going to have to step up to the plate and let me rate your skills myself."

Avery pulled away so she could look up at his face. "I doubt I'll measure up for someone whose third all-time-favorite pastime is eating."

"Sugar, if what I've seen of you already has any bearing, I have a feeling that nothin' you do is less than a perfect ten."

Avery's cheeks heated at the innuendo. No guy had ever told her that she was good in bed before. Hell, no one had told her she was good at *anything* before. She didn't think she was awful, but definitely not a ten. "If I'm a ten, it's only because you set a pretty high bar, Mr. Blackwell. I had no choice but to step up my game or get left behind."

"Not a chance."

Jase couldn't remember the last time he'd felt so at ease with a woman. Avery was funny, smart, and though he wished she'd own how great she was and quit being so self-conscious, good-natured. He had a soft spot for a woman who could take a little teasing, and he was willing to bet that Avery could give as good as she got. Goddamn did she ever turn him on.

Emotion bloomed in his chest as she flashed him a wide smile. The expression was so honest and open that it made his breath catch and he wondered how he could have ever suspected that she was nothing more than another football groupie. He didn't know her well, but Jase sensed that Avery wasn't the type of woman to use a person for her own selfish reasons.

"Maybe we're both perfect tens because we make a good team." He might've been pressing his luck referring to them as a "we" but Jase didn't care. "Sometimes even the best players have a shitty showing on the field because they're just not compatible as teammates. You and I just play well together."

"Mmm." Her green eyes sparked with fire and Jase's body responded, warming to her heated expression. "I have to admit, we do play well together . . ."

Jase grabbed Avery and pulled her up into his lap. He cupped the back of her neck with one hand while the other skimmed down between her breasts to the hem of her shirt. His palm found the smooth flat skin on her stomach and Avery's eyes became hooded as he ventured upward, cupping her bare breast in his hand and feathering over one pearled nipple with the pad of his thumb. She went liquid in his embrace, her body melting against his as her lips parted with shallow pants of breath.

He could stay here all night and simply pleasure her. Take in the sight of her furrowed brow, her teeth as they grazed her bottom lip, the flush that began to spread across her cheeks. Jase hiked up her T-shirt and bent his head to her breast, taking the dusky nipple into his mouth. He sucked deeply before drawing the taut peak between his teeth and nibbling. Avery moaned—a low, seductive sound that hardened his cock in an instant—and threaded her fingers through his hair, holding him against her.

"Jase . . . god . . . your mouth." Avery's words only stoked the fire of Jase's lust. No matter how much he wanted to bury himself to the root in her slick heat, he had to restrain himself. Especially if he wanted to be worth a shit for tomorrow's game. But just because he was forcing the torture of abstinence on himself, didn't mean Avery had to suffer right alongside him.

As he continued to suckle her, Jase's free hand found the waistband of her cotton shorts. He flirted with the elastic band for a moment, delving his fingers under the garment and then up her torso and around her belly button. Avery let out a whimper, thrusting her hips to meet his touch. He cupped her sex in his palm, stroking her through the fabric that was already damp with her arousal.

It was going to take an act of sheer will not to fuck her senseless at this point.

Avery reached between them and took his hand in hers, guiding him inside of her shorts. He slipped his fingers below the hemline, teasing the nest of curls and the slick wetness that clung to them. He dipped his forefinger between her already swollen lips and Avery bucked as he swept the pad of his finger over her clit. Then he broke the seal of his mouth from the tight point of her breast and circled the dusky nipple with his fingers, spreading her own sweet honey over her skin.

"Oh god," she panted as he covered her with his mouth, licking the sweetness from her flesh.

He reached down and dipped his finger into her pussy again, repeating the motion of slathering Avery's nipple with her own arousal. "You taste like clover honey," he murmured against her flesh before lapping it all up. "So damned good."

"Jase." She trembled in his embrace, stomach muscles twitching and contracting with each light brush of his fingers. Avery let out a whimper as though she couldn't push the words she wanted to say past her lips.

"What?" Jase reached down and eased her shorts down over her ass, taking her underwear with them. He repositioned them so that he was sprawled out on the couch, her body stretched out on top of his. Leaning up enough to strip off her shirt, he then guided one of her legs up until it was slung over the back of the couch, opening her up to him. With shaking hands, he stripped off his own shirt so he could enjoy the silky skin of her back pressed up against his chest. "What do you want, Avery?"

Her head fell back on his shoulders, the short strands of her dark hair like satin on his skin. "Don't stop touching me, Jase."

Avery craned her neck back and he leaned over, putting his mouth to hers. Their bodies fit together so well, her petite frame cradled by his much larger body. He reached around to fondle her breasts while his other hand returned to the slick flesh between her thighs. With one touch, she melted against him, their breaths becoming one as he continued to kiss her. Jase craved her body like a drug, couldn't get enough of her sweet mewling cries as he circled the swollen knot of nerves at her core. No woman had ever had this effect on him.

Women came, they went. One-night stands, though admittedly, none of those encounters had ever lasted more than a couple of hours before he hightailed it and headed back home. He'd never burned with the need to have any one of them more than once. But the woman in his arms now was different. His gut pulled into a tight knot as the realization dawned that Jase might not ever get enough of Avery. Once, twice . . . Fifty times wouldn't sate his hunger for her or quench his desire.

In just a couple of days, Avery had become as vital to him as water or air. "Come for me, sugar," Jase murmured in her ear. She arched into his touch, reaching around to cup the back of his neck in her palm. "That's it." He laid his lips to her throat, rolled her stiff nipple between his fingers. "Let me hear you." She cried out as he plunged one finger and then another into her tight channel. Adrenaline coursed through Jase's body, his cock throbbing in his jeans. "Come for me, Avery. Now."

The engine was running and the pickup was still in gear, but Jase couldn't bring himself to put it in park and turn the damned key off. He just sat there in his garage, knowing he needed to take his ass inside and at the same time, wanting to race back to Avery's apartment. Hands shaking, Jase gripped the steering wheel like it was the only thing keeping him anchored to the earth. It took an actual physical effort to finally put the truck in park and cut the damned engine. He was wound as tight as a fucking spring, his cock so hard it caused him discomfort. Being with Avery was supposed to be a release. A tension breaker meant to relax and focus him. But now, all he could think of was speeding back to her and fucking her into the early hours of the morning. He relived their moments together, reveled in the memory of her coming at his command and the way her pussy clenched his fingers, so tight. Her cries echoed in his ears, a plea for release that he'd been more than happy to answer one more time. His body was tense, his mind racing. He needed to come so badly, he hurt all over.

He needed *her*.

Instead of hitting the shower yet again and taking his

ass to bed like he knew he should, Jase took a detour, by-passing the staircase as he made a beeline for his weight room. Too wound up to relax, sleep would be impossible if he didn't do something to work Avery out of his system. And whereas the better option would have been to just jerk one off and call it a night, Jase knew that it wouldn't sate him. His own goddamned hand was a poor substitute for the real thing. The only option at this point was to distract the stiff bastard between his legs with physical exertion.

Lifting seemed like a promising way to beat his body into submission. He traded out the bumper plates for some-thing lighter since he wanted to wear himself down, not physically exhaust himself. It only took a moment to shuck his jeans and Jase settled onto the weight bench in noth-ing more than a pair of boxer briefs. The cold metal of the bar felt good in his palms and the weight as he hoisted the barbell up off the rest and high above his chest was a wel-come distraction. He pumped the weight down on a slow inhale and back up on an exhale. Up, down. In, out. He let the sound of his breath channel his focus, the weight press-ing down on him, clearing his mind of all distraction. If he didn't get Avery out of his head, he wouldn't be worth a shit tomorrow. His plan to use a little booty to break his bad-luck streak had totally fucking backfired.

Sweat beaded on his chest and trickled down his neck as Jase continued to pump the barbell up and down. Up and down, his once slow and measured breaths chuffing in and out of his chest. No amount of physical exertion would banish the memory of her, soft and willing in his arms, from his mind.

How could he possibly focus on his career right now when all he wanted was her?

EIGHT

"Jason, this is without a doubt the best game you've played all season. Maybe even your entire career. Can you tell us what brought on such a dramatic change?"

Jase stared into Erin Andrews's expectant face, knowing she was waiting for his response, but his brain was calling up an answer that he didn't want his mouth to deliver. "It's the playoffs," he finally said, flashing her a confident smile. "I wouldn't be doing my job if I wasn't giving a thousand percent on the field."

"Well, it certainly showed," she said as she pulled the microphone back to her mouth. "Your performance seems to improve with each game. You're one win away from the division title and with the stellar teamwork between you and Carson Rader, you helped to move the Cowboys one step closer to a Super Bowl bid. Congratulations."

"Thanks." Jase cast a quick look toward the camera before heading for the locker room. Carson was still fielding questions from the press. Erin wouldn't waste a second to snag him next. Jase was thankful for the distraction his teammate offered because right now there were only two things on his mind: taking a long hot shower, and getting to Avery ASAP.

Amid knocks to the shoulder and words of congratulations from his teammates as he passed, Jase hurried through the locker room and straight for the showers. Anticipation coiled in his stomach as hot water sluiced down his body. It helped to ease his sore and too tight muscles, but he wasn't planning to linger under the spray for long. He'd been seeing Avery for three weeks now. Easily the longest relationship of his life. The euphoric high of being with her hadn't lessened in the slightest. In fact, the more time he spent with her, the greedier he became for just another minute, one more hour of her time. If he had it his way, she'd be moved into his house by now.

"Blackwell's got himself a pregame lucky charm," someone remarked as though in answer to a question from the other room. "Wish I had a sweet piece of ass to give me a good-luck fuck before next week's game." Fucking Carson and his big mouth. Jase was going to kick his ass. He gossiped worse than a nosey old woman. "Hey, Jase, you wanna share? Give the rest of us some of that superpower pussy?"

His earlier anticipation congealed into anger. Cold and heavy like a boulder rolling around in his gut. Guys talked shit in the locker room. Period. And giving in to his urge to beat the piss out of some sorry fucker wasn't going to do anything for his team's cohesiveness. To the guys on the other side of the wall, Avery was nothing more than a faceless fuck. Another football groupie Jase was using to work off the stress of playoffs. But the depth of his feelings for her was his secret. One that he coveted and held close to his heart. He'd never felt this way about a woman before. There was a chance that maybe . . . Maybe he could love her.

Shit.

The once-famed playboy converted to monogamy? Stanger things had happened.

Catcalls and lewd remarks continued to drift to his ears from the locker room as Jase wrapped up his shower. If he hung around to listen to their bullshit, he wouldn't be able to stop himself from laying into someone. The team couldn't afford any rash, hotheaded behavior right now. Too much hinged on Jase keeping a level head.

"Sorry man." Carson turned on the nozzle next to Jase and stepped under the spray. "I never would have said anything if I had known they were going to give you so much shit."

"Yeah?" Jase shook out his hair like a wet dog and reached for a towel. "They didn't come up with 'good-luck fuck' on their own. I'm guessing you had something to do with that, too."

Carson cringed as he began to lather up his hair and body. "You've got to admit, you've been playing like a goddamned all-star since you started seeing her. Coincidence?"

Jase didn't know a single player who didn't harbor a superstition or ten. Some guys wore the same socks— unwashed—for the entire season. Others didn't shave. He'd played with a guy in college who never stepped out onto the field unless his girlfriend's panties were tucked into his jock. And yeah, a lot of them boasted pregame sex rituals. Could Jase really be mad over his teammates' shit talk? He'd gone after Avery in the first place with the single-minded purpose of getting her into bed to help end his unlucky streak. If the guys were calling her a good-luck fuck, he had no one to blame but himself.

"I know it started out that way with her." Jase paused and breathed in a lungful of steam. "But it's different now."

Carson gave him a pointed look. "How so?"

Jase snatched a towel from a hook on the opposite wall

and slung it around his waist. "Avery's not like any other woman. She's tough. Funny. She wants a career and is just as ambitious as I am. She just needs someone to help her realize how amazing she is."

"Do you hear yourself?" Jase stopped midstep but didn't bother to turn and face his so-called friend. "You're playing like a hard-core bad ass, but it's not because of some bullshit superstition. Do I think she has something to do with it? Yes. Because she's *changed you,* man. For the better."

Jase's spine stiffened. He didn't feel any different. Could she have really made such a huge impact on his life in such a short time?

"Your ass had better be at my party tomorrow tonight." The sound of the shower turning off was preceded by the slap of Carson's wet feet on the tile. "And you'd better bring her with you. No excuses."

"Yeah," Jase replied as he headed back toward the locker room. He knew that things had changed between him and Avery in the past few weeks, but damn. It must've been major if Carson could see it, too. Talk about scary. "I'll see you then."

"There's something different about you."

Avery kept her eyes on her saucepan and the béchamel sauce she was trying not to burn. "There's nothing different about me." Kristie had no idea what she was talking about. "I'm the same person I've always been."

"No," she said. "As a matter of fact, you're not."

Avery had a feeling that she wasn't going to like the direction this conversation was headed. "Okay, since you're so perceptive, how exactly have I changed?"

Kristie rolled her eyes as she whisked her white sauce. "You've got perma-grin. You're skipping around like a Disney princess. And you haven't burned, spilled, or broken anything in almost three weeks."

"That's not true."

"Dude." Kristie pointed her whisk at Avery for emphasis. "You *aced* your first attempt at hollandaise sauce this week without even batting a lash."

Was it really so hard to believe that she could get something right on her first try? "So?"

Kristie's blue eyes bulged. "Seriously? You know I love you, Ave, but you usually can't get through a day without at least one klutzy moment. You're like Cinderella post–glass slipper or something."

Avery laughed. Okay, so klutzy was her middle name. But she hadn't noticed any sort of Cinderella transformations in the past couple of weeks. "You're crazy. Maybe I'm just growing out of my awkward phase."

"Oh you totally have, and you have Jason Blackwell to thank for it."

"I—"

"Don't *even* try to argue with me, Avery. I've never seen you so head over heels for a guy before. You're happy. Your confidence is soaring. And it's awesome! Doesn't hurt that he's drop-dead gorgeous and rolling in money, either."

"I don't care about his money," Avery replied, low.

"Oh, I know. Which is why it's so obvious that you're falling for him. You *lurve* him!"

Avery's jaw hung slack. Did she love him? They'd only been hanging out for a few weeks and he'd yet to take her on an actual date. So far, they'd spent most of their hours together naked. Great sex wasn't enough of a foundation to build a successful relationship on, was it? "I don't love him," she said after a moment. Admitting she had feelings for Jase would only open her up for heartache later when he decided he was through with her. "At least, I don't think I love him."

"Oh, I see," Kristie said. "You're just using him for sex, then?"

"I'm not using him for sex." Avery grabbed a spoon to taste her béchamel sauce. She had to admit, it was pretty damned perfect. A first. "Jase is amazing. He's easygoing and so humble. You'd never know he was sitting on a billion-dollar nest egg if you hung out with him. He's so driven, too. His career means so much to him. He gives a hundred and ten percent all the time and he's one of the most ambitious people I've ever met." *He's gentle* . . . she thought. *Sweet.* His touch was like a salve that made everything better. God, she really was lost to him, wasn't she?

"Would it be so terrible if you did love him?" Kristie ventured.

"Of course not." Avery could think of a million things worse than loving Jase Blackwell. He was down to earth. Funny. Sexy as sin. And she had to admit that she enjoyed spending time with him. "It's just that a relationship with him wouldn't be as simple as just him and me. I think I'd feel like I was in constant competition with his team and his fans. The media, too. I don't know if I could handle the added stress of sharing him."

Kristie smirked. "Sounds like you've put some thought into it. Are you saying you're jealous of his adoring fans?"

"No." Avery looked away. "Okay, maybe a little. What if he's not interested in anything other than a casual fling? I mean, we haven't even seen each other outside of my apartment yet."

"It's a little weird," Kristie admitted. "But have you ever considered that he doesn't like to go out? You've never had to fend off crowds of autograph hounds and groupies before. Maybe he just wants a little privacy?"

"Could be." Avery wasn't convinced, though. "But he hasn't even introduced me to any of his friends yet. Maybe he doesn't want them to know he's slumming with a waitress."

"Hey, Negative Nancy, I refuse to hear that kind of

talk." Kristie brandished her whisk like a weapon. "You might be waitressing to pay the bills, but it's not who you are. And if Jase Blackwell is too closed-minded to see past what you do or where you live, then he doesn't deserve you."

Avery gave Kristie a sad smile. "Thanks." It shouldn't have mattered what Jase thought about her, but it did. She wanted him to be proud to show her off to his friends or take her out. And it's not like she expected him to drop loads of cash on a date. She'd be fine with burgers and a movie.

"You know, he might be keeping a low profile because of the playoffs," Kristie suggested. "The Cowboys have a good chance of going to the Super Bowl. That's gotta be stressful. He might be one of those superstitious sports guys who have to follow a certain ritual during the season. His might be living like a hermit."

Avery laughed. "It would be a heck of a lot better than wearing dirty underwear for four months."

"All right everyone, please present a sample of your béchamel and begin to clean up your stations," Chef Isaacs announced from the back of the classroom.

Thank god. Despite the fact that she couldn't wait to show off her béchamel, she was anxious for class to be over and call it a night. She wanted to check the score from tonight's game. With any luck, the Cowboys had racked up another win and Jase would be in a good mood. She loved his playful side and a lighthearted Jase was a lot of fun. Tonight would be one of their last nights together for a while. If the Cowboys won tonight, their next game would be out of town and she had no idea when she'd see him again. The thought of being away from him for even a day soured her stomach. Maybe Kristie was right and Avery's feelings for him ran deeper than she wanted to admit.

Her phone vibrated in her back pocket and she peeked to the rear of the classroom to make sure Chef was occupied before she checked the text message. A smile lit her face when she read Jase's name and she swiped her finger across the screen to read his text: **Booyah! We won! One step closer to the Super Bowl, baby! Heading over to your place in an hour to celebrate. Can't wait to see you. Preferably naked. Make sure you're free tomorrow. Taking you to a party.**

A party? A ribbon of hope unfurled in Avery's chest. Maybe Jase wasn't embarrassed to be seen with her after all. She smiled as she fired off a quick response: **Congrats! I'll see you in an hour. Maybe without my clothes. ;)**

Chef Isaacs approached her station and Avery quickly tucked her phone into her back pocket before dipping a spoon into her béchamel, anxious for him to taste. She'd aced tonight's assignment and tomorrow night she had an honest to god date with Jason Blackwell.

Could her life get any better?

NINE

Avery fidgeted in the passenger seat of Jase's Maserati as a riot of butterflies swirled in her stomach. She'd worked plenty of the Cowboys' team functions over the past few months, but she'd never attended one as a guest. Tonight's was another private party and thankfully, Peyton's catering service wasn't providing the food. Which meant no familiar faces, no prying eyes and whispering lips for her to worry about. Unless some of the players or their dates recognized her from previous parties, Avery could maintain a modicum of anonymity. She wouldn't have to make excuses for what she did or where she came from. At least, she hoped.

"So . . . the division championship game is in Miami?" Beside her, Jase was a picture of calm while Avery was so nervous she'd resorted to the most ridiculous small talk *ever*. "Have you been there before?"

Jase's affectionate smile was enough to turn her bones to mush. "Several times. Like, every time we play them. Avery, relax. It's just a party. You're about to vibrate right out of your seat."

She stilled her bouncing knees as heat rose to her cheeks. "I know."

"Then why do you look like you're about to lose your lunch?"

Avery shrugged. "It's just . . . I mean . . ." *Gah. Spit it out already!* "What if someone recognizes me from the events I worked?"

"So what if they do?"

She cleared her throat, forced the words from her mouth. "Won't you be embarrassed if your teammates find out that you're dating the hired help?"

Jase's expression darkened and Avery's heart plunged into her stomach. He put on his blinker and checked traffic before crossing over into the far right lane. At the first turnout he could find, Jase pulled off the road and brought the car to a complete stop. He threw the car into park and turned in his seat, facing her fully. "Jesus, Avery. Do you really think that I'm that shallow? That I'd be ashamed to be seen with you because you're a fucking waitress?"

"Come on, Jase. You have to admit, I'm not exactly the type of girl a guy like you goes for. And I assumed that we spent so much time at my place because you were worried about being seen with me." She'd never voiced her insecurities before and cringed at Jase's pained expression.

"Wow. I had no idea that you thought so little of me."

"What? No. Jase—"

His eyes burned with hurt and anger, making Avery wish she could take back everything she'd said. Damn it. Why did she always have to let her self-doubt get the best of her? Jase's nostrils flared and he settled back into his seat with enough force to cause it to groan in protest. She'd never seen him angry before, but her careless comment had obviously triggered one of his hot-button issues.

"You know, Avery, there is nothing worse than someone making assumptions about the type of person you are.

I've been called a snob, accused of using my money to advance my career, and yeah, of even being a shallow, insensitive dick. But you know more about me than most people. Like the fact that my childhood home makes your apartment look like the fucking Plaza. If I was embarrassed to be seen with you do you think I would've even asked you to come with me tonight?" His voice grew louder with each word.

"No." Avery averted her gaze, his hurt slicing through her. "I know you're not that sort of guy." She was letting her own stupid insecurities get the better of her. "I'm sorry, Jase."

He reached out and guided her chin up so she had no choice but to look at him. His expression softened and he said, "Avery, you're beautiful. Funny. Intelligent. And don't tell my mom I said this, but you cook the best food I've ever eaten. How could I not want to show you off to my friends? My teammates? Hell, the entire state. I haven't taken you anywhere because I'm a selfish son of a bitch and I haven't wanted to share your attention with anyone else. That's all. So can we please get back on the road before all of the good snacks are gone?"

A reluctant smile tugged at Avery's mouth. Emotion swelled in her chest at Jase's admission. His compliment about her cooking alone was enough to endear him to her. Falling in love with Jase Blackwell didn't seem so far-fetched anymore. "I think at a fancy party, they're considered hors d'oeuvres."

"If they're bite-sized, they're snacks. Period. So, are we good?"

"Yes." He caressed the line of her jaw with his thumb and Avery leaned in to the contact, letting her eyes drift shut. "We're good."

*   *   *

"Damn, Blackwell. I need a good-luck charm like yours. She's so tiny, I bet I could carry her around in my jock."

Jase's jaw was clenched to the point that he was pretty sure he'd taken the enamel off of his molars. Malcolm Willis was one bullshit comment away from getting cold-cocked.

"Maybe if I got her on her back, I could have a killer post-season, too."

If it wouldn't mean suspension, he'd beat the son of a bitch to a bloody pulp right in the middle of Carson's living room. Hell, if he could be guaranteed that he'd only be fined, Jase would pay upward of a hundred grand just to lay him out.

"Hell, I might even get to start Sunday's game if I could get a blow job out of her."

Jase took a step forward and Carson put a hand on his chest, urging him back. "Down, boy. The last thing you need tonight is to get into it with anyone on the team. He's just jealous that you're kicking ass on the field and he's trying to rile you into doing something stupid. Don't let him play you like that."

Jase tore his gaze from the younger man and focused on his friend's face. His chest heaved with labored breaths and his muscles ached with unspent adrenaline. He should have said something. Told the cocky little bastard to shut his mouth. But anger clogged his throat and Jase couldn't force the words out no matter how hard he tried. Instead, he let Willis insult Avery behind her back while he stood there and took it like some sort of pussy. And the worst part of it was, before he'd truly gotten to know Avery, he'd considered her as nothing more than a means to an end. The lucky piece of ass he'd needed to get his game tight. Christ. He was just as big of an asshole as Willis, wasn't he?

"Don't even think about it," Carson said as though

sensing Jase's thoughts. "You are not allowed to get down on yourself for being the bigger man."

"Yeah?" The word burned his mouth like acid. He sure as hell didn't feel like the bigger man. "Give me one decent reason why being the bigger man is a good thing right now."

"Because if you start shit at my house, Gena will have your ass in a sling for starters."

Gena, Carson's wife, was a notorious ball buster and one of Jase's favorite people. She kept Carson in line off the field and he was head over heels in love with her. Likewise, she ran a pretty tight ship and shenanigans of any kind were off-limits when you went to a party she was hosting. Jase knew better than to test her. "Willis oughta thank Gena for the fact that he's not picking his sorry ass up off the floor, then."

"So true," Carson said with a laugh. "Man, I'm sorry I even said anything about Avery. If I'd had any idea how you really felt about her or that some of the guys would take it so far—"

"I know," Jase replied. "Don't worry about it."

"If it's any consolation, your girl looks like she's doing just fine."

Jase followed Carson's gaze to where Avery was standing with a group of wives. He caught her eye and she flashed him a dazzling smile that made his heart clench and his gut curl up into a knot. Her expression shone like the sun, the happiness radiating from her. "I really wanted Gena to like her." As the queen bee of the group of Cowboys wives, Gena's approval meant that no one would give Avery an ounce of shit. Ever. Not to mention the fact that if the two women hit it off, Jase wouldn't have to worry so much about Avery feeling as though she didn't fit in. Truth be told, he couldn't give a shit what anyone else thought about her. The only opinion that mattered was his.

"Hey, are you taking her to Miami?"

Jase hadn't thought about it. She had school and work. But damn, having her there to support him during the championship would be awesome. "I don't know." His eyes were still glued to where she stood. He couldn't wait to get her home and into bed. "I hadn't really thought about it."

"Between you and me, I think you should take her." Carson put an arm around Jase's shoulder. "Because if you don't, I doubt you'll be able to focus enough to tie your shoes, let alone catch a pass."

"Are you saying I'm not a professional?" Jase ribbed.

"Not at all," Carson replied. "But if the way you're looking at her right now is any indicator, you'll play that much better if you know she's waiting for you at the end of the day."

"Are you speaking from experiencc?"

Carson chuckled. "You know it. There's nothing better than spending as much time as possible with the woman you love."

"It's only been a few weeks. Way too early for words like love."

"Jase, you're so far gone in love with that girl there's no comin' back. And the sooner you come to realize it, the better. Let's go get another beer before Gena cuts me off for the night. I ordered a new microbrew I want you to try."

As he followed Carson to the kitchen, Jase chanced a quick glance at Avery on his way out. Damn, she was beautiful. Smart. Independent. Funny. Not to mention sexy as all get-out. But love? Was that what this bone-deep ache in his chest was? He'd never felt this way about anyone before. Could he love her? And more importantly, could she love him back?

TEN

"Avery, will you excuse me for a second? I think we're just about ready to eat and I want to check in with the caterers."

"Sure. No worries."

Never in a million years would Avery have thought that she'd hit it off with Gena. Gorgeous, well-spoken, and built like a supermodel with long blond hair and bright blue eyes, she was the type of woman who couldn't help but project an air of self-confidence. Shorter, quieter, and a hell of a lot more introverted, it wouldn't have been tough for Avery to just melt into the scenery in the presence of the other woman. But Gena had coaxed her out of her shell, engaged her in the conversation, and seemed to be genuinely interested in what she had to say. She was welcoming, open, and friendly. The type of woman Avery could see herself becoming friends with. Why had she been so nervous about coming here tonight? So far, she was having a blast.

"So Blackwell finally let you out of your cage, huh?"

Avery recognized the guy speaking to her from some

of the other team parties, though she didn't know his name. A smarmy grin was plastered on his face and his words were slurred. Someone had clearly had too much to drink tonight. He leaned against the wall, eyeing Avery up and down and a nervous tremor ran the length of her spine.

"I don't think we've ever met." Her voice quavered as she tried to infuse confidence into the words. She held out her hand. "I'm Avery Lockhart."

"I know who you are," he said with a sneer. He didn't bother to take her hand. "You're Blackwell's good-luck fuck."

A wave of nausea crested over her and Avery fought for a deep breath. "Excuse me?"

The drunken jerk leaned in and she got a strong whiff of bourbon on his breath. "You're the talk of the locker room, sweetheart. I'm surprised the team hasn't erected a statue in your honor. You must have a magic pussy because Blackwell's never played so well. Maybe when he's done with you, you'll consider passing some of that mojo my way."

Oh god. She was going to be sick. Avery's heart raced, her rib cage constricting to the point of pain. It took a conscious effort to draw a deep breath, and even then it was ragged and shuddered in her chest. His words tore through her like a well-honed butcher knife, eviscerating her heart into a hunk of bloodied meat. *Good-luck fuck?* The term was so crass, so . . . disgusting that it made Avery feel dirty from head to toe.

Dark spots swam in her vision and she pushed her way past her verbal assailant and toward the foyer. "Avery?" Gena's voice called out from behind her but she didn't dare stop. Tears spilled over her cheeks, running in rivulets that dripped from her chin. Jase had *used* her and everyone on his team knew about it. Had he brought her here tonight— his lucky charm and the supposed reason for his outstanding performance the past few games—for the sole purpose of parading her around for the benefit of his buddies? Avery had never been so humiliated, so *hurt* in all of her life.

She burst through the front door gasping for breath. Kicking off her heels, Avery started off at a slow jog down the driveway. It was a forty-minute drive to her apartment, but she'd walk all night to get home and suffer blisters from hell before she'd stay another minute in that house and endure the humiliation of knowing she was nothing more than a pawn in Jase's stupid game. God, what a fool she'd been! Her heart ached from the betrayal. Her stomach twisted into a painful knot. To think that she'd fallen for his act; actually considered the possibility that she could fall in love with Jason Blackwell and that he could, in turn, love her. All the while he'd been bragging to his teammates about her, trivializing their time together as nothing more than something he used to get pumped up for his next game. What a joke!

She was finally starting to feel good about herself. Like her life was on track and things were going her way. School was better. Work was better. *Everything* was better because Jase had been in her life and knowing that it was all a lie made her feel like throwing up.

Avery had put about a half mile behind her when she heard the growl of an engine creep up behind her. She squared her shoulders and kept her eyes forward, unwilling to look back. The car accelerated with a roar and Jase pulled up beside her, leaning over the center console as the passenger-side window slid down.

"Avery, what happened? Gena said she saw you talking to Malcolm Willis and then you ran out of the house crying. What's going on?"

"Go away, Jase." The concern in his tone gutted her. The thought that he must've brought her here tonight to show off his *lucky charm* disgusted her. "I don't want to talk to you."

"What? Why? Avery, what in the hell is going on?"

His insistence on keeping up the pretense snapped Avery's control over her temper. "Oh, come on, Jase! I don't want or need your fake concern. You're an asshole! Go back to your stupid party and find some other girl to give you a *good-luck fuck* before the championship game!"

Jase hit the brakes so hard that the tires screeched on the pavement. Avery picked up her pace, ignoring the bite of the asphalt on her bare feet as she continued her trek out of the swanky subdivision. The car door opened and slammed behind her but she paid it no mind. Damn it, she'd left her damned purse at the house. Which meant no cell phone to call a cab to get her the hell away from Jase Blackwell for good. And she wasn't about to endure the shame of going back to get it.

"Avery, stop."

She ignored his demanding tone. "Go to hell, Jase!"

"Avery!"

The sound of his shoes pounding on the pavement behind her sent a jolt of anxious adrenaline through Avery's body. She refused to run from him, but a brisk speed-walk was totally acceptable. A hand gripped her elbow and Jase spun her around like a whip.

"Don't." Fresh tears pricked behind Avery's eyes but she stemmed the flow. She wouldn't give him the satisfaction of witnessing her pain. "I don't want to hear your excuses, Jase."

His brow furrowed, the depth of emotion shining in his light brown eyes enough to break Avery's heart all over again. Among his other talents, Jase Blackwell was apparently a pretty damned good actor.

"Avery, listen to me." Jase gripped her shoulders tightly

as though afraid she'd try to bolt. "I don't blame you for being pissed off—"

"Well, that's big of you."

"But you have to know that what that asshole Willis said couldn't be further from the truth."

"Do I?" Avery asked with a derisive snort. "It's funny, Jase. Now that I think about it, we've been together at least one night before every single game of the playoffs. I guess I should be flattered. I mean, I must be a hell of a good lay if I single-handedly managed to secure your team's spot in the championship. Maybe I should rent my services out. If I got the Cowboys this far, imagine what I could do for other teams?"

"Stop." Jase's fingers dug into her arms, not painfully, but enough to convey his urgency. "I can't control what those assholes say in the locker room. Hell, up until a few weeks ago, everyone still thought I'd bought my way onto the team. So of course, the second I up my game, those same haters are going to come up with another excuse to justify how I'm getting it done. Anything other than admit that I might actually be worth a damn on the field."

She knew that his skills on the field were a sore subject and that Jase suffered from a lack of confidence in his abilities. Under any other circumstances, Avery would have been thrilled that he'd finally come into his own and was being recognized for the talent she knew he'd had all along. But not now, and certainly not at the expense of her dignity. "According to that jerk back at Gena's, I'm the talk of the locker room. One more toss before the championship game? If that's the case, maybe we should just get it out of the way right now. I mean, we've screwed in the front seat of your truck, your car couldn't possibly be much less accommodating. I wouldn't be doing my duty as a Cowboys fan if I didn't do my part to ensure that you guys get a Super Bowl bid."

Jase released his grip at her acidic tone. "I would never disrespect you, Avery."

She leveled her gaze on him, the Maserati's headlights illuminating his strong features. "Really? Then look me in the eye and tell me that Willis is lying. Tell me that you never, *ever* considered using me as some sort of sexual good-luck charm."

Jase's jaw clamped down tight and he averted his gaze. He raked his hands through his hair and let out a rushed breath. "God damn it, Avery, if you'd just let me explain."

"That's what I thought. Don't blame yourself, Jase," Avery said without an ounce of emotion. "This is my fault. I knew better than to hook up with you. All I wanted was a meaningless fling and ended up letting myself believe that you were different than any other guy I'd ever met. The mistake—and the humiliation—are mine. Good luck on Sunday."

Avery turned and left Jase where he stood. With her back to him, she finally allowed the flow of tears to resume their path down her cheeks as a pained sob lodged itself in her chest. She might have left him behind to watch her leave, but she'd left her heart back there with him.

Jase slammed the door of his Maserati hard enough to bust the damn hinges. *Meaningless fling?* All this time he'd thought his relationship with Avery was going somewhere and instead, she'd all but admitted that she'd used him for sex. She'd thought he was different? Who had played who, here? She was obviously just like every other jock-riding, football groupie out there. *Fucking awesome.* He put the car into gear and sped back to Carson's house, all the while rubbing at his chest that ached as though someone had sliced him open between the ribs and scooped his heart out with a spoon.

No matter what she'd said in the heat of anger, Jase had

seen the hurt in her eyes and it laid him low. Hell, if he hadn't treated her like another conquest—a goal he had to achieve no matter the costs—in the first place, he wouldn't be sitting in his car now, wishing he could rip his beating heart out of his chest. *You really fucked up this time, buddy.* Because of his own selfish stupidity, Jase had just lost the only thing in this world he gave a shit about.

He parked in front of Carson's house and sat for a moment, gripping the steering wheel so tightly that it creaked in his palms. Anger mounted, the pressure building to a fever pitch, boiling and burning inside of him until Jase had no choice but to release the valve. Throwing himself from the car, he raced for the house, burst through the door, and beelined it for that rotten son of a bitch who'd ruined his life with nothing more than a string of malicious words.

"You're a piece of shit, Willis." Jase pulled back his fist and let it fly.

His fist connected with Willis's jaw and the other man went sprawling backward. The idiot was shitfaced drunk and could barely stand, but that wasn't going to stop Jase from beating the bastard to a pulp. He followed him down to the floor, throwing body shots and right hooks to the face. The ache in his chest intensified as the realization that he'd lost Avery—likely forever—burrowed itself into his core. He hit Willis again. And again. Jase's knuckles grew bloody and his breath sawed in and out of his chest in desperate gasps, but he just kept hitting. Damn it, he needed something, *anything,* to take away the hurt that was eating him from the inside out.

"Jase!" Carson grabbed him by the arm and tried to haul him off of Willis but Jase shook him off and renewed his assault. "Goddamn it, Jason. Knock it off!"

Bodies closed in around him, his teammates joining in to pull him out of the fight. Jase snarled, his shouts of protest scouring his throat as he fought against the many hands restraining him. "Let me go!"

"You've stepped in it now, Blackwell." Willis's words were slurred and he swiped at his bloodied nose. "You're done. Your career is fucking *done*! Let's see your entitled rich ass take the field on Sunday after this. McNealy is going to suspend you so fast it's gonna give you whiplash."

Carson released his grip on Jase and took several steps forward, hauling Willis up off the floor. He kept his hand wrapped around the other man's arm and said, "The fuck he is, Willis. Because you're going to keep your god-damned mouth shut about what went down tonight. And if you don't, there's not a man here who won't say that you started this."

"He came at me!" Willis argued.

"And you provoked him. The second you took your smart-mouthed bullshit out of the locker room, you violated the trust of your team. Not a single one of us will take the field with a man we don't trust."

A murmur of assent echoed from behind him and Jase's head cleared, albeit very little. He still wanted to pound the bastard to a pulp, but his violent streak was no longer mindless. His body relaxed by small degrees and the hands holding him in check slackened their grips as well.

"Stevens, take Willis's drunk ass home," Carson said to the monster linebacker still holding Jase. He steadied Willis on his feet before letting him go. "Cool off, sober up, and think about what the fuck you did here tonight and about what it means to be a part of a team. Do you understand me?"

Willis let out a grunt of acknowledgement and threw a caustic glare Jase's way before he staggered through the press of people toward the foyer. Stevens gave Carson a nod before he headed out behind him and said as he passed Jase, "Take it easy, Blackwell. We've got your back."

With the tension winding down, Gena stepped in like the good hostess she was and tried to restore some order to the night. Jase wasn't having it, though. He'd never felt so utterly wrecked. Destroyed. He wanted to get in his car and chase Avery down. Throw her in the front seat and keep her there until she quit being so stubborn and *listened* to what he had to say. Despite her insistence that he'd just been a fling, he knew there was more to it. She cared about him. She had to. He refused to believe anything else.

"Let her cool off, too, Jase," Carson said as though he'd read Jase's mind. He led him away from the group, into the study, and Jase reluctantly followed. His entire body had gone numb. Despite his swollen and bloodied knuckles, his heart that was damned near pounding out of his chest, and the buzz in his brain that beat out a steady rhythm between his ears, Jase felt none of it. He was a shell: a void of nothingness. Avery had taken his very soul when she'd turned her back on him and walked away.

"I love her, Carson," Jase said as his knees gave out. Thank god there'd been a chair to catch him. "I didn't realize it until just now, but *goddamn*. I fucking love her."

"It's about time you caught up," Carson said with a laugh. "I've been trying to tell you that for days."

"What am I going to do?"

"You'll figure it out."

Jase didn't appreciate the knowing smile on his friend's face, as though Jase was about to be inducted into some secret club. He didn't want to *figure it out*. He wanted answers. He wanted to turn back the clock. Fix everything between them. Keep himself from treating her like a fucking lucky charm in the first place. He wanted someone to bring Avery back to him, damn it. "What if I don't? What if she just turns me away?"

"Come on," Carson replied. "You're *the* Jason Blackwell. You don't know how to quit."

God, he hoped that was true. Because he knew without a doubt that Avery was the one thing in this world he couldn't afford to lose.

ELEVEN

"Super Bowl, baby!" Carson shouted with enthusiasm Jase wished he felt. "Best game of your life, man. I can already feel the weight of that ring on my finger. There's no way you won't get MVP with the post-season you've had, Jase. Phenomenal."

It was a dream come true. His life's goal so close to being realized. But the AFC championship win, hell, even the prospect of going to the Super Bowl was hollow and empty without the one person he wanted to celebrate with. As the plane touched down, Jase's stomach rocketed up into his throat. He'd never get used to flying. It was the flight that had him out of sorts and not the prospect of what he was about to do. A week had passed and Avery refused to answer his calls or texts. Tonight, though, she was going to hear him out whether she liked it or not. So yeah, it was the flight that had Jase tied into knots and not the prospect of Avery's negative reaction to him showing up at her apartment without an invitation.

"You want to come over? It's just Gena and me, but

she'd love to have you over for dinner. We can wind down and veg in front of the television."

"No thanks. I've got somewhere to be."

"Ah. Gotcha."

The plane taxied to a stop and the captain announced that they could move around the plane. Jase grabbed his bag and shouldered his way into the aisle, impatient to get the hell out of there. "Hey, Carson, can you grab my suitcase? I don't want to wait around."

"Got it!" he called. "And good luck!"

Jase didn't need luck. He just needed Avery to listen.

For most of his adult life Jase had been surrounded by false friends and hangers-on. Gold diggers and fame seekers all wanting a piece of what he had for one reason or another. But Avery had only wanted him. Jase. Not the rich kid. Not the football star. She hadn't cared about any of that other stuff. She was *real* and what they'd had was real, too. Jase refused to let her go without a fight.

Avery slid the soufflé into the oven and eased the door closed. Only a week in and semester break was already too long, leaving her with too much free time to let her thoughts run rampant. And each and every one of them centered on Jason Blackwell. She was supposed to be using the time off from school to find another job. The money she'd put away wasn't going to last forever, and since she'd given Peyton her notice the day after Carson and Gena's party, she'd been living off the meager savings. If she didn't find a job soon, she'd lose her apartment. And crappy as it might be, it beat sleeping in a Dumpster any day.

Instead, her every waking moment had been occupied with thoughts of him. How long did it take for a broken heart to heal? She'd quit her job to avoid seeing him at any team functions, and likewise, she'd further depleted her savings when she left a check in his mailbox to cover the costs for the car repairs he'd paid for. None of it gave her closure, though. It didn't help to sew up the gaping hole in her heart.

Avery gathered up the dirty mixing bowls and utensils and put them into the sink to soak as a knock came at her door. Kristie had been trying to get her to go out and have some fun for days. Maybe her friend was tired of being shot down. Little did she know that Avery didn't succumb to peer pressure. No forcible partying for this girl.

"Kristie, I don't want to go out . . ." The words died on Avery's tongue as she opened the door wide and looked up, up, and *up* until her eyes met Jase's. In just a week, she'd forgotten how tall he was, how masculine and imposing his presence. How damned *good* he smelled. "Jase." God, even the sound of his name was a sensory experience, the word tingling on her tongue.

His gaze bore through her, the whiskey-brown depths devouring her with an intensity that beaded her skin with sweat. The heat was unmistakable, enough to steal her breath. And even as her hand twitched on the knob, urging her to slam the door in his face, she couldn't bring herself to follow through with the action.

She didn't realize until this moment how much she'd missed him.

"Avery, just listen." He must have sensed what she was about to do and he took a step forward until his large frame took up the entire doorway. She took two steps back—afraid she'd be tempted to reach out and touch—and Jase followed her inside, easing the door closed behind him. "Sweet Christ, sugar." His voice was strained, the words ragged. "How can one woman become more beautiful in a week?"

A pang of emotion shot through her chest but Avery steeled herself against his pretty words. "Jase, what are you doing here?" Her own voice was nothing more than a whisper. "I can't . . . I can't do this with you right now." Try *ever*. Dredging up the pain of that night was too much.

His brow furrowed while his jaw took on a stubborn set. "Well that's too damned bad, Avery. You're going to hear me out. I won't let you turn your back on me again."

She opened her mouth to protest. To tell him to get the hell out. But the words wouldn't push past her lips. The thought of watching him walk out the door made her sick.

"Avery . . ." Jase raked his fingers through his tawny hair and blew out a gust of breath. So reminiscent of their last night together. "Damn. I . . ."

"What, Jase? Just say it."

"Damn it, I love you!"

Avery sucked in a breath. Had she heard him correctly?

"I love you so damned much it hurts. A month was all it took for you to crawl under my skin and now I can't live through one more day without you. I could stand here and try to apologize for what that asshole Willis said to you. But I'm not going to. Instead, I'm going to apologize for what I did to you. I'm so sorry, Avery." He took a deep breath and held it in his lungs. "If I could do it again, I'd take it all back so you wouldn't have to suffer an ounce of hurt and humiliation. I was a dick. A selfish asshole who never should have treated you as though you were a charm for me to keep in my pocket and use whether I truly felt that way or not. If my game was better, it was because you made me a better man. You made me *want* to be better. What we had wasn't some stupid superstitious ritual. It was *real*. I need you, Avery. I want it all with you. And I know you want me, too."

She wanted to believe him. The sincerity in his eyes, his words, was unmistakable. "You want it all?" she asked in a whisper, her voice quavering.

"Sugar, I want to take you home and show you off to

my family. I want to wine and dine you, buy you pretty things, take you on trips. Hell, I'll sit in this apartment all day, every day if that's what you want. Anything to spend time with you. Avery, I *love* you."

"You hurt me." Jase's chest tightened as his heart clenched. "Those words took away everything good I thought or felt about myself since I'd met you. You played with my emotions and decimated my heart. I appreciate that you're sorry, Jase, and I am, too. I never should have said the things I did. I was hurt and confused but . . ."

No. This sounded too much like good-bye. She had to forgive him, damn it. "Avery, don't push me away. Don't let my stupidity ruin what was so perfect between us. Please, just give me another chance. I won't let you down. I'll do whatever I have to do to prove that I'm good enough for you."

"It's not about being good enough. How can we have an honest relationship when it was built on dishonesty?"

"Avery." Jase pinned her with his gaze. "I never lied to you. Everything I said when we were together was the truth. And everything I felt about you—still feel about you—is real."

"Maybe you're just riding the high of your success. Maybe you're afraid of what will happen if we're not together."

Damn it. He refused to let her make excuses to push him away. "You're right. I'm fucking terrified to lose you, Avery. But not because of some stupid superstition. I wouldn't give a shit if I never played another game in my entire life. Because *none* of it—not the money, the success, anything—would matter if I don't have you."

Her gaze softened. "Jase."

He hadn't convinced her yet. There was still too much doubt in her voice. "Please give me another chance, sugar.

We can go slow, I'll do whatever it takes to earn your trust. Just . . . just please don't walk away from this. Us. You know we're good together. I love you, Avery. And I know you love me, too."

Avery's eyes drifted up to meet his, bright shining emeralds against a night sky. Never in his life had Jase laid eyes on a more desirable woman. One that knew him heart and soul and had seen past his wealth and fame to the man underneath. With a feather-light touch, he brushed her hair behind her ears and cupped her face in his palms. Avery's lips parted, her expression sad and unsure. It broke his heart all over again.

A week. Seven short days apart felt like years as he kissed her. Their bodies melted into one another, his arms encircling her waist, hers coming up to grip his shoulders. Jase savored Avery's taste, the softness of her lips, the heat of her mouth as he kissed her. Her hands wound into the fabric of his T-shirt and she held him as though afraid he'd pull away.

"I love you, Avery," Jase whispered against her mouth. He deepened the kiss, delving into her mouth with his tongue and stroking along her bottom lip. She pulled away and studied him. Her gaze conveyed the emotion he felt. "And I'm going to tell you every minute of every day for the rest of my life until you believe it."

She reached up to trace his jaw with the soft pad of her finger. "Maybe not *every* minute. You're going to need some of that time to play ball if you want to win a Super Bowl anytime soon."

There had been times growing up when Jase didn't think he'd ever have anything. But now? He had the life he wanted, the career and respect he'd worked so hard for, and most importantly, he had the girl. Avery was everything to him. Now that he had her, he knew that he'd never need anything else.

"Will you go?" he asked. She came up on her tiptoes and planted a sweet, soft kiss on his lips. "It would mean a lot to me if you were there."

"Are you kidding?" His lips met hers once again. "I wouldn't miss it for the world."

ROCKED
by the
Billionaire

ONE

The tires of Luke Blackwell's rental screeched on the pavement. He brought the car to an abrupt stop outside of what was once Joe's, the coffee shop and bakery where he'd spent most of his formative years playing guitar and singing for extra cash. Now a trendy wine bar and bistro, only the brick façade was left to remind him of his past as he tracked the woman darting across the street toward the building. His gut clenched at the sight of her, his mind flooded with memories of bare skin, panting breaths, and endless hours of teenage lust that had fueled more than a few of his Top 40 hits. *God damn.* Just thinking about Kayleigh Taylor got his blood up. Seeing her in the flesh was enough to cause his cock to perk up like a hound after a rabbit even eight long years later. He guessed she'd kept to her word and stayed close to home. And here he thought returning to his old stomping grounds to lay low for a while would be boring.

He'd done his damnedest to fly under the radar of the media, his manager and publicist, and just about everyone else who had nothing better to do than look through the window of social media for a peek into his life. The band was on hiatus—between records and tours—and Luke knew that he needed to get away from the cluster-fuck that threatened to take his career down in a tailspin. If he didn't take the time to gather his wits and form a game plan away from the spotlight, the stress of it all was going to send him over the edge. He needed to get his shit straight. Now. Before he lost it completely and someone checked him into one of those facilities where celebrities went to get a little R & R.

After watching Kayleigh duck into the building where they'd spent so much time together as kids, Luke wondered just how much peace and perspective he was going to get on his little reality check. Without thinking, he pulled off the street and into a parking space in front of the building and cut the engine. Ryder wasn't expecting him until to-morrow so it wasn't like he had to hightail it out to the ranch anytime soon. Only his immediate family knew he was coming to town and he'd wanted it to stay that way.

What would she think, seeing him again after he'd walked out on her? He'd been a stupid kid with a wild dream and more ambition than brains back then. Now . . . ? Now he was the fucking master of all things rock. A king, worshipped on the stage and off. Luke was far from hard-up and never lacking for female companionship. He didn't need the complications that hooking up with his high school sweetheart would bring but, damn. He couldn't re-sist the opportunity to see her again. Smell her intoxicat-ing scent. Allow himself to be entranced by the sweet tenor of her voice. There'd been a time when he would have sold his soul for just another night with her. Sort of fitting for the infamous "Lucifer" Blackwell . . .

She was the inspiration for every word he'd ever sung. Every note he'd ever strummed.

Luke pulled open the glass door and walked inside. The

space had been totally renovated, the back corner that had once been set up for open mic night now sported a mahogany bar and wine tasting station. No longer greeted by the aroma of coffee grounds and yeast, he was welcomed with heady oak and tapenade. As he approached the counter where Kayleigh stood with her back to him, a bottle of wine clutched in her fists, he was overcome by the sweet fragrance of sage and lilacs. His gut bottomed out as another barrage of memories burst from a single spark into a raging inferno. But that was the thing about Kayleigh Taylor: she took him immediately back to a time and place when he'd been a wild, reckless kid. And so fucking in love that he didn't know up from down.

Luke took his time. Watched her. As she dug through her purse, she knocked into an empty display table to her right and then tripped on her own foot as she tried to regain her balance. Totally oblivious to the world around her, he had forgotten how she had a tendency to get wrapped up in her own head. Luke suppressed the chuckle that built in his chest. She might have traded in English toffee lattes for wine, but there were some things that not even the passage of time could change.

Her hair was a little mussed, as though she'd been running her hands through it, and her shoulders hunched. Tired? Stressed? Had her day gone to shit, or were the auburn locks just wind tousled? Luke's feet itched to take a step closer to her and he obeyed his body's command. One step. Another. Until he stood right behind her in the checkout line. Empty-handed. As though that wasn't lame as fuck.

Words formed and dissolved on his tongue. Could he simply start up a conversation with her after leaving her alone all those years ago? He swallowed down a snort. He was Lucifer Blackwell, for shit's sake. Women threw their goddamned panties at him. Showed up in his trailer buck-ass naked, more than willing to fulfill *every single one* of his fantasies. In less than a decade, Luke's life had turned around. No longer the poorest kid in town with barely enough food to keep him full, now he had fame, more money than he could spend, and willing pussy in spades. He sure as shit had no reason to feel unsure anymore. So why did his goddamned heart feel like it was trying to pound right out of his fucking chest?

Why was currently standing in front of him in line, digging through her purse.

Kayleigh was beginning to think that kindergarteners were scientifically engineered to suck the life right out of her, leaving behind a dry husk of a woman with the mental capacity of a zombie. They were cute little buggers, but man did they tire her out. She'd left work and headed for the bistro with one thing on her mind: wine and how many glasses it was going to take to erase her hectic week. As much as she wanted to avoid the renovated coffee shop where she'd spent most of her teenage years—and every summer during college—it was the only place in town that sold the Merry Edwards Olivet Lane pinot noir that Spencer had specifically requested for tonight's dinner party. Did that make him a wine snob? Probably, since a bottle of Boone's Farm from the Quickmart would've gotten the job done for her.

The place was almost unrecognizable from the space it had once been. But despite the fancy plaster and paint, the high-end sofas and local art on display, she could almost smell the dark roast of coffee and her eyes inevitably wandered to the far corner where Luke used to play, his eyes glued to her like they were the only two people in the world . . .

"Can I help you?"

Kayleigh started as the cashier broke her from her reverie. Talk about being a nostalgic sap. She handed over the bottle of pinot and continued to root around in the bottomless pit that was her purse for her debit card. A line had formed behind her and her cheeks grew hot with embarrassment. "Sorry," she mumbled as she continued to dig. Good Lord in heaven, she really needed to clean out her purse. Besides too many tubes of lip balm and gloss, she was carrying around an extra pair of shoes, an empty bag of Swedish Fish, an unopened package of raw almonds, three packs of gum, and a Snickers. If anyone got a peek inside, they'd be sure to discover the bar by which she set her snacking priorities.

"I used to know a girl who said that when a guy shows up with a bottle of wine it's because he's hoping to get her out of her panties in a hurry. So in the interest of expediency, why don't you let me buy the wine?"

A long, muscular arm marked with tattoos reached over her and handed a stark white credit card to the cashier. Kayleigh's stomach toppled over her hips and landed somewhere near the soles of her feet. Her spine went starch-stiff as she took in the sight of the cashier, the other woman's eyes glazed over as a silly grin spread across her face.

Holy crap, that voice. Her own words quoted back to her in an almost lewd tenor rippled over her skin like rings on a pond, stretching outward until she was covered from head to toe in microscopic tremors. She didn't dare turn around. Couldn't. She was more afraid to confirm with her eyes what her ears were already telling her. It was impossible. Just, no.

"Aren't you a sweetheart!" The cashier gushed, effectively ignoring Kayleigh as if the floor had opened up and swallowed her whole. Big surprise there. Standing out amidst their present company was like being a twenty-watt lightbulb in the presence of the sun. "And ohmygod, can I just tell you that I absolutely *loved* your last album!"

Well, no need to turn around now to confirm that the one man she never thought she'd see again was standing right behind her, close enough that she could feel the heat from his body buffeting her back. Kayleigh took a step to the right, anything to put a little distance between them. Besides, it wasn't like the starstruck cashier was even remotely interested in dealing with her anymore.

Indecision warred within her, the need *not* to turn around and face him greater than her desire to hang around and accept his charity. Stupid freaking pinot! While the cashier continued to gush, proving her fan status by reciting lyrics and band trivia to Luke, their small talk faded to the back of Kayleigh's mind. She closed her eyes, blocking everything out. The old, *if I can't see it, it's not there* tactic seemed to work well enough for five-year-olds. Maybe she could get it to work for her as well. She gripped the straps of her purse to keep her hands steady even though the rest of her was shaking like a leaf. Every woman's fantasy was to run into her ex looking fabulous: thin, put together, and eat-your-heart-out gorgeous with an equally yummy stud attached to her arm. Too bad she was currently rumpled, wearing ten hours of exhaustion and the curves of almost a decade's worth of unhealthy eating habits. Not to mention she was covered with dried glue and glitter from today's art project. Totally impressive. Gah!

"If you've closed your eyes so you can picture me naked, you should know that all you have to do is ask to get the live show."

The remains of her splattered stomach rocketed up into her throat with the force of a projectile being launched into space. Cocky. Well, at least one thing about Luke Blackwell hadn't changed over the years.

"Or . . . maybe you're simply deep in thought."

Kayleigh's core clenched as the rough tenor of his voice vibrated over her skin. Blocking him from her vision only heightened the allure of the voice she'd heard countless times on the radio. And damn it if he wasn't better live.

"My manager has been suggesting meditation for years. It's never worked for me, but maybe that's because I've never tried it in the middle of a crowded bistro. You might have something there, baby."

Baby? An angry flush settled on her cheeks. He had no right to call her anything but Kayleigh. Or Miss Taylor. God, he'd probably get off on that . . . *Oh good Lord, would you suck it up already and just look at him!* You'd think that laying eyes on Luke Blackwell would cause her flesh to melt, or catch fire or something. Though, he was the only man who'd ever truly commanded her attention. Left her speechless. The only one to ever make her body tingle with sparks of electricity. The only one to shatter her heart into millions of tiny pieces.

And after eight years, it seemed that his effect on her hadn't diminished in the slightest.

Her eyes snapped open but she kept her gaze averted. "Funny, I'm the one buying the wine tonight. So I guess that means I'm trying to get someone out of their . . . uh, panties." Well, that was smooth. Rather than backpedal, Kayleigh sprung to action like a reanimated corpse, digging through her purse in a disjointed, frenzied effort to keep her gaze anywhere but focused on him.

"Sounds like a party," Luke remarked, smooth as aged bourbon. Even with her gaze averted, she knew his eyes had narrowed with humor, his full mouth spreading in a sensual smile.

"Let me pay you for the wine." She'd let him continue on with his current train of thought over her dead body. "I'm sure I've got a few twenties in here somewhere . . ."

She felt like an animal caught in a trap, readying to gnaw its arm off in order to break free. "I just have to find my wallet . . ."

"Are you going to look at me anytime soon or are you going to keep pretending that I'm not standing right in front of you?"

Damn it. Kayleigh let out a gust of breath that did nothing to slow the pace of her racing heart. Her eyes met his torso first, every bit as lean and muscular as she remembered, and up past the wide breadth of his chest and shoulders. She'd forgotten how tall he was. How overwhelming his presence. He towered over her, and she had to crane her neck up to meet his face. As though she couldn't help it, her eyes narrowed into a squint as she took in his whiskey-brown eyes, strong, square jaw, and full mouth. Exactly like looking into the sun.

"So, how've you been, Luke?" It took an actual effort to push his name past her lips. It felt stiff and rusty, like an old screen door that hadn't been used in a while. Her heart clenched at the sight of him as memories—mostly painful ones—assaulted her. It wasn't fair that he could look so self-possessed, so goddamned *gorgeous* after so many years living the fast and loose life of a rock star while she was the one who looked as though she'd been ridden hard and put away wet. What in the hell was he doing here, anyway? Shouldn't he be off in some hotel somewhere, sleeping off a night of hard-core partying beneath a pile of naked groupies?

"You've got something in your hair."

Kayleigh's breath left her lungs in a nervous rush as Luke reached out. His touch was gentle, slow as he brushed his fingertips through the length of her hair. Heat rose to her cheeks and she thought she might pass out from embarrassment. God only knew what was floating around in the tangle of wild curls. Dried macaroni? Tissue paper?

Glue? A groan rose in her throat and she swallowed it down. Somehow, almost a decade later, Luke found a way to add insult to injury.

He inspected the glittering plastic disk and a smile lit his handsome face. "Sequins? You leadin' a double life I don't know about, Ms. Taylor?"

Sweet Lord, that drawl. It was like fresh honey out of the comb, sweet and thick. The sort of cajoling tenor that could convince a woman to do just about anything. "You don't know a damned thing about my life." His sultry Texas charm might have coaxed the panties off droves of women—her included—but not anymore. Sexy and as tempting as the devil himself, he'd earned the nickname "Lucifer" long before he'd become famous. Though at thirteen, the moniker had been given to him more for his mischievous nature than his sex appeal. She dug through her purse, working hard not to lose her cool and finally found her wallet. Tucked in a side pocket were three twenties—her latte and snack money for the next couple of months—and she slapped the bills into his palm. "For the wine." His fingers grazed hers and Kayleigh suppressed a pleasant shudder as she turned away.

Luke wrapped his long fingers around hers and held her fast, pulling her gently back to him. "I just got into town and you're gonna turn away, just like that? Let's go get some dinner." He flashed her a wide grin. "Maybe we could share the wine after?"

So, *so* confident. Typical. It was her turn to feel smug for a change though. Kayleigh squared her shoulders and returned his smile. "No can do, Blackwell. I've got a date."

TWO

A fucking *date*? The smug confidence he'd felt evaporated under the fiery heat of her rebuff. Luke fought the urge to rake his fingers through his hair in frustration, opting instead to sling his thumb casually through his belt loop. Kayleigh's gaze wandered to his hips, her eyes lingering a bit too long and it stirred his cock into instant awareness. Not even five minutes in her presence and all he could think about was stripping her bare and pounding into her.

"A date, huh?" Kayleigh tried to pull away but he kept their joined hands between them. Her skin on his was a balm that quieted his racing mind and troubled soul. Luke took a step, completely closing the space that separated them and a flush of pink colored her cheeks. "Who's the lucky guy?"

She hadn't changed much. Sure, her auburn hair was longer and she'd lost a bit of the girlish innocence that had accentuated her wide brown eyes. Now her body was graced with supple, filled-out curves and a sensual maturity that stole Luke's breath. Still had a smattering of freckles across her nose, though. Thirty-two of them. Luke had spent an entire afternoon counting them as they lounged by Milton's Pond under the shade of an oak tree. If it was possible, she'd grown even more beautiful in the time that he'd been gone.

"Can I have my hand back?" Her eyes met his, and a spark ignited deep in the center of his chest. She could always get to him with nothing more than a look. Women threw themselves at him nightly. Hell, some of them vowed never to wash their hands again after one touch. But the one woman that had mattered—the only woman—treated the contact as though he were trying to spread some sort of communicable disease.

Awesome.

"All right." He released her hand, but damn, he didn't want to let her go. "Don't want to keep your boy waiting, do you?"

"No." Kayleigh's voice dropped to a murmur and she looked away. "I don't."

For a moment, she stood perfectly still and Luke's heart pounded in his fucking chest. The urge to crush her to him, to make her remember how good it had been between them was almost too powerful to resist. Deep down, she had to feel it, too. Why else would she still be standing there with indecision marring her brow?

"Don't get into too much trouble while you're here, Lucifer." Her body turned though her eyes lingered on him as she headed for the door. "This town is too small for the broken hearts you're bound to leave in your wake."

A gust of cool spring air wafted over him with her exit and Luke inhaled the scent of sage and lilacs, all Kayleigh.

"That was sort of rude."

Luke swallowed an agitated sigh and turned back to find the expectant cashier leaning over the counter toward him. Sometime between him paying for the wine and turning to talk to Kayleigh, she'd applied a metric fuck-ton's worth of lip gloss, making her lips look like plastic monstrosities. He was pretty sure there was a song in there, somewhere . . .

"Not everyone's a fan," Luke replied with a tight-mouthed smile.

"You'd have to be crazy not to be." She leaned over the counter, her arms hugged tight under her breasts giving Luke an unhindered—not to mention enhanced—view of her cleavage. "Good thing for you, Lucifer, that you've got a bona fide fangirl right here in front of you."

She wasn't even trying to play coy at this point, giving Luke a smoldering fuck-me gaze that traveled the length of his body and settled on his crotch before working its way back up to his eyes. A slow, seductive smile curved her mouth before she drew one corner of her over-glossed bottom lip between her teeth. "My shift's over in a couple of hours. Wanna stick around until I get off?"

The double entendre was about as subtle as a smack up-side the head. There was no doubt that Luke could screw his way through town and leave a few happy—and probably a couple of pissed off—women in his wake on his way out. But the thought of taking Glossed 'n' Ready to bed was as about as appealing as eating a handful of gravel after seeing Kayleigh again.

"I appreciate the offer, honey," Luke said, careful to keep the disdain from his voice, "but I'm already—"

"Not even in town an hour and you're *already* gettin' yourself into trouble?" Luke breathed a sigh of relief at the sound of his brother's voice. Talk about divine intervention. "Maybe I oughtta be carrying my checkbook for the next week or so. You know, in case you need to be bailed out of jail."

Ha. Ha. Okay, so sophomore year he got pinched joy-riding with Tommy Davis's dad's tractor. But that was the one and only time Ryder had ever had to come get him from the county jail. He turned to face his older brother and gave him an appraising stare. "You look a little thicker since I saw you last. I guess the little lady is feeding you all right."

Ryder responded with a snort and a bright smile that belied his show of annoyance. Luke had only met his brother's girlfriend Lara once—at the Super Bowl—but it had been clear from their love-struck grins, possessive expressions, and over-the-top grabby hands that this was a relationship that was going to go the distance.

"If you ask me, it's you that's lookin' doughy, little brother. A few weeks out on the ranch would do you some good."

Good-natured ribbing was the foundation of the Blackwell brothers' relationship. Something that Luke had missed while on the road. "I can still buck more hay than you." He sized up his slightly shorter "big" brother and shook his head. "You're not as young as you used to be."

"Neither are you," Ryder pointed out. "I wasn't expecting you until tomorrow."

"Yeah. I got antsy. Had to get the fuck outta L.A. I booked a room at the Holiday Inn for tonight since I didn't give you a heads-up," Luke said. "Pretty swanky digs, huh?" The cashier perked up at the mention of his hotel and Luke stifled a groan. He probably should have taken this conversation outside and away from eager ears.

"Like I need a heads-up," Ryder replied. "Just give me a sec to pay for this wine and we're out of here."

Thank. Fuck. The last thing Luke needed was a surprise visit from the lip gloss brigade at one in the morning or for a greedy hotel employee to tip off the paparazzi as to his whereabouts. "Thanks, man. But seriously, what is it with everyone turning into wine fanatics? What's wrong with a cold beer?"

Ryder chuckled. "When you have a woman to impress, we'll talk about it."

Much to the cashier's disappointment, Luke headed for the door as he waited for Ryder. Running from his problems wasn't ideal, but maybe he'd be able to shoulder the stress a little better with family at his back—and if he had anything to say about it, Kayleigh by his side.

"Okay, what in the hell is wrong with you?" Kayleigh's friend Rachael leaned in close and snatched a square of Beaufort cheese and a slice of pear from the tray. "And don't try to tell me it's work stress because you are straight-up rattled. There's no way those adorable little kidlets have you this distracted."

Why had Luke chosen tonight of all nights to show back up into her life? *Let's go get some dinner. Maybe we could share the wine after?* Just the memory of the low, suggestive timbre of his voice sent chills dancing over her skin. After so much time had passed, it pissed her off that he could still affect her so instantly. And with such raw intensity, turning her body traitor as she'd fought the urge to lean into him and get a hell of a lot closer.

"Kayleigh?"

"Sorry." She gave herself a mental slap to the face. Rachael was wearing a giddy, knowing grin that tied Kayleigh's stomach into knots. Did she know that Luke was in town? If so, who else knew? She swallowed down a groan as she pictured the gossip spreading like wildfire. "You're right. I am rattled."

"How did you find out?" Rachael whispered, her eyes as big as dinner plates.

Kayleigh's eyes slid to the right, where Spencer was chatting with Rachael's husband, Colton, and she brought her voice down to a whisper. "How did *you* find out?"

"Colton told me." Rachael picked up the fruit-and-cheese tray and followed Kayleigh from the kitchen to the dining room. "Spencer told him yesterday." She set the platter down next to the roasted game hens and rosemary-seasoned new potatoes and put her wineglass next to a plate.

Spencer knew Luke was in town? The churning knot of nerves in her stomach unfurled and took flight, rocketing right up her throat. "How in the hell did Spencer find out?" She damned near choked on the words as she tried to keep her voice down to a vehement hiss.

"What?" Rachael's brow furrowed. "Are we talking about the same thing?"

Her panic quickly turned to confusion. Were they? She had no idea . . .

"Okay ladies, what are y'all gossiping about over here?"

Kayleigh sloshed the wine over the lip of her glass as she set it down on the table. She'd only been seeing Spencer for a couple of months but he knew about her history with Luke. Hell, anyone who'd grown up in the county knew about it. Even though Spencer had graduated high school before Kayleigh was a freshman, and he didn't really know Luke, he'd always had a strange grudge against the Blackwell family. The fact that Kayleigh was still friendly with Ryder even rubbed him the wrong way. Needless to say, Kayleigh did her best to keep any talk of the Blackwells—or her history with Luke—off the table.

"Girl stuff. None of your business," Rachael teased.

Spencer eased up behind her and placed a kiss on Kayleigh's cheek. Rather than lean into the contact, every muscle in her body seized up. She'd rubbed her "date" in Luke's face and she was ashamed of it. And now, she was ashamed of the fact that she was standing next to an attentive, successful, generally decent guy and all she could think about was the not-so-decent one she'd left staring after her at the bistro.

"Hey?" Spencer asked close to her ear. "Are you okay?"

"Fine." Kayleigh gave a nervous laugh. "Just starved. Let's eat."

By the time her third glass of pinot kicked in, Kayleigh wished she was more interested in eating dinner. The table tilted at an angle and every word out of Spencer's mouth seemed a thousand times funnier than usual. Rachael was giving her some serious side-eye and after she'd served up a few pieces of poorly sliced cheesecake, Kayleigh was more than ready to put this miserable evening behind her and go to bed.

Spencer cleared his throat and picked up his wineglass as he stood from the table. His gaze landed on Kayleigh and a warm smile lit his face. Her mouth went dry and taking a deep enough breath to fill her lungs with the necessary oxygen to stay conscious was damned near impossible as her heart began to hammer in her rib cage like a stampede of wild stallions. What was he about to do? *Oh, god.* Kayleigh's gaze slid to Rachael, her eyes as big as dinner plates and glistening with happy anticipation.

Spencer wasn't going to do what she thought he was going to do . . . was he?

"Kayleigh." Spencer reached for his pocket, producing a black velvet box and her vision darkened at the periphery. "I know it hasn't been that long, but—"

"Luke Blackwell is in town." Kayleigh shot up out of her seat, the words exploding from her lips in a nearly incoherent rush. "I saw him at the bistro tonight and he asked me out for dinner."

A dark cloud settled over Spencer's once bright expression and an uncomfortable silence settled on the table. Colton shifted in his seat and Rachael's eyes were glued to Kayleigh, even larger than they'd been before and her mouth forming a silent "oh" of shock.

Are you insane? She hadn't meant to stand up and blurt

out some sort of confession as though she'd stripped naked and screwed Luke right in the center of downtown. Hell, aside from the spark on her skin when he took her hand in his, their encounter had been as innocent as a run-in with one of her students' parents at the grocery store. Though admittedly, none of her students' parents greeted her with an offer to get naked . . . But the prospect of what Spencer had been about to do sent a tremor of fear through her center and she'd used the first available excuse at her disposal to stop him.

She liked Spencer. But he wasn't Mister Right. More like . . . Mister Right Now.

"I have an early morning tomorrow, maybe we should take off, Rach." Colton placed his napkin on the table and scooted his chair back. Rachael, on the other hand, seemed to be glued to her seat, her eyes bugging out of her head. They'd been friends since elementary school, Kayleigh didn't need to have telepathy to know the questions spinning around in her friend's head.

"Rachael."

"What? Oh, yeah." She looked over at Colton and then from Spencer to Kayleigh. "I have to show a house in the morning, too. So . . . yeah . . ." Colton was already up and headed out of the dining room leaving Rachael to bring up the rear. "Thanks for dinner, guys. I'll talk to you later, Kayleigh."

Spencer remained silent, his lips drawn into a tight line, blue eyes as hard and cold as ice. When the door shut behind Rachael, Kayleigh sank back into her chair but Spencer remained standing. He let out a forceful sigh and pinned her with an accusing glare. "I think we need to talk, don't you?"

It was going to be a long night.

THREE

The great thing about small communities: you didn't have to search too hard to find what—or who—you were looking for. Especially when she was living in her parents' old house. Luke pulled up into Kayleigh's driveway, his gut churning like an angry sea. Jealousy burned him from the inside out even though he knew he had no right to feel it. His heart still had a claim on her, even if she'd chosen to forget it.

For a few minutes he simply sat in the car with the engine running, headlights off. A man with even a lick of common sense would have turned his ass around and gotten out of there. But Luke never was one to play it safe. Besides, the spark that had ignited in Kayleigh's eyes when he'd taken her hand was more than enough evidence that no matter how many years separated them, there would always be a fire that burned hot between them. And he wasn't leaving there until she begged to feel the heat from those flames.

The porch light sparked to life and Luke recalled the many times that same light had flicked on when Kayleigh spent a little too much time out in the driveway with Luke after one of their dates. Fuck, he could practically taste the sweetness of her mouth now, feel the petal softness of her lips. His fingers tightened on the steering wheel as the front door swung open. So help him, if the boyfriend was standing on the other side of that door, it would be all he could do to keep from pressing his foot on the gas pedal and running the fucker over. Lucifer Blackwell, indeed.

He eased his foot off the gas when Kayleigh stepped out onto the porch. Bathed in the soft light of the bulb, her skin all but glowed. Luke's gaze traveled down the length of her body and the baggy T-shirt that hung down just below her hips. The boyfriend's? The steering wheel creaked under his grip.

He rolled down the window and drew a deep breath of crisp spring air. She placed a hand on her cocked hip. Her head fell to the side and with it, a cascade of auburn curls. "Are you going to sit out in my driveway all night, or are you coming in?" Without waiting for a response, she turned and went back inside, leaving the front door wide open.

Hot. Damn.

Luke's brain short-circuited at the sight of Kayleigh's ass, the round half-moons of her bare cheeks peeking out from her booty shorts. He fumbled with the key and the engine grated in protest as he turned the ignition on rather than off. He'd be buying this rental if he didn't watch out, but with his brain so full of Kayleigh, there wasn't room for anything else.

Like one of those zombie parasites that took control of its host's brain, lust dug its way into his, taking over his motor functions, and he had no choice but to obey. He killed the engine and hopped out of the Escalade, strolling up the front porch steps with a swagger that contradicted his pounding heart. He kicked the door closed behind him and froze just inside the tiny foyer. Christ, the place hadn't changed much since he was a kid. Talk about surreal. It made him feel even more like he was crossing some sort of line. Pushing the boundaries of what was decent. And it sent a thrill chasing through his bloodstream.

Kayleigh was curled up on the couch, a fluffy blanket tucked around her legs and hiding all of that glorious bare skin from his view. Luke's mouth went dry and his tongue might as well have been coated with a layer of fur. He couldn't have talked if he'd wanted to, which was probably a good thing because the only thoughts in his head were of how beautiful she looked, and how badly he wanted to fuck her.

There was *definitely* a song there . . .

"I broke up with my boyfriend tonight." Kayleigh gave a rueful laugh that was tinged with sorrow. Her eyes came up to meet his and for the first time, Luke noticed that they were red and puffy as though she'd been crying. "Who in the hell does that? I mean, seriously? Who in their right mind breaks up with a perfectly good guy because her ex blows into town?"

Luke's heart soared at her words despite the grief that lined her face. He'd never intended to hurt her by approaching her at the bistro, but damn it, he couldn't deny that her loss was his gain. "I'm sorry, honey." That was the truth. He was sorry she hurt. Wished he could take that pain from her. "But if it was so easy to cut him loose, then maybe he wasn't the guy for you."

Her bark of laughter ended on a sob. "No, I guess he wasn't. Apparently I'm a glutton for punishment. I only want men who don't want me back."

The words sliced through him like a razor blade, cutting deep into his flesh. Luke stayed rooted to his spot on the carpet, incapable of taking a single step. God, just standing near her cleared the clutter from his mind. For months he'd suffered artistically. Emotionally. Gone through the motions like a fucking zombie. Regurgitated lyrics that no longer meant a damn thing to him. He'd been hollow. But in Kayleigh's presence, he felt full to bursting.

Kayleigh sniffed and wiped at her eyes. "What are you doing here, Luke? *Why* did you come back?"

"The truth?" Was that even an option? If she knew how badly he'd fucked himself over would she kick him out the door before he even got the chance to explain himself?

"I think I deserve it, don't you?"

She deserved so much more than the truth. So much more than him. But Luke was a selfish bastard and he'd decided a long time ago that life wasn't worth livin' if he wasn't willing to go balls out for everything he wanted. Right now, he wanted her. A slow smile crept onto his face and he hiked a casual shoulder. "What would you say if I told you that I came home because of you?"

A slow shuddering sigh released from between her parted lips. "You really are a son of a bitch, Luke."

Probably. She wasn't the first woman to tell him that at any rate. Luke put one foot in front of the other as he stalked toward her perch on the living room couch. The deep chocolate brown of her eyes glistened with unshed tears and her cheeks flushed crimson. Sorrow and rage, soft rain and a raging fire. Kayleigh had always been a walking contradiction. His muse. The basis for every raw emotion he'd ever put to paper. She took his breath away.

"I drive a Prius and I teach kindergarten. Most nights I crawl into bed with a book and on the weekends, I'm either hanging out at the lake or catching up on laundry. My life is far from exciting and I'm okay with that. I haven't changed, Luke. I'm still all of the things you were trying to get away from, so you'll excuse me if I think that your excuse for showing up here is total bullshit."

* * *

Kayleigh had come to terms with the fact that life wasn't fair a long time ago. If it had been, her parents wouldn't have saddled her with a house that was rotting into the ground while they retired on a beach in Mexico, she wouldn't have to tutor snotty middle-schoolers over the summer to make ends meet, and she'd be living happily ever after with the man of her dreams, *not* kissing every frog within a hundred-mile radius only to be disappointed time and again.

It only added insult to injury that the man she'd thought she was going to spend the rest of her life with was standing in her living room in the exact same spot he'd been in eight years ago when he broke her heart and told her he was leaving. She'd dreamed for countless nights that first year that he'd come back. That was the thing about Luke, though. He was every woman's dream. Sensitive, yet aggressive when it counted. Raw. His emotions always close to the surface. He didn't lack for words; they flowed from his tongue like the sweetest nectar. And even after so many years, the memory of his kisses left her flushed and breathless. He was everything Kayleigh had ever wanted. After he'd broken her heart into so many pieces, she'd feared that she'd never be able to put herself back together again.

"You're right," he said in that confident tone that gave her chills. "I am a son of a bitch."

Luke closed the distance between them and snatched Kayleigh by the wrist, hauling her up from the couch. The blanket covering her waist dropped to the floor between them as he wrapped his free arm around her. Her breath raced, heart thundered as she jerked her wrist free from his grasp. Big. Mistake. Luke used the opportunity to his advantage, reaching around to cup her nearly bare ass. Dear Lord, how was it possible for something so simple to feel so good? Luke held her gaze, his nostrils flared with his heavy breaths as he searched her face, drank her in with a laser intensity that made her pussy wet as though on command.

She was a switch that only he could flip. Her body was fine-tuned to Luke Blackwell's touch and it didn't give a shit about past heartaches. Only this moment, and getting as much of him as she could.

A very male smirk accentuated his full mouth. He had her and he knew it. Damn him. "God damn, baby," he murmured as he lowered his mouth to hers. "It's been a long time since a woman made me want to lose control."

How could eight years feel like a lifetime and a matter of hours all at once? Luke's mouth on hers was a homecoming. It filled her with a sense of rightness that Kayleigh had never felt with anyone else but him.

"*Fuck*." Luke's breath brushed her mouth in a warm whisper that caused a ripple of chills to slide down her spine. "You taste like heaven." His tongue traced the seam of her lips and she opened her mouth to him. Such a simple act and yet, that intimate welcome ignited something between them. A spark that flared to life and burned through his body into hers. "I'm gonna taste every inch of you, too."

What was she doing? The day he'd walked out of her life, Kayleigh had vowed never to let him back in. Their breakup had been brutal. Emotionally crippling. She'd taken an entire year to heal from the wounds he'd inflicted on her heart. Starting college long after all of her friends just to get her head straight. How could she let him do this after everything that had happened between them?

"Luke . . ." She turned her head to the side and placed her palms on his chest. Tried not to lose herself in the warmth of him that soaked through his T-shirt into her palms. Kayleigh took a steadying breath and gave a weak shove at the wall of muscle pressed up against her, a totally futile effort. "I don't think I can do this."

"Sure you can." His heated breath caressed her neck and Kayleigh shuddered. "Just follow my lead."

For as long as she'd known him, Luke had always played to win and he wasn't going to make putting him at arm's length easy for her. As convincing as the devil himself, he could coax a nun right out of her panties if he set his mind to it. Getting Kayleigh out of hers wouldn't exactly take a whole lot of effort on his part.

"Come on, baby. Let me touch you. Kiss you. *Lick* you. Ever since this afternoon, I haven't been able to get you out of my head. Your hair . . ." He stroked his fingers through the tangle of curls. "Your breasts . . ." He ventured downward, his fingers brushing the aching points of her nipples. Kayleigh sucked in a breath that caused a wicked grin to spread across Luke's sensual mouth. "Your tight, sweet pussy . . ." His fingertips teased the low waist of her shorts and a tremor vibrated through her causing that very part of her body to throb. "I remember how wet you used to get for me. Are you wet right now, baby?" He dipped one finger below her waistline, the heat of his breath tickling her lips as he spoke. "Is your pussy dripping for me?"

Rather than push him away like she'd intended, Kayleigh's arms wound around his neck. He reached around to cup one palm over her ass while his other hand came up to wind in her hair, holding her firmly in place as he brought his mouth back to hers.

Holy shit, could Luke Blackwell kiss! Like the perfect composition, his kisses struck chords in Kayleigh's body, crystal-clear notes that resonated through every inch of her in a harmony that left her weak and gasping for breath. He'd learned a trick or two over the years, no longer hurried and unsure, now he took his time with her as though each soft caress of his lips had been well rehearsed beforehand. She was shameless, her body responding to him in exactly the way she knew it would. Her underwear grew damp with arousal and her sex was so swollen with want that the brush of fabric over her skin was torture. Luke always could play her like a finely tuned guitar.

Yeah, and he's probably rehearsed the same song on every woman over eighteen from L.A. to New York City.

The thought helped to wake her from her lust-induced stupor and Kayleigh pulled back, only to have Luke hold her fast against him. "Don't. Stay with me, baby." He released his grip on her hair and brushed his thumb across her jaw, feather light. Her stomach clenched at his dark, seductive tone and a renewed rush of wet heat spread between her thighs. "Let me taste you, touch you, drink you into my soul."

She trembled under the onslaught of his words. Pure seduction. Raw sex. Her pussy clenched and Kayleigh was sure he could talk her straight into an orgasm if he wanted to. "Luke . . ." She couldn't draw a breath deep enough to talk. "Please . . ."

The hand cupping her ass slid around her hip, teasing the waistband of the spandex booty shorts. He slid his fingers past the elastic barrier and Kayleigh sucked in a hissed breath as the heat of his skin met her mons. "Soft as rose petals against my skin," he murmured as he continued to pet her. Her clit began to throb, aching for the same attention he paid to her clean-shaven mound. "Lie to me, baby. Tell me this is for me. This soft skin. Tell me it's mine."

Was there ever any part of her that hadn't belonged to him? Her thighs trembled, her knees dangerously close to giving out. She clung to him, spreading her legs wider. The words were little more than a whisper when she said, "It's all yours, Luke."

He rewarded her for her words by sliding his fingers through the slick, swollen flesh as he worked them over her clit. Kayleigh cried out, the intense sensation rippling from her core, outward with a heat that made her break out into a sweat. Luke groaned into her ear as he circled the tight bundle of nerves, light, teasing strokes that coaxed desperate moans from Kayleigh's throat, each one hitching on a pant of breath.

"Come for me, baby," Luke crooned in her ear. "Let me feel you break apart."

FOUR

The fire that sparked to life inside of him from simply touching this woman could never be replicated. Faked. Kayleigh was his. She'd always been his.

His cock throbbed behind his fly as his fingers slid through the slick, swollen lips of her pussy. The scent of spring clung to her skin, intoxicating him, and his head swam in a giddy, drunken blur. He stopped his ministrations only long enough to free her of the restricting fabric and urged her legs to spread as he cupped her dripping pussy once again. Her mouth parted on a moan and he swallowed the sound, tasting of red wine. He thrust his tongue past her lips. He'd meant what he said: he wanted to drink her in, take her passion into his soul when she came apart. Keep a part of her. *His*.

No longer the shy, awkward girl, the woman in his arms was a creature born of fire and passion. She gripped onto the back of his neck, her nails biting into his skin as he deepened the kiss. The sting spurred him on and he wanted more. Wanted her to break the skin and pull his hair. Demand that his pain was equal to her pleasure. Sick?

Probably. But Luke's mind was always clearer when he hurt a little.

So fucking wet.

He guided her to the couch and urged her to sit. Kneeling on the floor beside her, Luke drank in the sight of her, naked to his gaze, her legs spread wide so he could see the glistening arousal coating her thighs. God, he wanted to bury his face in her gorgeous tits and suckle her until he marked her skin. Branded her as his and no one else's. He wanted to tie her up and tease her with gentle strokes and soft kisses, touch her with whispers of caresses that would make her beg for his cock. But all of that would take time that Luke wasn't willing to spare. His need to bring her to that point of abandon that already consumed him, raging like wildfire. With the pad of his thumb, he circled her clit and Kayleigh gave a desperate thrust of her hips in time with each pass. She groaned with frustration and pushed herself away from the couch, clinging to him as her nails dug into his neck. "God, yes. Just like that, baby. Stay with me and I'll give you what you need." He increased the pressure on her clit, sliding one finger inside of her tight channel. The answering sounds that vibrated in her throat were pure relief. His cocked pulsed hot and hard and Luke welcomed the discomfort. A sweeter torture, he'd never known . . .

Kayleigh's back bowed. A tremor vibrated up her thighs through Luke's arms, lewd and raw in its intensity. She tried to pull away but Luke wouldn't let her, thrusting his tongue in her mouth in time with every deep thrust of his finger. Her pussy clenched and he slid a second finger in, maintaining a slow, steady pace to prolong her pleasure as he swallowed down every desperate whimper that accompanied her orgasm.

Time ceased to exist in that moment. Nothing had changed in eight years. Not a goddamned thing. Kayleigh still belonged to him every bit as much as she owned him. She had to have known it, too. Felt it right down to her bone marrow like he did.

He brought her down with slow, gentle caresses and she became liquid in his embrace. He missed the bite of her nails in his skin, her hard edges as she strained against him. Even her mouth had softened, her lips swollen and pliable from his kisses. Luke kissed her once. And again as he withdrew his fingers from her constricting heat and reveled one more time in the petal-softness of her sex. And he couldn't wait to feel that satin heat hold onto his cock.

For a moment Luke held Kayleigh in his arms, listening to the sounds of her heavy breaths. He brushed the tangles of her hair away and cupped her face in his hands as he took in the sight of her dark, glazed eyes and flushed cheeks. "I'm gonna love you so good that no other man will ever have a chance to break your heart ever again."

In his arms, her body went rigid. She pulled away and looked at him, her brows furrowed and her expression dark, making Luke wish he could take back the words. The hurt he'd caused her was obviously still close to the surface and unlike the countless other women who'd fallen for his lines, all he'd managed to do with Kayleigh was re-open wounds that hadn't completely healed.

Fuck.

"Oh my god." The words left her mouth with a rueful laugh. She scrubbed her hands over her face. "I am *such* an idiot!"

"Kayleigh." An apology sat at the tip of his tongue. A tome's worth of purple prose that would dampen the panties of droves of women. But Kayleigh would see through those trite words. Even after all this time, she knew the barest parts of him. The exposed and raw nerves that he'd never shown to anyone but her. "Come on, baby. Let's leave the past where it belongs, yeah?" He tried to pull her close once again but she resisted. "Can't we just be in the moment? Enjoy each other? There's nothing wrong with living in the present. Let me make you feel good."

She stared at him, aghast. Yup, he'd fucked that up royally. God*damn* it. Kayleigh had his number. He wasn't going to get away with shit.

She disengaged from his embrace, snatched the discarded blanket from the floor, wrapping it around her body like a shield. It didn't matter that she'd blocked her body from his view though. Luke knew every inch of her. All he had to do was close his eyes to be back in that moment when she'd been his.

"Why are you really here, Luke?" Tears glistened in the dark depths of her eyes and his heart clenched. "You don't get enough of playing with women's emotions on tour so you came home to fuck with mine? Or are you running from something?"

Yep, she had his number all right. He took a step back to give her a little space. How could he possibly make her understand? "Baby—"

"*Don't* call me that." Her hurt flared into an indignant fire in an instant. "I'm not that fifteen-year-old girl anymore that you can manipulate with your pretty words. It was stupid of me to invite you in. I should have turned my back on you like you did on me. It's a mistake I'm not going to make again, though."

Fire and ice. That was Kayleigh to a tee. He deserved every one of her harsh words. All of her anger and then some. He wanted it all from her. He wanted to feel something real and honest for a change. "I told you I was a son of a bitch, baby. I won't say I'm sorry for coming here tonight or for what just happened. But I will apologize for what went down when I left you. I owe you that much."

She gave a derisive snort. "Well, isn't that big of you. You know, *Lucifer,* that whole 'it's better to ask forgiveness than permission' thing was cute when you were a kid but it's not going to fly now. I don't want or need an apology for what happened a lifetime ago."

"Jesus, Kayleigh. We were *kids*!" Was she going to hold what happened against him forever? "The ranch had just barely started turning a profit and Ryder had Jase's tuition to pay. What in the hell was I supposed to do? Sit around here and play at the fucking coffee shop? I had to go out there and make something happen. You're going to hold my ambition against me?"

"I never had a problem with your ambition, Luke. Or your bank balance. What I have an issue with is the way you left me in your wake as soon as you had your diploma and your mama's blessing to leave town. You didn't even try to include me in your future. Do you know how that made me feel?"

Her angry shout only served to fuel Luke's own ire. Walking away from her had been like tearing out his own goddamned heart and leaving it behind. "You didn't want *any* of it! You wanted to stay! For someone not interested in an apology, you're sure enjoying rubbing the past in my face."

Kayleigh backed away until she was nestled in the corner of the couch. She let herself fall back on the armrest and let out a forceful sigh. "It's not the apology I don't want, Luke. It's your empty, poetic words that I don't give a shit about."

It wasn't fair to take her anger with herself out on Luke, but it was what it was. Truth be told, those pretty, poetic words were one of the things she'd loved the most about him. Luke had always worn his heart on his sleeve, even when they were in middle school and he'd had to endure the malicious teasing of their classmates. Growing up poor in a tight-knit community hadn't been easy on any of the

Blackwell brothers. But they'd overcome adversity with a fierce determination that was admirable. Luke could've let the unkind ribbing of his classmates tear him down. Despite his hotheadedness, he'd turned that hurt into something beautiful. His music had elevated him above ugly pettiness. And now Kayleigh was throwing it back in his face, condemning him for a decision that simply didn't matter anymore.

If anyone recognized the power of words, it was Luke. And Kayleigh knew she'd cut him to the quick with hers.

His warm whiskey eyes hardened and Luke's jaw squared. Leaner than his twin brother, Jase, Luke was no less imposing. He towered over her, all six and a half feet of him corded with unyielding muscle. No matter how she felt about him showing back up in her life, he was a sight worth her admiration.

"I've never once lied to you. Never played games with you. I was straight with you when I left and you're going to hold my honesty against me? What the fuck is up with that?"

Even tinged with anger, his voice was a seductive purr that caressed her from head to toe. Kayleigh suppressed a pleasant shiver as she wrapped the light blanket tighter around her waist. "I don't hold your honesty against you. Hell, I'm not even mad that you left. It's the fact that once you were gone, you never looked back! Jesus, Luke. Did I cross your mind at all after you blew out of town or were you too busy with the revolving door of willing tail to give me a second thought?"

Her voice broke on the last word but Kayleigh refused to let him see how badly she hurt. It was her own foolish pride that took a hit tonight and she was so angry with herself that she had no choice but to project that anger on the first available target. Good Lord, she'd spread her legs for him as eagerly as any hopeful groupie. Hadn't even batted a lash when he stuck his hand down her shorts as though it was a common occurrence for men to bring her to orgasm while she sat in the middle of her living room.

Kayleigh had humiliated herself tonight and opened the door for Luke Blackwell to break her heart all over again. If she didn't steel herself against his charm now, she'd be nothing more than a lump of clay in his palm. Malleable. His to shape and command. *As if you wouldn't love to be worked by those hands again.*

Luke's expression softened and he sat down in a nearby wing chair as though his legs couldn't support his weight for another second. His gaze drilled into her, so full of honesty that it stole her breath. "I'm drowning, Kayleigh. I need you to anchor me."

The desperation in his voice tore her composure to shreds. "I can't be that for you, Luke." He'd reduced her importance to that of a security blanket. Something familiar and comforting to help him weather whatever storm he'd found himself in the eye of. "I can't let you in again just so you can crush me after you get over this hump."

"I still love you."

The words eviscerated her. Shredded every ounce of tissue in her body until all that was left was raw nerves and searing pain. "You have no right to show up on my doorstep after eight years of silence and say those words to me. *None.*"

Luke pushed himself forcefully from the chair. A trickle of fear spiked through Kayleigh's bloodstream causing her heart to race and her breath to quicken. "And you have no right to tell me what to feel or what time frame I'm allowed to feel it in."

Kayleigh wasn't sure what was worse: his ridiculous proclamation of love, or her own foolish desire to want it to be true. "You don't even know me anymore, Luke! How can you possibly love me?"

"I know you." His anger was replaced by the trademark Blackwell self-confidence that piqued female interest throughout the county. Hell, the *world*. In a few quick steps, he'd crossed the living room and stood before her. Kayleigh slid from the arm of the couch down onto the sofa, her brain too full of Luke to function properly and her mouth too damned dry to form a single word.

He braced a heavily muscled arm on the back of the couch behind her and the other on the rest beside her. Kayleigh's breath stalled as he leaned down, his mouth mere inches from hers. If she leaned in she'd get to kiss those full lips again . . .

"We're a force of nature when we're together. Unmovable. Unstoppable. Fierce and frenetic. You know it as well as I do. Get used to seeing me around, baby. I ain't going anywhere anytime soon."

He put his lips to her forehead. Such a simple, innocent kiss compared to what they'd done not thirty minutes ago. There wasn't an ounce of guile in his expression as his gaze bore into hers. "I'll see you tomorrow. Get some sleep."

And as easily as he'd breezed through her front door, he took himself back out, closing it silently behind him. Kayleigh released the breath she'd been holding and it vibrated through her in microscopic tremors that tightened her abdomen. He was right. She couldn't stay away from him any more than she could stop the sun from rising. Her body craved his on a primal level.

Get used to seeing me around . . . Luke Blackwell was nothing if not stubborn. When he set his sights on something he got it. She'd given him her body easily enough tonight. Would she be able to resist him a second time? Or would she give him the opportunity to break her heart all over again?

FIVE

Luke slumped against the wall in the guest bedroom, his guitar cradled in his lap. He hadn't slept at all after leaving Kayleigh's house last night. Too keyed up for rest and much too wound up to just toss one off and call it a night. Going off into his own goddamned fist sounded about as appealing as getting a blowjob from a hammerhead shark. Nothing short of Kayleigh's tight, wet pussy wrapped around his cock would satisfy him. The night hadn't been a total loss, though. He hadn't experienced such a surge of creativity in a long goddamned time. The words flowed, the music trickled from his fingers as though on its own. He had one song completely composed and another nearly finished. All thanks to Kayleigh.

Who knew a serious case of blue balls was the key to great writing?

Hell, there was no use kidding himself at this point. The inspiration that seized him had nothing to do with the need to get off. If that had been the case, he could have marched on down to the bistro and fucked the glossy-mouthed cashier senseless. What he'd gotten from Kayleigh last night was a hell of a lot deeper than a quick orgasm. And he wanted *more*.

"Lara says to tell you that you're never allowed to leave." Ryder poked his head in the doorway and leaned against the jamb.

Luke didn't look up from his guitar, just kept strumming. "Why's that?"

"Apparently, she enjoys being serenaded first thing in the morning. *I,* on the other hand, don't like it quite as much."

Luke snorted. He'd learned at an early age that the best way to deflect his classmates' scorn was to impress them into silence. Girls had especially found his musical abilities swoon-worthy. Kayleigh hadn't cared about any of that, though. She'd been his friend long before he'd ever picked up a guitar. And after they'd started dating, she'd made it clear that she loved him for himself and not because of his talent. Luke stopped strumming and grabbed his pencil, rearranging the hook and changing the chord to A minor. "I can get a room at the hotel if you want."

"Mom would have my ass if you did," Ryder remarked with a laugh. "Besides, I'm just giving you shit. I don't suppose this sudden surge of inspiration has anything to do with where you went after dinner last night?"

"Maybe." Not that it would take an investigative genius to figure out where he'd gone, but he didn't feel like discussing Kayleigh with Ryder—or anyone else—right now.

"You know I've got your back, Luke, but . . ."

Oh great. After their dad had left, Ryder had taken up the role as head of the household. A position he'd taken seriously. You'd think he was decades older than Luke, not just a few years, with his father-knows-best attitude. "I don't need a lecture, Ryder. My shit is straight."

"Is it?" Ryder pinned him with a knowing gaze.

"Because if you ask me, your shit is as far from straight as it can get."

Why did he have to be so goddamned parental? "I know what I'm doing."

"You *think* you do. And that's what I'm worried about."

Luke stopped mid-strum and covered the strings with his palm, creating an abrupt halt to the melody he'd been working on. "What in the hell is that supposed to mean?"

"Is this meltdown you're having worth hurting her again? Spencer Jackson was going to propose to her. Did you know that?"

Spencer Jackson? *Seriously?* That was the douchebag Kayleigh had been seeing? The dude had two first names for Christ's sake. Good riddance. "What does that have to do with me?"

"According to the local gossip, she interrupted him right in the middle of it last night to tell him that you were back in town."

Despite his effort, Luke could do nothing to hide the self-satisfied smirk that crept onto his face. He began to strum again and shut his eyes, picturing Kayleigh, soft and willing in his arms, her breath mingling with his as he swallowed her impassioned cries.

"Luke."

Aaannndd . . . there it was. The stern, you'd-better-listen-to-me voice that Ryder had perfected over the years. He stopped playing and looked at his brother, his jaw clamped down tight.

"I get that you needed time away to get your head on straight. But I'm warning you, don't drag her down with you."

"Duly noted."

Luke returned to his guitar in earnest, effectively blocking his brother out. Ryder let out a long sigh and closed the door, leaving Luke to his thoughts. He didn't want to drag Kayleigh anywhere but right on top of his stiff cock. And hurting her was the last thing on his mind. He simply needed a little bit of clarity and for some damned reason, the only place he'd ever been able to find it was with her.

Fucking Ryder.

Guilt twisted Luke's gut, rose in his throat like bile, and choked the air from his lungs. Had he really hurt Kayleigh's chance at happiness by inserting himself back into her life? Sure, they had history, but if she could so easily cast Spencer Douche-Canoe Jackson to the curb, then she hadn't been truly happy with the loser. Right?

He penciled in a revision to the bridge and played it over again. Much better. Kayleigh could never have been happy with a guy like Spencer. The dude had no soul. She deserved to be with a man who understood her. Who recognized her dark moods and could pull her out of them. A guy who realized that her supposed scatterbrain wasn't a result of flakiness, but rather a quick, clever mind that was always thinking one step ahead. What Kayleigh needed was a man like . . .

Him.

There were worse choices. Luke had money. A decent career. A trust fund that guaranteed security. He could make her come in thirty seconds flat with the right motivation. What was so wrong with him?

Ryder seemed to think he was damaged goods or some shit. Jase had always been the "good" brother. The kind, conscientious one. The kid with good grades and an even more pristine reputation. He never broke hearts or stepped a toe out of line. Never got caught with a bottle of peppermint schnapps at school. Didn't walk out on people who counted on him.

You're a first-class fuck-up, dude. His own brother didn't think he was good enough for Kayleigh. Didn't he deserve to be happy, though? Ryder had Lara, and Jase had hooked up with a hot little chef who rocked his world. Didn't Luke deserve that, too?

The doorbell rang, the sound pinging around in his brain like a pinball against the bumpers. Thanks to Ryder's visit, Luke's mood had soured past the point of salvation. There was no way he'd be able to work now and the walls of the bedroom were starting to close in on him. Maybe he'd saddle up one of the horses and go for a ride to clear his head. He hadn't done anything like that in a long time.

From the top of the stairs, the sound of a woman's voice caught Luke's undivided attention. It latched onto his heart with sharp hooks, digging deep until he felt the bite. What was Kayleigh doing here? His feet moved of their own accord, taking him down Ryder's handcrafted staircase. He stopped short of the living room and leaned against the archway, careful to stay out of sight.

"Can't you make him leave, Ryder?"

Luke's stomach plummeted to the soles of his feet, taking his heart with it. Kayleigh didn't want him beneath her, beside her, or anywhere near her.

She wanted him gone.

Ryder's lips pursed as he regarded Kayleigh with an emotionless stare. The eldest Blackwell was steel under pressure, never revealing his hand. Not much had changed since they were kids. He was still as intimidating now as he'd been when she was fourteen.

"This is his home, Kayleigh, and he hasn't been back for so much as a visit since he left. I'm not kicking him to the curb. Sorry."

She should have known that Ryder would side with his brother. What in the hell was she thinking coming here?

"You're right. I'm the one who should be sorry for suggesting it. It's just . . . seeing him again. It's too much. You know?"

Ryder's eyes bored through her, the exact whiskey brown of Luke's. "Just because he's in town doesn't mean you have to see him."

True. But when he showed up on her doorstep looking like sex on a freaking stick, what was she supposed to do? "I'm twenty-six-years old. You'd think I could be an adult." She gave a rueful laugh. "But there's something about your brother that turns me into an irresponsible kid. One that can't make a mature decision to save her life."

"Is this about Spencer?"

Kayleigh groaned. "You know about Spencer?"

Ryder laughed. "*Everyone* knows about Spencer. Did you forget what living in a fishbowl is like?"

Their tiny suburb might as well have been freaking Mayberry. Not much had changed in a decade. People still talked. Gossip flowed like a river in spring. "We'd only been dating for a couple of months. Seriously, I have no idea what Spencer was thinking! I would have turned him down either way. I was—Luke just—God, it's like my brain short-circuits when he's within a five-mile radius of me."

Ryder's brow furrowed and a flush rose to Kayleigh's cheeks. She was standing here talking to Luke's older brother like he was her therapist or something! Good Lord, they were friends, but this had to cross some sort of line. "I'm sorry, Ryder. This really isn't anything you should have to worry about and I'm just standing here blathering like an idiot. I shouldn't have wasted your time. This is my problem. I'll deal with it on my own."

Kayleigh spun on a heel and hightailed it for the foyer. She couldn't get out of there fast enough and her stomach was churning and bucking like the thirty-year-old washing machine in her basement. The cherry on top of this miserable morning would be to puke all over Ryder's fancy hardwood floors.

"Oh shit!" Her face met a solid wall of muscle that knocked her off balance. Strong arms reached out to steady her and her previous mortification rose to new heights as she looked up to find Luke staring down at her, his expression pinched.

She'd assumed Luke would be staying with Ryder and she'd come anyway. But hadn't that been the point? Some small part of her had hoped she'd see him.

His big body crowded her, but Kayleigh stood her ground. She refused to let Luke think he had *any* effect on her. His expression further darkened and a thrill of anticipation shot through her. He leaned down over her head and his deep, heady words were for her alone. "Back for more? I laid in bed, wide awake all night. The smell of you on my fingers drove me fucking *crazy*. I'm ready for round two."

He was trying to shock her, or hell, maybe to embarrass her. To make her pay for throwing him out last night. Well, too damned bad, buddy. "I told Ryder I wanted you to leave town. Unfortunately for me, he likes having you around." She looked down at his hands still wrapped around her upper arms and he let go, cupping the back of his neck with one large palm. "Rejection hurts like a bitch, doesn't it?"

His whiskey gaze hardened but he kept his cocky smile intact. "I don't mind a little pain." Kayleigh's eyes met his and a flash of heat licked up her spine. "As long as you promise to follow it up with pleasure."

So much for standing strong against Luke's advances. When he talked to her like that, his words smoldering with heat and innuendo, her knees went weak. He leaned back and her body followed, metal drawn to a magnet. How could she possibly keep her distance when everything inside of her screamed to get closer? An uncomfortable silence descended and Kayleigh's throat went bone dry. "I . . . um, I was just leaving."

"Let's go for a ride."

She'd just told him that she wanted him to leave town forever and still he was coming on to her? The man was *relentless.* "That's probably not a good idea."

His eyes sparked with mischief, reminding her of the Luke of her childhood. "What's the matter? Worried you've lost your touch in your old age? Or maybe that you can't keep your hands off of me?"

Kayleigh snorted. As far as keeping her hands off of him went . . . any time spent with Luke would be a test to her restraint. "Don't flatter yourself, Lucifer. You're not that irresistible." World's biggest lie, right there. But his ego didn't need any more stroking.

"Hey, it's not my mind that's in the gutter, honey. I was talking about horses. But if you'd prefer to mount up, I'm sure I could—"

"If I'm not mistaken, cattle and horse thievery is still frowned upon around here. I doubt Ryder would appreciate us taking off with any of his stock," she interrupted with a nervous laugh. Anything to keep him from finishing that sentence.

Luke reached out and took her hand in his. So gentle. So unlike the cocky bravado he readily displayed. It wasn't that his gentleness was better, just . . . different. Tentative. His touch was the plea that pride refused to allow him to speak. He didn't want her to leave. And despite her earlier words to Ryder, Kayleigh wasn't sure she wanted to leave, either.

"Ryder doesn't own every horse on this ranch. Come on, do you have something better to do this morning? Maybe a stack of macaroni art that needs to be graded?"

A challenging brow arched over one eye and Kayleigh couldn't help but laugh. "I can spare a couple of hours to help you relearn how to ride. L.A. has probably brainwashed every ounce of cowboy out of you."

He headed for the door and Kayleigh went after him as though she had no other choice. Luke had always had a magnetic pull that was too strong to fight. "There are a lot of things L.A. hasn't managed to flush out of my system." She shivered at the dark tenor of his voice and the way his eyes held hers when he turned to hold the door open for her. He leaned in over the top of her head and took a deep breath. Kayleigh's eyelids fluttered as he released it. "Riding is one of them."

So much for getting him out of town. At the rate they were going, Luke would be sticking around for good.

And if Luke decided to stay, Kayleigh knew that it would surely ruin them both.

SIX

Luke's bravado had definitely gotten the better of him. He owned three of the ranch's stock horses, but it had been almost a decade since he'd saddled up and it showed. His ass was killing him and Lucifer—Ryder's idea of a joke—was living up to his name, making the trip to the back forty as hard on Luke as possible. Damned gelding nearly threw him after coming to a dead stop at the bottom of the knoll. It had given Kayleigh something to laugh about, though, so he'd let the bastard's ornery streak slide for now.

It might have been stupid to press his luck with her, especially after hearing her beg Ryder to get him out of town. Short of stripping her naked and licking her from head to toe right there in the foyer, he'd all but dared her to look him in the eye and tell him that she didn't want him. And the fact that she hadn't further proved that she couldn't stay away from him any more than he could from her. He wasn't ready to throw in the towel yet. Not as long as there was still this spark of electricity between them.

Kayleigh brought her mare to a stop near a narrow stream that ran through the pasture. Short, brilliant green spring grass had begun to poke up through the dry white stubble of last season's hay. In L.A. the seasons weren't quite so marked. Nothing poked up through the sidewalks to indicate the coming of spring. Luke missed the rolling open fields and quiet solitude. Kayleigh hopped down from her mount and let the mare graze while she walked a few yards to the north and sat down under a giant oak tree, its newly sprouted leaves rustling in the light breeze.

For a moment Luke just stared. Took in the sight of her, absorbed the calm that she projected. He'd taken more deep breaths in the past twenty-four hours than he had in the last five years. And each one of them smelled of lilacs and sage.

"Do you remember that time we made a fort with Jase in Rich Davis's wheat field?" Luke asked as he led his horse down to the creek. He tried to dismount without looking like a fool, but his foot got caught in the stirrup and he damned near fell flat on his face. If Kayleigh noticed, she didn't let it show. Thank fuck. "I thought the old man was going to have a heart attack when he saw what we'd done."

"I remember thinking that it was so beautiful. A sea of gold and so thick you couldn't see through it."

Luke could barely remember the field. But he remembered the way she'd looked that day, her cheeks flushed from running and her smile wide with laughter. He left his horse to graze next to hers and walked to the tree. She'd found a bed of spring clover to sit on.

She looked out across the field and tucked her legs beneath her. "I also remember the split lip Jase ended up with after you hit him."

Jase was his twin and there was no one on the planet he was closer to. But that day, Jase had pushed him too far. Teasing Luke about his crush. Of course, Luke had denied it. When Jase threatened to kiss Kayleigh though, Luke had lost his cool and popped his brother in the face. They'd been fifteen at the time and that was the moment that he realized Kayleigh meant more to him than a simple friendship. Lying in the circle of wheat that they'd laid flat, her hand resting in his, Luke knew that he was in love with her.

"I don't sleep much anymore." He sat down beside her, his back against the tree and angled away from her. He'd been nothing more than a cocky, horny asshole with her since the second he'd laid eyes on her. He missed the ease with which he could talk to her. The way he could lay his soul bare to her without the threat of judgment. Talking to Kayleigh was like going to confession: just by listening, she lifted a burden from his soul. "Not for the past year, anyway. I can't get my brain to quiet down. It just runs and runs until I feel like I'll fucking explode if I don't do something to make it stop. I tried pills but all they did was give me fucked-up dreams and make me feel like shit. I haven't written anything in as long. I feel like everyone wants a piece of me. Wants to tell lies about me. The guys told me that if I didn't get my shit together they were going to replace me." A bark of disdainful laughter erupted in his chest. "Can you believe that shit? I founded Riot 59 and they're going to kick me out?"

Kayleigh remained quiet beside him, but he didn't need her to talk. He knew she was listening and that's what mattered. It's what loosened the knot that had been lodged in his chest for months.

"My manager suggested one of those spas where celebrities go to get over exhaustion. Meditate. Get two or three massages a day. Live on apple and kale juice for a couple of weeks to 'cleanse my system.' I stayed at one place for a full forty-eight hours before I started to unravel. All the meditation did was give me more time alone with my thoughts. And I can't live on juice." One thing would never change and that was his love of a perfectly grilled T-bone. "Food fads and new age bullshit weren't going to center me."

Luke let the sound of the breeze in the grass fill his ears and his eyes drifted shut. It felt so damned good just to sit beside her. There wasn't a drug on the planet that could calm him the way she did.

"And you thought that after almost ten years, you could come home and everything would be the same?"

The words weren't much louder than the breeze, but he heard them. "Not at first." His hand found hers and Kayleigh let him twine his fingers with hers. "But then I saw you crossing the street . . ." How could he possibly explain to her that by simply seeing her, she'd set his careening world right? "No one knows me like you do. Nothing can calm my mind like you can. I missed you, Kayleigh. *Every fucking day.* It damned near killed me to walk away from you."

Her fingers twitched as though she wanted to pull away. "It seemed easy enough for you at the time."

The lyrics of the song he'd finished last night left his lips, not quite singing, not quite speaking: "Part of me stayed behind that day. The part that couldn't bear to let you get away. Through the noise and the chaos, you found me. And I was a fool not to see that everything I'd ever needed was right here in front of me."

When the last word faded into silence, Kayleigh pulled her hand away from his. "Don't do that do me, Luke. It's not fair to use your pretty words against me."

Maybe not. But since when was life fair? "Every song I've ever written has been about you. You're my muse."

A strangled sound escaped her throat and Luke glanced over to see Kayleigh push herself up from the ground and take off at a near-run. "Kayleigh, wait!" Luke used the tree for leverage and sprung to his feet to chase after her.

"That's the problem, Luke!" Kayleigh whipped around to face him, her eyes full of fire and her cheeks flushed. The breeze stirred the loose curls of her hair, sending strands across her face. God damn she was fucking breathtaking. "I've *been* waiting! For years! Waiting on fantasies. Memories. For something that was never going to happen. You didn't show up out of the blue because you'd left your heart behind. It sounds to me like what you needed was a little goddamned inspiration and you knew you'd find the drama to make it happen here."

"Kayleigh . . ." If only his reason for coming home was that simple. But was she right? Was everything he felt just an echo of some creative drive?

"I was trying to move on." Her voice broke with emotion. "And now I'm going to have to start from square one when you leave again."

Could she be more pathetic? Luke Blackwell was the prime example of why girls fell for musicians. His artistic soul, willingness to push boundaries, and fearlessness to lay himself bare was like catnip and wasn't she the horny feline to go after him?

"I don't want to hurt you, baby. I never wanted to hurt you."

"I'm not your baby." Who in the hell pined after their high school sweetheart for *eight years*? A drug she couldn't quit, the second she'd laid eyes on him he'd held her rapt. "In fact, I'm pretty sure you've called a fair share of women 'baby' since you left."

She wanted him to deny it even though she knew better. To profess his faithfulness. If only to give her a good reason to walk away from him once and for all. She'd seen proof of his many hookups plastered all over the media. A space of silence stretched between them and Luke's dark brows came down sharply over his eyes. "I fucked my way from one end of the country to the other and not a single one of those empty encounters could come close to even five seconds with you."

God damn his honesty. He'd never lied to her. Not once. And apparently he wasn't going to start now. Kayleigh hadn't exactly been abstinent, either, but a pang of jealousy speared her heart just the same. "You know, it would hurt less if you'd just blown into town for a quick fuck. At least I would've known where I stood with you. What you're doing now is a thousand times worse."

"What am I doing, Kayleigh?" God, the way he said her name. A low, seductive caress that she felt on every inch of her skin.

"I don't want to care about you, Luke. I can't."

"I can't *not* love you," Luke replied without guile. "No matter the distance or years between us. I won't ever love anyone else."

He was *killing* her. Plying her with emotion that she couldn't resist. Words that she'd been dying to hear for too long. Tears stung at her eyes but she refused to let them flow. "And because you won't let me go, *I'll* never be free to love anyone else."

Luke rushed at her, cupped her cheeks in his hands. He searched her expression, his own pinched with pain. The air sizzled between them and Kayleigh's chest tightened as Luke seized her mouth in a brutal kiss.

Passion had never been their problem. They'd had it in spades. There was a synchronicity between them that Kayleigh had never experienced with another man. His arms came around her, one gripping the hair at the base of her neck, the other curled around her waist. Their mouths slanted, tongues meeting in a wild tangle that caused Kayleigh's stomach to twist into delicious knots. Kissing Luke was like riding a roller coaster. Always had been. One exciting twist and turn after another.

He took a few stumbling steps back and she followed, their mouths joined in a frenzy of hungry kisses. The shade of the oak blocked out the reflection of sunlight behind her lids and a cool kiss of spring air caused a chill to ripple over her skin. Luke released his grip on her, fumbling with the buttons on her shirt. The last one released with a pop of thread as he shoved it down over her arms. Her bra went next, the clasp unhooked with a simple flick of Luke's hand.

Their lips parted as Luke stripped his T-shirt off and Kayleigh drank in the sight of his naked torso, covered with tattoos. She reached out, traced the outline of her name in swirling black ink, nested in a pattern of swirls on his left pec. "I doubt many of your other girlfriends were crazy about this tattoo."

His eyes smoldered. Embers in a dying fire. "I told you, Kayleigh, no one else matters. I've never given a shit about any other woman but you."

She should have felt bad for the trail of broken hearts Luke had no doubt left in his wake. But had she treated any of her past boyfriends any better? Hell, she'd broken up with Spencer the second Luke showed up in town. Mid-proposal! Luke had branded his body with her name. A piece of her that he always carried with him. She might not have had any ink of her own, but he'd branded her heart. And it was a mark that would never fade.

"Luke, touch me."

She needed the reassurance of his hands on her. She craved this man she'd tried to send away. Wanted him as badly as she feared the emotional damage he'd inflict on her. The breeze kissed her naked skin and her nipples puckered into tight, aching peaks. Luke took her in his arms and pulled her close. He eased her back, supporting her with his strength as he bent and covered one pearled nipple with his mouth.

"Oh god." He scraped his teeth over her sensitive flesh

and she gasped. His hands kneaded her shoulder and hip as he held her and with each pass of his tongue, Kayleigh became more mindless in her need of him. Her underwear dampened and her clit throbbed with each frenzied beat of her heart.

Luke's knees bent as he shifted and scooped Kayleigh up in his arms. He abandoned one breast for the other, licking, biting, sucking until she could no longer take a deep breath. Gently, he set her down on the bed of clover, his eyes devouring her as he unfastened her jeans and jerked them—along with her underwear—free of her body.

A moment of uncertainty sent a burst of adrenaline through Kayleigh's bloodstream. She wasn't an old hag by any means, but she wasn't that tight-bodied teenager anymore, either. Her hands crept up to her abdomen, a little rounder than it used to be and Luke reached down and seized her wrists.

"Don't." Luke's brow furrowed as he guided her arms high above her head. "Let me look at you." A sigh that ended on a groan left his parted lips. "You're so beautiful, baby."

"Compared to the barely-legal hard-bodies who throw themselves at you nightly?"

"Compared to every other woman on the face of the fucking earth," he replied in a rough, sensual tone that made her break out into delicious chills. "Christ, Kayleigh, just thinking about your pussy makes me hard. The way you taste, how tight you are, the way you squeezed my fingers when you came last night." Luke reached down and cupped her breasts, kneading her flesh in his large palms. "And don't even get me started on these," he groaned. "The most gorgeous tits I've ever seen." She arched into his touch and he bent to suck one taut nipple, and then the other into his mouth, releasing it with a wet pop. "Cotton-candy pink and oh, so sweet."

Another jolt of excitement shot through Kayleigh's body. The roller coaster climbing its way to the top of the track. A renewed rush of warmth spread between her thighs and she moaned, rubbing them together as though the simple act would release some of the tension that wound her body tight as a spring. Slick with her own arousal, all she managed to do was apply pleasant pressure to her sensitive clit. God, if he didn't take her soon, she'd explode! She sat up and worked loose the button and eased down the zipper of Luke's pants. "You'd think I was sixteen again with the way you've got me all wound up."

His finger slipped beneath her chin and he guided her face up to meet his. "Every time I look at you, I'm sixteen again."

Kayleigh's stomach lurched up into her throat as she prepared to speed down the steep incline of the virtual track, her heart thundering in her ears. Oh, boy. This was going to be a wild ride.

SEVEN

Luke shook with the need to take her. He shoved his jeans and underwear off, kicking them somewhere behind him. Kayleigh's gaze warmed and his cocked throbbed from the attention she bestowed on him. Hard to the point of pain, if he didn't find release soon, he'd go out of his fucking mind. He took his erection in his fist, just a stroke or two to ease his discomfort . . .

"Let me."

Kayleigh's voice was a low seductive purr that vibrated down his spine. A shudder passed over him as she replaced his hand with her own, stroking from the thick base to the top of his swollen head. She came up on her knees and they faced each other, naked under the shade and mottled light of the oak. Luke couldn't remember another moment in his entire life that was more perfect than this one. God, the way she stroked him . . . Her closed fist glided over him, squeezing just tight enough to cause him to swell in her palm. The pad of her thumb caressed up and over the head of his cock and Luke sucked in a breath. She repeated the motion, the sensitive skin there prickling with thousands of nerve endings that sparked to life all at once. So damned good. Her small, pale hand wrapped around his shaft and pumping with slow precision was a sight he could watch all day.

They'd both been a couple of kids the last time he saw her. Nervous, unsure, and inexperienced. The woman whose palm slid up and down the length of his cock was confident, a force of sex and nature. Skilled. Her eyes locked with his as he thrust into her hand. The intimacy between them, the soul-deep connection, shook Luke to his foundation. He'd always felt too deeply, his emotions too close to the surface. But Kayleigh never shied from the intensity of his personality and she didn't shy away from him now.

He took her face between his hands and crushed his mouth to hers, lips slanting, tongue lapping at hers in a desperate frenzy. There wasn't an inch of her that he didn't want to taste, touch, explore. His mouth wandered from her lips to her throat and Kayleigh's head lolled back, a cascade of auburn curls spilling over one shoulder. "I can breathe again," he whispered against her fragrant skin. "Think again." How could he possibly convey to her how being with her made him feel when there weren't any words worthy of the explanation? "You make me whole."

He'd lied to plenty of women in his life, but he'd never once lied to Kayleigh. Lying to her would be like lying to himself. And just like that day in the wheat field, Luke knew without a doubt that his heart would sit still in his chest if she wasn't there to make it beat.

The wind picked up in earnest, whipping her hair around them in a wild tangle. Luke latched his mouth over her throat and sucked. Nipped at her tender flesh. Goose bumps rose on Kayleigh's skin and he moved lower, tracing the swell of her breasts with the tip of his tongue.

"I want to taste you, Luke."

The desperate plea in her ragged voice sent him over the edge of his control. Wanton and sweet all at once. "Oh, hell yes." He rocked his hips against her, thrusting into her hand. "I want your mouth on my cock."

Luke leaned back on his heels, bracing his arms behind him on the ground. His erection stood out proud and thick from his thrust hips and Kayleigh continued to stroke him, the glide of her hands like silk as she lowered her mouth to the engorged crown. Her fingers wrapped tightly around the thick base as her tongue flicked out. "Fuck," Luke ground out on a sharp exhale. The sensation rippled down his shaft and tightened his sac. "That's so good, baby."

She took him deeper, enveloping his shaft in the wet heat of her mouth. Luke gave a shallow thrust of his hips and was answered with a low moan from Kayleigh that vibrated down the length of his cock. He continued to thrust, urging her to take him deeper, meeting every plunge of her mouth. She sucked hard, swirling her tongue over the sensitive head before gliding down his shaft. Luke panted through the intense pleasure. "Mmm. Just like that, baby. Feels so fucking good."

She cupped his balls in her free hand, massaging the delicate flesh. A low, drawn-out moan escaped from between his teeth as she tugged gently, causing a surge of sensation to rocket through him. "You're driving me crazy." It wouldn't take much to make him go off. Just a few deep pulls of her mouth. "Kayleigh." Her name buzzed around in his head, rushed from his lips in a desperate moan. "Kayleigh."

His sac drew up tight as she continued to fondle him and he sunk back on his heels. She released him with a wet pop that damned near sent him over the edge but he was unwilling to finish before she had her pleasure as well. He snatched her up by the waist and repositioned her so she lay on her back. Her legs fell open, revealing the swollen pink lips of her sex, glistening with arousal that coated her thighs.

"Jesus fucking Christ," Luke said on a shuddering breath. He settled himself between her thighs and took his erection in his hand, guiding it to her opening.

"Promise me, Luke." She put a staying hand on his left pec where her name was inked permanently into his skin. "That you haven't been with anyone else like this. Otherwise . . ."

"I promise. I've never been like this with anyone but you." Most of Luke's many hookups had been one-nighters. Anonymous fucks that meant nothing to him. And he never mixed alcohol and sex because it opened the door for mistakes he couldn't afford to make. Kayleigh was the only woman he'd ever made love to. And the only one he'd been irresponsible enough not to wear protection with.

He hadn't wanted anything to separate their bodies then, and he didn't want anything to separate them now.

Kayleigh reached for him, her eyes hooded. Luke slid the head of his cock through her wet folds and a shiver raced down his spine. She bucked from the contact and a quiet whimper escaped her. Her mouth parted and Luke dragged his shaft over her clit once again, his eyes glued to her face as he gauged her response.

She was perfection.

"Luke." She kept her eyes on his as he continued to tease her. "Ooooh. God. That feels *so* good."

Yeah it did. But he wanted more than just a simple tease. He needed *all* of her. With gentle care he eased himself in, his jaw welded shut as he resisted the urge to pound into her. Impatience had nothing on Luke and he shook with restraint, sliding into her tight slick heat, a groan lodged in his throat. Arms braced on either side of her, he stared down at the woman he'd loved for most of his life.

"I lo—"

"Don't say it, Luke." Instead of letting him tell her how he felt, Kayleigh rose up and seized his mouth in a kiss. His arms bent at the elbows as he lowered his weight on her, wrapping her tight in his embrace as he thrust home.

"Fuck." The word grated in his throat as he pulled out to the tip before driving back in. "Baby, you're so tight. So fucking wet." She didn't want to hear his tender words, and so he held them back until his chest burned from the backup.

He fucked her slowly, enjoying the slide of his flesh on hers, the way her pussy held him tight. Kayleigh's nails bit into his back and she locked her legs around his waist, her heels digging into his ass. "Harder, Luke. Faster."

Lust battled with anger as she took one more step at erecting an emotional wall between them. Did she want an emotionless fuck from him? Hard and fast. No loving words spoken softly between them, no chance of being hurt.

Fine. If that's what she wanted, that's what he'd give her. "You want to be fucked hard? Tell me, Kayleigh."

"Yes." She dug her nails in deeper, the exquisite bite of pain causing his sac to tighten. "Do it."

He hitched her hips up higher, taking her ass in his palms. His first forceful thrust coaxed a low moan of pleasure from Kayleigh's throat. On the second, she cried out as her back bowed off the ground. She squeezed her eyes shut, but Luke refused to let her block him out completely. He wound the length of her hair in his fist and gave a little tug at the base of her neck. "Look at me, Kayleigh."

She refused. Luke pulled out to his engorged head and fucked into her harder. Her fingers curled around his shoulders and she bit down on her bottom lip to quiet the sound of her pleasure. "Look at me." Another quick, deep thrust and she gasped. "Look at me."

Luke pulled out and buried his cock as deep as it would go. Kayleigh's eyes fluttered open as though she fought against her own body for control. He lowered his mouth to hers in a desperate, frenzied kiss as he continued to fuck her. The taste of her mouth intoxicated him. Her scent sent his head to spinning. Harder and faster, his ass clenched on each drive home. When he pulled away, her eyes were wide and smoldering with desire. Her lips swollen from his kisses and her cheeks flushed.

"Don't stop, Luke," she said through panting breaths. "God, don't stop."

The moments of intimacy they'd shared scared the shit out of Kayleigh and she needed to put distance between them now before she irrevocably lost her heart to Luke Blackwell once and for all.

His heartfelt words, unabashed honesty, and untamed passion hadn't changed, nor had Kayleigh's own recklessness when it came to him. She shouldn't have been so cavalier in regards to sex with him. She was on the pill, but that was no excuse for being careless. Never once since the day she'd met him had she doubted his honesty, though. He'd never lie to her and she'd been so caught up in the moment. Craved that skin-to-skin closeness that they'd once shared. There was little about Luke that was different from the boy who'd been her first love. Hell, her *only* love. She couldn't deal with the emotions he was reawakening in her. So instead of letting him make love to her the way he'd wanted, Kayleigh opted to be treated like a stranger. One of his random hookups.

How could something that felt so damned good, hurt her so badly?

Luke's firm grip on her was heaven. The heat in his gaze caused her to break out in a sweat that cooled her skin when it met the crisp spring air. His breath sawing in and out of his chest with every hard thrust of his hips sent a riot of butterflies swirling in her stomach. A creature created with the sole purpose of pleasuring a woman, it would be a triumph to belong to a man like Luke. To own him, heart and soul.

Stop.

Kayleigh forced her mind to still and instead shifted her focus to her body. His gaze didn't break with hers and she allowed herself to drift. To lose herself to sensation and every detail of Luke's face. He filled her completely, their bodies fitting together as though they were made to be joined. Two pieces of a puzzle locked together to complete the picture.

Her back arched as he pulled out and slid the length of his shaft against her clit. She sucked in a gasp at the intense pleasure and cried out when he once again impaled her on the length of his cock. He bared his teeth with each roll of his hips, a feral expression that squared his jaw and sharpened the angles of his face.

"Is this what you want, Kayleigh?" His body slapped against hers with the force of his thrust and she cried out. "Tell me."

"Yes!" She couldn't stop the word from leaving her lips in a desperate shout. "Fuck me." She couldn't love him. Couldn't let him love her. They'd destroy each other if either one of them made a single sacrifice for the other.

It was better this way. They could enjoy each other's bodies, and let that be enough. He increased his pace, giving her exactly what she wanted. His expression fierce, full of fire and passion, Kayleigh focused on his face and her own pleasure building and coiling low in her core.

So close. His face blurred out of focus as Kayleigh looked up at the light filtering through the leaves, bathing him in a halo of gold. It set fire to his tawny locks, a little too long and shaggy, damp with sweat. She drew a deep breath into her lungs and held it there, her jaw clamped down as the pleasure mounted to an almost unbearable level. Her clit ached and her pussy clenched around him, drawing him even deeper inside of her. A low throb in her core grew to thundering intensity and when she came it shattered her completely.

"Luke!" His name echoed on a desperate shout. She cleaved to him, rising up from the ground as he pounded unmercifully into her. Wave after powerful wave of sensation crested over her and her throat became raw, her voice ragged from her cries.

His mouth covered hers and he kissed her as hard as he was fucking her, swallowing every whimper of sound. Her body jolted from the force of his thrusts and his body went rigid above hers, every inch of him sculpted marble. His grip on the back of her neck tightened and his steady rhythm broke.

His mouth left hers and came to rest at her ear. "Oh, god, Kayleigh." The emotion in his voice shattered her again, this time breaking her heart into myriad shards that pierced her soul. He pulled out with a quick jerk of his hips and jet after jet of delicious warmth striped her stomach as he came. A low moan vibrated in his chest and Kayleigh shuddered as the remnants of her own orgasm rippled through her, waves on a pond that had yet to subside.

Before he left again, Kayleigh knew that Luke would destroy her. And the scary part of that realization was that she was going to let him.

For long moments, Luke lay still, cradling Kayleigh in his arms, his face buried in the crook of her neck. His breath warmed her skin and she shivered when the breeze picked up again, so cool in contrast to Luke's heat.

"When I left here, I thought I had nothing," he murmured against her skin. "And now that I have everything,

I've realized that the only thing I ever needed was right here all along."

Tears sprang to Kayleigh's eyes, but she held them at bay. Why couldn't he have had this epiphany eight years ago? There was no use lamenting their shitty timing, though. All that mattered was this moment. The chance to be with him one more time before he came to his senses and left her behind again.

"We should get back to the house. It looks like a storm might be moving in." She couldn't acknowledge his words. Not when the pain of losing him all over again would crush her so completely.

Luke sighed into her hair, laid his lips to her temple in the gentlest of kisses. "All right. I'll take you back."

EIGHT

Luke couldn't remember a time in the past eight years that he'd been so at peace. He was probably rocking a goofy, pussy perma-grin, but he didn't give a single shit. Nothing else mattered with Kayleigh in his arms. The world could burn around them and he wouldn't even notice.

They'd tied Tallulah to Lucifer's saddle and Kayleigh rode in front of Luke, her back molded to his chest. The horse knew his way back to the stable and Luke let the reins out loose. Lucifer didn't seem any more anxious than Luke to go home. He meandered through the pastures at an easy gait as though sensing Luke's need for just a few more minutes with her. He didn't want to face the reality of the situation. No matter how much he wanted to, Luke knew he couldn't stay there. The life and problems he'd left behind in L.A. hadn't been put to bed quite yet.

Fucking hell, he was a bastard. And of course, Kayleigh knew it. Why else had she erected an emotional wall between them? But the thought of just turning his back on her and leaving her a second time tied his stomach into an unyielding knot. There was so much more he wanted to do with his career and he couldn't do it in their sleepy Texas suburb. He wanted a life and successes apart from Ryder and the family's fortune. He had a hell of a lot more to prove. There were plenty of schools in California. Why couldn't she come with him? Get a job at some swanky private school or a local public elementary. Hell, she wouldn't even have to work at all if she didn't want to. He had more money than he knew what to do with. She could come on tour with the band, see the world. They could be together all the time. As far as he could tell nothing was keeping her in Texas. Her parents weren't there and she didn't have any brothers or sisters to worry about. Why the hell couldn't she leave with him?

Because she doesn't want the sort of life you'd give her, dipshit.

Even as kids it had been a bone of contention between them. The only one, in fact. He wanted more than to work on the family's ranch and she craved familiarity. They were the only thing each other needed and at the same time, not enough. But now that he'd come home to her, Luke didn't think he could live without her. No, he *refused* to live without her.

"Do you remember the time you tried to get Jase to trade places with you so you wouldn't have to take the history final?"

Luke smiled at the memory. Their shared history was comforting. Why couldn't that familiarity be enough to anchor Kayleigh and keep her by his side? "It totally would have worked if Mrs. Baker hadn't noticed that we'd forgotten to trade shirts."

Kayleigh laughed, the sweetest music to his ears. "It totally would not have. You sucked at history. She would have been on to your switch after she graded the paper."

"True."

"Do you like your job?" Maybe he could use this time

to lay the groundwork, convince her that life outside of Texas might be a good thing. "Does hanging out with rug rats all day do it for you?"

She chuckled. "Teaching kindergarten doesn't make my eyes roll back in my head if that's what you mean. But I like it. The kids are great and if I can ever get my student loans paid off, I might get to enjoy my summers for once."

"How much more do you have left to pay?"

"More than I'd like," she admitted. "But those are the breaks. Tutoring over the summer pays pretty well, though I should get a bonus for dealing with hormonal middle-schoolers."

"God, I hated middle school." He'd dealt with his fair share of assholes in his teen years. Smug sons of bitches who had nothing better to do than tease him and Jase for being poor.

"I know." Kayleigh placed a gentle hand over his. "Kids can be such assholes."

"The only good thing about it was you. High school, too. I never would've gotten through it without you."

Two peas in pod. That's what Luke's mom had called them. The best of friends and later, so much more. "Hey, remember the time we tipped the hay bales off the trailer and Ryder had to pick them all up by himself? He was so mad I thought his head was going to explode."

On and on it went for the entire ride back to the ranch. One memory relived after another. It was a welcome distraction, one that kept Luke's mind off the future and what would happen when it was time to return to the real world.

"Luke, what do you want from life?" The question came out of the blue as they made their way to the stables. Her voice was unsure and her body stiffened against his.

"I want to be happy with who I am and what I've done. I want to know that I didn't cut any corners and did my best no matter what. I want my success to be measured by my talent and drive and not by who I know or how much money I have. And I want to share my life with someone I love."

"Oh," she said, barely audible over the bluster of wind. "What do you want?"

"I don't know," she said with a rueful laugh. "Pathetic, right? I have no freaking idea what I want out of life. I'm sort of jealous that it's all so clear for you. But then, it always was. You knew what you wanted, even as a kid, and you weren't afraid to go after it."

"You're talking like you're old and gray, Kayleigh." He'd never known her to be so introspective. That was usually his hang-up. "You're not even thirty. You don't have to have all of the answers now, you know. You can go after what you want—live the life you want—at any time. You're in control of your life, baby. No one else."

"I'm supposed to be the rational voice of reason and you're supposed to be the dreamer, remember? Not the other way around."

It was true that she'd always been the calm that balanced him out, but why did it have to be that way? If, in the course of their relationship, he'd made her feel that she had no choice but to be the reason to his chaos, then he'd hurt her far more than he realized. And the thought damned near stopped his heart.

Luke reached up and smoothed her hair behind her ear, letting the silky strands pass through his fingers. "You only get one life, Kayleigh. Live it right so you don't end up with regrets later. Don't apologize for it, and don't feel like you owe anyone anything. Ever. Okay?"

He choked up on the reins, bringing Lucifer to a stop inside of Ryder's posh stable. They sat still for a moment and Luke wrapped one arm around Kayleigh's waist, hugging her tight against his chest.

"I've missed you, Luke," she said.

He helped her down from the saddle but held onto her hand. When her eyes came up to meet his he replied, "I've missed you, too, honey."

If she could, Kayleigh would've lived today over and over again in a continuous loop. Despite the sadness she felt, she wouldn't trade today with Luke for anything in the world.

Every day could be like this. All you have to do is ask him to stay.

No matter how badly she wanted to, Kayleigh knew she'd ruin him if she asked him to stay just as surely as she would have suffocated if she'd left with him all those years ago. His words of assurance resonated with her, though. Maybe it wasn't too late to lead the life she wanted. She simply had to be brave enough to go after it. The question was: What did she want?

Luke?

She couldn't remember a time that she hadn't wanted him. For a long time she couldn't imagine a future without him in it. A long-distance relationship never would have worked and it wouldn't now. Neither of them would be able to cope with the strain of being apart. There was no halfway for them. It had to be all or nothing.

"How was the ride?"

Kayleigh turned with a start at the sound of Ryder's voice. His knowing smile did little for her already frazzled nerves but she met him look for look, daring the older Blackwell to lend a voice to his suspicious expression. "It was nice." She flashed him a pleasant smile as she hauled the tack from Tallulah's back and stowed it. "The creek is high this year."

"Uh-huh." Ryder folded his arms over his wide chest and smiled.

"Luke's putting Lucifer away." She wished he'd quit looking at her with that know-it-all grin. "Nice name, by the way."

"I gave him to Luke as a Christmas present a few years back, hoping it might get him to come home for a week or two. Guess what I should have given him was a kindergarten teacher."

Heat rose to Kayleigh's cheeks and she averted her gaze.

"Ryder, about what I said earlier, I—"

"Are you harassing this lovely lady?" Luke emerged from the stall at the far end of the stable, dusting his hands off on his jeans. "Leave her alone and go find your own woman to pester."

"Lara's making dinner reservations in the city. She wants to know if she should make it for four."

"Oh. No." Any more time with the Blackwell clan and she'd be helpless to make a rational decision. She needed to decompress, weed through what she was feeling. "You all go ahead. I think I'm going to—"

"Kayleigh and I already have plans for tonight," Luke interrupted. "You two have fun."

Crap. Once again, he'd steamrolled her, refusing to give her an out.

"Back at ya, brother." Ryder winked at Kayleigh before turning to leave. "You two have a good time tonight."

As Luke walked by and shut the door on Tallulah's stall, he said, "You should know better than to think I'd let you get away that easily. You're mine tonight. Don't even think about trying to weasel your way out of it, either."

Mine.

The word settled as a deep ache in her chest. Kayleigh rubbed at her sternum and gave him a weak smile. "I wouldn't think of arguing with *the* Lucifer Blackwell. You always get your way."

"Damn straight." He crossed the space between them and chucked her under the chin. "And you'd best get used to it. Because I won't be happy until I get *everything* I want."

That's what she was afraid of.

NINE

You'd think he was going to the prom or some shit with the way he'd preened before leaving Ryder's house. Hell, he hadn't taken this much care with his appearance when he went to the Grammy's last year. Luke wanted tonight to be perfect, though.

Kayleigh could put up all the walls she wanted, but he wasn't stepping a foot out of town until she admitted that they belonged together. Nothing was going to stop him from making her his, once and for all. He wanted her, he was going to keep her, and that's all there was to it. He'd gone too goddamned long without her and he wasn't wasting another hour, let alone another day. Nothing she could do would change his mind or scare him away. He knew her better than anyone. Probably better than she knew herself. There would *never* be another woman for him.

When he pulled up to her house, his heart began to race and the damned thing slammed against his rib cage like a bass drum. All he could think about was this afternoon in the pasture and how damned good it felt to be with her again.

Kayleigh stepped out of the house before he could cut the engine and Luke's breath stalled in his chest. The woman was raw sensuality in a pair of heels. To-die-for gorgeous. She'd talked about herself as though she were already a withered old hag. *So* not the case. As she strolled down the front steps, a smile playing on her full mouth, she put all of L.A.'s beauties to shame.

Her short, billowy skirt showed off her shapely legs and the light cotton fabric of her V-neck top showed off the tantalizing swell of her breasts. He swallowed hard as he thought about teasing the hardened peaks with a flick of his tongue. A long necklace hung between them, something with a flirty silver tassel that swung with every step she took. A wide leather cuff graced her left wrist and she'd pulled her hair up into a ponytail, letting her thick curls trail down the center of her back.

Fuuuuck.

Focusing on a civilized meal was going to be nearly impossible when all he could think about was hiking up that skirt and burying his face between her thighs. He hopped out of the rental and rounded the front end just as she hit the driveway.

"Gonna open my door for me, Mr. Blackwell?" He could practically taste the sweetness of her tone on his tongue. "Aren't you a gentleman?"

"Hardly." He flashed her a wicked grin as he pulled open the door. When she stepped past him, he slid his palm around her waist and let it trail down her thigh and around to the curve of her ass. He put his mouth close to her ear and whispered, "I was just looking for an excuse to get my hands on you."

"Talented *and* resourceful." She flashed a saucy grin and climbed up into the Escalade giving him a tantalizing view of the very ass he'd just been admiring. "I might be in over my head with you."

"Baby, you have no idea."

Luke shut the door. Walking the few feet to his side of the truck was already posing a problem, considering he was currently sporting a hard-on the size of the Florida panhandle. Come to think of it, any brain function whatsoever was going to be next to impossible thanks to his blood supply being rerouted to his dick.

He climbed up into the driver's seat and readjusted several times until he found a position that was marginally comfortable. Kayleigh cocked a brow, her lips pursed. "Having a little trouble?"

"Nothing I can't handle."

Her answering smile knotted his stomach. Sweet Jesus, she was perfect.

As they drove to Angus—a newer steakhouse Ryder had suggested—in companionable silence, Luke marveled that even though things had changed since he'd left, they'd also stayed the same. The familiarity—or the rut as he'd thought of it—that Kayleigh wanted to live in didn't seem quite as distasteful now. Was it a sign that he was maturing that trading in night after night of heart-pounding excitement on the stage for a quiet life of routine didn't seem so bad?

"I'm not going to lie, I'm pretty excited to eat here," Kayleigh remarked. She looked over at him, her eyes sparking with heat. "They've only been open for a couple of months."

On the outside, Angus looked swanky enough. The sort of place couples went to celebrate anniversaries or engagements. Not quite the sort of high-end dining he'd been used to in L.A. and New York, but still, nice. "You mean Super Spencer didn't wine and dine you here?"

Her expression fell and Luke wished he could take back the words. He'd tried not to think about the fact that Kayleigh had been seeing someone prior to his reappearance.

"He said that eating out was a waste of money," she remarked in a quiet tone. "We usually just ate at my place."

Real progressive making the little lady sweat over a hot stove after a long day at work. What a douche. Luke hopped out of the Escalade and opened her door for her. He offered his hand and she took it, sliding down from the seat in a way that hiked her skirt up dangerously close to her hip. He swallowed down the lust that clouded his brain and focused on pretending he was housebroken. "Come on," he said. "Let's get some eats."

As the hostess led them to their table, Luke endured the usual commotion that accompanied a public outing. Whispers. Curious stares. Cell phones pointed at him as people snapped off pics that would inevitably end up on Facebook or Instagram. Kayleigh stiffened beside him, her shoulders hunching in and gaze directed at the floor. Her discomfort angered him, but there wasn't much he could do about it. This was his life. Maybe it was better that she see it on a smaller scale now before she experienced the batshit craziness of L.A.

If Luke got this much attention at a local restaurant far from the city, she could only imagine the sort of commotion he caused when he went out in L.A. A nervous tremor skittered up Kayleigh's spine. How could she possibly think of a life with Luke beyond the little bubble she lived in here? Sure, when contained in this microcosm of a community, Luke had eyes for her and only her. But what would happen if she allowed him to take her away from here? How long would it be before an eager fan showed up on his bus, sans panties and up for anything?

"I'll be right back." Kayleigh slid her chair out from the table. Adrenaline buzzed through her system, making her a little light-headed and her breath sped in her chest. Passing out at the table: not cool.

"What's the matter?" Luke's brow furrowed and he leaned across the table. "Talk to me, Kayleigh."

Damn him for being so in tune with her emotions. "Nothing." She tried to laugh it off but the sound was more like a choke. "I just have to use the restroom." He frowned at her answering smile as she deposited her napkin on the table and took off in the wrong direction. Crap. "Oops," she said as she turned back past their table. "Wrong way."

By the time she made it to the bathroom, Kayleigh thought she might throw up. She didn't suffer from anxiety but what she was experiencing right now was a full-blown panic attack. What in the hell was *wrong* with her?

She turned the faucet on to cold and bent over the sink. The door creaked behind her and Kayleigh looked up at the mirror to see Luke standing just behind her in the reflection. "Jesus, Luke." Her hand came down on the lever, shutting off the water. "This is the ladies' room!"

He didn't seem fazed. "What's wrong, Kayleigh? And don't tell me 'nothing' because I know better."

"Luke, I . . ." Why was it so hard to be up-front with him? In all of the years she'd known him, he'd never pulled any punches. Was always 100 percent honest with her. "I don't know if I can do this."

"Dinner?" The smile he gave her didn't reach his eyes. "If that's the case we'll order to-go and take it back to Ryder's house. I've been dying to see what you're wearing under that skirt."

Kayleigh let out a sigh that did nothing to loosen the knot that lodged in her chest. "When we're alone together . . . we're *us*. You know?" She jerked her head toward the door. "I don't know if we can still be us out there."

Luke backed up to the door and turned the lock.

"Luke! You can't do that." He smiled at her scandalized whisper and she rolled her eyes. "What if someone has to use the bathroom?"

"They can wait." He moved toward her like a lion stalking a gazelle, all sinewy grace and silent power.

"We can't just abandon our table." His eyes pinned her in place, blazing with a heat that left her breathless. "Our waiter will be back to take our order any time."

Luke hiked his shoulder in an unconcerned shrug. "That," he mimicked her head jerk toward the world outside, "doesn't mean shit to me."

Kayleigh backed away, the natural state of prey in the presence of a predator and stopped when the counter met her lower back. He continued to advance on her until they were chest to chest, his long, muscular arms braced on either side of her.

"Do I like the attention that comes with being a celebrity? Yes. I'm an entertainer, Kayleigh. It's what I do, it's not who I am. Those people don't know a fucking thing about me apart from the words I'm singing and the notes I'm playing. You treating that attention like it's some sort of relationship is as bad as them treating my private life like it's theirs to invade."

She'd never thought about it that way. To her, Luke's life in the spotlight made her think that there was no division between Public Luke and Private Luke. And here she was, having a stupid panic attack over that attention as though she were fighting the world for a piece of him when she had more of him than anyone else ever had.

"I don't want to share you." Admitting her selfishness caused a flush of shame to heat her cheeks. "And I don't want to come second."

Luke's gaze burned through her, the intensity sparking a low thrum in her core. He seized her by the waist and hoisted her up on the counter, spreading her legs wide as he took a step away from her. "I've been gone for eight years, Kayleigh." His palms passed up her inner thighs and her breath hitched. "And there wasn't a day of that time that you weren't the first thing I thought about every morning and the last thing on my mind before I went to sleep."

Oh.

His hands found her underwear and he gripped either side, jerking them down over her hips. She rose up, letting her hands brace her as he whisked them from her thighs and stuffed them in the pocket of his jeans.

Looked like she wasn't getting those back anytime soon . . .

Luke didn't look away as he feathered the pad of his thumb over her already swollen and throbbing clit. Kayleigh shuddered as pleasure rippled through her as a whimper escaped her lips. His nostrils flared and he grabbed her by the waist again, this time lifting her as though she weighed nothing until she had no choice but to stand on the counter.

"Luke," she said with a nervous laugh, "What are you do—*Oh. Oh, wow.*"

As he fisted her skirt and lifted the hem well above her waist, Luke buried his face between her thighs. The heat of his tongue plunged between her labia and Kayleigh bit down on her cheek to keep from crying out. Her hips thrust out as her shoulder blades came to rest on the mirror behind her. She spread her legs wider and Luke gripped onto the backs of her thighs to steady her, his fingertips digging deliciously into her flesh.

He lapped at her hungrily, his tongue swirling over the sensitive bundle of nerves. Kayleigh's jaw hung slack, her breath coming in desperate pants as her fingers dove into the soft, tangled locks of his hair. "Luke. Don't stop."

His mouth on her felt so good, Kayleigh didn't give a crap about where they were or who might be standing on the other side of the locked door. Luke was her entire universe, there was nothing—and no one else. His tongue swirled over her clit, flicking out before he took her in his mouth and sucked. Her thighs trembled and her stomach muscles went taut.

Only Luke could evoke such raw, unabashed passion in her. She reached down and grabbed one of his hands, guiding it up her shirt. He jerked down the cup of her bra and rolled the hardened peak of her nipple between his thumb and finger. The roughened calluses from years of strumming only heightened her pleasure. A low moan vibrated in her throat as she rolled her hips in time with each pass of his tongue.

His hand left her breast and Kayleigh let out a disappointed whimper only to gasp as he gripped her ass, his fingers venturing downward through the crease. He dipped his fingers into her pussy, spreading her slick arousal upward as he ventured back up between her cheeks and the tight ring of nerves that clenched with his questing touch.

"Luke." It was a breathy gasp. No one had touched her there before, not even him. But the sensation was amazing as he continued to tease her there, lapping at her pussy while he increased the pressure on her ass. "Don't stop what you're doing." He was driving her insane with lust, his finger venturing past the tight ring just enough to elicit a low moan of pleasure. Kayleigh's breath caught somewhere between her lungs and throat as her muscles contracted and her body coiled in on itself. "You're going to make me come."

Luke pulled away and Kayleigh continued to thrust her hips at empty air. She was wound tight and if she didn't find release soon, she'd lose her damned mind. He snatched her down from the counter and set her on her feet. His mouth found hers in a ravenous kiss and the taste of her on his lips only drove her further past reason. He spun her quickly around and bent her over the counter.

"I've gotta fuck you, baby. I don't want you to come until I'm inside of you."

She was mindless. Wanton. Past the point of rational thought. She'd scream her pleasure right here for everyone in the restaurant to hear if that's what Luke wanted her to do. Anything as long as he gave her what she needed.

He kept one hand tightly wound around her waist while the other jerked at the button of his jeans. The hiss of his zipper echoed off the tile walls and Kayleigh looked up to find him watching her in the reflection of the mirror.

"Oh god, Luke. Hurry up and fuck me."

TEN

Luke was abso-fucking-lutely mindless in his need to take her, his cock throbbing and tight and his balls aching. Kayleigh worried about having to share him with complete strangers? He was going to make her believe once and for all that no one else mattered to him but her. He shoved his jeans down around his hips and grabbed his cock, so sensitive that he shuddered from the contact.

He drove home in a forceful jerk of his hips that coaxed a moan from Kayleigh, resounding through the small bathroom and shivering down his spine. Her pussy squeezed him like a fist and he fucked her hard, steadying her around the waist while his other hand came around to hold her gently by the throat. Her eyes locked with his in the mirror and the rush of excitement surging through his bloodstream was gasoline on a raging fire, fueling his lust. He couldn't take her deep enough. Hard enough. Desperation welled up inside of him and intensified with every drive of his hips. Without her, he'd never be whole, never feel a sense of calm again. If they parted ways this time, it would kill him as surely as a bullet to the head.

"Tell me you want me."

Kayleigh's lips parted, her hands splayed out on the smooth surface of the countertop. On the heels of her sharp intake of breath, she exhaled the words, "I want you, Luke."

He pounded unmercifully into her and Kayleigh brought her balled fist to her mouth, biting down to muffle her passionate cries. The sight of it spurred Luke on and he drove his cock as deep as it would go into her slick heat. "Tell me you need me."

"Yes," she gasped. "I need you."

Harder. Faster. His jaw clamped down. He fucked her with mindless abandon, the only gentleness his delicate grip on her throat. Luke's balls tightened and his shaft swelled inside of her, the pressure building to an unbearable level. His eyes held hers in the mirror, wide and wild. "Tell me you love me, Kayleigh. Me and no one else."

Her pussy constricted around his shaft and she collapsed on her arms as the orgasm took her. Pulse after powerful pulse drew his cock deep inside of her and Luke came in a violent spasm, rushing on him too fast for him to have the good sense to pull out.

"I love you, Luke," Kayleigh rasped as she came. "I've always loved you."

Another powerful wave stole over him, shaking Luke to his foundation. He gulped in lungfuls of breath as he buried his face in her neck to muffle the sound of his own victorious shout.

"I love you, baby," he murmured in her ear. He gave shallow, disjointed thrusts as his cock twitched inside of her. He'd never come so hard, the sensations so intense. "And I'm never letting you go."

The moment some semblance of clarity returned to him, Luke regretted taking her like this, like some random hookup after a show in a public restroom. Jesus fucking

Christ, what had he been thinking? She deserved so much more than this. Being with Kayleigh was sort of like being an addict, though. His need for her overrode common sense, self-preservation, his own well-being. Consequences be damned.

"Don't move. Let me clean you up." He tended to her as best he could, and then himself, making them both presentable before they returned to their table. He kissed her neck, the small of her back as he pulled down her shirt, and the mouth-watering swell of her ass as he yanked her skirt back into place.

"What about my underwear?"

The smile in her voice put him at ease. "Sorry, but those are mine. The spoils of war."

"You just want to think about me sitting across from you at dinner with nothing on under my skirt."

Her husky tone stirred his cock. *Down, boy.* There'd be time for an encore later. Right now, he needed to salvage this evening and try to restrain himself long enough to get her fed. "True. And so you know, I'm planning to get dessert to go. Something with hot fudge. I'm going to lick it off you later."

Kayleigh stood up straight and her gaze warmed as it caught his in the mirror. She pulled the elastic band from her hair and smoothed out her ponytail. "That sounds like a great end to a perfect day."

Perfect.

Luke returned to the table first, giving Kayleigh a quick peck on the cheek before ducking out. Only Luke Blackwell could get her to do something as brazen and reckless as fucking in a restaurant bathroom. But oh, god, it was worth every bit of the embarrassment she'd feel as she took the walk of shame back into the dining area. Which . . . surprisingly, wasn't very embarrassing at all.

Was it a sign of how completely under his spell she was that she didn't give a damn what anyone thought about their long absence from their table?

As though he'd sensed her presence, Luke turned in his seat. His smile was more brilliant than the sun, displaying so much tender emotion that Kayleigh's heart stuttered in her chest. "What?" she asked with a grin as she sat down. Luke's gaze smoldered, raking over her in a way that made her feel devoured.

"You look so good, I want to bend you over this table."

Kayleigh giggled and tapped the white tablecloth. "This table?"

"Right here. Right now."

She slipped off her shoe and rested her foot in Luke's lap, stroking the length of his erection that was still hard enough to press tight against the denim. He sunk low into his seat in order to spread his legs wider and slung an arm casually over the chair. "Maybe not on top of the table . . ." she said with a sly smile. "But I can think of a few things I can do *under* it."

Their waiter stepped up to them and cleared his throat. Without even giving him an opportunity to speak, Luke said, "Two of whatever the special is tonight and two molten lava cakes. With a side of hot fudge. To go. And a two-hundred-dollar tip if you can get the chef to put a rush on it."

Kayleigh couldn't help her seductive laugh as the waiter beelined it for the kitchen. "Impatient, Mr. Blackwell?"

"Baby, I wasn't kidding when I said I'd take you right here and now on top of this table."

So. Freaking. *Hot*.

Luke's expression fell, his lips forming a thin, hard line. His eyes sparked with angry fire and Kayleigh turned around to see what had soured his mood so quickly. Not what. Who.

Spencer.

The past two days had been like a dream. A roller coaster of emotions and a visit to her past that had virtually erased the rest of the world. Despite the impetuousness of his decision to propose to her even though they'd been seeing each other for only a couple of months, Kayleigh had failed to acknowledge how Spencer might be feeling amidst all of this. And seeing her out with Luke—his perceived reason for their breakup—was no doubt going to be like a shot of bourbon on an open wound.

"It's not taking you long to make the rounds, Blackwell," Spencer said with a sneer. "I guess it doesn't matter to you that you're going to leave her in hundreds of shattered pieces when you blow out of here again."

Kayleigh cringed. Her history with Luke was well-known, as was the way she'd fallen apart the first time he'd left her. And though she didn't always consider herself a pillar of strength, she was better than what Spencer had just reduced her to. As though she'd simply quit living without Luke in her life.

"Don't worry about Kayleigh," Luke drawled. His cocky smile elicited a hateful glare from Spencer. "She's going to be *well* taken care of."

The innuendo didn't help to cool Spencer down. "You might think you're hot shit, Blackwell, but I know better."

Kayleigh's stomach clenched. The conversation was heading down a dangerous road. One that was sure to ignite Luke's ire. A superior smirk accented Spencer's lips. He slapped a glossy page that had been ripped from a magazine down in front of Kayleigh and leaned over her, the pad of his index finger jamming down on the headline: Lucifer Blackwell, Deadbeat Baby-Daddy? Below the headline read: *Riot 59 front man flees to avoid being slapped with a paternity suit.*

The words blurred out of focus and Kayleigh swallowed

down the lump that rose in her throat. Her jaw hung slack as her eyes met Luke's. His brows came down sharply over his eyes. "What?"

"Luke . . ." She could barely push the words past her lips. Didn't want to believe the picture of Luke shying away from cameras on one side and on the other, an overdone hottie smiling at the camera with smug satisfaction. The thin paper vibrated in her shaking hand as she handed it to him across the table. "Is this true?"

Luke snatched the article from her hand and glanced down at it before bringing his gaze back to hers. His mouth turned down, his jaw squaring. He focused his attention on Spencer and grated the words from between clenched teeth, "You fucker."

"Spencer, you have every right to be upset. I'm the one who ended our relationship, not Luke." Guilt ate at her. This was all her fault. If she hadn't ended things so badly with Spencer, he wouldn't be here now trying to publically humiliate Luke. "It's not fair to come over here and use petty gossip to hurt him when it's me you should be angry at."

Spencer scoffed. "Petty gossip? If he's not trying to get out of something, then why has Blackwell missed two court appearances in the past six months? I checked, Kayleigh. The court records are legit."

She didn't want to believe Spencer, but his expression told her just how serious he was. Had she been a fool to fall for Luke's romantic, tortured artist sensitivity and his bullshit line that he couldn't live without her? All along he was hiding out from the press and a woman he couldn't even be responsible enough to practice safe sex with!

"Kayleigh." Luke's warning tone told her that he sensed the storm brewing. "You need to let me explain."

Luke had never lied to her. Not once in all of the years they'd known each other. Even when he left eight years ago, he'd been up-front with her, no sugarcoating whatsoever. But the care he took with his words now made her wonder if Luke was attempting some sort of damage control. Softening the blow so she wouldn't freak the hell out.

"There's nothing to explain." Kayleigh forced her mouth into a complacent smile and kept her tone soft and even. She refused to add to tonight's spectacle by making a scene.

"Kayleigh, he's a loser." With her attention focused solely on Luke and his on her, she'd completely forgotten there was anyone else in the restaurant, let alone standing beside her. "The entire family is trash. He misled you and I can understand how—"

"Who are you calling trash, you piece of shit?"

Luke pushed out his chair with enough force to topple it backward as he stood. His roots and impoverished childhood had always been a sore spot. Spencer knew that and was using it to push Luke's buttons. Every set of eyes in the place turned toward them and Kayleigh's heart fluttered in her chest as a wave of anxiety crested over her.

"Luke." She reached out in an attempt to get him to sit back down, but his temper flared past the point of reason. She'd only seen him this angry one other time, and it had been after a group of kids had scrawled "white trash" across his locker with a sharpie. He'd been thirteen at the time and was suspended from school for a week after giving Ken Malheur a bloody nose over it. Not only was Luke considerably bigger now, but bulkier, his entire body corded with sinewy muscle. He'd pound Spencer into a pulp before anyone could do anything to stop it.

"Luke, don't do this." Kayleigh pushed her chair out and got between him and Spencer. She lowered her voice to a whisper. "You can't afford any more negative press."

ELEVEN

She thought he was worried about some bad fucking press?

Luke trembled with unrestrained rage, his hands curled into tight fists ready to strike out. Yeah, he knew that the story made him look bad, and that fucker Spencer hadn't exactly helped his case. And the fact that Kayleigh was so quick to believe that son of a bitch was a knife straight through his goddamned heart. Hell, he wasn't even worried about that fucking tabloid article Spencer had decided to wave in Kayleigh's face. It was total bullshit anyway and nothing he couldn't explain given the chance. It was the insult to his family that sent Luke toppling over the edge of reasonable anger management.

He was going to beat that mouthy son of a bitch to a bloody pulp.

Spencer puffed out his chest, real fucking macho with Kayleigh standing between them. "I said you're trash, Blackwell." He flashed a superior smirk as he laid a hand on Kayleigh's shoulder. "I'm just saving her from your bullshit before it's too late and you take off again."

Luke glanced down at Spencer's hand wrapped possessively around Kayleigh and jealous rage flared deep in his chest. "Take your fucking hand off of her before I shatter it."

"You were a ratty piece of shit when you were a kid and you still are now," Spencer remarked with disdain. He smoothed his free hand over his silk necktie as though the simple act would proclaim his social grace and standing in the community.

Luke snorted. What a fucking wanker.

Luke met his superior gaze and quirked a half smile. "I sure hope you don't have any meetings tomorrow, Jackson, because I'm going to beat the fuck out of your face."

"Luke, stop it." Kayleigh took a step forward, shrugging off Spencer's hand. "You're making this worse than it already is. Just . . . go back to Ryder's."

His eyes narrowed. "So I should just take this asshole's shit? Turn the other cheek and crawl back to my brother's house like a fucking pussy?"

"Yes." Her eyes shone with hurt and Luke looked past her to Spencer's ugly, smirking mug. He could walk away, for *her*. They had a lot to talk about, namely that fucking trash mag and the lying fame seeker who'd contacted them. "All right." He held out his hand and though he'd begun to calm, his breath still raced in his chest. "Let's get out of here then."

"No, Luke." The corners of her mouth tugged down into a frown. "*You* go back to Ryder's. Alone. I need . . ." She rubbed at her temples and sighed. "I need some time to think."

"Bullshit." How could she possibly be buying into this crap? "Come on, Kayleigh. This is me. You know I'd never do anything to—"

"She said she doesn't want to see you!" Spencer pushed his way past her and shoved at Luke's chest. "So take your low-class, white trash ass out of here and—"

Luke socked the fucker in the nose before he could say another word.

A cannon of gasps from every person in the restaurant was followed by a collective raising of the smartphones. Photos and video clips were no doubt being uploaded en masse to the Internet at the speed of 4G. Fucking great.

Spencer pushed himself up from the floor and took a stumbling step toward Luke. Blood gushed down his face, dripping all over the fancy blue silk tie that he'd been so goddamned proud of.

Luke squared his shoulders, more than ready to knock him flat on his ass again when the sound of a siren howled outside. *Shit.* Red and blue lights flashed through the wall of picture windows on the north side of the building.

"Let's see you bullshit your way out of this, asshole." Spencer snatched Kayleigh's napkin from the table and pressed it to his nose. "Kayleigh, I'll be at my place if you want to talk." He brushed past them both, knocking his shoulder into Luke's as he passed.

Like the pussy he was, Spencer went straight to the nearest cop to file a complaint. A silent comedy, the little prick provided plenty of entertainment as he pointed and railed, lifting his bloodstained tie to the officer's gaze as though his swollen nose and bloody face weren't indicator enough that Luke had assaulted him.

He fixed Kayleigh with an emotionless stare as he turned his chair upright and sat his ass back down. No use in standing around looking foolish while he waited for the cops to slap the cuffs on him. Hopefully Ryder had his checkbook on him and was in a generous mood, because his brother's prediction that he'd have to bail Luke out of jail had come to fruition.

"I'm not going anywhere, Kayleigh." One of the officers stepped into his line of sight and cleared his throat.

"And I'm not going to let a bunch of lies someone told give you an excuse to push me away."

"Mr. Blackwell, would you stand up please?"

The cop didn't sound too happy with him. Whatever. Looked like it was never too late to live up to one's nickname. He turned his back to the officer and put his hands behind his back. All around him, cell phones continued to snap off shots but he ignored every last one of those voyeuristic assholes. Instead, he kept his gaze locked on Kayleigh.

Silence answered him, as though she couldn't bring herself to speak. "I've never lied to you, baby. Don't forget that."

"Luke Blackwell, you're under arrest for assault . . ."

The cop's words were nothing more than inane chatter in the back of Luke's mind. Who gave a shit about going to jail when a possible future with Kayleigh balanced on a razor's edge? As he was dragged away, Luke fought to turn. To get just one more eyeful of her. She slumped down in her chair and buried her face in her hands. Goddamned Spencer. Because of his bullshit, Luke might have lost the only thing in this world he gave a shit about.

Oh, who in the hell are you kidding? Luke thought as he was dragged from the restaurant to more eager amateur paparazzi. *You have no one to blame for this but yourself.*

Kayleigh sat in her chair, her skin crawling with the multiple sets of eyes on her, unable to move.

She was too numb for embarrassment. Too stunned for confusion. Much too concerned for Luke to think about her own hurt. The crazy thing was, she *did* trust him. Even so, by the way he'd spoken to her, Kayleigh knew that no matter how much of the article Spencer had shown her was a lie, somewhere buried inside of it was a kernel of truth.

Did she really want to know how much?

"Um, here are your dinner specials and desserts." The waiter gingerly set a white plastic bag on the table along with the check. Kayleigh looked up at him, incredulous. Not only had her date been arrested, she was now saddled with more food than she could eat *and* the bill. Riotous laughter bubbled up Kayleigh's throat and the waiter looked at her like she'd lost her mind. Tears pooled in her eyes as she fished her credit card from her wallet and plunked it down on the table. The waiter retrieved it like he was reaching into a bowl full of scorpions and another bout of uncontrollable laugher burst from her that quickly turned into painful, wracking sobs.

She wiped at her eyes in a desperate attempt to stem the flow of tears. She stared at the table, unwilling to acknowledge the people still staring at her when the waiter returned with her receipt. As she gathered up the bag of food she dialed Ryder's number on her cell. "It's Kayleigh. Luke's been arrested. Can you meet me at the county jail?"

"*Shit.*" She could only picture Ryder's enraged expression. "What did he do?"

"He punched Spencer in the middle of Angus."

"Is that all?" Ryder snorted. "Hold tight. I'll be there as soon as I can."

Kayleigh sat outside of the county sheriff's office, the keys to Luke's rental car clenched tightly in her fist. Was it stupid to trust a man that she hadn't seen in years just because of something they'd shared almost a decade ago? And why did the prospect of hearing his explanation for the magazine exposé make her stomach tie up into myriad unyielding knots?

"You've been sittin' out here all night?" Ryder took a seat on the bench next to her and leaned against the brick wall, stretching his long legs out in front of him.

Kayleigh let out a slow sigh and allowed her head to fall back. She turned toward Luke's brother. "You look nice." His custom-tailored suit probably cost more than she made in a month. "I'm sorry if I ruined your date night."

"You didn't ruin anything," Ryder remarked. He tilted his head up toward the star-filled sky. "Luke, on the other hand, owes me big time."

"Is Lara mad?"

Ryder snorted. "Nothing ruffles her feathers. She thinks having Luke around makes life more entertaining."

Entertaining. That was one way to describe Luke.

"How are you holdin' up? Those two idiots didn't hurt you when they went at it, did they?"

Ryder was like the big brother she'd never had. It warmed her heart that he was still looking out for her. "I'm fine. Really, it was only Spencer who got hurt. His face had a run-in with Luke's fist."

"Sorry to say this, darlin', but Spencer has always been an asshole."

Rather than debate Spencer's shortcomings, Kayleigh reached into her purse and handed Ryder the folded-up magazine page. "Did you know about this?"

He scanned the article and crumpled the paper into a tiny ball in his palm. "I did," he said with disgust. "I take it this is what tonight's scuffle was over?"

Kayleigh shrugged. More like years of pent-up aggression and grudges were what tonight's scuffle had been about. It wouldn't change what had happened to tell Ryder that Luke had been defending his family by decking Spencer, though. "More or less. Is it true, Ryder? Did that woman have Luke's baby?"

Ryder didn't look at her, just stared at the sky. "What do you think?"

The knots in her stomach tightened and Kayleigh hugged her torso as if it would keep her shattering world intact. "I don't know. Whether or not it's true, I think he had a relationship with her."

"And that bothers you?"

Of course it did! "Yes. I mean . . . no." She'd been seeing Spencer when Luke showed back up. And before that, she'd had other boyfriends. Could she really be angry with him for seeing other women? "I don't know. *Ugh.* I just wish that loving Luke wasn't so damned complicated."

"Let me ask you a question. Would you love him if he wasn't complicated? If he was calm and level-headed? Dispassionate? Would you love Luke if he was boring and safe?"

She didn't even have to think about it. "No."

Ryder turned and fixed her with a stern, almost fatherly stare. "Then what are you doing sitting out here? Don't you think you should go bail him out?"

Right. Like she had bail money.

"Here." He handed over a blank check with his signature scrawled across the bottom. "Just tell me the damage tomorrow. I don't want to think about it tonight. I told him that I'd be bailing his ass out of jail before he went home."

Kayleigh stared down at the check and then stretched her hand out to Ryder. "I can't." He took the check from her, a crease digging into his brow. "I need some space and I need to think. I thought I could do this but I'm not so sure. Tell him I'm sorry, Ryder." She pushed herself away from the wall and stood, handing him the keys to Luke's car. "Tell Lara I'm really sorry for ruining your night."

Ryder frowned, and the weight of his gaze settled heavily on her as Kayleigh jogged across the parking lot. She had no idea how she was going to get home, but one thing was for certain: she needed to get as far away from Luke as possible before her composure crumbled once and for all.

TWELVE

Luke supposed he could add a civil lawsuit to his paternity suit after tonight. His manager and label would be *thrilled*. He supposed his lawyer would be genuinely happy, though. Nothing like racking up the legal fees at six-hundred-plus-dollars an hour to save him from utter self-destruction. And now, he could add cutting a check to whoever had bailed his ass outta jail to his mounting list of debts.

He'd only been home for a couple of days and he'd managed to fuck everything up. That fucking tabloid. What a bunch a vultures. Luke hadn't been running from Minnie or her allegations per se, he'd just reached the level of shit he was willing to take and decided that it was time to clear his head and set his priorities.

As the deputy slid a manila envelope with his possessions across the counter, he gave Luke a lopsided grin. "Think you could sign an autograph for my daughter before you leave? I have to listen to your songs on repeat every morning on the drive to school. No offense, but I'm hoping she finds a new band to obsess over soon."

Nothing rounded out a stellar night like autographing swag for the dude who'd booked him. "Sure, man. Have you got anything I could sign?"

He handed Luke a large yellow notebook. "Will this work?"

He'd signed odder things than a legal pad. "What's your daughter's name?"

"Hailey."

Luke scrawled out a quick note and scribbled his name beneath it. He handed the notebook back to the deputy and he traded it for a clipboard. "Sorry, Mr. Blackwell, but I need you sign this as well, acknowledging that we've returned your personal belongings to you. Also, you'll get a notice within thirty days regarding your court date. If you have any questions, you can call the courthouse."

"Right." Luke scrawled his name on the necessary paperwork. His lawyer was going to blow a gasket that he didn't call before putting his name to all of this shit, but it didn't matter. Spencer Jackson could get in line behind all of the other assholes who wanted a piece of him and sue him for everything he was worth.

He snatched the envelope from the counter and headed for the lobby. He pushed open the glass door, his heart lodged somewhere in his throat. *Please let her be here. Please let her be here . . .*

"Hey, brother. I told you I'd be bailing you out of jail before you left." Ryder stood from his seat and crossed to where Luke stood rooted to the floor.

Disappointment settled in his gut like a heavy stone. He knew that he'd fucked up, clocking Kayleigh's ex, but she wasn't even going to let him explain the tabloid article? How could she just walk away from him like that?

Like the way you walked away from her eight years ago?

He really was a bastard.

"Obviously, I'm not who you wanted to see," Ryder remarked. He clapped a hand on Luke's shoulder and urged him to move along. "Don't sweat it, Luke. Maybe it would be a good idea to give her a little space."

Luke stopped short of the exit and stared at his brother. "So she can have the time to overthink everything and make her own assumptions about this bullshit paternity case before she shuts me out for good?"

"Have you considered that if you put too much pressure on her too quickly that you might push her away for good all on your own?" Ryder held open the heavy glass door, staring down his brother. Luke let out an aggravated sigh and strode out into the cool night air. "Luke, you show up out of nowhere, *eight years* after leaving her and expect her to pick right up where you left off."

"Why is that a bad thing?" It's exactly what they'd done and he marveled at how easy it had been. They'd fallen back into their rhythm as though no time had passed at all. If that wasn't a sign that they were meant to be together, he didn't know what was.

Ryder hit the key fob, disengaging the alarm on Luke's rental. "Of course it's all well and good for you. You left her in this town, sitting on a virtual shelf while you went out and sowed your oats. In the view of *public eyes*. We live pretty far from L.A., Luke, but it's a far cry from a cave in the woods. She watches TV, has Internet access. You don't think it hurt her to bear witness to your wild antics over the years?"

Luke climbed into the passenger seat—he wasn't in the mood to drive—and leaned the seat back. "Since you're so *old and wise,* what do you think I should do?"

Ryder frowned, probably because Luke couldn't help but point out that he was totally pulling the dad act on him. "If I were you, I'd get my shit together with my old life before trying to start to live a new one. Go home, Luke.

Take care of business and set the record straight. Think about what you *really* want."

"I know what I want." He wanted Kayleigh.

"Fine, then think about why you want it." Ryder started the car and flipped on the headlights before pulling out into traffic. Luke rested his forearm over his eyes, as much to block out Ryder and his nagging voice of reason as the streetlights passing by. "Do you want to be with her because you know in your heart that's what's best for both of you, or are your reasons totally selfish?"

Yup. That voice of reason was abso-fucking-lutely annoying. "What if I leave and she goes back to that asshole?"

Ryder snorted. "What if you stay and she goes back to that asshole? Look, I know that life wasn't easy for us growing up, but you've got to do something about that chip on your shoulder. Spencer is an asshole. So what? So are a lot of people. Get over it and move on. Are you going to let the hang-ups you had as a teenager ruin your life as an adult?"

"Are you over all of it?" Ryder had shouldered all of the responsibility after their asshole of a dad had left and that included helping to support them financially. It was a wonder he'd graduated high school, let alone built their cattle ranch into the empire it now was. Didn't it bother him that jerks like Spencer considered them nothing more than white trash despite their success?

"There's no point in worrying over people who aren't worth my time," Ryder said. "I'd rather spend it on the people who *are*. The rest can go screw themselves."

"Easier said than done," Luke grumbled.

"You can't have a future with Kayleigh if you keep trying to relive your past." Ryder was certainly rocking the Zen vibe tonight. Did he have to be so damned mature and levelheaded? "Think about that when you're taking care of shit in L.A."

It looked like he was officially being run out of town on a rail. By his own brother, no less.

"Keep an eye on her while I'm gone?"

"Always have," Ryder replied.

Luke supposed it was finally time to grow up and let go of the past. He just hoped that the future he wanted would survive the changes he was about to make.

From the back porch swing, Kayleigh stared up at the stars dotting the inky night sky. You couldn't see the stars when you lived in a big city like L.A. The air was heavy, birds didn't sing. Too many people congested every nook and cranny. At least, that's how she perceived it.

If she was being truly honest with herself, maybe she'd used tonight's drama as an excuse to put distance between her and Luke. She could have taken Ryder's check and bailed him out. Come back here and listened to his explanation. Really, though, what was there to explain? Kayleigh had spent years following Luke's life through social media and the crap that passed as news reporting lately. As a young man, Luke had been no saint and as an adult, not much had changed. He was still wild. Reckless. Dismissive of authority. He still had a chip on his shoulder the size of Texas. His appetites were still insatiable. Each time she'd read the gossip or seen a picture of him with a new, drop-dead gorgeous starlet, model, or musician, it had broken off another shard of her heart.

Was she just one in a string of hookups for an ambitious rock star hell-bent on living up to his name? Or could she truly believe that Luke was still the same boy she'd fallen in love with? The one she'd promised forever to.

He'd only been home for a couple of days. In that time, they hadn't once sat down and really *talked*.

Her cell rang and Kayleigh reached over to the antique milk can that doubled as an end table. Her heart beat with the speed of a hummingbird's wings and then seized up as she read Ryder's name on the caller ID.

"Hello?"

"Hey," Ryder said. "How are you doing?"

How stupid was she that Kayleigh actually hoped it would be Luke on the other end of the line? She let out a slow breath and willed her heart to start beating at a nice even pace again. "I'm fine. How's Luke?" Was he mad at her? Hurt that she'd ditched him? Worried? She hoped that Ryder would read between the lines and answer all of the questions that had gone unspoken.

"Mad at the world as always," Ryder remarked with a laugh. "But relatively unfazed. What's a little assault charge with everything else he's dealing with, right?"

God, Kayleigh couldn't even pretend to know what Ryder was talking about. She hadn't taken the time to ask how his life was. She'd been more interested in protecting her own heart. A couple of great sexual interludes didn't equal an emotional reconnection. Instead of treating him like the Luke who'd been her best friend, she'd treated him with as much carelessness as everyone else who wanted a piece of him.

"Ryder, I know it's late, but do you think it would be okay if I came over and talked to him?"

Damn it, she should have stayed at the jail. It should have been her to pick Luke up and not Ryder. She should have been there for him and not hung him out to dry. She was such a *jerk*!

A space of silence passed and Kayleigh's mouth went dry. "He's not here," Ryder finally said. "He took the red-eye and flew back to L.A."

"W-what?" How could he just leave her again? Anger swelled like a rising tide, hot in the back of her throat.

"Settle down, Kayleigh," Ryder said. "I told him to leave. You're both worse than a couple of teenagers still, you know that? He needs a break. *You* need a break. He's not gone forever. Just for a while."

"A while" had been eight long years last time. How long would he leave her in a state of inertia this time? "Thanks for bailing him out, Ryder. I'll talk to you later."

Before he could continue to lecture her, Kayleigh disconnected the call. Ryder was right, though. They were both behaving like a couple of brainless, hormonal teenagers. She was twenty-six years old for Pete's sake! She should be past this sort of drama. In fact, her life should be about her career, retirement plans, starting a family of her own. Her skin flushed with warmth as she remembered her moments with Luke in Angus's bathroom. God, they'd been so careless. She was on the pill, but still . . . Consequences meant nothing when she was with Luke. Good decisions? What are those? But despite the fact that she knew she should put the past in the past and start looking toward a more stable future, Kayleigh couldn't bear to think of a future that didn't have Luke in it.

Maybe it was time for both of them to make a change.

THIRTEEN

"Okay guys, time to clean up your stations."

Little bodies scattered like ants on a hill. The prospect of a few minutes to play outside before the busses showed up was enough to spur any little kindergartener into action. Such a cute group of kids, she'd miss them next year. In fact, she'd miss all of the kids at Riverview Elementary next year. She'd fallen in love with their sweet—and sometimes ornery—faces, not to mention the friends and colleagues she'd be leaving behind.

It's not too late to change your mind. You could just stay home and play it safe.

No. It *was* too late. With only two months left before summer break, the school district was already looking for someone to replace her. It might have only been a few weeks since Luke had left, but Kayleigh was sure of the decision she'd made. It was time to take life by the horns and stop being scared.

"Wow, the stations are so clean!" Smiling, expectant faces looked up at the sound of her words and a rush of emotion crested over her. "This is great, you guys. Because you did such a great job, we're going to go outside and play for the rest of the day. Who's the line leader?"

"I am, Miss Taylor!" A wild arm waved from the back of the room.

"Everyone get your backpacks and line up behind Samantha. Let's show the first and second graders how quiet we can be when we walk down the hall."

Like good soldiers, they fell into line, their little chests puffed out with pride before they even had a chance to walk out of the door. Such a group of sweeties.

The entire class walked to the playground with nary a peep. Positive reinforcement worked wonders with the K-through-sixth set. Too bad she couldn't have used the same tactics on a certain bad-boy rocker she knew.

As the kids raced to the playground equipment, Kayleigh strolled across the playground, enjoying the late afternoon sun. Spring was her favorite season. Everything was new and fresh and clean. Green grass, beautiful flowers. Not too hot and not too cold.

Perfect.

Her cell buzzed in her pocket and she took stock of each and every one of her little charges, making sure that they were all where they ought to be. She pulled out her phone and looked at the text message. Ryder never texted. In fact, she was surprised he even knew how to access the message screen. Attached to the text he'd pasted a link—wonders never ceased—and the sentence: *You might want to watch this.*

A squeal of delight grabbed her attention and Kayleigh made a precursory check, counting little heads to make sure all twenty-three little bodies were accounted for before clicking the link that took her to the E! News site and a video clip.

"Riot 59's sexy front man is an errant baby daddy. True or False . . . ?"

The breath caught in Kayleigh's chest as Giuliana Rancic waited to pronounce the verdict. It would have been nice to hear the words from Luke himself, but since she hadn't seen him in almost three weeks, the odds of being hit by lightning were better. She gripped her phone so tightly in her hand that her knuckles turned white.

"The answer is . . . *So* false."

Kayleigh emptied her lungs of the air she'd held hostage. "Kyle! Take turns, please!"

She turned her attention from the slide back to her phone as Giuliana recapped the story.

"Luke 'Lucifer' Blackwell addressed allegations that he'd fathered a child with Minnie Ramsay, a professional dancer who'd toured with 'Round the World who'd opened on tour for Riot 59 last year. Blackwell went so far as to submit to a paternity test upon returning to L.A. in order to quiet rumors that he was running from a potential law suit."

The screen cut to Luke talking to a group of paparazzi. "It's true that Minnie and I dated last year, but our relationship ended a long time ago. There's only one woman for me. There always has been. And if *anyone* is going to have my baby it's going to be her."

"Luke! Luke!" Voices off camera shouted his name. "Who is she? Who are you seeing right now?"

He turned away and strode to his car amidst a flurry of bodies and shouts. The footage ended and the camera panned back to Giuliana. "Shortly after submitting to the paternity test, Blackwell made the results public, confirming that he was not, in fact the father of Ramsay's baby. But now we're left to wonder . . . who is this mystery woman who's won one of rock's most eligible bachelor's hearts?"

"Miss Taylor, are you okay?"

Kayleigh blinked back the tears that pooled in her eyes

and smiled. "I'm fine, Emily. I think the busses are pulling up, you'd better go grab your backpack and get ready to go."

Emily trotted off with a smile of her own and Kayleigh stuffed her phone in her pocket. Even if Luke wasn't here to say the words in person, hearing them warmed her heart just the same.

"It's true, you know. If *any woman* is gonna have my babies, it's you."

Luke tensed as he waited for Kayleigh to turn around. Showing up at school probably hadn't been the best idea, but the thought of spending another second away from the woman he loved was unacceptable. Three weeks had been three too many. And now that he was here, within touching distance, he was overwhelmed with the need to reach out and take her into his arms.

She turned slowly as though afraid to confirm that he was in fact standing behind her. His heart dropped to the souls of his feet. His mouth went bone dry. This was fucking torture. Was she happy to see him? Angry? Was she hoping he'd left her alone and never come back? Her face was an impassive mask, giving nothing away as her deep brown eyes pinned him in place. *Say something, you stupid son of a bitch!*

The bell rang and a swarm of older kids and teachers flooded the playground, reminding him of a concert crowd. The teachers worked together, herding the kids to where they needed to go while keeping them on task. Organized chaos. There was probably a song in there somewhere . . .

"I need to get the kids on their busses." Not even her tone betrayed her emotions. Good Lord, she was killing him! Kayleigh took a slow step backward and then another. "Don't go anywhere. I'll be right back."

A slow breath of relief deflated Luke's lungs. "Don't go

anywhere" was a hell of a lot better than "fuck off." He'd taken Ryder's words to heart, and was ready to do things right this time. He'd settled that bullshit with Minnie, and met with the guys about the future of the band. Some of it had been positive and proactive, but there'd been a shit ton of negativity and disagreement, too. After everything was said and done, Luke was happy with the decisions he'd made. He'd made choices that were for his music and career, but more importantly, he'd done what was right for his *life*.

A smile grew on his face as he watched Kayleigh usher all of her little rug rats to their respective busses. The smile on her face as she helped one with his backpack, and another with a loose shoelace, caused his chest to swell with emotion. The woman was fucking spectacular. It showed just how far lost he was to her that he could stand there and watch her wipe runny noses and zip up jackets all day.

The playground began to empty until every kid was either on a bus or in the care of their own parents. Even the teachers dispersed, heading back into the building like horses trotting back to the barn.

Luke strolled over to the swings, not far from where Kayleigh was talking with a mother whose little girl was tugging on her jacket. He squeezed himself into the U-shaped rubber seat and pushed back, setting the swing in motion. When the little girl apparently became too impatient to wait another second, Kayleigh gave a little wave, watching as the two walked toward the parking lot.

A peaceful calm settled around him. Kayleigh stood staring out at the parking lot for a few more minutes and Luke gave her the space she needed to gather her thoughts as he continued to sway back and forth, his knees almost up to his chin in the tiny swing. She turned, that same impassive expression on her face, and made her way to him, taking a seat in the swing beside his.

"I had to go to court today." Nothing like addressing her ex's broken nose to start off a conversation.

"Oh yeah?" Her voice bore a hint of playfulness and Luke's heart soared. "Was the judge anxious to throw the book at the infamous Lucifer Blackwell?"

"I got community service," he said with a laugh. "I look good in an orange vest though so it's no big deal."

"Sort of hard to pick up trash when you're supposed to be a few thousand miles away, isn't it?"

"Yep, which is why I bought a house here."

The swing stopped abruptly and she turned to face him, her brow furrowed. "What?"

Luke smiled. "Familiarity can be nice. My mom's already planning family dinners and it'll be cool to be closer to Jase and Ryder." He stopped the sway of his own swing and turned in the tiny bucket seat to face her. "I never should have shown up out of the blue like a selfish asshole, demanding to pick up where we left off without so much as a conversation. I won't apologize for wanting you, Kayleigh. I'll *always* want you. But I should have been mature enough to explain myself and let you decide what you wanted instead of putting so much pressure on you."

"What about the band? Your career? Luke, you can't just walk away from it."

"I'm not." He'd found a way to make it work, though this year would be more of a trial run. "I don't have to live in L.A. to make music. I'm going to build a recording studio here. Chase, Toby, and Eric are staying in California and that's cool. I've agreed to commute when I need to. We'll still tour. But we'll record our music here. I know it's not ideal, splitting my time like this. But I think it's a decent compromise. I used to think that I couldn't have it all. But maybe I can. Maybe . . ." He reached over and took her hand in his. "Maybe I can slow down and enjoy the ride for a change. I could take you out to dinner again sometime. I promise not to punch anyone."

Laughter bubbled in Kayleigh's chest, her amusement growing to the point that Luke wondered if she'd finally snapped. Hell, for all he knew she was already back with Spencer, and he was much too late for compromises and sentimentality.

"I quit my job last week," she said through another bout of laughter. "I was planning to move to L.A. over the summer. To prove to you that I could step out of my rut. That I could brave change and the prospect of sharing you with other people. I shouldn't have walked away from you that night, Luke. I should have been more understanding. I thought that if I could go where you needed to be for your career that we could try to make this work. I've missed you so much. I don't want to live another day without you."

He grabbed the chain that suspended her swing, pulling her until they faced each other. His mouth found hers in a slow, tender kiss that set him ablaze with want, uncontrollable lust, but most of all, love. "I love you, baby," he murmured against her mouth. "I've always loved you."

"I love you, too, Luke." Her lips found his and he deepened the kiss. He'd never, *ever* get enough of her and for the first time since he'd left her, Luke felt the final piece of the life he wanted click into place. "And I'm ready for anything, as long as we're together."

"Baby," he smiled against her mouth, "you aren't *ever* gettin' rid of me."

There was *definitely* a song in there somewhere.

THE
Billionaire
SHERIFF

ONE

"Someone oughtta put a disclaimer on that sign: Welcome to Sanger . . . Don't blink or you'll miss it."

Noah Christensen let out a soft snort at his deputy's observation. She might have acted as though she had nothing but disdain for the small Texas town, but he knew better. "Come on, Ali. It's not that bad."

They cruised past the sign toward town after a routine checkup on an unattended dog complaint just outside the city limits. As the local sheriff, Noah could have left it up to a couple of the on-duty deputy's to take care of, but he liked to be out and about. He wanted to know what was going on in his community.

Ali gave him a sidelong glance and her mouth puckered. "You only think that because you didn't grow up here."

"You've got a point." Noah had grown up in Dallas in a world so far removed from the one he lived in Sanger it might as well have been on another planet. He'd been raised surrounded by wealth and privilege. Wealth he hadn't ever enjoyed and privilege he'd inherited simply by being a Christensen.

Texas oil royalty.

Yee-haw.

His family name brought with it a lot of clout, but Noah wanted to earn respect. Having it handed to him on a silver platter had never been appealing. He guessed in the long run, his dad had been right to cut Noah and his three older brothers off by not giving them a single dime and no legs up in life. Byron Christensen's faults had been many, but he'd loved his sons in his own strange way. As was evidenced by the billions they'd inherited when he died. Funny, Noah had never wanted the money. Or the clout. Now, it seemed he was stuck with both.

"I would have traded you childhoods in a second," Ali remarked. "I'm pretty sure I wouldn't have complained about being the Paris Hilton of Texas."

Noah cut her a look. "Are you seriously comparing me to Paris Hilton right now?"

Ali grinned wide. "Of course not. You're *much* prettier."

"And still your boss," Noah remarked without an ounce of humor.

"Pfft." Obviously, Ali was scared to death of him. "I was thinking more along the lines of evil dictator. But if you think *boss* encompasses it . . ."

Noah tried to hide his grin. "You're not funny."

"Please," Ali scoffed. "I'm a regular comedienne."

The Sweet 'n' Sassy BBQ and bar came into view and Noah's foot eased up on the gas pedal. "Are you hungry?" he asked as though the thought had sprouted magically in his head. "I skipped lunch. I could go for an early dinner."

"I bet you could," Ali replied all too knowingly. "You eat there so often, I'm surprised you don't permanently smell like smoked meat."

Noah cringed. He doubted his expression went unnoticed in the dusky interior of the truck. "This is Texas," he said. "Barbeque is a staple food."

"Uh-huh." Ali bit back a laugh and Noah's grip on the steering wheel tightened. "I'm sure that's what you tell yourself every time you walk through her door."

His spine straightened and Noah cleared his throat. "I don't know what you're talking about."

"Okay," Ali said. "Whatever you say, boss."

Noah might have pretended not to have a clue about what Ali had insinuated, but her observation proved that he'd been unable to downplay his infatuation. Ever since the bar and barbeque joint had opened six months ago, it had become a regular stop for Noah. And not only because the pork ribs were spectacular.

"I like the ribs," Noah remarked.

"You like the woman who serves them."

Noah cleared his throat again. Had someone turned up the heat? It suddenly felt a little too stuffy inside the confines of the truck. He infused his voice with a nonchalance he certainly didn't feel. "She's all right."

"I'd say you think she's better than just *all right*."

His foot eased farther off the pedal as he flipped the turn signal. Stopping would only strengthen Ali's argument but Noah couldn't help himself. "Do you want dinner or not?" He doubted that Ali would turn down a free meal—or the opportunity to continue to give him a hard time.

"Of course I do," she said with a laugh. "Being on shift with you all day works up a girl's appetite."

Noah's lips puckered as he pulled into a parking space. He'd learned a long time ago that in a war of words, Ali would always win. He'd seen her shake down suspects and bring speeding teenagers to tears. If he continued to deny his motives in stopping for dinner, she'd continue to counter his argument until he had no choice but to admit defeat. He wasn't ready to come to terms with it himself why he stopped here day after day. No way was he going to admit it to his nosy deputy.

Ali hopped out of the truck and headed inside. The bounce to her step only made Noah's heart pound faster in his chest. He swore, if she did—or said—anything to embarrass him, he'd take her badge. Okay, so he probably wouldn't do that, but he'd make sure she worked a month-long shift with Charlie Johnson. Sanger's oldest deputy could drive anyone to drink with his endless tales about the good old days. Yep, if Ali so much as glanced Naomi's way, she'd be hating life for the next thirty days.

Noah paused just inside the door as Sweet 'n' Sassy's owner flashed him a bright smile. *Damn.* Naomi Davis could stop him dead in his tracks.

"Hey there, Sheriff! Take a seat anywhere."

Yeah, Noah definitely didn't come here for the ribs. The knot in his gut was all the confirmation he needed. "Thanks." Unfortunately, he also turned into an inarticulate asshat the second he walked through her door.

He wanted to sit at the bar but that wasn't going to work while he was in his uniform. Noah was on duty and rumors would fly if the locals saw him bellied up to the bar. Instead, he followed Ali toward the restaurant seating at the far end of the building. Might as well have been miles away from where he wanted to be. *Damn it.*

Noah watched Naomi from the corner of his eye. Holy shit, she was beautiful. But not in the traditional sense. No, Naomi was beautiful like the night was beautiful. Quiet and dark. Secrets hid behind her smoky gray eyes, and her dark chestnut hair, run with streaks of violet, reminded him of a late winter sunset. Her features were soft and expressive, her lips almost too full in contrast with her sharp cheekbones. A tiny silver bar glinted from the piercing at her eyebrow and coupled with her leather cuff bracelets, rounded out her look to paint a decidedly edgy picture. Edgy and goddamned sexy.

And Noah wanted her so damned bad he could barely think straight.

Naomi watched with appreciation as Noah Christensen walked past the bar area and took a seat across the table from one of Sanger's other deputy sheriffs. The man could certainly fill out a uniform and Naomi's considerably shitty day was suddenly looking up. The small town of Sanger didn't offer much in the way of dating prospects, but the sheriff supplied her with the eye candy necessary to get her through the week. Tall, with gorgeous hazel eyes, short clipped dark hair, and a smile that absolutely *melted* her. She'd actually grown to anticipate his almost daily visits to the bar, evidenced by the riot of butterflies that took off in her stomach the second he walked through the door.

Funny that since she'd moved here, a visit from the sheriff was all the entertainment she needed.

Life in Sanger was a far cry from her previously wild Dallas existence. But that's exactly how Naomi wanted it. Anything was better than living in the city. Especially when living in the city had only ever brought her a world of trouble. A string of bad decisions and even worse dating choices had convinced her that she needed to get her butt out of Dallas ASAP. She might've stuck out like a sore thumb in the tiny conservative town, but even so, she'd never felt such a sense of belonging.

She really hoped she wouldn't have to pack up and leave this place soon.

Naomi stuffed the sudden wave of anxiety and sadness to the soles of her feet as she grabbed two glasses and a pitcher of water and headed for Noah's table. There wasn't any point in worrying about things she couldn't change. Especially not now when her night was finally looking up.

"How goes the keeping of the peace, guys?" Naomi asked as she poured two glasses of water. "Any dangerous criminals I need to worry about?"

Deputy Brown gave a soft snort of laughter but Naomi couldn't seem to drag her eyes from Noah. Her lips curled into a smile at the same time her stomach twisted into a tight knot. The only thing criminal in Sanger was Noah Christensen's sex appeal. Freaking mouthwatering!

His deep voice rumbled through her. "Unless you consider a dog dispute as dangerous, I think you're safe tonight."

Deputy Brown rolled her eyes and Noah shifted in his seat. Naomi had a feeling she was on the outside of an inside joke. She had no idea how someone as drop-dead gorgeous as Noah could come across as so nervous. He really was the epitome of the shy, small-town guy.

Totally adorable.

"Mrs. Dickerson again?" In a town as small as Sanger, everyone knew everyone's business. It could be a blessing and a curse. This time, it wasn't Naomi's business that people were nosing into, which was fine by her.

Deputy Brown laughed. "How'd you guess?"

"Rich was in here yesterday complaining about it," Naomi said as she poured a second glass of water. "He caught poor little Zeke in a live trap by his garbage cans. I can't imagine Mrs. Dickerson was too thrilled about it."

Noah laughed. The rich and decadent sound caused chills to break out over Naomi's skin. She clutched the water pitcher in her hands closer to her chest. "No," he said. "She wasn't. But I think we got them both settled down. Rich promised not to trap Zeke as long as Amelia agreed to have the hole in her fence fixed. Their truce should last a couple of weeks before they find some other reason to pick a fight with each other."

Naomi loved that the biggest problem the local law enforcement had to deal with today was a dispute between neighbors. Sanger was a safe place and she craved the sense of security it offered. "So, what are you two eating tonight?" She flashed a wide smile at Noah. "I know you're having the half rack of ribs. How 'bout you, Deputy Brown?"

Deputy Brown gave Noah a knowing smile and he looked like he wanted to kick her from under the table. Naomi's brow furrowed as she realized she was once again not in on the joke. Maybe there was more to Noah's relationship with the other woman than she thought. Her heart sank at the realization that he might not be as single as she'd thought. All of her best flirting gone to waste . . .

"It's Ali," Deputy Brown said with a friendly smile. Too bad Naomi wasn't feeling very friendly back all of a sudden. "I'll have the French dip sandwich with fries."

"I'll get your dinners started for you," Naomi said as she scribbled their orders on her pad. "Just holler if you need anything else."

"We will." Noah's answering smile nearly blinded her. "Thanks."

Naomi stumbled as she turned too quickly to leave. She caught herself before she went face-first to the floor and rushed toward the kitchen without looking back to see if Noah or Ali had seen her near wipeout.

"Smooth." Carl, the part-time cook winked at her from the kitchen's service window.

Naomi grimaced as she hung the order slip on a little wheel hanging from the corner of the frame. "Ugh. You saw that?"

"Oh yeah." Weathered skin crinkled at the corners of Carl's eyes as he grinned.

"Do you think he noticed?" Naomi didn't mind embarrassing herself in front of Carl, but she didn't really want Noah to see her trip over her own feet.

"The truth?"

Her stomach twisted. "I can take it."

Carl's smile widened. "That boy can't take his eyes off of you. He'd notice if you wobbled a half inch to the right."

Naomi groaned. But she didn't actually think Noah had noticed her clumsiness because his head was currently bent close to Ali's and the two appeared to be deep in conversation. "I'm pretty sure he's into her," she said as she jerked her chin toward Noah's table. "They were giving each other looks and she smiled at him."

"Ali?" Carl scoffed. "Nah. There's nothing goin' on there. Trust me. Noah Christensen is into only one girl around here and it *isn't* Ali Brown."

Naomi's cheeks flushed with heat. She'd hoped the electricity she'd felt between them over the past few months wasn't imagined. Yeah, he came in to eat a lot, and over the course of six months, they learned almost everything about each other, but she didn't want to read too much into it. He was single and for all she knew he simply didn't like to cook. Besides, she did smoke the best rack of ribs in the entire county. "Maybe he just likes the food?"

Carl clucked his tongue at her as he swiped the order slip from the wheel. "Somehow, I don't think it's the ribs he keeps coming back for."

A zing of excitement shot through Naomi's bloodstream. She averted her gaze and turned from the service window to prevent Carl from once again witnessing how Noah affected her. Naomi had always been overconfident and street-smart. She didn't get twisted up when a guy smiled at her. She was much too tough for those sorts of girlie emotions. But when Noah Christensen leveled his hazel stare at her, all bets were off.

He was the first truly good guy to ever turn her head. And that was a *huge* problem.

TWO

Noah gripped the steering wheel as he cruised down the highway toward home. Another night. Another missed opportunity. He was a total pussy. Even Ali had given him a hard time on their way back to the station, joking about how if he kept eating there every night, he'd weigh three hundred pounds before he got up the nerve to ask Naomi out.

Good lord, she was probably right.

What had changed so much in the past six months that he no longer wanted to live the free and single life? In a town with less than seven thousand residents, Noah couldn't exactly be a serial dater. Like hanging out at the bar, no one wanted to hear that the sheriff had been whoring around town. That's not to say he'd gone dateless the past couple of years. His brother Nate had hooked him up with his fiancée's assistant eight or so months ago. And he'd gone on a blind date arranged by his brother, Carter, not long ago. The only one of his brothers who hadn't tried to hook him up was Travis and that was only because his wilder sibling had suggested that one-night stands were so much better than dates.

Heh. Even Travis had abandoned his no-strings-attached policy a few months ago after he'd fallen in love with the woman tasked with improving his image. A bad boy no longer, Travis had been officially domesticated. Which made Noah the last remaining bachelor of the Christensen clan. He'd been totally okay with that, too. Until Naomi Davis came to town.

She tied him into knots. The way she dressed, skinny jeans or leggings, paired with a superhero T-shirt or long flowing tank top, with scuffed black motorcycle boots, drove him crazy. Her purple hair and precise makeup suited downtown Dallas more than sleepy Sanger, but she didn't seem to notice or didn't care. She was who she was and she didn't make excuses or apologies for it. Noah liked that about her. And all he'd wanted since their first meeting was to get to know her better.

Which he'd wasted no time in doing. He knew more about her than he did half of the cops that had worked for him for the past couple of years. Her favorite color was black. She took her coffee with cream and sugar. Cheesecake was the one dessert she refused to share, and she'd rather listen to EDM music than anything else. She didn't watch much TV, opting for a good book instead. She owned two cats and no dogs, but secretly wished she had a couple of pygmy goats in her backyard.

Despite their easy rapport, he'd been too nervous to ask her out time and again. Tonight was another example of one of his many wasted opportunities.

Noah hit the brakes and brought the truck to a skidding stop. What in the hell was he waiting for? If he didn't man up, some other guy was going to scoop her up. Women like Naomi didn't stay single for long. Hell, for all he knew she had a boyfriend somewhere. Probably a big, MMA-looking SOB who worked security at a trendy Dallas club or something.

He'd never live it down if he didn't do something about his infatuation. Hell, it's not like he wanted to marry her or anything. He could start with dinner and go from there. But he'd never know if she was interested in more than a simple friendship if he didn't ask.

Noah pulled back out onto the street and turned around to go back the way he'd come. He resisted the urge to flip on his lights and speed back to the bar. He had no idea what time she closed up for the night but if he didn't do this now, he'd lose his nerve and god only knew how much ribbing he'd have to endure from Ali if that happened.

The drive back to the bar on the outskirts of town was only about five miles but it felt like five hundred. Nervous anticipation churned in Noah's gut as he imagined every scenario possible from Naomi laughing hysterically in his face, to her tackling him in the parking lot and stripping him bare. Okay, so that might've been pushing it, but it painted one hell of a mental picture.

Noah turned into the parking lot. The glow of head-lights near the rear of the building illuminated the dust particles swirling in the air as he brought the truck to a slow stop. The hairs prickled at the back of his neck and he reached to his right hip to unclasp the strap that stretched across the grip of his gun.

Something wasn't right.

He killed the engine and jumped out of the truck. The usually brightly lit windows of the bar were now dark and only the floodlights at the front of the building had been left on. A high-pitched grunt of pain echoed from the rear of the building and Noah took off at a sprint, gun drawn. His heart lodged in his throat as Naomi's outline came into view. A man held her by her shoulders and gave her a rough shake.

"Police! Get your hands in the air!"

At Noah's barked command, Naomi's assailant shoved

her to the ground. He dove into his still-running car and took off with a spray of gravel. Noah shielded his eyes but could do nothing to protect himself from the bits of rock that peppered his arms and chest. He squinted in the direction of the fleeing car. It was too damned dark to get a good bead on the make and model and forget about reading the plates. As he hustled toward where Naomi had fallen, he grabbed his radio mic from where it was secured to his shoulder and called dispatch.

"Assault suspect, heading north on Main Street. Dark sedan. I couldn't read the plates." The dispatcher responded, but the words barely registered. His heart beat a million miles per hour and his breath raced in his chest. "Naomi?" He holstered his gun and went down on his knees beside her. "Are you okay? Are you hurt?"

Noah brushed the dark strands of her hair away from Naomi's face. Her eyes were wide and she shook with so much force that her fear vibrated through her into him. "Are you hurt?" he asked again. Her teeth chattered and she simply stared. Noah clamped his jaw down as a wave of anger crashed over him. "Dispatch, I need an ambulance at—"

"No!" The urgency in her voice made him pause. "No ambulance. I-I'm okay."

"The ambulance can stand down, dispatch," Noah said into his mic. "But keep a deputy en route to look for that sedan."

The dispatcher replied, "Copy that."

"Can you stand?" Noah turned his attention to Naomi.

She let out a shuddering breath and leaned against him. "Yeah." Her voice trembled on the word. "I'm not hurt."

Naomi might not have been hurt, but she was definitely shaken up. Noah swore under his breath as he helped her upright. If he'd been even a couple of minutes later, god only knew what might have happened to her. A wave of fear crashed over him and Noah forced it away. She was okay and that's all that mattered.

"Can you tell me what happened?"

She looked up into his face with wide, fearful eyes. Her gaze darted low and to the right. "I'm not sure. I was headed to my car when he jumped me. He grabbed me by the shoulders and . . ." She brought her eyes up to his for the briefest moment. "When you showed up, he pushed me down."

Noah's jaw clamped shut. It could have been the fact that Naomi was traumatized by what had just happened, but he couldn't shake the sense that she was keeping something from him. "Did he say anything to you?"

"N-no," she stammered. "Not that I remember."

Her response was too evasive for Noah's peace of mind. Then again, she'd been through a lot. Victims of crimes sometimes forgot details when they were still in shock. Maybe when she'd had a chance to calm down, and her mind wasn't muddied by the adrenaline rush, she'd remember something.

There was more to it than Naomi being rattled, though. Instinct tugged at Noah's senses and his gut sank. Was she hiding something from him? And why? He steadied her on her feet and Naomi gave him a weak smile as she straightened. The heat of her body left his and Noah missed it in an instant. He wanted to hold her. Comfort her. Protect her and beat the son of a bitch who'd done this to her to a bloody pulp.

Sort of going above and beyond his duties as the local sheriff, wasn't he? Damn it. There was a distinct possibility he was too close to this one. He couldn't let his feelings for Naomi get in the way of doing his job.

When Naomi was sure she could stand on her own two feet, she let out a slow, steadying breath. If Noah hadn't shown up . . . She didn't even want to think about what might have happened if he hadn't shown up.

"Are you cold? I have a blanket under the backseat."

She looked up at the sound of Noah's concerned words. Still shaking, with her arms hugged tightly around her middle, she probably looked as though she were freezing. "I'm okay," she said. "Just a little shaken up." Truth was, Naomi couldn't feel anything but the white hot fear that coursed through her. She'd really screwed up this time. There was no running from her bad choices anymore. It was time to face the music.

She'd learned to gamble from the best. Her dad had been betting against the house all of his life—and losing. You'd think that watching him sink lower and lower over the course of her childhood would have been enough to keep her on the straight and narrow. Or at the very least teach her how to make marginally mature decisions.

Yeah, right.

Naomi had known she'd needed to get herself out of Dallas before she self-destructed. The problem was, she hadn't had the cash to start the new life she wanted. So she'd done what anyone with her life skill set would've done: she went to a loan shark to get the cash she needed to make her dream life a reality.

Now, it was time to pay up.

"Can you remember anything at all about the guy that attacked you?" Noah's warm voice reached through her troubled thoughts to bring her back to reality. "Maybe something about his hair or eyes? Did he have any tattoos?"

Naomi knew *everything* about the man who'd attacked her. Including his name. "No." Her gaze slid to the right. She couldn't bear to look Noah in the eye while she lied to him. "It was too dark and it happened too fast."

"Okay." He was slow to respond and his brow furrowed.

"Maybe something will come to you later. Are you sure you don't want to go to the hospital? You've got some nasty scrapes."

She'd forgotten all about that. The pain didn't even register. When Jack had shoved her to the ground, she'd been so grateful for the reprieve, the rocks and gravel cutting a path through the skin on her knees and palms had seemed pretty damned inconsequential. Noah's concern did nothing more than intensify the guilt that congealed in Naomi's stomach. She'd gotten herself into this mess. She wasn't some random victim. And Noah treated her as though her safety and comfort were the only things in the world that mattered.

"I've had worse scrapes," she said with what she hoped was a reassuring laugh. "A little hydrogen peroxide and a couple of Band-Aids should fix me up."

Noah's lips thinned. If it was possible, the severity of his expression made him even more handsome. "Worse scrapes, huh. You get thrown to the ground often?"

Great. Every time she opened her mouth it seemed she dug herself a deeper hole. "Not really." Why did she feel more like a suspect than the victim when Noah leveled his stern gaze on her? "I just mean that there's no reason to rack up an ER bill when my scrapes are pretty superficial."

"You could be in shock, Naomi."

Oh, she was definitely in shock. Shocked that Jack hadn't even given her a stern warning before roughing her up. Shocked that, thanks to her dad's history with the same men, she wouldn't be given an extension on her loan. Shocked that by the end of the month, she'd have to come up with fifty grand or kiss her ass good-bye. At this point, *shock* was an understatement.

She was officially screwed.

"I'll be all right." She hoped that her now-steady voice

would help to convince Noah. "I just need to get home, clean myself up, and unwind."

"If you say so." Obviously Noah wasn't buying it. *Crap.* "I'll take you home."

"You don't have to—"

"Yes, I do," Noah interrupted. He tucked her legs into the cab before he eased the truck door shut. "No arguments."

Without another word, Noah shut the door. Silence settled in the cab and she watched Noah cross the parking lot toward one of his deputies. She'd been so shaken up, she hadn't even noticed the other vehicle pull in. The two exchanged a few words before he headed back for the truck. Naomi didn't want to admit it, but she was glad he'd insisted on taking her home. Jack might have taken off upon Noah's arrival at the bar, but that didn't mean he wouldn't be waiting for her at her house. It was dangerous to get Noah involved in her problems, whether inadvertently or not. Naomi didn't want to see him hurt, but she couldn't muster up the courage to tell him the truth, either.

"The bar's all locked up?" he asked as he climbed into the truck.

"Yeah," Naomi replied. "I'd closed down for the night and was leaving when you showed up."

Residual fear trickled into Naomi's bloodstream and she shivered as Noah started the truck and pulled out onto Main Street. He eased his foot off the gas and reached to the backseat. "Here. Cover up with this." He handed her a fleece blanket and this time, Naomi did as he said and wrapped herself up in its soft warmth.

"Thanks."

"You really should carry a can of pepper spray with you." Noah looked straight ahead as he drove. In the dark interior of the truck, his profile appeared sharper, stern.

"I know that Sanger is a small town, but even small towns can be dangerous after dark."

Was he chastising her? She'd grown up in the city and not under the best of conditions. She knew all about what dangers lurked after the sun went down. "I do," Naomi replied. "On my key chain. I just didn't think to use it." More to the point, she'd known better than to use it. She was already in deep shit with Jack's boss. Hitting the to-ken henchman with pepper spray would have only made a bad situation worse.

"Okay," Noah said. "Where am I headed?"

"Oh, right." Her brain spun so fast, it took a second to remember her own home address. She recited it mechanically, the words and numbers barely registering.

Noah obviously knew Sanger like the back of his hand. He didn't ask for any further directions, simply took off toward her house.

The rest of the drive passed in relative silence and that was okay by Naomi. She wasn't ready—or willing—to answer any more of Noah's questions and she felt her resolve slip each and every time she looked into his beautiful hazel eyes. He'd saved her bacon tonight and she wouldn't soon forget it. No man had ever thrown himself in the path of danger for her before. If anything, she'd lost another small part of herself to Noah Christensen tonight and that scared the hell out of her.

"This is me." She barely recognized her own voice as Noah pulled into her driveway. A cold knot of fear con-gealed in her stomach as she stared at the dark exterior of her house. She had no idea what waited for her inside the door. *Shit.* She turned to Noah and said, "Would you mind walking me inside?"

His gaze searched hers and his brows drew down over his eyes. "I absolutely don't mind."

Thank god. Without him, Naomi wasn't sure she'd be

able to muster the courage to go down the walkway, let alone go inside the house. "Thank you," she whispered.

"Don't worry." The warmth of Noah's voice banished the chill that settled on her skin. "It's going to be okay."

Somehow, Naomi doubted that.

THREE

Something wasn't right. Naomi didn't act like the victim of a random burglary attempt. It was only natural for her to be a little shaken up, but her behavior went beyond that. Noah couldn't shake the sense of certainty that Naomi had not only gotten a good look at her attacker tonight, but that she knew him. A violent ex-boyfriend, maybe?

He'd searched every nook and cranny of her house, checked the closets, under the bed, even the storage shed in her backyard as well as behind the trees and bushes that surrounded the property. He'd made sure every window was locked and even then, Naomi had been on edge. Despite her constant reassurances that she was fine, Noah sensed otherwise. And when he'd told her he was leaving, the fear in her gray eyes had left him nervous and shaken.

Shit, you'd think he'd been the one who'd been roughed up tonight as on edge as he was. That nervous anticipation churning in his gut had never steered him wrong. His intuition told him something that he was reluctant to admit to himself. Naomi was in serious trouble. He only wished she'd open up and tell him exactly what sort of trouble it was.

He settled into his seat, reclining it slightly before he scooped up the fleece blanket Naomi had discarded earlier. Her scent clung to the fabric, roses in full bloom, and Noah inhaled deeply. It was pathetic how far gone he was, which was further evidenced by his decision to camp out in his patrol rig in her driveway for the night.

"Noah? What are you still doing out here?"

He started at the sound of Naomi's voice, muted by the window. He turned the key in the ignition and hit the button to lower it, letting in the cool fall breeze as well as more of her delicious floral scent.

"I'm just keeping an eye on the place." It's not like he didn't think she'd notice his pickup parked out in her driveway, but he'd hoped she'd accept it as a nice gesture and let it be. Marching up to the window and calling him out only made him feel like a fool. "I'm not entirely sure that what happened tonight was random."

Naomi averted her gaze, confirming Noah's suspicions. "I appreciate that you're looking out for me, but I'm fine. Really. You don't have to sit out here in your truck all night."

"I know I don't have to," Noah replied. "I *want* to."

The corners of Naomi's lips hitched in a reluctant smile and Noah's gut clenched. "All right," she said. "Suit yourself."

She turned and walked away and his earlier elation crashed to the soles of his feet. He'd hoped the gesture would endear him to her, but it obviously had the opposite effect. *Great.* Noah raked his fingers through his hair and watched as Naomi's shadowed form crossed in front of the pickup. She rounded the vehicle to the passenger side, pulled open the door, and hopped into the passenger seat. "If you're going to sit out here all night, I guess I will, too."

Noah studied her in the dark, trying to discern her expression. "There's no need for you to sit out here with me," he said. "This is my job."

"So, if it had been Carl who'd been jumped tonight, you'd be sitting out in his driveway right now?"

"The safety of my constituents is important to me."

"That's not an answer," Naomi replied.

True. Because Noah didn't want to admit that if it had been Carl—or anyone else who'd been jumped tonight—he probably wouldn't be sitting in their driveway right now. His worry for Naomi might have seemed extreme and maybe even a little unnecessary, but Noah had learned a long time ago not to discount his feelings. He knew there was more to what had happened tonight than she let on. It didn't feel right to leave her alone.

"All right." She wanted the truth? Noah could give her that. "*Your* safety is important to me."

Naomi started as though taken aback by his words. Certainly a boost to the old ego. She studied him for a long, silent moment. Her whispered reply was barely audible in the quiet interior of his pickup. "No one's ever looked out for me before."

The words cut through him. No one had ever cared enough about her to make sure she was okay? "I'm going to look out for you," Noah said with every ounce of conviction he felt. "I won't let anyone hurt you, Naomi."

She looked away as though she couldn't bear to hear the words. Noah's need to get to the bottom of what had happened tonight burned through him like a fire through dry grass. She didn't trust him and until she did, he wouldn't be able to help her. In the meantime, he could keep an eye on her and make sure that she was safe.

"You can't sit out in your truck all night." She kept her gaze focused outside the window.

"I told you, I've done it before. I'll be fine."

"If you're hell-bent on keeping an eye on the place, you can do it from inside. The couch is a hell of a lot more comfortable than this seat."

She turned to face him. Shadows accentuated the delicate lines of her face and hollowed her cheeks. The graveness of her tone was a warning that Noah couldn't heed. She didn't want him to get too close. Well, too damned bad. He'd already made up his mind and he wasn't going *anywhere*.

"Thanks," he said. "The couch would be great."

She let out a sigh that was more relief than regret. Naomi might have acted like she didn't need Noah's help—or protection—but her reaction told another story. Noah would be damned if she ever felt afraid or unsure again.

He followed her back into the house. Every light in the place was on as well as the TV. Naomi gave him a sheepish grin. "I guess I'm still a little more shaken up than I want to admit."

Which was why he wasn't going anywhere.

"Anyone in your situation would be," Noah replied. "And I think once you've had some time to calm down and process everything that happened, you'll remember more about the guy that attacked you."

Naomi averted her gaze once again. Lucky for Noah her tells were easy to spot. "Maybe . . ." She looked around the room as though for a distraction. "Like I said, it was dark and everything happened so fast."

"Don't worry about it right now." Noah wanted to put her at ease. She'd never open up to him if he kept badgering her. "What's important is that you're okay."

"I am." She brought her gaze up to his and graced him with a soft smile that damn near brought Noah to his knees. "Because of you."

If he was ever in danger of developing a hero complex, it was now. He'd move the sun and moon for her if she asked him to. Anything for another one of those smiles.

"Just doing my job," he said.

Her expression fell. Had she been hoping for a different answer? Noah cursed himself for his insufferable lack of game. If it'd been Travis in his situation, he would have hooked up with Naomi months ago. At the rate Noah was going, he'd be old and decrepit before he did and said the right things.

"I'll get you a blanket and a pillow." Naomi headed for her bedroom in a nervous rush. "Be right back."

"Sure."

His eyes were drawn to the delicate, hypnotic sway of her hips as she left the room. He'd fallen hard for her and there was no turning back.

It showed just how big of a coward Naomi was that she'd been relieved to see Noah's patrol truck parked in her driveway. And yeah, she'd put up a brave front, pretended to scoff at his offer to stake out her house for the night, but on the inside, she'd said a little prayer of thanks for Noah Christensen's knight in shining armor persona.

For all she knew, he was the last of the truly good guys out there that wasn't married or attached. And he was spending the night under her roof. The thought of Noah camped out on her couch suffused Naomi with warmth. What would he do if she stretched out beside him on the cushions? Would he be a gentleman and suggest she go back to her room? She'd rather imagine he'd take her in his arms and do wonderful, naughty things to her. A pleasant shiver ran the length of Naomi's spine and she let out a rush of breath. Without even trying, he affected her. Made her stomach clench and her legs feel weak.

Naomi went to the closet and grabbed a blanket and took one of the pillows off of her bed. Noah wanted to protect her, but would he feel the same if he knew she'd done business with gangsters and loan sharks? Would his concern for her evaporate if he knew she'd dated one of those lowlifes at one time and that her father had taught her everything she knew about how to game the system? An anxious rush sped through Naomi's bloodstream as she walked back into the living room to find Noah perched on the couch. His gaze devoured her, so full of heat and longing that it made her sweat. Would he continue to look at her that way if he knew the sort of person she really was? Or would that heat cool to send a chill over her skin?

"I can rustle up another blanket if you want." She handed over the blanket and pillow.

Noah took the bundle with a smile and set them on the couch to his left. "I'm sure this'll be fine. Thanks."

"No," Naomi said. "Thank you. No matter what you say, I know you're going above and beyond. I just want you to know that I appreciate it."

Noah's eyes searched hers. She felt naked, too exposed, and at the same time, safe. She couldn't explain it, but she couldn't deny it, either. Maybe it was the badge. Or the fact that Noah was her closest friend in Sanger. Or maybe it had been so long since someone had been genuinely concerned for her that Naomi didn't know how to react.

"Sit." Noah patted the couch beside him and Naomi sat down as though she had no choice but to obey.

Naomi swallowed down the lump that formed in her throat. She sensed an interrogation on the horizon, one she didn't think she'd enjoy. Instead, Noah snatched the remote from the coffee table and settled back onto the cushions. He turned the TV on. "Do you like *The Tonight Show*?"

Every ounce of stress melted from Naomi's body. "Jimmy Fallon is hilarious." She leaned back, close enough to Noah that their shoulders touched, and propped her feet up on the coffee table.

Noah followed suit and the action caused the taut muscles of his upper arm to brush fully against hers. Naomi's breath caught as a molten rush of excitement coursed through her. The heat of his body soaked right through their clothes and she fought the urge to let her eyes roll back into her head from the sheer ecstasy of it all. Pretty pathetic that the most exciting sexual contact she'd had in months was arm-to-arm. At this point though, she'd take what she could get.

"I used to watch *The Daily Show* religiously," Noah remarked. "But now that Jon Stewart is gone . . . I don't know if I can watch anymore." He chuckled. "I hate change."

"Me, too." It was why she'd stayed in Dallas for so long despite her shitty circumstances. "It sort of freaks me out."

"Do you miss Dallas?"

They'd gotten to know each other well over the months. Not surprising with Noah's regular visits to the bar. Naomi knew more about him than anyone in Sanger. He loved sweet tea and anything barbeque. He had three brothers and two nieces. Country music was his favorite and he always teased Naomi for her own musical tastes. He considered law enforcement one of the best and most important jobs out there and he was proud of the fact that he'd climbed the ranks at such a young age. Noah was her friend and she'd felt comfortable around him since the day they met. But their conversation felt more intimate tonight. Probably because they were camped out on her couch. Or it could have been the warm timbre of Noah's voice that was more like a caress than mere words.

"Not even a little bit." It felt good to make the admission. "I only wish it hadn't taken me so long to leave."

"I know what you mean," Noah said. Jimmy Fallon's monologue in the background faded to a lull in contrast to his voice. "I never had much use for Dallas, either."

"You used to live there?" Naomi thought she knew everything there was to know about Noah. Apparently not.

"Born and raised," Noah said with a snort.

"Why did you leave?" Noah's brow furrowed and heat rose to Naomi's cheeks. "You don't have to answer that," she added. "I'm being nosy."

"I left because I didn't want to be reminded of my life there." Noah kept his gaze straight ahead as he fiddled with the remote. "I wanted to define myself beyond the boundaries that had been set by my father and what he stood for."

Naomi's breath stalled. Noah had talked about his brothers, but never his dad. He might as well have been talking about her own reasons for leaving the city. "I know what you mean."

Noah turned to face her. His brow furrowed and his jaw squared as he studied her. Naomi found it hard to take a deep breath in his presence. He overwhelmed her. Excited her. Heated her blood to the boiling point. "Did your dad place impossibly high standards on you right before he pulled the rug out from under you, too?"

The hurt in his somber tone settled on Naomi's chest and she resisted the urge to massage the ache away. "More like he wanted me to aspire to his impossibly low ones."

Naomi straightened on the cushion. She shouldn't have said anything. She didn't want Noah to get even a glimpse of what her life had been like before she'd moved to Sanger. It made her sick to think that while Noah's father had set the bar so high for him, her own dad had been teaching her that nothing beat easy money and honesty was over-rated.

"Hey." Noah's concern broke her from her reverie. He reached out and smoothed her hair away from her face. "Are you okay?"

No. How could she possibly be okay when he touched her with such care? As though she was something precious. Emotion clogged Naomi's throat and she pushed herself up from the couch. She needed to put distance between her and Noah before she started to believe about herself what she saw in his eyes every time he looked at her.

"I'm just tired," she said. "It's been a hell of a night."

"Naomi—"

"I'd better get some sleep." She couldn't let him finish his sentence. Couldn't bear the tenderness in his voice. "I'll see you in the morning, Noah."

"Good night, Naomi."

She paused and her eyes drifted shut. How was it possible to feel so much from three simple words? "Good night, Noah," she said as she headed for her bedroom.

FOUR

"I think I've got a lead on the guy that assaulted Naomi Davis."

Ali's words ripped Noah's attention from the budget report he'd been working on. "How? Where?"

Ali's smirk only served to goad Noah's impatience. "What? Didn't think I had the investigative chops?"

He wasn't about to admit that her getting one up on him rankled. He'd been looking for possible leads for days to no avail. "Just spill it already."

Ali chuckled. "Okay, so I could be a little overconfident. It might not even pan out. But a dark sedan ran a stoplight on the way out of town the same night Naomi was attacked. I ran the plates and got a hit."

Sweet Jesus, did she have to build the damn suspense? "And . . . ?"

"The car is registered to a Jackson Fletcher. Dallas address. Guy's got a record and some pretty spiffy criminal connections."

Damn it. Noah's gut sank. No way was what happened

to Naomi a random robbery attempt. "What sort of criminal connections?"

Ali's smile melted away. Anxiety trickled into Noah's bloodstream and his heart picked up its pace. "Duane Parker."

Noah shot up out of his chair. He slapped his palms down on the desk and braced his arms as he leaned toward Ali. "Are you sure?"

"Yeah," she replied. "I'm positive."

Shit. If Ali's research into Jackson Fletcher was legit, Naomi could very well be mixed up with Dallas's most notorious crime syndicate. Or at the very least, a man who was associated with it. Duane Parker had a reputation that reached far past Dallas. Hell, past Texas. The guy had ties to the cartel and crime syndicates in Los Angeles, Nevada, and god only knew where else.

"What do you want to do about it?"

Noah looked up at Ali as he gathered his thoughts. "Nothing." Yet.

"Nothing?"

"Naomi hasn't broken any laws."

Ali's brow furrowed. "I meant about Fletcher. Want us to bring him in?"

Noah had a few contacts with the Dallas PD. He'd have to follow the proper chain of command if he wanted face time with Fletcher. And since Naomi had claimed not to have gotten a look at the man who attacked her, they didn't have enough on him to outright charge him with the attempted assault.

"No," Noah said after a moment. "We'll be chasing our tails if we bring him in right now. I need to do some digging first."

Realization dawned on Ali's face. "You think Naomi's hiding something, don't you?"

Noah's shoulders slumped. "I don't want to think so, but

yeah. Carl pulled me aside at the bar the other night and told me she's been getting harassing phone calls. Started about two weeks ago. He's not sure who's calling or what they're saying, but he said that she's always rattled afterward."

"Could be a jealous ex."

"Yeah, that was my first thought, too." It made sense, anyway.

Ali settled down at her desk. Her fingers moved over her computer keyboard and flew over the keys. Noah's stomach tied into a knot. Ali was a good deputy because she didn't let her emotions sway her. Her quest for the truth wouldn't be influenced by her feelings. The *tap, tap, tap* of the keyboard stopped and Ali brought her gaze up to meet Noah's. His lungs compressed.

"She doesn't have a record," Ali said. "Not even a speeding ticket."

He let out a gust of breath. Somehow, it felt like a betrayal to have thought for even a second that Naomi could have had a criminal past. Still, having her innocence confirmed did little to put Noah at ease. "It wasn't random," Noah replied. "But she won't open up to me about it."

"Maybe you need to confront her," Ali suggested. "Instead of being the nice guy I know you are."

Noah cringed. Ali made "nice" sound like an insult. He knew she didn't mean it that way, but it stung just the same. Maybe it was because he was the youngest of four brothers that Noah had always been the quiet one. The "nice" one. His oldest brother, Nate, was the leader. Assertive. At times severe, but always in charge. Carter was the golden boy, good at everything he tried. Travis was the laid-back party boy. Confident and easygoing. Noah didn't share any of his brothers' traits. He was the peacemaker. The protector. Quiet and a little shy. Hell, it had taken almost six months for him to muster the courage necessary to ask

Naomi out. Maybe it was time to take a few pages out of his brothers' books and step up his game.

Noah raked his fingers through his hair. "I can't help her if she refuses to trust me."

"So," Ali said. "Make her trust you."

Noah pulled into the parking lot of Sweet 'n' Sassy. With every passing mile, he'd convinced himself that Naomi was dealing with a stalker. The attempted assault, the random phone calls, all pointed toward a romantic entanglement that had gone sour. Her reluctance to open up to him about it could have been fueled by embarrassment, but Noah wasn't so sure. More than likely, she knew that Jackson Fletcher had criminal connections. If she was aware of how dangerous he was, it stood to reason that she wouldn't easily give him up to the cops. Especially if he'd threatened her.

Was it wrong to want to give Naomi the benefit of the doubt? It showed that insufferable nice guy side of Noah that he was willing to offer himself an explanation that would inevitably make Naomi the victim. She might not have had a criminal record, but that didn't mean she was innocent. Damn it, he needed to get to the bottom of this before he drove himself crazy. Doubt ate away at him. Concern for her knotted his gut. As he put the truck in park and hopped out, he decided that he wasn't leaving here tonight until she told him every single secret she'd kept from him.

"Hey there!" Naomi greeted him with a bright smile that sent an electric rush through Noah's bloodstream. "You're right on time. I just took a brisket out of the smoker for tomorrow's sandwiches. Want me to cut you off a few slices?"

The way to Noah's heart was through good barbeque and she knew it. "Sure." There was no use in marching through the door and interrogating her. Noah needed Naomi to trust him. He needed to ease her into opening up to him. "I'll sit at the bar if that's okay."

Naomi's eyes widened with her grin. "Really? Not worried about what people will say?"

Normally, Noah would never sit at the bar. But since he was off duty and in plain clothes, he figured it would be safe enough to sit there. Besides, Naomi was always stationed at the bar. He couldn't have a real conversation with her unless he sat there.

"I'll risk it tonight," he said as he perched atop one of the high stools.

"You drinking?" Naomi tucked a violet-streaked lock of hair behind one ear as she plucked a bottle of Tito's from the top shelf.

Damn, he needed a drink. But in a town as small as Sanger, one drink would amount to him stumbling out of the bar completely shit-faced once the story made its way through the gossip mill. "I'll have a sweet tea."

Naomi's smile lost a little of its shine. "Mind if I drink?"

Noah's shrewd, hazel gaze narrowed. "Rough day?"

She recovered her sour expression with a wink. "No rougher than any other."

Noah's lips thinned and Naomi's stomach twisted into an anxious knot. She swore he could see right through her. "You got another phone call today, didn't you?"

The man didn't miss a beat. She'd tried to keep up appearances. Wanted him to think that life had gone back to normal after her run-in with Jack last week. Despite her smile and flirty banter, Noah saw past the façade. It was one of the things she liked best about him. And also one of the things that would probably get her into deeper trouble than she already was.

She had enough man problems right now, thank you very much.

Naomi dropped some ice and poured a shot of vodka into a copper cup. She finished it off with a little ginger beer and a squeeze of lime before swirling it all around and taking a healthy swallow. It was going to take more than a Moscow mule to calm her nerves at this point.

"Not sure what you mean. I get calls all day long," she said with a laugh. "Sort of comes with the business." She grabbed a tall glass and filled it with ice and sweet tea for Noah. He took the glass from her outstretched hand. His fingers grazed hers and Naomi drew in a tight breath from the electricity of the contact. Her heart beat a mad rhythm in her chest and her lower abdomen clenched. Every second spent in Noah's company only served to further unravel her. What would he think of her if he knew the truth?

"Naomi." Noah's serious tone sent a shiver of trepidation down her spine. "I think we need to talk."

No, they didn't. As far as she was concerned, they had nothing to say to each other that didn't have to do with the food or the iced tea. She took another swig from the copper mug before setting it down on the bar with a little too much force. The bell in the service window chimed and Naomi let out a sigh of relief for her reprieve, however short it might be.

"That's your brisket," she said. "I'll be back in a jiff."

The ten-foot trek to the kitchen was far too short. A nice long walk to Oklahoma would have been better.

"You look like you're about to swallow your tongue."

Naomi turned a caustic eye on Carl as she snatched the plate with Noah's dinner. "Glad to see my discomfort is a source of entertainment for you. Did you tell Noah that I was getting threatening phone calls?"

"I'm not entertained," Carl replied. His dark brown eyes shone with concern and his weathered lips puckered.

"Yeah, I told him. I know you're tough and can take care of yourself, but that doesn't mean you should have to. I'm hopin' you'll let go of that stubborn streak long enough to let the sheriff help you."

Naomi's stomach knotted and she swallowed down the bile that rose in her throat. "Help me with what?"

Carl scoffed. "I was born at night, but it wasn't last night. Whatever you've gotten yourself into, you're gonna need help gettin' out of. You're a good girl, Naomi. I don't want to see you get hurt."

That made two of them. Truth was, she'd spent most of the day trying to calm her frazzled nerves. Jack had called her every day this week with not-so-gentle reminders of what she owed and what would happen to her if she didn't come up with the cash by the end of the month. She might as well owe fifty million. The bar wasn't turning a solid profit yet and even if she sold her car and emptied out her bank account, she'd only have about ten thousand dollars to offer up to him when he came back to collect. Hardly enough to satisfy those bloodthirsty bastards she'd been stupid enough to do business with.

"You think I'm a good girl, Carl?" It was stupid, but those words meant a lot to her. Most of her life, Naomi had only ever thought of herself as a screwup.

"I know you are, kiddo." His affectionate smile caused her chest to ache. "Everyone makes a mistake now and then."

Problem was, Naomi's bad decisions far outweighed her good ones. "I'll think about talking to Noah." No use confirming what he already knew. "Thanks, Carl." She grabbed a set of silverware and headed back toward the bar.

Noah stabbed his straw down into his iced tea over and over again. It wasn't an angry gesture, more contemplative. He stared at some far-off point. His strong jaw squared and his brow furrowed as though he fought some internal battle. The muscles in his forearm flexed with every downward stab of the straw. Noah Christensen was too damned good to be true. So handsome it was almost painful to look at him. She had no doubt that he'd try to help her if he knew what she'd gotten herself into. Noah was the most honorable man she'd ever met. But really, what could he possibly do? She'd borrowed money from dangerous people. People who wanted their loan repaid. Aside from him cutting a check she *knew* a small-town sheriff couldn't cover, there wasn't much he could do to help her.

Her secrets would have to stay secrets. *Sorry, Carl. I'm on my own for this one.*

"Here you go." Naomi plastered a cheerful smile on her face and set the plate and silverware down in front of Noah. "Carl's trying out a new recipe for the beans. Let me know if you like it."

Noah grabbed a fork and dug into the beans first. "They're great," he said without any real enthusiasm. "Even better than the last batch."

"Excellent!" She might have gone a little over the top with her own excitement, but she hoped that she could do something to derail Noah's plans to talk to her about whatever the hell it was he thought they needed to talk about. "I'm more interested in what you think about the brisket, though. I whipped up a dry rub yesterday that I think is pretty fantastic. I smoked that sucker for nineteen hours, too. It might be the best one I've ever done."

Noah stabbed the brisket with his fork. Dang, it was a wonder he didn't take a piece of the plate off as well. He shoved the bite into his mouth and chewed. "It's good, too."

"Jeez, don't get too excited, Sheriff," Naomi said with a nervous laugh. His agitation with her caused a tingle to travel up the length of her arms and settle at the base of her neck. "I'd hate for you to have a heart attack right here at the bar."

"Everything you cook is great," he continued in that same insufferably deadpan tone. "Obviously, since I eat here almost every night."

Naomi grabbed her drink and drained it in a couple of swallows. She reached for the bottle of Tito's, more than ready for round two, minus the ginger beer. Noah's arm shot out and he gripped her wrist before she could get ahold of the bottle.

She should have been scared. Or at the very least, shaken up by his sudden assertiveness. Instead, a thrill chased through Naomi's bloodstream. The sharp lines of his expression gave him a decidedly dangerous edge. The hold he had on her wrist wasn't painful. Instead, he exercised just enough of his strength to let her know who was in control. And his hazel gaze, piercing in its intensity, told her that from here on out, he wasn't going to put up with her games.

This was a side of Noah she'd never seen. And damn, did she ever like it.

"I want to know how you got mixed up with Jackson Fletcher," Noah said. "And don't even think about lying to me. Understand?"

FIVE

She could try to deflect all she wanted. Feed him delicious barbeque, make small talk, flirt. Work her charm with that seductive smile and warm, honeyed voice. But Noah was through playing games. He wasn't going to let her distract him. He was going to help her . . . whether she wanted him to or not.

The smile melted from her expression and her wide gray eyes glistened with unshed tears. Noah cursed under his breath as he relaxed his grip on her wrist and then let it go completely. He hadn't wanted to scare her. Hell, she was already scared enough. Being the nice guy wasn't getting him anywhere with her, though. It was time to switch up his tactics.

"Jackson who?" Naomi's cheeks flushed with color. "I'm not sure who you're talking about, Noah."

He let out a slow sigh. *Damn it.* She certainly wasn't going to make this easy on him, was she? "I know he's the guy that roughed you up last week. And I know he's involved with a crime syndicate in Dallas. Men like that don't blow through a small town and hold up the local bar for what's in the register."

"Noah—"

"Don't." He leaned over the bar until only a few inches separated them. He lowered his voice for Naomi alone. "Don't play games with me. I know you're in trouble. I want to help you. Damn it, *let me*."

"I can't talk about this right now." Her voice hitched on a breath and tears pooled in her eyes. She swiped them away before they could fall down her cheeks. A shuddering breath left her lungs as she straightened and looked Noah dead in the eye. "Later, after I close up for the night. Okay?"

It might've been another attempt at deflection, but at this point, Noah would take what he could get. "Fine. I've got a hot meal, a cold drink, and all the time in the world. I'm not going anywhere."

She gave him a wan smile. "You seem pretty sure of that. You might change your mind."

The sadness in her words cut through him. What in the hell could she possibly be mixed up in that would make her so sad and so afraid? So sure that it would push him away. And why did Noah want to beat the bastard who'd stirred that sadness and fear to a bloody pulp? Oh, right, he was fucking crazy about her. That's why.

What a mess.

He should have handed the matter of Naomi's attempted assault over to Ali to investigate. He was too close, his feelings for Naomi too deep already. How could he possibly be impartial when all he wanted to do was protect her?

Noah's mood continued to plummet with every passing hour. He barely tasted his dinner and was on his fifth sweet tea of the night when the last straggling patrons filtered out of the bar. And still, Naomi kept her distance. She cleaned up, chatted with Carl, stacked chairs on top of tables as though Noah wasn't even there.

Naomi would learn soon enough that Noah was a stubborn son of a bitch. He'd told her he wasn't going anywhere until they talked and he meant it.

"I'll see you tomorrow."

Noah looked up at the sound of Carl's voice. His eyes locked with Naomi's and her expression transformed from casual dismissal to sheer terror. She wasn't scared of Noah, though. He knew that what had her spooked was coming clean about what was going on and that did nothing to calm his already frazzled nerves.

The door closed behind Carl and Naomi let out a slow sigh. "Noah, it's late. Can we talk tomorrow?"

The exhaustion and stress in her tone wasn't faked. Even so, Noah couldn't give her an inch. "No, I think we'd better talk now."

"Why do you even care about what's going on with me?" Her harsh tone cut through the silence. "Some guy jumped me. Big deal. It's not as though something like that never happened to me in Dallas. And I can guarantee you the cops didn't give a shit about it then. It's over and done with. Just let it go, okay? Jesus."

Naomi thought if she got angry, acted like the tough girl, Noah would cave and leave her alone. That wasn't going to happen. "I don't give a shit what the Dallas PD does or doesn't do. This is *my* county. *My* town. Nothing you say or do is going to convince me that Jackson Fletcher showing up here was *random*. You're going to come clean with me Naomi, whether you like it or not."

Naomi's brow furrowed. She chewed the inside of her cheek before she let out a frustrated breath. "You know what, Noah? You're a bossy asshole."

Noah crossed the room to where she stood. For the first time since they'd met he felt like shaking some sense into her. "Keep pushing my buttons, Naomi. It's not going to keep me from getting to the bottom of what's going on."

Her jaw squared and indignant fire lit her gray eyes, like a lightning storm on a summer night. Beautiful. "Mind your own business, *Sheriff*."

"You are my business."

Naomi's eyes went wide. "The hell I am!"

"You're a constituent in my county. What happens to you is *absolutely* my business."

Naomi scoffed. Noah hated to admit it, but she was doing a damn fine job of getting under his skin. "Anyone ever tell you that you sound like an evil dictator?"

He fixed her with a stern glare. "Every day."

She stalked past him. Noah reached out and grabbed her upper arm to stop her. "What did Fletcher want from you, Naomi?"

She pulled her arm free with a jerk. "None of your damn business, that's what."

"Are you involved in something illegal?"

Her eyes went wide. "You'd be the last person on the planet I'd tell if I were."

She'd pushed his buttons and Noah pushed right back. This wasn't getting them anywhere. "Don't make me find out on my own."

"Please, Noah." Naomi's voice trembled. "Let it go."

The vulnerability in her words and frightened expression broke him. He closed the distance between them in three purposeful strides. His arms went around her waist and he hauled her body against his. Naomi's mouth went slack and he couldn't resist the invitation of her soft, full lips.

He'd thought about kissing her every day for the past six months. Imagined what it would feel like. She was heaven and hell, the sweetest self-inflicted torture. And even though he knew blurring the lines between wanting to help her and simply wanting her wasn't a good idea, Noah did nothing to stop it.

Tiny sparks of electricity ignited over Noah's body with each caress of their lips. His cock hardened to stone behind his fly and he groaned as he pressed his hips against Naomi's. Her arms came up to wind around his neck and she scraped her nails along the nape, coaxing chills to the surface of his skin. Noah couldn't get enough of her. Wanted *more*. He'd lost himself to Naomi Davis and there was no going back.

Naomi's head swam. Her senses were awash with Noah: his scent, taste, the firm command of his lips on hers. He gripped the back of her neck and pressed his body against her as he deepened the kiss. His tongue thrust past her lips in a sensual caress that made her thighs quake.

Her attempts to put distance between them had been a futile effort. Noah had artfully deflected her anger and hurtful words, refusing to let her erect that wall she'd been so desperate to build. He'd shattered her defenses the second his lips met hers. How could she possibly put him at arm's length now when all she wanted to do was pull him closer?

They stumbled backward until Noah's back met the wall. Naomi reached up and raked her fingers through the close-cropped hair at the base of his neck. Noah moaned and the sound rippled through her, settling in a deep throb between her legs. He gave a gentle thrust of his hips and the length of his erection pressed against her. Naomi's breath caught as a molten rush of pure lust shot through her.

What had started out as a slow burn grew frantic. She couldn't kiss him deeply enough as her mouth slanted across his. She couldn't get close enough as she pressed her body against him. Naomi groped for his belt, ripping it free from the buckle before tugging loose the button of his jeans. If she didn't get her hands on bare flesh, she was going to go out of her damned mind.

"I want you." Noah's murmured words against her mouth only added fuel to Naomi's fire. "I've wanted you for too damned long."

They'd skirted their mutual attraction for months and it had taken an actual crisis to bring them together. That sort of instant combustion could be dangerous, Naomi knew that. And yet, as Noah's tongue slid against hers in a warm, wet caress, she couldn't be bothered to worry about the consequences of what had sparked between them.

What was one more mistake in a lifetime of bad decisions?

Naomi worked down the zipper of Noah's jeans. He sucked his breath in on a hiss as she slid her hand past the waistband of his boxers and stroked the length of his cock. "Oh god," he said on a groan. "Fuck, that feels good."

Naomi tucked away the smug satisfaction that she could affect him with so little contact. If that was enough to make him groan, she could only imagine his reaction when she put her mouth on him. She wanted to see the usually tight-laced sheriff come completely undone.

She crouched down and dragged Noah's jeans and boxers around his thighs. His erection sprang free as though as eager for her touch as she was to touch him. Noah pressed his back tight against the wall and let his head fall back. The only sound in the empty bar was that of his breath, ragged with anticipation.

Naomi's blood heated to the boiling point and her own heart beat a mad rhythm in her chest. She took him into her mouth and Noah let out a low groan that Naomi swore vibrated over every inch of her skin. His hands came down on her head and his fingers threaded tentatively through her hair. The care with which he handled her caused tender emotion to swell in Naomi's chest. He shook with restraint, unwilling to move even an inch. She wanted him to know that she wasn't as breakable as he thought and she drove the point home by taking him deeper into her mouth and sucking hard.

"Jesus." The word left his lips on an emphatic breath.

Noah gave a shallow thrust of his hips and she let out a soft moan of approval. His fingers threaded deeper into her hair and he gripped the strands. Another electric rush hit Naomi's bloodstream as she worked her mouth over his shaft. She dragged her mouth from the thick base to the crown, letting her teeth scrape lightly over his delicate flesh. If it felt this good to have him in her mouth, she couldn't wait to know what it would feel like to be fucked by Noah Christensen.

Naomi enjoyed every minute spent crouched between Noah's legs. She licked, sucked, bit down lightly on his engorged head. She hollowed her cheeks as she took him as deep as she could and he released a ragged breath when she cupped his sac and massaged it gently.

"You're going to make me come."

She wasn't ready for this to end.

Naomi pulled back. A little of the tension released from Noah's body and he let out a slow breath. She switched up her tactics and flicked out at the head of his cock with her tongue. She followed it up with a slow, languid lick that caused his breath to hitch. Keeping him on the edge would be well worth the wait for both of them. She ran the flat of her tongue up the length of his shaft and he shuddered.

"Do you like that?" she murmured.

"Are you kidding?" Noah looked down at her. His bright hazel gaze burned as he took her in. "It feels so good, I don't know how much more I can take."

A smile curved Naomi's lips. She'd never felt any particular amount of pride at being able to get a guy off but with Noah, it was somehow different. She wanted him to feel good. Wanted to know that it was *her* that had brought him to that mindless state of passion where nothing mattered but finding satiation.

She wrapped her lips around the crown and sucked gently before releasing him. "What about that?"

Noah's deep, rumbling laughter peppered her skin like rain on a summer day. "Now you're just teasing me."

She was, but he didn't seem to mind. Naomi let her nails lightly rake down the length of Noah's powerful thighs. She cupped his firm ass with one palm and let her fingertips trace the length of his crease. All the while, she continued to tease him with her mouth, light licks and kisses alternating with deep powerful sucks that brought him close to the edge without letting him topple over it.

With every touch, his body reacted and she loved gauging his pleasure by the twitches and flexes of muscle, the tensing and releasing of his body, each and every breath that expanded his wide chest. Noah fascinated her. She could watch him, explore his body for hours. Nothing mattered in this moment. Not her many troubles, her shitty past, the life she'd tried to leave behind in Dallas but had managed to bring with her anyway. Noah became her entire universe. Her past, present, and future. It might have been irresponsible to let herself fall headlong into the blissful reprieve that Noah offered from her life but she didn't care.

Nothing mattered but this moment and the way he made her feel.

Noah's thighs quaked and his quick breaths became desperate pants. He hauled her up to her feet and kissed her with furious intensity before pulling away to study her face. "Goddamn it," he said on an exhale. "I've got to taste you. Right now, Naomi."

Her pussy clenched at the words. The mere thought of Noah's mouth on her was almost enough to make her come. "Yes," she whispered. "Oh god, Noah. Do it."

SIX

From the moment they'd met, Noah realized that Naomi wasn't tame. It was what had first attracted him to her. She'd represented an abandon that Noah had never known. He was always the safe one. The shy one. He erred on the side of caution. But not tonight.

Tonight, Noah wanted to be reckless.

He was mindless with want. Driven to that point of longing where nothing mattered but finding satisfaction. Naomi kissed him. She nipped at his bottom lip and his cock pulsed in time with his racing heartbeat. He gripped her hips and spun her in his grasp so her back was molded to his chest. A low moan escaped her lips as he reached beneath her T-shirt to cup her breasts. The thin, lacy bra was a like a second skin and her tight nipples pressed eagerly against the fabric as he brushed the tips with the pads of his thumbs.

Her breath hitched. Noah reached past the elastic waistband of her leggings to cup her pussy. The lips were swollen and slick with her arousal. He let his finger slide between them and Naomi's tight whimper of approval sent Noah into a frenzy. She wanted this as much as he did.

Noah reached to his right and gripped the back of the nearest chair. The legs scraped on the concrete floor as he dragged it in front of Naomi. He brushed her hair to the side and kissed the nape of her neck, inhaling her delicious floral scent. She bent at the waist and braced her arms on the seat of the chair, thrusting her ass against Noah's stiff cock in the process.

Sweet Jesus.

Like she'd done to him, he took the waistband of her pants in his fists and dragged them—along with her underwear—down and around her thighs. He took a step back and admired the gorgeous view, the swollen lips of her pussy protruding from between her thighs in such a wanton way that he had no choice but to indulge in tasting her.

He went to his knees before her as though praying to some ancient goddess. Naomi's thighs trembled in anticipation and Noah's gut clenched. He gripped her hips and pressed his mouth to her sex, kissing her there before thrusting his tongue between her lips.

"Oh, god, Noah."

His name ended on a low moan that tightened Noah's sac. To hear her say it with such unrestrained passion nearly made him come. He found the tight bead of her clit and swirled the tip of his tongue over the swollen knot of nerves. Naomi's thighs clenched as she let out quick pants of breath. She leaned back to increase the pressure of his mouth on her, but Noah held her hips steady. He was in control now. And he wanted her to know it.

"That feels so good." Naomi's words strung together in a desperate rush. "Don't stop. Please don't stop."

He had no intention of stopping. She was the sweetest thing he'd ever tasted. She intoxicated him. Her scent spun in his head and dizzied him. Noah couldn't get enough of her. He'd been dying of thirst for months and she was a cold mountain stream.

Noah's fingertip dug into her soft flesh as he continued to grip her hips. He thrust his tongue inside of her pussy before taking her labia into his mouth and sucking. Naomi let out a surprised gasp that ended on a drawn-out moan. Her thighs quivered and Noah dragged his teeth along her flesh as he released her from his mouth. He wanted to feast on her, lap and suck and nip at her until she screamed her pleasure. He wanted his name on her lips as she came. In fact, he wanted his name to be the *only* name on her lips. His want of her was absolute.

The trembling in her thighs intensified. Her quick panting breaths became desperate sobs. Her body tensed as a tremor passed over her body. She was close. Noah couldn't wait to see her shatter, feel her come apart.

"I want you inside of me when I come, Noah."

The words barely registered. Noah continued to lap at her and swirl his tongue over her clit. Naomi straightened, almost abruptly, ripping him from the moment. She turned and grabbed him by the wrists as she urged him to stand. Noah was helpless to do anything but follow where she led as she guided him to sit in the chair. He watched, rapt, as she kicked off her boots, shucked her pants, and stripped off her T-shirt and bra. She stood before him, naked, vulnerable, and so goddamned beautiful that it stole Noah's breath.

He followed her lead and kicked off his shoes and got rid of his jeans. He reached for his back pocket and pulled a condom from his wallet before discarding it somewhere beside him. Her attention wandered to his stiff cock and she pulled her bottom lip between her teeth. The expression caused his erection to bob as though in anticipation of what was to come and without preamble, Noah ripped open the packet and rolled the condom on. He'd imagined this moment for damned near six months, he wasn't going to waste another second.

Naomi straddled him. She gripped the back of the chair as she lowered herself over him. The head of his cock prodded her opening and Noah held his breath. Her heat enveloped him as she slowly took him inside of her and a groan gathered in his throat at the tight constriction.

The sensation was so intense, it was a miracle he hadn't gone off the second she'd settled herself on his lap. For a moment, they didn't move. Noah panted through his pleasure as did Naomi. Her heavy-lidded gaze met his and one corner of her mouth hitched in a sexy smirk as she began to slowly ride him.

This moment had no equal.

So sensual, so full of passion. Naomi was everything he'd ever wanted in a woman and more. The intimacy of the moment left Noah shaken. The bar was still brightly lit, they'd wound up in the middle of the vast space for any-one to see if they peeked in the window. Noah didn't give a single shit about the possibility of discovery, though. The place could burn down around them and he wouldn't notice. All that mattered was how he felt, the intense pleasure that radiated through him, and the woman in his arms. The rest of the world could go to hell.

Naomi's back bowed as she rode him. Noah leaned forward and latched onto one pearled nipple with his lips. Her steady rhythm faltered for the barest moment. He sucked her nipple to an even stiffer point, laved it with the flat of his tongue, and bit down gently. Naomi's thighs clenched around him and her pussy squeezed him tight. Her pace increased with her rapid breaths and Noah didn't know how much longer he could wait before the orgasm tore through him.

But he'd be damned if that happened before Naomi

found her own pleasure first. She rose up and allowed the head of his cock to glide over her clit. For a few torturous moments, she pleasured herself on his shaft, rubbing her pussy against his cock until the delicious friction nearly drove Noah mad. She seated herself fully on top of him once again and he breathed a sigh of sweet relief. Her head lolled back on her shoulders as she gripped the back of the chair and ground her hips into his.

"Noah," she gasped. "I'm going to come."

He gripped her hips and pulled her down hard on top of him. He fucked her as deeply as he could go and she cried out as the orgasm took her. Chills broke out over her skin and her inner walls squeezed him tight. Noah gritted his teeth, willed himself not to come until she was finished. The sight of her, completely undone, held his attention like nothing else could.

He was lost to her.

Naomi shuddered as the last pulses of her orgasm rippled through her. The intensity of it stole her breath and her cries left her throat raw. *Dear lord.* She'd never been fucked like that before. The passion, the *intimacy.* It was almost more than Naomi could bear. When she came, it exploded through her, wave after powerful wave. Her legs were left weak and shaking, her limbs were deliciously heavy. And still, she wanted more.

"Noah." His name left her lips on a sigh. "Noah." She couldn't find the words to finish her thought. There were no words. Nothing could adequately convey what she felt. In a single moment, he'd ruined her.

He stilled beneath her.

Naomi pulled back to study him. His bright hazel gaze delved into hers. He reached up and swept a lock of hair away from her face. No man had ever looked at her the way Noah did. With so much heat, so much tender affection.

Awestruck. Her entire life, she'd been told she was worthless. A screwup. When Noah looked at her, she felt priceless. Her chest swelled with emotion that rose up to clog her throat. Did he realize the effect he had on her? Did he know that his presence put her at ease?

His fingertips traced from her temple, down and over her cheekbone, to her mouth. His thumb brushed against her bottom lip before he leaned in to kiss her. She tasted herself on his lips, reveled in the silky glide of his tongue against hers. His arms went around her and he held her tight against his body. The heat of his skin met hers and she sighed against his mouth.

"Waiting for your second wind?" she teased.

"No." His voice didn't bear even a trace of humor. "Just want to make it last."

He kissed her bare shoulder and Naomi shivered. The heat of his mouth met her throat, her jawbone, and the hollow beneath her ear. His fingers danced along her back in a haphazard pattern that made chills break out over her skin. She felt Noah smile against her collarbone before he kissed her there as well.

"I love to give you chills."

His tongue flicked out at her skin, wet, hot, slick. Naomi swallowed down a groan and said, "You do?"

"Mhm." He kissed the swell of one breast, and then the other. "When you came, chills broke out over the backs of your thighs. It was amazing."

No man had ever paid attention to her the way Noah did. He seemed eager to learn her body's secrets. What made her shiver and moan. What made her wet. His attentiveness caused a riot of butterflies to swirl in her stomach. He could have pounded away, kept his grip on her hips and helped her ride him straight into an orgasm. Instead, Noah had put on the brakes and took his time to simply enjoy her.

Noah Christensen was one of a kind.

Long moments passed. Naomi lost track of time as they caressed, kissed, whispered in the empty space. He kept himself seated deep inside of her, only giving shallow thrusts of his hips now and again to keep the fires of their passion stoked. Noah was an artful lover. Naomi would have never thought of considering a man in that way before but there was no other way to describe it. The way Noah fucked her was as close to art as anything she'd ever experienced. Hours—days—could pass and she wouldn't know or care. Nothing mattered but her, Noah, and this moment that seemed to stretch infinitely before them. Now that they'd passed this point of no return, Naomi knew that things between them would never be the same. Friends no longer, an intimacy had been forged between them. Already she felt the strength of that bond. And it scared the hell out of her.

Noah's hips rolled upward and he thrust deeper. It caught Naomi off guard and she gasped.

"Are you okay?"

Always looking out for her. She laughed softly. "Better than okay," she replied. "That felt amazing."

"You like it?" She pulled back to find a cocky—and extremely sexy—grin plastered on Noah's gorgeous face.

She reached up and feathered her thumb across one sharp cheekbone. "I *love* it."

He thrust again. Harder and deeper this time. She rolled her hips into the contact, inviting him to go deeper still. Noah sucked in a breath and his hips gave an involuntary buck. Her own smile grew, realizing she could turn the tables on him. "Do you like that?"

His wicked grin turned her insides to mush. "I fucking *love* it. You feel so good, Naomi." The rough timbre of his voice vibrated through her. "I don't know how much longer I can last."

He was worried about sticking it out? They'd been at it for over an hour. Noah had taken his time with her, drawn out their pleasure. A smile curved her lips. She'd been so impatient to come, she'd nearly toppled from his lap in her haste to find release. It was Noah's turn to feel that. She wanted to be right in the moment with him, too. To feel the evidence of his pleasure.

"Come, Noah," she whispered close to his ear. "I want you to come."

Their previous gentle playfulness evaporated in a blaze of fiery passion. Noah's grip settled at her hips once again as he guided every roll of her hips against his. Naomi's breath sped, her quiet moans once again became desperate sobs of pleasure. What had dimmed to a warm glow in the pit of her belly grew into a supernova, ready to shatter her at any moment.

As though he sensed her building passion, Noah slowed his pace. She let out a frustrated whimper and pressed herself down to take him deep and hard. "Don't stop, Noah. Oh my god, don't stop!"

Her words sent him into a frenzy. Noah pounded into her, his hips coming up off the chair with each forceful thrust. Naomi's pussy clenched. He filled her completely, the friction of their bodies meeting and parting drove her once again to the edge of her own release. She drew in a breath and held it as she lost herself to the moment. They'd fall over the edge together. And it was going to be amazing.

"I'm close, Noah," she said.

"Wait for me." The command was firm. "I'm almost there."

Noah thrust wildly and she could no longer quell her release. He let out a shout and his body went rigid as he came. Deep, throbbing pulses shook Naomi from head to toe as Noah's hips thrust and his cock jerked inside of her.

A rush of wetness spread between her thighs and she was suddenly suffused with delicious warmth.

"I knew it would be amazing," she said between panted breaths.

"Honey," Noah replied. "We left amazing about five miles back."

Naomi smiled. She couldn't agree more.

SEVEN

Noah gathered Naomi in his arms. So maybe the setting hadn't been where he'd imagined for their first time, but if he had it to do all over again, he wouldn't have it any other way. Naomi's passion and heat had no equal. Her unabashed enjoyment of his body—and her own pleasure—excited him beyond reason.

She was the most amazing woman he'd ever met. And Noah knew that once with her would never be enough. He wanted more. But as long as her secrets stood between them, tonight would be all he'd get.

"My dad used to place bets with Duane Parker's bookies." Naomi's voice was barely a whisper. She rested her head on his shoulder as she pressed her body tight against his. Noah let his fingers wander down her bare spine and she shivered in his embrace. "That's how I met Jack."

Noah drew in a slow breath as he recalled Naomi's comment about her father holding her to his low standards. He let his hands wander over her bare skin, over the silky length of her hair. He wanted to reassure her, to let her know that she could trust him. He let his actions speak for him in the gentle caresses. He didn't need to talk, simply listen.

"You resent your dad for holding you up to high standards," Naomi said with a quiet laugh. "I wish mine had given a damn about anything I did. He let me run wild. Didn't care when I came home or who I was with. He was too busy ruining his own life to worry too much about me ruining mine."

Noah's heart ached for her. Byron Christensen might've taken away his sons' financial advantages, but they'd never been completely discarded.

"I made a lot of stupid choices, Noah, but I never broke the law. I watched my dad do shit like that for years. Steal, gamble, con, game the system. I didn't want that to be my life. I wanted to get away from all of that. And from guys who weren't any better than the one who raised me."

Noah put his mouth to her throat and inhaled her sweet rose scent. "So you found a small town out in the middle of nowhere?"

"I saw the bar listed on Craigslist. It was perfect. I had some money saved up, but I didn't have enough to buy the building."

Noah could connect the dots from there. Naomi had been so desperate to escape her life that she'd gone to the very people she was trying to get away from for help. "I wish you'd told me sooner," he murmured against her cooling skin. "Jackson Fletcher is Parker's collection agent, right?"

"Fifty thousand dollars." Naomi's breath hitched on the words and she shuddered. "Because my dad managed to swindle a week's worth of bets out from under Duane's nose, they called in my debt. I'm officially two weeks late paying it back. I have until the end of the month and because they've been so lenient with me"—she let out a bark of sarcastic laughter—"I only have to tack on five thousand in interest for every week I'm late instead of the standard ten."

"That's why Fletcher showed up at the bar last week." Noah didn't really need confirmation. "To collect."

"Yeah." Noah's neck and shoulder became damp from Naomi's tears and she sniffed. "He's been calling me every day to remind me of what will happen if I don't have the money when he comes back for it."

For days, Noah had been imagining one terrible scenario after another in his head. He'd considered that Fletcher was a violent stalker ex-boyfriend. He'd imagined that Naomi had been a witness to one of Fletcher's—or Parker's—crimes and was on the run. Through sleepless nights and stressful days, he'd worried nonstop for Naomi's safety. Knowing the truth—that she'd borrowed money from slimy loan sharks—was so low on his list of possible scenarios that he almost laughed with relief.

Sixty thousand dollars and all of Naomi's troubles went away. Hell, Noah had that much sitting in his checking account. It would be nothing to pay off her debt and get Jackson Fletcher—and his low-life boss—out of her life for good.

He kissed her throat and across her collarbone. He couldn't get enough of the contact. His tongue flicked out at her silky skin and a sigh escaped from between her lips. "Noah, I don't know what I'm going to do."

His mouth found the hollow of her throat. He kissed her there, a wet, openmouthed kiss that brought goose bumps to the surface of Naomi's skin. Noah smiled, deeply satisfied that he could so easily evoke that physical reaction in her.

"First of all," he said. "You're going to stop being so damned stubborn and secretive. Secondly, you're going to let me handle this from here on out."

Naomi pulled away to look at him. Her brow furrowed

and her mouth parted invitingly. Noah reached out and swiped the wetness from her eyes before brushing her hair back from her face. Damn, she was the most beautiful woman he'd ever laid eyes on.

"I can't let you do that," she said.

"I thought I told you that you can't be stubborn anymore."

Her lips curled at the corners, hinting at a smile. "Look who's talking. I could learn a thing or two about stubbornness from you."

True. Noah flashed a proud grin. "I'm allowed to be stubborn in this situation. You're not. When it's your turn to be stubborn, I'll let you know."

"Stubborn," Naomi remarked. "And a little high-handed."

"Yup." Noah wouldn't make any apologies for wanting to protect her. "I'm going to take care of this for you, and you're going to let me."

Naomi's gaze softened and her smile became sad. "Noah, these guys are dangerous. They don't mess around. If they find out the cops are involved"—she looked away—"it could be bad for more than just me."

When her eyes met his again, Noah saw the worry there. "Your dad, right?"

"When Duane Parker wants to make a point, he makes it by hurting every single person you care about."

Did she count him as one of those people? Noah brushed his thumb across Naomi's cheek. Her eyes drifted shut as though she reveled in the contact. The simple expression stirred his cock and he grew hard between her thighs once again. Would he ever not want her?

"I can help you, Naomi," Noah said. "Let me."

Naomi had never known a better man than Noah Christensen. She'd worried that once he knew the truth about her situation that he'd drop her in a hot second. She hadn't been prepared for the depth of his concern or the ferocity in his expression when he said, "I can help you, Naomi. Let me."

And it was because of his fierce protectiveness, his gentle touch, and fiery passion, that Naomi *couldn't* let him. Noah was the sort of man who'd give a person the shirt off his back to help them. What chance could they have at an honest-to-goodness relationship if he always wondered if Naomi was with him out of some sense of guilt? As though she owed him a relationship in return for his help. Besides, what could he possibly do to get her out of this mess? He was a small-town sheriff and Sanger might as well be on another planet compared to Dallas. She doubted Dallas PD would let him march into the city to shake down Duane because some idiot girl got in too deep with a loan. If Noah tried to get involved, Jack would hurt him. He might kill him just to prove a point. Naomi would never be able to live with herself if she allowed Noah to put himself in danger because of her stupid choices.

"You're too good for me, Noah." Saying the words nearly gutted her.

"No." The conviction in his tone brooked no argument. "I'm not."

"You're caught up in the moment now but when your head is clear, you'll realize it." Tears pooled once again in Naomi's eyes and she willed them not to flow. "I won't bring you anything but trouble."

For a long moment, Noah simply stared at her. The attention didn't make her feel uncomfortable or nervous. Instead, she lost herself in his bright hazel eyes, and met his gaze head-on. From the moment they'd met, Naomi had felt at ease with Noah. When she looked at him she felt a sense of comfort and rightness that left her shaken. And knowing she had no choice but to let him go filled her with empty sorrow. Losing Noah was better than the alternative, though. She couldn't bear to see him hurt.

"You can try to push me away, but it's not going to work."

It would work because it had to. "Can't we just have tonight?" She wanted so much more, but admitting it would only encourage him.

"Can you honestly say that tonight will be enough?"

His guileless expression refused to let her answer with anything but honesty. "No. But that's how it has to be."

"Naomi," Noah said with a laugh. "I'm not afraid."

"I am, though." Tears pricked at her eyes once again. "I don't want you to get hurt because of my bad choices. I'll figure this out. I always do. But in the meantime, I think it'll be best if you keep your distance."

"That's not going to happen."

Noah thought he was stubborn? Stubborn had *nothing* on him. "You can't help me."

He raised a sardonic brow. "What makes you so sure?"

"Do you secretly own a bank that I don't know about?" Naomi had done some shitty things, but allowing Noah to give her even a dollar was too low even for her.

"Maybe. You don't know everything about me."

Her brow furrowed. True, she didn't know everything about Noah. And his dead-serious tone piqued her curiosity. Then again, she didn't doubt that he'd try to convince her that he did in fact own a bank if it meant she'd let him help her. He was gallant like that.

"Well, now you know everything about me," she offered in response. "There's nothing else to tell. I'm a class-A screwup who's in deep with loan sharks. Impressive, right?"

"That's not all you are," Noah replied in his deep, warm voice. "You're not the sum of your choices, Naomi. You're strong, funny, smart. You cook the best food I've ever eaten. You're beautiful, fiery, passionate. You're so much more than what you think you are."

"Noah."

"I won't take no for an answer," he said. "I'm going to help you whether you like it or not."

There was no arguing with him. For tonight, she could let him think that he'd won. But tomorrow, when his brain wasn't fogged by lust, she'd convince him that it would be best for him to keep his distance. He needed to let her protect *him*. Whether he liked it or not.

She reached between them and took his hardening cock in her palm. She stroked him slowly, building his pleasure until his gaze burned from it. She kissed him once, twice, and again, until he deepened their kisses into a frenzy of slanting mouths and panted breaths. She broke the contact only long enough to retrieve another condom from his wallet. He took it from her and rolled it on before his mouth found hers once again. She could distract him with her body, let them both feel something real and intense for the rest of the night.

In the morning, Naomi would allow herself to mourn the loss of cutting Noah out of her life.

EIGHT

Last night had been one of the best of Noah's life. He'd gotten everything he'd ever wanted and more. The memory of Naomi's mouth on him, the silky glide of her skin against his, and the sweet sounds of every impassioned cry were permanently ingrained in his memory. She thought he could simply have one night with her and walk away? There weren't enough nights in his lifetime to satisfy him.

He could no more walk away from her now than he could disregard his own heart.

Noah stared down at the check in his hand. He hadn't even thought twice about writing it. Knowing that Naomi would be free and clear of those bastards was worth every last cent. Hell, he'd pay ten times that amount if he needed to. He didn't give a damn about the money. All he wanted was *her*.

He took a deep breath before he pushed open the door and strode into the bar. This early in the day, the lunch crowd had yet to show up, which gave Noah a few private moments with her before Naomi would have to direct her attention to her customers. This might not have been the best place for him to hand over a sixty thousand dollar check, but she'd given him little choice in the matter last night when she'd implied that it would be best if they didn't see each other anymore.

Noah wasn't going to let her go without a fight.

Determination squared his jaw as Noah stalked to the bar. Naomi looked up and her expression brightened for a moment before she hid her excitement behind a mask of passivity which only fortified his determination.

"Noah, I can't do this right now."

Without a word, he slid the check across the counter toward her. Naomi's brow furrowed. She scooped the check up with her fingers and studied it for a moment before dragging her gaze to his.

"Is this some sort of joke?"

She couldn't conceive of anyone actually wanting to help her? Noah's jaw clamped down and he leaned over the bar. "I told you I was going to get you out of this mess and I meant it."

"You can't afford this," Naomi replied as she waved the check at him. "This is a check for sixty thousand dollars! Good lord, Noah, this must be an entire year of your salary."

From the kitchen's service window, Carl's gentle snort drew Noah's attention. It didn't surprise him that Naomi didn't know anything about his family. In the course of their many conversations, the subject had never come up. What did surprise him was that Carl hadn't told her about him sooner.

"A year's salary?" Carl poked his head out of the window and Naomi turned to face him, her jaw slack. "He probably found that sixty grand in the cushions of his couch this morning."

Naomi looked from Carl to Noah and back again. "What are you talking about?"

"You've never heard of Christensen Petroleum?" Carl asked. "Our sheriff is worth *billions*."

Ugh. It always made Noah feel dirty when anyone talked about his family's wealth. He'd never benefited from it in his youth, and truth be told, he didn't have much use for it now. He liked his life. His modest house and patrol truck. He wasn't flashy or fancy. He didn't give a shit about expensive clothes and gourmet food. Once people found out who he was and what he had, they always treated him differently. He didn't want that from Naomi. He wanted her opinion of him to be untarnished by the numbers in his bank account.

"Noah? Is that true?"

He hiked a shoulder. "More or less."

Her arms dropped to her sides. "So basically, you're loaded?"

Noah scowled. "Does it matter?"

Naomi's gray eyes went wide. "Are you fucking kidding me? Of course it matters! What is this? Payment for services rendered?"

A slap to the face wouldn't have stung more. Noah's jaw clamped down so tight that the enamel scraped. "You *know* that's not what this is."

"You two, outside." Carl's commanding tone caught both of their attention.

Naomi turned in a huff and headed for the kitchen. Noah followed her past Carl as he negotiated the food prep counter and flat top. They made their way in silence through the kitchen to the rear exit. Naomi shoved open the door and Noah caught it before it bounced back to smack him in the face. She was angry but Noah was livid. How could she possibly think that he was such a slimy bastard as to pay her for sex?

Once outside, Naomi whipped around and shoved the check against Noah's chest. "Keep your money. I can't be bought."

"You've got a hell of a chip on your shoulder, you know that?" Noah kept his voice to a controlled burn. He'd never known a more hardheaded woman. "I don't want to buy you, Naomi. Even if last night hadn't happened, I'd still be giving you this check right now. I'm trying to help you, damn it."

She placed a hand on her hip and fixed him with a stern, cold stare. "So you write people outrageous checks with no strings attached on a daily basis. Is that it?"

"No, but—"

"Exactly."

It showed just how hardheaded Naomi was that she refused to let him get a word in. Noah raked his fingers through his hair and let out a frustrated breath. "You don't want me to investigate this. You don't want me to get Dallas PD involved. And now, you won't even let me pay off your debt even if it means saving your damned life? What in the hell do you expect me to do?"

"Nothing," she said. "This isn't a problem for you to fix, Noah."

"Oh yeah?" His temper flared. "How are you planning to fix it?"

"I-I don't—"

Noah hit her with a dose of her own medicine. "*Exactly.*"

"It doesn't matter." Her voice escalated with every word. "It's not your problem!"

She could be as indignant as she wanted. Noah wasn't going to let her stubbornness get in the way of him helping her. "And I told you that anything that has to do with you *is* my problem!"

"Why?" Naomi's voice broke on the word. "Because I

live in Sanger? Because I'm one of your constituents and you can't bear for anything to be out of line in your perfectly ordered town?"

"Because I'm in love with you, damn it!" The words exploded from Noah's lips. "I've been in love with you for a long damned time."

"You think because—wait." Naomi's expression softened and her brow furrowed. "What did you say?"

"You heard me." Noah closed the space between them. He gripped Naomi's shoulders and bent his head close to hers. "I'm in love with you."

"That's what I thought you said," Naomi murmured.

Noah's admission nearly knocked her off her feet. Of all the things she'd expected him to say to her, that he was in love with her was at the very bottom of her list. Their night together had been beyond amazing, and Naomi couldn't deny that her chest swelled with tender emotion every time she thought about Noah. But love?

"Whether you love me or not, you can't just walk in here and plunk down a sixty-thousand-dollar check like you're giving me a few bucks to buy a candy bar or something. Noah." Naomi let out an exhausted sigh. "Do you know what sort of guilt you're placing on me by asking me to take that money?"

His expression fell. A groove cut into his forehead right above the bridge of his nose. His gaze delved into hers and a shiver danced down Naomi's spine. "There are no strings attached to this money." His strained tone broke her heart. "I'm not trying to buy you."

Shame heated Naomi's cheeks. She'd insinuated as much and she hadn't stopped to think about how her words might hurt him. If Carl hadn't said something, she never would have known about Noah's family—or his wealth. He wasn't the sort of man to flaunt what he had. Noah was honest and modest. Passionate and caring. Honorable and protective. She'd never known a better man and he was in love with *her*.

"I know you're not," she said, low. "I'm sorry. But Noah, I don't deserve your help." She averted her gaze. "I don't deserve this money."

"It's my money to give. Why don't you let me decide if you deserve it or not?"

She was so tempted. Such a seemingly simple gesture on Noah's part and all of her problems would disappear. "It's too much money."

"You heard Carl," Noah said with a laugh. "I found it in the cushions of my couch this morning."

"How rich are you really?" She cringed, wishing she could take the words back the second she'd said them. It was none of her business how much money Noah had. Sure, it might've eased her conscience a bit, but in reality, she didn't care how much money he had in the bank. It wouldn't change how she felt about him.

His lips curled into a sardonic smile. "Rich enough to assure you that you should take that check and not feel even an ounce of guilt when you cash it."

Wow. So sixty grand really was like spare change to him. "Why didn't you tell me?"

"What? That my father's company is worth a shitload of money and he left it all to me and my brothers when he died? Is there ever a good time to work something like that into a conversation?"

Naomi laughed. "I guess not."

She looked down at the check still clutched in her hand. Silence settled between them and Naomi let out a gentle sigh. Noah kept his hands on her shoulders, kneading the tightness away until she felt absolutely boneless.

"If I take this money," she said, "you have to let me pay you back."

"It's not a loan."

She smiled at his sternness. "It has to be. Otherwise it'll get in the way of our relationship. I don't want that."

Noah's expression perked at her words. "Relationship?"

"Yeah." She looked up to meet his gaze. "I mean, if you want one."

Noah bent his head close. His mouth met hers in a slow, soft caress that damn near curled her toes in her Chucks. There was more emotion in that simple kiss than anything Naomi had ever experienced and it caused her heart to pound in her chest and tears to prick at her eyes. She went up on her tiptoes and kissed him back with everything she was worth. Naomi wasn't quite ready to say the words she knew Noah wanted to hear, but maybe he'd feel in their kiss every bit of deep affection she felt for him.

The moment might have lasted a few minutes or a few years. Naomi wasn't quite sure. Either way, Noah's decadent kisses continued to rain down on her and she allowed herself to be lost to the moment. To him. To the feelings that rose inside of her like a tide, threatening to crash over her and take her out to sea.

When he finally pulled away, Naomi was drunk on his kisses. She swayed on her feet and he reached out to steady her.

"Thank you, Noah. There aren't even words to explain how thankful I am."

"I think your lips did a damn fine job of conveying what you couldn't find the words for."

Heat rose to her cheeks and she looked at him from beneath lowered lashes. "Are you sure about this?"

"I already told you to cash the check. Don't make me come back here with a suitcase full of cash."

She gave him a soft smile. "No, I mean, are you sure about me?" She wasn't exactly the clean-cut, small-town girl. She had a wild past and enough baggage to make any man want to run in the opposite direction. Noah deserved a better woman than her. It still hadn't completely sunk in that he wanted her.

He kissed her. "Damned sure. And there's nothing you could do or say that's going to change my mind. I love you."

A girl could get used to hearing those words on a daily basis.

"What now?" It wasn't every day that a guy told you he loved you *and* bailed you of a big-time cluster fuck.

Noah gave a gentle laugh. "Well, first things first, you're going to put that money in the bank. I've got to get to the station and you've got delicious barbeque to make." He bent to kiss her forehead and Naomi smiled. "I'll stop by after work tonight. How does that sound?"

It sounded like an honest-to-god normal adult relationship. "It's perfect."

"Good." Noah kissed her one last time. Just a quick peck that only made Naomi want more. "I'll see you tonight."

Instead of heading back inside, Noah went the opposite direction, back toward the parking lot. Naomi watched him leave, appreciating the way his pants hugged his muscular thighs and the curve of his ass. She knew now that there was nothing weak or shy about Noah. He exuded power. Jack and the crew he rolled with used intimidation, guns, and violence to show their strength. Noah could do all of that and more simply with his powerful strides.

He was amazing. Perfect. The best thing that had ever happened to her. He was caring, generous, strong, and passionate. When he looked at her, Naomi felt like she *mattered* for the first time in her life.

Noah Christensen was in love with her.

And she was pretty sure that she was in love with him, too.

NINE

"What do you mean she never came back?" Noah leaned over the bar, ready to grab Carl by the collar of his shirt. "And why are you just now telling someone about it?"

Carl glanced away and Noah's heart sank into his gut. It didn't take a genius to figure out what Carl had assumed. Was it possible that Naomi had taken his money and run?

"I didn't want to think it," Carl said as though he'd read Noah's mind. "But you know, she's had a hard a life. Her dad's a hustler . . ." He let out a gust of breath. "She's a good girl, Noah, but I know she's scared of whoever she's in trouble with. She might not make good choices."

As much as she'd lamented the crappy choices of her past, and her shady upbringing, Noah couldn't imagine that she'd fall back so easily into old habits. "When did she leave?"

"A couple of hours after you did this morning," Carl replied. "She made a phone call right after you left. I don't know who she was talking to or what she said. She put a few racks of ribs in the smoker and told me she'd be back in about a half hour but she never came back."

Damn it. Noah swallowed down the string of curses that rose in his throat. Seven hours unaccounted for. An entire fucking day! "Jesus Christ, Carl."

Noah couldn't remember the last time he'd been so pissed off. Or hurt. Or confused. Doubt gnawed at him. The possibility that Naomi had stolen his money and took off sucked every ounce of oxygen from his lungs. Had she been working an angle the entire time? Had Naomi known all along about his family and his wealth? Jesus, had the attack on her even been legit or had it been staged to gain Noah's sympathy?

His ass landed on the bar stool behind him. The worry that tied his stomach into knots burned in the indignant fire that flared up in its place. He'd spent months pining over her, working up the courage to even ask her out. And then, when they'd given in to their desires, Noah thought he was about to get everything he'd ever wanted. He'd told her he loved her. *Shit.* As if that wasn't humiliating as hell. He'd spilled his guts and she'd run off with his money. He had one hell of an investigative instinct, didn't he? Snowed by a beautiful con artist with a flirty smile.

"Noah? Did you hear me?" He looked up to find Carl studying him. His weathered brow puckered with concern and his lips thinned.

"Sorry." Noah had been so lost in his own damned tortured thoughts he'd had no idea Carl had even been talking to him. "What did you say?"

Carl held the phone up in his hand. "Ali called. She said you need to get back to the station ASAP."

Why hadn't she called his cell? He reached for his pocket to find it empty. *Damn it.* He'd been so excited to see Naomi that he'd left his phone in the truck. He could only imagine what was up that Ali didn't think she could relay to him over the radio. Noah pushed the stool out from the bar and stepped down. No matter what Naomi might have done, he still had a job to do. Sitting around like some sad sack wasn't going to do the people of Sanger any good.

"Thanks, Carl. If you hear from Naomi, can you give me a call?" Her sudden disappearance left a sour taste in Noah's mouth and put his nerves on edge. Whether or not she'd conned him, he wanted to know that she was safe.

"You'll be the first person I call," Carl replied.

"Thanks."

Noah headed out the door and got in his truck. The five-minute drive to the station felt like five hours as he continued to contemplate the possibility of Naomi conning him out of sixty grand. When he walked through the station to his office at the back of the building, Ali looked as though her head was about to explode right off her shoulders.

"Where in the hell have you been?"

His jaw squared and Noah swallowed down his angry retort. "Left my cell in the truck. Carl told me to head back to the station so I did. Why didn't you radio me?"

Ali's exasperated expression intensified. "Couldn't. I got a strange phone call about a half hour ago."

Noah's attention piqued. A nervous tremor rolled over him and he stretched his neck from side to side in an effort to release the tension pulling his shoulders taut. "What sort of phone call?"

"Glad I finally have your attention," Ali scoffed.

Noah folded his arms across his chest and fixed her with his most intimidating stare. If Ali knew how quickly his afternoon had gone to shit, he doubted she'd be quite as snarky right now.

Her answering expression carried none of its usual sarcasm. "It was about Naomi."

And just like that, Noah's stomach dropped to the soles of his feet. "What about her?"

"I'm not sure," Ali said. "That's the weird part. "The

guy who called asked for you. I told him you'd gone home for the day and asked if there was anything I could help him with. He said that he'd be calling back in a half hour and that it was in Naomi's best interest if you were here to take the call. Then, he hung up."

"Naomi's unaccounted for." The words had no emotion as they left Noah's mouth. "Carl hasn't seen her since around eleven this morning."

"Unaccounted for?" Ali's eyes bulged. "What does that even mean?"

"I'm not sure." But Noah was starting to suspect that his shitty evening was about to get a whole hell of a lot worse.

The office phone rang. Noah and Ali locked gazes for the barest moment before he crossed to his office. Ali picked up the extension at her desk and answered, "Sanger Sheriff's Office." She looked at Noah as she listened to the caller before giving him a quick nod. "He is. I'm putting you on hold. Don't go anywhere."

Noah settled into his chair and took a couple of deep, cleansing breaths. His heart beat a mad rhythm in his chest and his mind swam with too many thoughts to separate a single one. He picked up his extension and answered, "This is Sheriff Christensen."

"I've got your girl. What's she worth to you?"

Adrenaline dumped into Noah's bloodstream. "Who is this?"

"None of your fucking business, that's who this is."

Noah's teeth ground. "Jackson Fletcher, am I right?"

Silence answered him. "You want to see Naomi again, it's going to cost your rich-as-fuck ass. Ten million. Unmarked bills. You've got three days to get it together or she dies."

Bastard. Noah's earlier suspicions dwindled, but there was still the possibility that Naomi and Fletcher were playing him. "What makes you think I've got ten million dollars sitting around?"

Fletcher laughed. "Naomi shows up with a check for sixty grand outta nowhere to pay off her debt, you don't think I'm going to do a little research? I know exactly who you are, Christensen. And what you've got. So don't treat me like I'm a fucking idiot."

Well, it was worth a shot. He wasn't about to roll over, though. Or buy in to what Fletcher was selling him. Not until he talked to Naomi. He'd know from her tone whether or not she was really in trouble. "I want to talk to Naomi first," he said. "Then, we'll negotiate."

"He wants to talk to you." Jack smirked.

A thousand vile curses sat at the tip of Naomi's tongue. He brought the phone to her ear and she let out a slow breath to stem the flow of tears that stung her eyes. "Noah?"

His sigh of relief on the other end of the line nearly shredded her composure. "Are you okay? Did he hurt you?"

"I'm not hurt," Naomi said. "I'll be okay. I'm so sorry, Noah." Her voice hitched and she willed it to stay strong. "I never should have gotten you involved in this. This is all my fault."

"Naomi, listen to me." Noah's words conveyed so much emotion. "*None* of what happened is your fault. Do you understand me? I'm going to get you out of this."

Naomi knew what Jack wanted. Money, and lots of it. With the ten million dollars he'd demanded from Noah for her return, Jack would find the opportunity to break from Duane's syndicate where he'd no longer be someone's stooge.

"Don't." She couldn't let Noah pay her ransom. Jack was ambitious but stupid. Once Duane found out what he was up to, he'd shut Jack down. That didn't necessarily mean Naomi would make it out of this alive, but as long as she could protect Noah, she didn't care what happened to her. "Please, don't give him a single dime, Noah. I'm not worth it. I'm not—"

Jack pulled the phone away from her ear before she had a chance to finish her sentence. "All right, you know she's alive and not hurt. But she's not going to stay that way for long."

Naomi strained to hear even a word or two of Noah's response. She might not have been able to make out what he said to Jack, but his anger was apparent. Up until last night, Naomi had always thought of Noah as easygoing and a little shy. But there was a fire in his hazel eyes and a sternness in the set of his jaw that let her know he could be a force to be reckoned with when riled. Noah was a protector to the pit of his soul. No matter how much she wanted him to turn his back on her, she knew he never would. Jack had no idea he was poking an angry bear.

She had a feeling that this wouldn't end well for him.

"Tuesday at eleven o'clock," Jack said. "You'll hear from me before the drop. In the meantime, if I get wind that you've told anyone about this, she's dead. Understand?"

The sound of Noah's voice was a low growl on the other end of the line. Jack chuckled and ended the call without another word. "Your boyfriend sounds pissed." He took the burner phone he'd used to call Noah and dropped it on the cement floor before smashing it to pieces with his boot. Bits of plastic scattered around her feet and Naomi cringed. She had no doubt Jack would rough her up far worse than that if Noah failed to come through. "You must be some piece of ass if he's willing to pay ten million to get you back."

Naomi infused her glare with every bit of hatred she felt. "You're an asshole, Jack."

He laughed. "Yeah. I know."

"When Duane finds out what you're up to, he's going to kill you," Naomi remarked. "Is that what you want? To be on the run for the next decade or so of your life?"

"He's going to be busy tracking you down for his sixty grand." Jack's shit-eating grin made Naomi want to wipe it off of his face. With a shovel. "I'll be long gone before he's even realized what's happened."

"Oh yeah?" Jack really was an idiot if he thought he could get away with this. "What about when I tell him that you ran off with the money I owed plus ten million of Noah's? You don't think that's going to bring some serious heat his way as well as yours? It won't take long for the cops to connect the two of you. He'll have every guy on his payroll out looking for you."

Jack's eyes narrowed. "Not if you're not around to tell him what happened."

Fear seized Naomi's heart and gave a tight squeeze. The air left her lungs in a rush and drawing a new breath to replace her depleted oxygen was an almost impossible feat. Sure, she'd considered the possibility that Jack would put a gun to her head. He'd done worse for Duane Parker in the course of his employment with the gangster. But having it confirmed did nothing to calm her nerves or slow her racing heart. She'd told Noah not to give in to Jack's demands knowing damn good and well that he'd play the hero and do whatever it took to protect her. In the long run, it didn't matter, did it? Jack was going to kill her either way. And if he couldn't allow Naomi to stick around to rat him out, odds were good he was planning on getting rid of Noah, too.

They were as good as dead.

"Jack, think about what you're doing." Her attempt to scare him into changing his mind had crashed and burned. Maybe it was time to reason with him. "You've got a good thing going with Duane's outfit. Would you really want to jeopardize all of that for a few million dollars that you're bound to burn through in a few years?"

"So I can be like your old man?" Jack said with a sneer. "Indebted for the rest of my fucking life because I don't have no place else to go?"

Naomi cringed. The reminder of how she'd gotten mixed up with guys like Jack in the first place stung. "You're smarter than my dad," she replied. "You know better than to bite the hand that feeds you."

"Do I?" Jack asked with a snort.

"Even if you do kill Noah and me to cover your tracks, Duane isn't stupid and neither are the police. They're going to figure it out and they'll question Duane. He's not going to want that sort of attention. When he realizes what you've done, he's going to hunt you down."

"By the time he does," Jack said, "I'll be long gone."

Their conversation had come full circle. Jack was so confident he could pull all of this off. He wasn't the brightest bulb in the box, which was why he hadn't advanced within the syndicate. "Noah's got three brothers," Naomi said. "You don't think he's going to tell one of them what's going on?"

"Not if he wants you back in one piece."

The threat inherent in his tone sent a spike of fear through her chest. She didn't doubt for a second that he'd take off a finger or two in the next couple of days just to prove to Noah how serious he was. "Jack, you don't have to do this."

"Yeah," he replied. "I do."

He walked up to Naomi. Every step placed on the concrete floor echoed deep in Naomi's chest. She swallowed down the bile that rose in her throat as Jack leaned down to eye level. "Take the sixty grand and let me go," Naomi said through the thickness in her throat. "I'll deal with

Duane, get my debt to him paid by the end of the month, and you've got a nice little nest egg while you work your way up the ranks. I won't tell anyone about it, I promise."

"I've got shit to do tonight. Gotta make a living, right? In the meantime, you sit tight. I've got eyes and ears on the house. Try anything while I'm gone, and I'll put a bullet in your boyfriend's head. Understand?"

There was no swaying Jack. He'd made up his mind and nothing Naomi said or did would change it. She couldn't bear the thought of Noah being hurt. If he tried to buy her freedom, Jack would kill them both. "I won't try anything," she choked out. "I promise."

Jack gave her a pat on the head. "Good girl." He turned and his footsteps faded into silence as he climbed the basement stairs and left.

Was there anything she could do to protect Noah from this world she'd been drawn back into? She'd told him he was too good for her and she'd meant it. Because he'd loved her, wanted to help her, he was going to die.

"I'm sorry, Noah," Naomi whispered into the dark. "I'm *so* sorry."

TEN

"You're not seriously going to pay that asshole, are you?"

Noah pinched the bridge of his nose between his thumb and forefinger. His brother Nate had done nothing but shout and swear for the past five minutes. If he would let Noah get a word in edgewise, maybe they could avoid one of them having a stroke tonight.

"I don't care about the money, Nate."

"This isn't about the money and you know it."

Deep down, Noah did know it. None of his three brothers gave a shit about their wealth. They'd been raised to work for what they wanted and over the course of their lives had proven themselves independent of their family name and fortune. The money was more of a burden than a gift. And now more than ever, Noah wished he could shuck the Christensen name as well as the wealth. If he'd been a poor city cop, Jackson Fletcher wouldn't have considered the possibility of taking Naomi hostage.

"I love her, Nate." He'd disregarded the notion that Naomi was somehow in on the scam from the moment he heard her voice on the phone. She'd tried to hide her fear and worry but the tremor that vibrated behind each word had sparked Noah's protective instinct. "Even if I didn't love her, I'd do whatever the hell was in my power to help her."

"Let me hire a private security team," Nate replied. "I don't know if I trust local law enforcement to take care of this."

One of the things Noah had always hated about being the youngest was that his brothers treated him like he was the youngest. He was twenty-seven years old and already the managing sheriff in Sanger. That wasn't a ladder easily climbed even in a small town. He had to have done something right, but instead of trusting him to manage the situation, Nate wanted to hire someone to take care of it for him. "You do realize that *I'm* local law enforcement, right?"

"I'm not saying you're incompetent," Nate said, exasperated.

"Oh, good." Noah couldn't keep the snark from his tone. "Because there for a second, I was a little confused."

"Damn it, Noah, you know I don't mean that *you're* incompetent."

Noah swallowed down a snort.

"At least let me come with you," Nate said. "You shouldn't do this alone."

As a former Navy SEAL, Nate was more than qualified. Hell, it probably wouldn't be a bad idea to take him along. That didn't mean Noah would, though. He'd worked out a plan and it was solid. All he needed Nate for was help getting the cash together.

"I've got this," Noah said. "But I appreciate the offer."

"If you change your mind . . ." Nate said.

"I know. You've got my back."

Nate chuckled. "Damn straight. You know, it's ridiculous that you even need me to get your hands on the money.

I need to talk to my lawyer and figure out how to change the terms of the trust."

Noah didn't give a shit about the trust. He had access to an account with a half million that had been set aside for "living expenses" and he hadn't touched the damn thing until he'd written Naomi the check to cover her loan.

"Nah, don't worry about that," Noah said. "You know I wouldn't even be bothering with the trust if I didn't need it."

"I know," Nate said. "But I still don't think you should give that son of a bitch a red cent."

Noah wasn't planning to. "I'll see you Tuesday at the bank."

"Yeah, I'll see you then. Later, brother."

"Later," Noah said, and ended the call.

Ten million in cash wasn't exactly easy to gather up. Without the considerable strings Nate was pulling, there's no way Noah could get the cash within Fletcher's timetable.

"We're all set?"

Noah turned to John Quinn, the head of the FBI's kidnapping and missing persons task force in Dallas. It wasn't that he didn't trust Dallas PD, but he knew that Duane Parker had eyes everywhere. The implication of a sting operation to get Naomi back was already risky. There was no point in attracting the attention of one of the city's most notorious crime syndicates in the process.

"Ready to roll," Noah replied. He sat down at his desk and cracked each one of his knuckles. "You guys still think Fletcher went rogue?"

"Parker's got millions of his own. He's one of the most successful—not to mention hard to prosecute—traffickers in the country. There's no way he'd bring this sort of heat on his organization for ransom money. Especially by extorting cash from one of the state's most famous families."

Famous families. The words weighed down Noah's shoulders and pushed them toward the floor. "None of this sits well with me." Not knowing where Naomi was or if she was okay, killed him. And the two-day wait to get the money together wasted precious time.

"You have nothing to worry about," Quinn replied. "Obviously Jackson Fletcher isn't a criminal mastermind. But arresting him would be a boon to our investigation into Parker's operation. With any luck, he'll flip."

That's what Noah was afraid of. "And what if he does and Parker comes after Naomi because of it?"

Quinn fixed Noah with a contemplative stare. "I don't see that happening. Think about it, Noah. This is Fletcher's fuck-up. Period. Parker will know that."

Noah wasn't so sure. But he planned to make sure that Naomi was off the hook with the bastard, regardless. He couldn't leave anything to chance. The FBI would do everything in their power to make sure Naomi got out alive, but their priority was Fletcher. Noah didn't care if that son of a bitch burned. If he so much as scratched Naomi, Noah vowed to make him pay.

"We'll meet Tuesday morning and go over the details one last time before we meet Fletcher." Quinn packed up the files he'd brought along and stuffed them in his brief-case. "You have nothing to worry about, Noah. This is going to go off without a hitch."

He gave Quinn a nod of acknowledgment. "Yeah."

Quinn's parting words barely registered as he left Noah's office. His brain buzzed, his heart pounded, and his gut churned like an angry sea. He hadn't slept a single minute since yesterday's conversation with Fletcher and now, he had two long days to sit and wait and do absolutely fucking nothing to help the woman he loved.

Noah had never felt so helpless in his entire life. The lack of control he had in the situation galled him. If he had any idea where Naomi was, not Nate or the FBI or anyone could stop him from going to her right now. He wanted to pummel Jackson Fletcher. Make him bleed. Terrify him in the way Naomi was no doubt terrified.

Naomi was tough, though. Tougher even than Noah. Tougher than anyone he'd ever known. She'd get through this. And when he got her back, he wasn't *ever* letting her go.

Naomi worked her wrists back and forth as she tried to loosen the zip tie Jack had bound her with. Another tie bound her ankles and she used all of the force she could muster to spread her ankles apart and stretch the thick plastic. She bit down on her lip to keep from crying out as the zip ties bit into her ankles. Wet warmth trickled over her skin. Pain radiated from her wrists; she knew they weren't in much better shape.

The son of a bitch had done a damned good job of making sure she wouldn't be able to free herself.

Every muscle in Naomi's body bunched and ached. She rolled her shoulders, stretched her neck from side to side. The act did little to relieve her discomfort and she let out a frustrated gust of breath. The least Jack could have done was let her lie down. Two days spent sitting upright with little sleep would kill her long before he had a chance to.

Hunger gnawed at Naomi's stomach. Thirst scratched at her throat. Her chapped lips burned and her head pounded. Of all of the shitty situations she'd found herself in over the years, this was by far the shittiest.

"Son of a bitch!"

Her frustrated shriek echoed in the basement Jack had stuffed her in. A chill settled over her sweat dampened skin and she shuddered. A single bulb illuminated the tiny corner of the room that had been her jail cell for the past few days. Naomi had lost track of time, but she was pretty sure sunrise wasn't too far off. That would make today Tuesday. The day that Noah was supposed to pay her ransom. She was both hopeful he'd get her out of this mess and terrified he'd even try.

Deep down, she knew he'd never abandon her. *Damn it, Noah. Why do you have to be so goddamned honorable?*

Naomi continued to work her wrists in the zip ties. The thought of how far Noah was willing to go to protect her washed over her in a wave of warm emotion. She thought about the many months they'd known each other. Every conversation they'd shared had endeared him to her more. Every smile wormed its way deeper into her heart.

Naomi had known very few good men. And even fewer selfless men. Noah trumped them all.

She was in love with him.

The realization sucked the air from her lungs. She'd suspected that her feelings for him ran far deeper than she was willing to admit to herself. It had taken her swallowing her pride and admitting to Noah that she was a class-A screwup to realize it. He accepted her for who she was. Unconditionally. He forgave her for the mistakes that she'd been unable to forgive herself for. Even now, he was willing to pay an ungodly amount of money to a gangster to get her back. If that didn't prove how much Noah loved her in return, she didn't know what did. There was no way she was going to let him sacrifice anything for her. She'd get herself out of this mess. She couldn't let Noah think that the only thing she needed him for was rescuing.

If she could just get her damned feet free, at least she'd be mobile.

It was tough to plan an escape and at the same time be quiet. If she woke Jack up, she'd be screwed. Naomi brought her knees up. As forcefully as she could, she brought her feet down to the floor while spreading her ankles to put tension on the zip tie. The plastic cut deep into her skin and Naomi swallowed down the shout that threatened to burst from her lips. She brought her knees up again and slammed her feet down hard on the cement floor. The rubber soles of her Chucks slapped down and Naomi winced. She repeated the motion again and again until tears spilled over her lids and down her cheeks.

Slap! Slap! Slap!

Naomi brought her knees up one last time. Her breath sawed in and out of her chest and her muscles burned. Her feet made contact with the cement floor and a shock of pain radiated from the balls of her feet up the length of her shins.

Snap.

She nearly toppled forward when the zip tie broke. Her legs flew open and Naomi braced her feet wide apart as she reveled in the freedom of movement. *Yes!* Relief flooded her. Freeing her feet was a small victory, but it was a step in the right direction.

It took several more minutes for Naomi to work the knot loose that wound around the zip tie and secured her wrists to the back of the chair. Jack was an idiot to have tied the knot within her reach but she wasn't going to complain. After that, it took a moment for Naomi to get her bearings. Pins and needles pricked her calves and thighs and she wobbled as she put weight on her feet for the first time in two days. She stretched for a long, luxurious moment before she sat back down on the floor with her arms tucked beneath her thighs. After a couple of tries, she managed to shimmy her legs through her arms so her hands were no longer behind her back. A sigh of blissful relief escaped from between her lips. Her shoulders were so damned stiff that every tiny movement hurt.

She wasn't out of the woods yet, though.

Mobility was a huge step in the right direction. When

she was sure she wouldn't fall over trying to walk, she made her way up the steep basement steps. Each creak of the old wooden steps made her cringe. Hopefully, the basement was soundproof. When she got to the door, Naomi said a silent prayer before taking the doorknob in her bound hands and turning. The knob moved an eighth of an inch before it met with resistance. *Damn it!* Naomi swallowed her disappointment. It was silly to have thought that Jackson would leave the door unlocked.

Okay, so the door was a no-go. But maybe the window would prove more fruitful.

Naomi pushed the chair to the window at the top of the far wall. If her ass fit through the tiny rectangle it would be a miracle. Her booty might just be her undoing, but even so, she vowed to give up cornbread when they pried it from her cold, dead hands.

A sound somewhere on the floor above her drew Naomi's attention. Her heart leapt into her throat and her pulse shifted into high gear. She hopped up on the chair and released the latch on the window before swinging it open. Though tall, Naomi wasn't quite tall enough. With her fingers gripping the sill, she stepped up on the back of the chair to give her a little extra height. A precarious perch to be sure, but if she managed to get through the window, it would all be worth it.

She pushed off with her feet. The chair crashed to the floor but it gave her the necessary leverage to propel herself upward. A grunt left her lips as Naomi squeezed her head and shoulders through the window. *Almost home free!* Just a few feet more and she'd be out—

Whoof!

The air left Naomi's lungs in a rush as she was hauled out and down from the window. She kicked out with her legs, tried to wriggle free of the unyielding grip on her torso. "Let me go!" she shrieked. "Jack, you asshole!"

The freedom she'd grasped slipped through Naomi's fingers as Jack hauled her down and tossed her over his shoulder. With one foot, he set the chair upright that she'd used to climb up to the window and deposited her on the hard wooden surface none too gently.

"You're lucky I don't beat the shit out of you!" he growled close to her ear.

"Do it!" Naomi seethed. Jack seized her ankles and slammed them together as he secured them once again with a zip tie. "Lay a single finger on me and see what happens."

Jack let out a derisive snort as he secured her ankles. "Your boyfriend gonna lay into me if I do?"

"No," Naomi said. "*I* will."

Jack chuckled. "I bet you would." He let out a slow breath as he tested the lock on the zip tie. "You just sit tight for a few more hours and you won't have anything to worry about. As long as your boyfriend shows up with the cash, that is."

Naomi sneered. "Like I'm supposed to believe that you're not going to kill us both, either way?"

Jackson's leering smile confirmed what she already knew. He went to the far end of the basement and dug through some boxes until he found a longer bundle of rope. He tied Naomi to the chair, making it impossible for her to free herself again.

"You've got a few more hours to wait," he said. "You try to pull anything again, and I'll send you back to Christensen in pieces. Understand?"

Naomi swallowed down the fear that rose in her throat like bile. She was going to die and she'd never get to tell Noah how she truly felt about him. "I understand."

"Good." Jack finished tying the rope into knots. He gave Naomi one last apprising look before he headed for the stairs. "You're about to make me a very rich man," he remarked. "Thanks for that."

"Go to hell."

His answering laughter was the last thing she heard before the door closed to once again shut her up in dark silence.

ELEVEN

"You ready?"

Noah glanced over at John Quinn. He'd been ready since the night Fletcher had called to tell him he had Naomi. Now that he was close to getting her away from that asshole, Noah had to beat back the nervous anticipation that skittered up his spine. He'd been in his fair share of dicey situations, but this was different. Noah had never been responsible for the safety of someone he loved before.

"Yeah," he said after a moment. "I'm ready."

"Good. Don't worry, Noah. We know what we're doing."

He wasn't worried. Not about the FBI or the handoff. What had Noah's gut churning was that Fletcher had to be pretty damned desperate to ruin the good thing he had going with Parker to kidnap Naomi. Desperate men had nothing to lose. And right now, Noah had *everything* to lose.

They waited in the parking lot of the Kay Bailey Hutchi son Convention Center. Cell service sucked in the area right now due to the large concentration of people attending Dallas Comic Con. It was smart, really, to have arranged the handoff here. The crowds would offer Fletcher a buffer, not to mention an escape route. It was obvious that he didn't trust Noah to keep up his end of the bargain no matter the threats he'd made against Naomi.

Fletcher was desperate, but not stupid. Luckily, neither was Noah.

"Anyone have eyes on Fletcher yet?"

Noah gave Quinn a sidelong glance. The agent's silence indicated that no one on his team had spotted Fletcher yet. For a second, Noah wished he had one of the tiny earbuds in his ear so he could listen in on their conversations. Then again, maybe he was better off not knowing.

A few quiet minutes passed. Noah swore if something didn't happen soon he was going to crawl right out of his damned skin. Quinn tapped him on the shoulder. He turned to face the FBI agent. "Black SUV headed to the drop point," he whispered. "Get ready."

Noah drew a deep breath into his lungs. He stepped out of the van the FBI used for their mobile command center and climbed into his own rig. He couldn't help but laugh as he pulled out of the parking lot and headed toward the drop point. In the movies, ten million dollars could easily be handed off in a large duffel bag. The reality of transporting that much cash required a pallet and a goddamned pickup truck. If Fletcher had thought the handoff would be inconspicuous, he had another think coming.

With a quick look in the rearview mirror, Noah pulled out and headed to the north end of the convention center where the docking bays were located. How Fletcher managed to circumvent security was beyond him but Noah figured he'd leave it up to the FBI to figure that little detail out. He'd no doubt used Parker's connections to get it done. Something that'd probably help to seal his death warrant with the gangster once he realized the heat Fletcher had brought down on him.

Noah pulled into the rear lot and brought his pickup to a stop. He'd opted not to wear a wire despite Quinn's insistence. FBI agents were stationed around the convention center and it was not like they needed verbal confirmation of Naomi's kidnapping to arrest Fletcher. If he had her—and he'd *better*—they had all of the evidence they needed to arrest him. Naomi's testimony alone would put Fletcher away for a good, long while.

Noah's heart pounded in his chest as he got out of the truck. His hands balled into fists at his sides as Fletcher got out of his SUV and crossed the lot toward him. The urge to pummel the bastard into a bloody pulp was almost more than Noah could resist. But until he knew for sure that Naomi was with him—and unharmed—he had no choice but to be patient and play Fletcher's game.

"I gotta tell you," Fletcher said with a sneer as he approached Noah. "I still can't figure out why a guy with as much money as you've got would waste your time with a nine-to-five gig. My ass would be on permanent vacation."

"Where's Naomi?" Noah had no interest in having a conversation with a slimy asshole like Jackson Fletcher. He was here for one reason and one reason only.

"Right down to business, huh?" Fletcher said with a laugh. "I'll give you props for that. She's in the backseat." He jerked his head toward the SUV. "Once our transaction is complete, I'll let her go."

Noah didn't buy it even for a second. The last thing Fletcher would want was witnesses. His jacket gaped at his chest, revealing the gun holstered under his arm. Yeah, once he had his ten million in cash, Noah and Naomi were as good as dead.

Fletcher was going to be disappointed more than once today.

"No." Fletcher raised a brow at Noah's harsh tone. "I want to see her before you get even a dime of my money."

"Funny," Fletcher remarked. "I don't remember you making the rules here."

"Funny," Noah countered. "I don't remember giving you a choice in the matter."

Fletcher's eyes narrowed as he studied Noah. Quinn had agreed not to move in until they had confirmation that Naomi was with Fletcher and not in any direct danger. It was not as though Noah had expected any of this to go down smoothly—or easily. They'd circle each other like bulls, stamping their hooves and stirring up dust, for god only knew how long until one of them backed down. It sure as hell wouldn't be Noah who bowed his head first.

"I could put a bullet in her head and walk away from this," Fletcher said.

A jolt of adrenaline dumped into Noah's bloodstream. He clenched and unclenched his fists. Swallowed down the anger that prompted him to do something rash. "You could," he replied with much more composure than he felt. "But you won't."

Another tense moment of silence followed before a wide smile split Fletcher's face revealing a row of crooked teeth. "Pretty confident, considering I've got you by the balls, Christensen."

"Do you?" Noah asked. "I'm the one with the brick of cash in the back of my truck. You want it? Then let me see Naomi."

"You're a stubborn son of a bitch," Fletcher said with a chuckle. "I like you."

He wouldn't once the FBI showed up to arrest his ass.

Without another word, Fletcher turned and headed back toward his SUV. Noah dug his heels into his boots to keep from following after him and ripping the door open himself. Tension gathered his muscles into tight knots and

Noah rolled his shoulders as he waited. The time it took for Fletcher to get to his rig was only a few seconds, but to Noah it felt like years. When he finally opened the door to reveal Naomi, bound and gagged, her expression fearful, Noah was ready to beat the bastard to a bloody pulp.

"Here she is," Fletcher said with a sneer. "Now, give me my fucking money."

Naomi cried out in relief at the sight of Noah watching her from less than fifty feet away. His dark brows drew down sharply over his hazel eyes and his jaw squared with anger. She'd never seen him so enraged, or so undeniably gorgeous.

"All right, you've seen her. Now, I want to see the money."

Noah gave a sharp nod of his head. He climbed up into the bed of his truck and released ratchet straps from around a canvas-covered brick that sat in the bed. He pulled the canvas back and Naomi's jaw dropped as he revealed a solid block of cash wrapped in clear plastic. *Holy crap.* Noah wasn't messing around, was he?

"Now that's a beautiful sight," Jack said with a chuckle. "Load it in the back of my rig. Then, you can have Naomi."

Not a chance.

Noah hopped down from the bed of his truck. He took several steps toward Jack who narrowed his gaze and reached for the gun holstered under his jacket. Naomi turned her full attention on Jack who'd grown antsier with every step Noah took toward him. Her almost-escape had put him on edge and Noah's behavior wasn't helping. Now that he was about to get what he wanted, she knew that it wouldn't be long before he tied up all of his loose ends.

"FBI! Don't move, Fletcher!"

A swarm of activity erupted around Naomi. Men in bulletproof vests jumped out from what seemed like thin air, guns drawn and shouting commands at Jack. Noah lurched forward at the same time Jack reached for her. He wrapped his arm around her chest and hauled her out of the backseat and against his body. Naomi's heart pounded, her lungs constricted from Jack's tight grip, and black spots swam in her vision. He pulled the gun fully from its holster and pressed the barrel against Naomi's temple. "Anybody takes even a step closer, she's dead!" he shouted.

Oh god. Panic seeped into Naomi's bloodstream. Her eyes met Noah's and she was taken aback by the unabashed rage she saw there. His jaw squared and he held out his hands, palms up, as though to placate Jack and diffuse the situation.

"Calm down, Fletcher," Noah said from between clenched teeth. "No one has to get hurt."

"You dumb motherfucker," Jack spat. A tremor passed through him and Naomi swallowed against the lump that rose in her throat. He was twitchy as hell. If his finger so much as flinched on the trigger, she was dead. "I told you what would happen if you got anyone involved!"

A cacophony of sound assaulted Naomi's ears. Noah, Jack, and the men in the FBI vests seemed to all start shouting at once, barking commands, threats, and insults that blurred into a single ear-shattering sound. Naomi knew better than to fall apart right now. She needed to keep her shit together if she wanted to get out of this in one piece.

"Here's what's going to happen!" Jack's voice rang out above all the others and a stillness settled over the tense scene. Noah's lips formed a hard line as he tore his gaze away from Naomi to focus on Jack. Damn it. She needed that eye contact to ground her. "Christensen is going to finish loading that block into the back of my rig. You're going to stand down and let me drive outta here. Understand?"

Noah scoffed. "That's not going to happen, Fletcher."

"Yeah," he said. "It is. Because I'm taking Naomi with me and if any of you fuckers try anything, I'll kill her."

So not good. She'd known since the day Jack had nabbed her that at the end of all of this, he was going to kill her. He had absolutely nothing to lose. Not the FBI, nor Noah's sheer fury was going to derail his plans now. Jack would kill her in a heartbeat, if only to create a distraction so he could try to escape.

Noah focused his attention back on Naomi. She let out a shaky sigh of relief and gave him a slight nod to let him know she was holding it together.

"You're going to be okay, Naomi," Noah said. "I promise."

Noah's arm swept behind him in a blur of motion. He reached behind his back and whipped out a gun that he fired off without a second thought. Naomi flinched at the explosion of sound. Her eyes squeezed tightly shut as she waited for a bullet's impact—either Jack's or Noah's—but instead felt only Jack's grip on her slacken before he fell to the ground.

Violent tremors rocked Naomi's body and she went to her knees. Pain radiated upward through her thighs as she made contact with the pavement below and she opened her eyes to find Jack beside her on the ground, gripping his bleeding shoulder.

"You're going to pay for this, you son of a bitch!" he seethed. "You're a dead man, Christensen!"

Shock kept Naomi frozen in place. The ringing in her ears deafened her. Her limbs grew cold and almost completely numb. When Noah reached down and scooped her up into his arms, it barely registered. The activity swarming around her as Jack was handcuffed by the FBI stole her focus. *Jesus*. What in the hell had just happened?

"Naomi?"

She looked around, wide-eyed and stunned. Her brain

cranked into overdrive as it tried to keep up with what was going on around her. Strong arms held her against a wide chest and she rested her palm on a broad shoulder.

"Naomi? Talk to me."

She shook herself from her stupor as her head came slowly around to face Noah. Concern etched every line of his face and his brows drew tightly over his eyes. "W-what?" she stammered.

"Are you hurt?"

Was she? Naomi shivered in Noah's embrace and her teeth chattered. "I don't think so."

Relief cascaded over her as the realization of the situation finally hit her. Jack had been ready to kill her if need be and Noah had saved her. She threw her arms around him and sobbed against his chest. "Noah." He held her tighter and she let out a shaky breath. "Noah, I'm *so* sorry."

"Shh." He soothed her as he smoothed a hand over her hair. "It's okay, honey. You're okay. Everything's going to be fine."

It would, wouldn't it? Because Noah would never let anything bad happen to her. "I love you," she said on a rush of breath. "I love you so much."

He let out a quiet chuckle. "I love you, too."

Noah carried her to his truck. He set her down in the front seat and she was reluctant to let him go. He kissed her forehead, her cheek, the tip of her nose, and once gently on her mouth before he pulled away. "Do you need to go to the hospital?"

"No hospitals," she said.

He cocked a dubious brow. "All right. Can you sit tight while we wrap up here?"

She could wait as long as he wanted. "Don't go too far."

"I won't," he assured her. "Be right back."

Naomi let out several shaky breaths before she felt as though her heart rate had returned to some semblance of normal. In the distance, Noah chatted with one of the FBI guys while the others transferred the large block of cash to an armored truck. He'd gone above and beyond to protect her. Noah Christensen loved her.

And she loved him, too. He was it for her. Period.

TWELVE

Naomi nestled closer to the warmth of Noah's body and drew the covers up around them both. It was hard to believe that just forty-eight hours ago, she'd been held at gunpoint, not sure if she was going to live or die, and praying that she'd be given a chance to at least tell Noah how she felt about him. The details of that day were still a blur in her mind. Naomi had been terrified, certain that once Jack was arrested, Parker would come after her for retribution. Ever the hero, Noah had assured her that he'd taken care of her debt and that Parker had no interest in retribution. He'd get that from Jack, she supposed. Unless the FBI managed to break him first. Either way, it wasn't any of Naomi's business anymore, and that's how she wanted it to stay.

She ran the flat of her palm up the ridges of Noah's abs to the wide hills of his pecs. He stirred beneath her touch and a deep sigh escaped from between his lips. "If you don't stop touching me like that, we won't be getting out of this bed anytime soon."

Naomi pressed a kiss to his shoulder and said against

his skin in a husky murmur, "Who says I want to get out of bed?"

A shiver danced over her skin at Noah's approving groan. Her hand wandered south and she reached between his legs to take the length of his cock in her hand. She stroked to the base of his shaft and he sucked in a breath that caused Naomi's stomach to tighten and her thighs to clench. A familiar throb settled between her legs and she put her lips to his solid shoulder once again.

Her eyes drifted shut as Naomi reveled in the sensation of stroking Noah. His flesh in her palm was smooth and hard as marble. She brushed the pad of her thumb over the sensitive head and he shuddered, coaxing a smug smile to her lips.

In a flash, Noah had her on her back. A sinful grin spread across his full lips as he settled himself between her thighs. "You're impatient this morning." Naomi let her knees fall open and Noah's gaze heated as it wandered to her pussy.

"I am," he agreed. He grabbed a condom from the bed-side table and ripped the packet open. "It took me six months to get up the courage to tell you how I felt about you. I'm not going to waste a second to show you."

Noah might have thought that those six months were a waste of time, but Naomi might not have fallen in love with him otherwise. She'd gotten to know him, trusted him, *liked* him long before she'd loved him. He'd been her friend when she wasn't sure if she could open herself up to trust anyone. Without even realizing it, she'd fallen for him. Hard.

"Actions do speak louder than words," she teased.

Noah grinned. The expression was like the summer sun, bright and shining. Naomi's eyes wandered down the length of his exposed torso, over the perfect V that cut into the skin where his thighs met his hips. Heat flushed her cheeks as she took in the sight of his erection and it grew even harder under her appraising stare. Noah ripped the packet open and rolled the condom on in a fluid motion before bracing his arms on either side of her. Her breath hitched in her chest as the engorged head prodded her opening and she let out a low moan as he drove home and filled her completely.

The sensation of their bodies joining had no equal. Naomi let out a low moan as Noah moved above her, pulling out to the tip before driving home once again. She hooked her ankles behind his knees as she thrust her hips up to meet his.

Naomi had never had it so good.

He fucked her slowly, taking his time the way he had their first night together. They'd had wild nights since then, passion that swept them up into a frenzy until they were tearing at each other's clothes. But this morning, Noah loved her slowly. Thoroughly. Enjoyed her body and allowed her to enjoy his. He made love to her and in every deep thrust of his hips, she knew what he felt for her.

Naomi's back arched off the bed. She gripped his shoulders as she came up to meet him. His mouth found hers and his tongue thrust past her lips in time with each drive of his hips. The sensation coiled within her, giving the illusion that she was nothing more than a tiny sphere floating in the ocean. Noah rode the waves of her orgasm with her, lifted her to heights of passion that made her cry out and beg for more. He knew her body. Knew how to touch her, how to kiss her, how to make her purr. Not for the first time, Naomi marveled at the man she now called hers.

Noah was the total package. Brave, smart, caring, sinfully handsome, and sweet. Funny, sexy, playful, and serious when he needed to be. He was passionate. Affectionate. Honest and honorable. He was much too good for Naomi and yet, she'd been lucky enough to have won his love.

For the longest time, Naomi had lived by the adage, if she didn't have bad luck, she'd have no luck at all. Moving to Sanger had been her saving grace, despite the desperation that had led her to borrow money from someone she shouldn't have. That one bad decision had been a blessing in disguise, though. It had brought her closer to Noah. For the first time in her life, Naomi didn't regret one of her mistakes.

"What are you thinking about?"

In the aftermath of her pleasure, Noah threaded his fingers through her hair. He rolled his hips against hers, shallow thrusts that brought her down from the high of orgasm slowly and rekindled the fire between them that smoldered in the peaceful lull.

"I'm thinking about you," she murmured close to his ear. He thrust harder and Naomi's back arched off the bed as renewed lust surged within her.

His low chuckle tingled over her skin like rain. "What about me?"

"How lucky I am to have you." He gripped her ass and angled her hips upward as he ground into her once again. She let out a soft moan that ended on a sigh. "And how I'm never letting you go."

"Never, huh?" Noah increased his pace and Naomi drew in a sharp breath. Wet warmth spread between her thighs and she rolled so that Noah was on his back and she straddled him.

"Nope." She braced her arms on his wide chest as his hips undulated. "You're stuck with me, Noah Christensen. What do you think of that?"

What did he think of that?

Noah reached up to cup the perfect roundness of

Naomi's breasts in his palms. His thumbs brushed over her nipples and she shuddered as she rode him, which only added to the intensity of sensation. Naomi thought she was damaged. Imperfect. Undeserving of his love. All he saw when he looked at her was perfection. A woman with a fiery soul and a fierce heart. She gave herself wholly to him, heart and soul, and without fear. She was unlike any woman Noah had ever known. He'd lost himself completely to Naomi from the moment they'd met. And he knew that there was no turning back from that love. Not ever.

She was it for him. Noah had met the love of his life in a barbeque joint in tiny Sanger, Texas. He wouldn't have wanted it any other way.

"I think it's a damn good thing," he answered after a moment. "Because, honey, you couldn't get rid of me if you tried."

Her tight, panting breaths as he slowly fucked her nearly drove Noah mad with want. It took everything he had not to pound into her and find his own release. He wanted this to last. He wanted to make love to Naomi for hours. They had all the time in the world, though, didn't they? Noah had meant what he'd said to her, she wouldn't get rid of him so easily. Now that he'd found her, he wasn't ever letting her go.

Noah thrust his hips up to meet hers. She let out a luxuriant sigh that sent a zing of electricity through him. His hands wandered from the swell of her breasts to her hips and he gripped her tight as he guided her motions until they found a nice, easy rhythm. "Just like that, honey," he said. "Don't stop."

She bent over him and put her mouth to his. The dark curtain of her hair framed her face and her intoxicating rose perfume went straight to Noah's head. She was the most dangerously sexy woman he'd ever laid eyes on. Her gray, smoky gaze met his, unabashed and full of heat. It was enough to bring him to the edge of release. Goddamn, she was perfect.

"Noah, I'm going to come again," Naomi said on a tight breath.

No way was he going off until she did. He pulled her down with more force, driving up to meet her with every roll of her hips. She bent over him and her hands wandered from his pecs to his shoulders. Noah let out a low groan as her nails bit into the skin as her muscles grew taut. A renewed rush of wet warmth bathed his cock and her inner walls squeezed him tight as she came.

The intense sensation caused his sac to tighten. Noah increased his pace, thrust wildly up as he pounded into her. Naomi's impassioned cries echoed in the quiet bedroom and with every sob of her pleasure, he edged closer to his own release.

"I want to feel you come, Noah."

Her words pushed him over the ledge of his restraint. She squeezed her inner walls around him as he came and Noah let out a ragged shout as his hips left the mattress. Waves of sensation rolled from his sac and up his shaft. With each deep pulse, Naomi's hips jerked. Noah clamped his jaw down and pushed himself up to kiss her while he rode out the orgasm.

"That was amazing, Noah." Naomi pulled away to whisper in his ear. "So warm. I felt how hard you came."

He guided her face to his and kissed her again. Naomi said exactly what was on her mind and she didn't make apologies for it. Where he was shy, she was brazen and he loved her for it.

"You drive me crazy," he panted against her mouth.

"I hope that's a good thing," she replied with a throaty chuckle.

"Oh, it is," he said. He kissed the column of her throat,

up to the delicate flesh below her ear. He flicked out with his tongue and goose bumps broke out over her skin. He'd have to remember that spot for next time. He wanted to learn every single place on her body that she liked to be touched, kissed, licked. He wanted to drive her mad with desire every single day so she'd never have a reason to leave him. "I can't get enough of you."

Her answering smile was pure seduction.

Naomi bent down to kiss his chest, his shoulders, his neck. She didn't move to separate their bodies and Noah enjoyed the connection between them and the warmth of her body as it enveloped him. A peaceful silence descended on them and Noah marveled at the rightness of it all. He stroked the silky length of Naomi's hair, inhaled her sweet scent. Her skin was as soft as flower petals against his and he let his fingertips wander over every exposed inch. She let out a dreamy sigh before propping herself up on an elbow.

Naomi's dark eyes shone with emotion as she studied him. "Good guys like you aren't supposed to fall for bad girls, you know."

Noah stroked up her spine and she shivered. "What makes you so sure I'm a good guy?"

"You can't fool me, Noah Christensen." Naomi's tongue flicked out at this throat. The wet heat made his stomach muscles go taut. "You're the best guy I've ever met."

Noah knew he was a good guy. But he'd always considered himself uninteresting because of it. A pale representation of his more dynamic brothers. When Naomi said he was a good guy, however, pride swelled in his chest. That was love, though, wasn't it? Finding that one person who made you feel like you were worth something. Like you were the best person in the world.

"I love you, Naomi," Noah murmured close to her ear.

"I love you, too, Noah." Her lips met his throat, his jaw, the corner of his mouth. "I've never loved anyone more."

Those were the best words he'd ever heard. And he'd never get tired of her saying them to him. Minutes passed into hours. They spent the time touching, kissing, and whispering sweet loving words to one another. They laughed. Sighed. Teased one another and made solemn vows. It was the best day of Noah's life and this was only the beginning. He'd spend the rest of his life making sure that each day with Naomi was better than the last.

"You know what would hit the spot right about now?" he asked.

Naomi brought her gaze to his and grinned. "A platter of ribs?"

He couldn't love any woman more than he loved Naomi. He put his mouth to hers and kissed her slowly before he pulled away with a smile. "You read my mind."